THE
CYCLONE'S
EYE

T.J. FARLOW

The Cyclone's Eye

First edition December 2023

Copyright © T. J. Farlow 2023
tjfarlowauthor@gmail.com

Edited by Sarah Dronfield,
proofread by Rachael Mortimer.
Cover design by Miblart.

Internal Design by Book Whispers

All rights reserved. No part of this publication may be reproduced, stored in a retrieval system, or transmitted in any form or by any means, electronic, mechanical, photocopying or otherwise, without prior permission of the author.

ISBN 9780975643808

This is a work of fiction which incorporates references to historical events, real people and real places. Other names, places and events are products of the author's imagination. Any resemblance of characters in this novel to real persons, living or dead, is purely coincidental.

CONTENTS

DRAMATIS PERSONAE

Characters whose names are in bold are historical figures. Ranks, titles and honours are in accordance with their first mention in this novel. Many of these people were subsequently promoted, knighted, and even elevated to the British peerage.

Admiral Jean-Marie Abrial

Lieutenant General Ronald Adam

Major General Harold Alexander

Brigadier Kenneth Anderson

Major Archdale

Clement Attlee

Gaius Ambrosius Artorius

Private Baker

Lieutenant General Michael Barker

Air Marshal Arthur Barratt

Group Captain Bishop

Lieutenant General Alan Brooke

Benita, Kathleen and Victor Brooke

Sergeant Brown

Sergeant Burford

Lieutenant Colonel Dudley Clarke

Winston Churchill

Commander James Clouston

Able Seaman Collins

Commander Harold Conway

Lieutenant Colonel Ronald Darcy

Captain Michael Denny

Lucy Deverey

Commander Alastair Denniston

General Sir John Dill

Chief Petty Officer Driscoll

Sergeant Dwight

Air Chief Marshal Sir Hugh Dowding

Wing Commander George Edwardson

Molly Edwardson

Sophie Edwardson

General Bertrand Fagalde

Admiral of the Fleet Sir Charles Forbes

Gunner Brian Fahey

Sergeant Hockey

Lieutenant Hoffmann

Major General Hastings Ismay

Dr Kenneth Jackson

Private Jones

Admiral Sir Roger Keyes

Dr Bleddyn Kendrick

Lieutenant James Langley

Private Mackenzie

Lieutenant MacLean

Second Lieutenant Edward Mann

Major General Bernard Montgomery

Air Chief Marshal Sir Cyril Newall

Major Philip Newman

Sergeant Owen

Gunner Parry

Private Pascal

Mr and Mrs Percy and family

Signalman Perkins

Lieutenant General Henry Pownall

Brigadier Neil Ritchie

Vice Admiral Bertram Ramsay

Major General Erwin Rommel

Toby Smith

Oliver Strachey

Lieutenant Smith

Major David Strangeways

Lieutenant Charles Sweeney

Captain William (Bill) Tennant

Private Turner

Unnamed German spy in Axleigh

General John Vereker V.C. (Lord Gort)

Colonel Whitfield

Martha Wrigley

Lieutenant Willingham

Professor Helen Wodehouse

The tomb of Arthur is nowhere to be found –
whence ancient fables claim that he will return.

William of Malmesbury, 1125 A.D.

PART ONE

AVALON

CHAPTER 1

Monday, 13 May 1940
2050 hours
Cambridge Recruitment Office

Bleddyn propped his bicycle under the 'Dig for Victory' poster. He checked his watch. Ten minutes early.

There was a black Austin parked in front of the recruitment office, and a lady's bike leant against the wall on the other side of the steps. The blackout curtains were drawn, but a faint glow emanated from underneath the door.

Bleddyn approached, hesitated, drew his breath, and knocked.

'Just a moment!' a man called from inside.

Bleddyn swallowed. He was about to find out why they'd summoned him. Why they needed him for an assignment. Why they wouldn't tell him anything over the telephone.

The door creaked open. A gaunt face peered out from the darkness. 'Dr Kendrick?'

'Yes,' replied Bleddyn.

'Come in, come in.' The man ushered Bleddyn through, closed the door, and switched the light back on. The feeble incandescent bulb barely illuminated the poster-clad walls, but Bleddyn could now see the man's corporal epaulettes and ribbon bars. He had probably fought in the Great War.

'You're younger than I expected, being a doctor and all,' the corporal remarked.

'I only graduated last year.'

'Ah. Well, take a seat over there.' The corporal gestured to a bench against the far wall, where a young woman sat. 'I'll inform the group captain that you're both here now.' He limped off in the opposite direction, his gait and the dull thud of his left step indicative of a prosthetic.

Bleddyn approached the bench. The woman's strong, angular features gave her a striking appearance that was captivating and intimidating at the same time. Golden hair flowed around her neck and disappeared behind her shoulders. Her ice-blue eyes followed him as he approached. She could have cut diamonds just by looking at them.

Bleddyn was still on his feet when the corporal called, 'Dr Kendrick, Miss Edwardson, Group Captain Bishop will see you now.'

Bleddyn stepped aside for Miss Edwardson. Only when she stood did he fully appreciate how tall she was. She must have been six foot two, if not six-three – nearly a head taller than he was. Her tight blouse and skirt also revealed an unusual frame for a woman of her height, curvaceous and athletic at the same time. All in all, she could have passed for a Norse goddess.

Don't stare. He averted his gaze and followed her into Bishop's office.

An overweight man in an RAF officer's uniform sat behind a heavy wooden desk. His ruddy face was set with a bushy imperial moustache, a pipe and a monocle. Tobacco smoke hung in the air. The corporal shut the door as he left, sealing them in with Bishop and the noxious emissions of his pipe. The sooner this meeting finished the better.

'Be seated.' Bishop pointed to a couple of chairs.

Miss Edwardson remained on her feet. 'My father's behind this, isn't he?' she demanded, her scowl fixed on the group captain.

'Miss Edwardson, I understand that you and your father have a somewhat terse relationship, but he specifically asked for you because of your command of Latin.'

Miss Edwardson continued to scowl at Bishop for a few more seconds before she took her seat.

Bleddyn sat, too. It sounded as though he was about to be caught in the middle of a family feud.

'Kendrick,' said Bishop, 'I heard you've been called up for national service in the Royal Army Medical Corps. Is that correct?'

'That's right, sir, and I'm supposed to commence service in two—'

'Captain Fairleigh remembered your Welsh-sounding name, "Bleddyn". Are you from Wales, and can you speak Welsh?'

'It's pronounced "Ble*thyn*" – but yes, sir. As I already told Captain Fairleigh, I'm from Wales, and I speak Welsh.'

'What business has a Welshman in this part of England?'

As much as Bleddyn didn't like Bishop's tone, telling a high-ranking officer to mind his own business was probably a bad idea. 'I won a scholarship to the University of Cambridge,' Bleddyn replied. 'I stayed here because I'd been invited to train in pathology after the completion of my residencies.'

'A university scholarship, eh?' Bishop didn't bother to hide a sneer.

'Is that a problem, sir?' Bleddyn asked.

'Not one you would see, I suppose,' Bishop muttered, 'but at least national service will let you repay the debt you owe the taxpayers of our great nation.'

Bleddyn dug his nails into his palms, but he said as calmly as he could, 'It was a private scholarship, sir. Don't worry, your tax contributions didn't pay for my education.'

The group captain's eyes narrowed. 'And I suppose your parents put you through Eton before you came here?'

'Group Captain,' Miss Edwardson said in a firm voice, 'I'm sure you didn't summon us here to interrogate Dr Kendrick about his personal circumstances in front of me. By the way, a true gentleman doesn't smoke in a lady's presence.'

Bishop's affronted scowl evaporated under Miss Edwardson's burning glare.

At length, the group captain said, 'My apologies, Miss Edwardson –
I'd lit my pipe before you arrived and hadn't given it a second thought.'
He laid the pipe in an ashtray.

Bleddyn glanced back and forth between them, unsure if he should
be embarrassed or grateful.

Bishop clasped his hands and placed them on the desk. 'The reason
you're here is because Wing Commander George Edwardson needs to
question a man arrested at his airfield. This man doesn't speak English,
but Edwardson thinks he speaks Welsh and Latin.'

'Translate for a man in custody?' Bleddyn asked. 'That's all you
want us for?'

'Well, can you?' demanded Bishop.

'I-I suppose I could, sir, but aren't there professional translators for
this sort of thing?'

'Indeed,' added Miss Edwardson. 'Why us?'

'Edwardson wants to keep this confidential,' Bishop replied.

She sighed. 'All right. Tell us about this man.'

'He was caught trespassing at your father's airbase just after a
platoon from the Royal Engineers opened up an old burial mound.'

'I beg your pardon?' Miss Edwardson leant forward. 'There's a
burial mound on-base? I've been to Axleigh before, and I don't recall
anything like that.'

Bishop checked a note on his desk. 'It seems to be a recent
acquisition. The airbase has just expanded.'

'Oh. I recall a hillock just north of the airbase perimeter.' Miss
Edwardson nodded. 'Yes … yes, that *could* be a pre-Norman burial
mound, now that I think about it – but why were they opening it up?'

'To convert it to a munitions dump.'

'*What?* They're destroying an ancient monument to make a
munitions dump?'

'Miss Edwardson, I'm just repeating what your father told me,'
Bishop said. 'If you don't like it, take the matter up with him.'

Bleddyn clenched his fists under the desk. Surely they could have found another place to build this munitions dump.

Miss Edwardson leant back into her chair and placed her hands in her lap. 'I most certainly will take it up with him,' she said in a menacingly soft tone.

Bishop cleared his throat. 'As I was saying, the man appeared to a platoon of sappers at a construction site. None of them saw him until he was near the entrance of the tomb, and Wing Commander Edwardson thinks the intruder was … ah … masquerading as the occupant.'

'He was inside?' Miss Edwardson asked.

'It appears that he was – although your father has no idea how he got in. Anyway, he needed medical attention, so they sent him to the hospital at Axleigh. Unfortunately, civilians have seen him, so rumours are bound to be flying around the village already. He's in police custody now. This man appears to identify by two different names …' – Bishop checked a note on his desk – '*Gaius Ambrosius Artorius* and *Arthur ap Emrys.*' He looked at Bleddyn. 'Do those names mean anything to you?'

Bleddyn shrugged. 'The first name isn't Welsh. The second one is close to *Arthur ab Emrys*, which would mean … Wait a minute. Emrys? Ambrosius? But those names only come up in the Arthurian legend.'

'Group Captain,' said Miss Edwardson, 'are you telling us this man claims to be King Arthur?'

'That's what your father thinks,' replied Bishop, 'although he's speculating. Remember, the intruder hasn't spoken English. That's where you two come in.'

'So why the secrecy?' asked Bleddyn. 'Just because some fool calling himself King Arthur appears … oh, of course.' He rolled his eyes. 'The burial mound. I suppose that's meant to be Avalon.'

'I still don't understand the need for secrecy,' Miss Edwardson said. 'Do you really think anyone will fall for such nonsense?'

'That's all too likely, I'm afraid,' Bishop replied. 'The war's going badly right now. Britain needs a miracle, and people might cling to any offer of hope, however preposterous it is. What we *don't* need is a false prophet rallying the masses for an ill-fated crusade.'

'Sir, is this wing commander sure the man speaks Welsh?' Bleddyn asked.

'I don't really know how confident he was in identifying any of the languages. There's probably a reason he asked for both a Welsh and a Latin speaker.'

'In that case, I may not be the right person to help with this. Welsh has probably changed a lot since King Arthur's time.'

'Oh, don't be a fool, Kendrick,' snapped Bishop. 'He won't be speaking ancient Welsh. He's probably a Welshman who's hoping his native tongue will be enough to convince people in Yorkshire that he's King Arthur.'

'And if he's speaking Cornish or Breton?' Bleddyn asked. 'I won't be able to help you there.'

'Dr Kendrick makes a good point,' said Miss Edwardson. 'I could recommend—'

'The fewer people who know about this the better,' Bishop said. 'Let's hope at least one of you will understand him.'

Bleddyn closed his eyes and drew a slow, deliberate breath. With only two weeks before he had to start national service, dealing with this nonsense was the last thing he wanted to do. 'Sir, if this man's a threat to the public interest, why hasn't MI5 taken charge?'

'From what I understand, MI5 isn't interested in this case. They just want the local police to charge him or have him committed, depending on whether he's a fraud or a lunatic.'

'He's a fraud,' Bleddyn said.

'You sound sure about that, Kendrick.'

'Well, I'm not a psychiatrist, but the burial mound, the languages – that's not what I'd expect from a man suffering from delusions. He's planned this.'

'If you say so. Edwardson said there was more to this, but he wouldn't elaborate over the telephone.'

An unsettling thought hit Bleddyn. 'Sir, I hope I'm only here because you need a Welsh speaker. You didn't call me in because I'm a physician, did you?'

'Of course not. Why would a physician be needed to interrogate … oh.' The group captain peered at Bleddyn through his monocle. 'Yes, yes, I see what you mean. Your medical knowledge could be useful for extracting confessions from uncooperative suspects.'

'No, it would not,' Bleddyn retorted. 'The Hippocratic oath forbids it.'

Bishop snorted. 'Calm down, Kendrick. The RAF doesn't carry out those sorts of interrogations. The Security Service might, but they're not involved.'

Bleddyn relaxed a little.

Bishop opened a manila folder and handed them each a train ticket. 'These will take you to Doncaster, where Wing Commander Edwardson will meet you. A compartment will be reserved for the two of you, so you may discuss the matter in private. I'll have a driver pick you up from your respective lodgings around 0730.'

Bleddyn and Miss Edwardson rose.

'Oh, and Kendrick,' added Bishop, 'when you commence national service, you'll be expected to salute senior officers. It would be wise to get into the habit early.'

Bleddyn saluted. Had a lady not been present, he might have been tempted to reply with a different gesture.

Back in the waiting room, the corporal dimmed the lights and let them out.

Miss Edwardson looked back at Bleddyn as she walked towards her bicycle. The pained grimace on her face was in stark contrast to her glacial demeanour back in the recruitment office, but she said nothing before she broke eye contact. She must have been embarrassed. After all, it was her father behind this stupid task.

Bleddyn cursed under his breath as he grabbed his bicycle and rolled it towards the road. Thanks to this 'King Arthur' rubbish, he had even less time before he had to report for duty. He still needed to pack things and send them home. There was tax, too; should he contact the Inland Revenue, or would the Medical Corps cover that for him? Who could he ask? He'd been in Cambridge for nearly six years, but he still didn't know any tax accountants …

Then it struck him.

He turned around. 'Miss Edwardson?'

'Yes?'

'This place, Axleigh – how many people live there? In the village, I mean.'

'Oh … about five hundred or so. Why do you ask?'

Bleddyn looked around. Nobody was in earshot, but he stepped towards Miss Edwardson and lowered his voice nevertheless. 'It just occurred to me that this "King Arthur" must have known the hill was an old burial mound. He couldn't have planned this "emergence" otherwise. However, you said you'd seen the hill, and you didn't know what it was.'

'Oh – so if he knows the district's landmarks that well, he's probably a local.'

'And yet, nobody at the village hospital or police station has identified him.'

A contemplative frown crept across her face. 'Yes. Yes, you're right. That *is* odd.'

They stared at each other.

At length, Miss Edwardson shrugged. 'Perhaps Bishop misunderstood something. We won't know for sure until we go there, but I'm sure there's a reasonable explanation.'

Bleddyn nodded. 'I suppose we'll find out tomorrow. Until then, Miss Edwardson, good evening.'

'Until tomorrow, then.'

Bleddyn turned his bicycle back to the road, but the intrigue continued to play on his mind. Perhaps Miss Edwardson was right. After all, Bishop was conveying an account of events he hadn't personally witnessed.

However, if this 'King Arthur' fellow was indeed unknown to the Axleigh community, this whole matter could turn out to be more interesting than Bleddyn had first thought.

CHAPTER 2

Tuesday, 14 May
0740 hours
Girton College, Cambridge

Sophie Edwardson paced back and forth at the college entrance. She went to kick the base of the stone archway, but stopped herself. Such an exhibition would be immature, no matter how strong the urge to vent her frustration.

It was unusually clear this morning, and she could see all the way across the college grounds. A pedestrian came into view. Even from a distance she recognised her supervisor, Dr Percy White, by his limp.

'Sophie?' he asked when he was close enough to talk. His gaze rested on her suitcase. 'It looks like you're going somewhere.'

'My father wants me to help him out with something,' Sophie replied. 'I should only be gone for a couple of days.'

'Help with a task?'

'He's in the Royal Air Force. I can't tell you any more, I'm afraid.'

Dr White crinkled his forehead. 'That sounds intriguing. Well, I hope you'll be back by next Monday.'

'Oh, good grief – the departmental meeting.'

'You're one of the few students not at risk of being called for national service, so I hope we can preserve your scholarship,' Dr White said. 'Nevertheless, it would be better if you were here to argue your case in person.'

'I hope to be back by then,' Sophie replied, 'but it depends on my father now. If I'm not back by Monday, could you please impress on everyone that my absence is related to the war effort?'

'I'll try. Well, I wish you a good trip.' Dr White continued towards the Faculty of Classics.

Sophie took a deep breath. A curse on this war, a curse on her father, and a curse on this King Arthur impersonator.

It wasn't long before a Morris pulled up, driven by a woman in a khaki uniform. Dr Kendrick was sitting in the front.

'Sorry I'm late, Miss Edwardson,' the driver said as she got out of the car.

'No need to apologise.' Sophie regarded the woman's uniform as she picked up her suitcase. 'Are you in the ATS?'

'No, miss. MTC – Mechanised Transport Corps.' She unlocked the boot. 'Here, I should take that …'

'Not at all.' Sophie put her suitcase into the boot.

'Which seat would you prefer, Miss Edwardson?' Dr Kendrick asked. He had also stepped out of the car.

'Oh … here is fine, thank you.' Sophie pointed to the back left seat.

He held the door for her, then took the seat behind the driver.

'You're not in uniform, Dr Kendrick?' Sophie asked after the car started moving.

'Not yet. I don't officially start for another two weeks.'

She glanced at him from time to time as they drove to the railway station. Short and wiry, but clean-shaven and well groomed, he held himself with an air of humble dignity. Sophie cast her mind back to the meeting last night, and the snide remarks Bishop had made about Dr Kendrick's background. It was almost comical, really. Dr Kendrick may have come from a working-class background, but at least he was unambiguously human. Bishop, on the other hand, could have been mistaken for a walrus had it not been for his monocle and that putrid pipe.

At the railway station, Dr Kendrick took both suitcases as soon as the driver opened the boot. He ignored her protestations and Sophie's outreached hand.

They found their platform and sat on a bench underneath a 'Careless Talk Costs Lives' poster.

While they waited, a porter came up to Dr Kendrick, twirling a cigarette between his fingers. ''Scuse me, got a match?'

Dr Kendrick shook his head. 'I don't smoke.'

The porter grunted. 'Well, you should. It's good for you.'

'No, it's not. Quite the opposite, in fact. It causes cancer.'

The porter walked off, muttering under his breath.

'Dr Kendrick is a medical practitioner,' Sophie called out.

'He's a Mrs Grundy, that's what he is!' the porter replied without a backward glance.

Sophie turned to Dr Kendrick. 'Cancer, you said?'

'Well, lung cancer, definitely. Possibly others. The smoke probably contributes to obstructive lung disease, too.'

'I must let my father and brother know. Thank you.'

'Just bear in mind that smokers usually don't care to hear it.' He glanced in the direction of the porter, who was now trying to procure a match from another passenger.

Sophie rolled her eyes.

Eventually, their train pulled into the station and came to a stop. Sophie reached for her suitcase, but Dr Kendrick had already picked it up.

They pushed their way into the front carriage and found a compartment with their names on a card hanging from the door. An entire compartment to themselves was extravagant when the train was so tightly packed, but Sophie was privately grateful for the space. She closed the door behind them, shutting out the worst of the noise and tobacco smoke.

'Thank you, Dr Kendrick,' she said after he heaved her suitcase onto the overhead luggage rack. She settled into the worn leather seat.

'You can call me Bleddyn, if you wish,' he replied as he sat opposite her.

'In that case, Bleddyn, please call me Sophie.' An irritating realisation hit her. 'Oh – we'd better revert to formal address when in Doncaster. My father shares Bishop's opinions about class, and he wouldn't approve if he heard us address each other by our first names.' She returned Bleddyn's stung expression with a pained smile. 'I'm sorry, Bleddyn, but a man of my father's rank could make things difficult for you.'

'Does that mean I'll hear another lecture about reimbursing the taxpayers?' Bleddyn asked.

'Heaven forbid – I hope not. Anyhow, didn't you say it was a private scholarship?'

He nodded. 'The Frederick Cavendish Scholarship.'

'The Frederick – oh my God, that means your father …'

Bleddyn sighed. '… Died in the Great War.'

'I'm sorry,' Sophie murmured.

Bleddyn contemplated the backs of his hands. 'To be honest, I don't know if I fully understood my loss, really. He died at Gallipoli just before I was born.'

A guard blew the whistle outside.

'If my father asks how you came to study in Cambridge, mention that scholarship,' Sophie told him. 'He's a military man through and through, and he'll think twice before deriding the son of a fallen soldier.'

Bleddyn looked up and nodded.

The train began to move.

'Anyway, Sophie,' he said, 'Bishop was after a Welsh speaker and a Latin speaker, it seems. I take it that you read Latin at Cambridge?'

'I've read Latin, ancient history and a little archaeology. I'm undertaking a master's thesis in British Vulgar Latin. Titular degrees, of course.'

Bleddyn frowned. 'Vulgar Latin?'

'It's the proper term for the colloquial or slang Latin spoken by the common people, as opposed to Classical Latin.'

'Ah, so nothing to do with obscenities …'

'No, no. Vulgar Latin is to Classical Latin what Cockney and Liverpudlian English are to the King's English.' She smiled. 'It's a common misunderstanding.'

'So, this British Vulgar Latin – is that what King Arthur would have spoken?'

'We don't know if King Arthur even existed; but if he did, then he probably spoke a similar dialect to the one I'm studying.'

'It sounds as though you're better qualified for this task than I am, then,' he remarked.

'For the next day or two, perhaps. I don't think a classics education will be much use for the war effort.'

Bleddyn tilted his head. 'Do you wish you'd read another field?'

'Well … I've thrown myself into Latin, and I do have a natural talent for it. Nevertheless, engineering, or science, or medicine would have been interesting, and certainly more useful.' She sighed. 'Alas, I had to agree to study the classics even before I started my HSC. My father would never have supported me otherwise, and even then, he only did so reluctantly. That's the sort of man he is, Bleddyn. A university education, especially in the sciences, doesn't conform to his idea of a suitable endeavour for his daughter.'

'That's ridiculous,' Bleddyn said. 'If anything, there aren't enough women in medicine, especially obstetrics and gynaecology. And as for the pure sciences – well, I'm glad Marie Curie's parents didn't think that way.'

Sophie couldn't help but smile. 'Bleddyn, if only more men thought as you do. I don't just mean my father, either – do you have any idea how hard it is for a woman at Cambridge?'

'I think I can imagine.' Bleddyn fiddled with a button on his cuff.

The train was beginning to pick up speed now.

'Didn't you say you were training to be a pathologist?' Sophie asked when he looked up again.

'No, not yet. I'm still in my first year out. I've been invited to study chemical pathology on the completion of my residencies, but I don't know how long that invitation will remain open, and national service could take years.'

'Oh, the war could ruin your career, too?'

'Well, I'd still at least … What, you as well?' Bleddyn straightened. 'What happened?'

'The department's budget has been cut. My master's scholarship is in jeopardy.'

'Oh.' Bleddyn rubbed his forehead. 'I'm sorry, Sophie, I really am.'

They moved on to other subjects to while away the journey. Bleddyn turned out to be one of the most engaging men Sophie had ever met. His passion for learning was at least as strong as hers, and although he was more enthusiastic about science than archaeology or the evolution of languages, he was attentive when she discussed these subjects. It was no surprise that a man with such an inquisitive mind had won a scholarship.

As the conversation flowed, it transpired that financial hardship had overshadowed Bleddyn's childhood. Things Sophie had taken for granted, such as sports club memberships and music lessons, had 'never really been an option' for him. His matriculation at Cambridge was the first time he'd left Wales. She tried to avoid topics that were likely to highlight the disparity between their upbringings in order to spare him discomfort.

It was past four o'clock when the train finally pulled into Doncaster station. They stepped onto the platform and were walking towards the station office when a familiar towering figure in an RAF uniform approached.

Sophie tensed. 'Hello, Father.'

'Good afternoon, Sophie.' As usual, her father's words were devoid of any emotion. He turned to Bleddyn. 'Didn't they teach you to salute a senior officer, Kendrick?'

Bleddyn placed one suitcase on the ground and did as he was instructed.

'Bishop warned me you were an impertinent conscript,' her father said.

'Come on, Father, you can see Dr Kendrick isn't in uniform.'

'*Dr* Kendrick? Oh. Bishop just told me he had a posting in the RAMC.' Her father shrugged. 'Oh, well. Follow me.'

An attractive blonde MTC driver was waiting outside the station. She saluted and unlocked a black Austin Twelve.

'Lucy works on-base, and she's privy to this matter,' her father told them as Bleddyn put the luggage in the boot. 'It's safe to discuss it in front of her.'

Sophie chose the seat behind the driver, while Bleddyn sat beside her.

After they left the station, her father said, 'Well, Sophie, I'm pleased you're able to help out on this matter. I never thought your university degree would be of any practical use, but one could never have envisaged such a bizarre incident. Even so, I was wondering if you had given any thought to a more practical occupation – one that would be of greater use to the war than studying dusty old manuscripts in Cambridge.'

Sophie dug her nails into her palms. He had some nerve criticising her 'superfluous' education while calling on her expertise.

'Nursing is a good option for a woman. In fact, that's how Colonel Godfrey and his wife met – she was in the QAs in the Great War, you know.'

Oh, for God's sake, can't you wait until we're in private? 'We'll discuss it later, Father. Tell us more about why we're here.'

'All right. This business occurred yesterday morning, when a team from the Royal Engineers was constructing a munitions dump.'

'Group Captain Bishop told us about the destruction of the cairn,' said Sophie. 'Did you recover anything from inside?'

'We recovered plenty, but I don't think anything was authentic. I'll come to that in a minute. Anyhow, this man appeared soon after the sappers opened the burial mound.'

'How soon?' Sophie asked.

'I wasn't there, but they claimed it was barely a minute after they opened it. He collapsed soon after they saw him. They thought he might have been concussed by the explosion, so they sent him to the hospital in Axleigh – but he'd already started babbling in whatever languages he speaks before he left the base. The engineer worked out that his names invoke the Arthurian legend, so I had the police restrain him to the hospital bed. There was nothing seriously wrong with him, so he's now in police custody. He made a commotion while they were taking him in, and too many people saw it.'

'Has anyone identified him?' Sophie asked.

'No. He doesn't seem to be from around these parts.'

Sophie and Bleddyn exchanged looks. It seemed Bleddyn was right. 'So why didn't you call MI5?' she asked her father.

'I did. I called them first. It turns out they're stretched thin looking for spies and traitors, and they believe this man is too eccentric to be either. According to the agent I spoke with, they get plenty of imposters masquerading as historic and legendary people during wars. King Arthur and Sir Francis Drake impersonators were particularly common in the Great War, along with blasphemers claiming to be Jesus Christ.'

'People who are supposed to return one day,' Sophie mused.

'Ah.' Her father nodded. 'Yes … yes, that makes sense. Anyway, the Security Service is fed up with these crackpots, and they want me to deal with it. That's why I called RAF Fulbourn and asked Group Captain Bishop to send you here, and a Welsh speaker if he could find one. Incidentally, what were you doing in Cambridge, Kendrick?'

'I studied under the Frederick Cavendish Scholarship, sir.'

'Oh.' Her father nodded. 'Anyhow, there are a couple of rummy things about this case. It appears he was hiding inside the tomb. I haven't a clue how he got in, but we recovered fresh food.'

'There must be a concealed entrance,' Sophie said. 'Have you stopped demolishing it?'

'We haven't had time to stop work. There's a war on, you know.'

'Then in that case, you will have destroyed the entrance and any chance to prove he wasn't already inside. You'd better hope he confesses.' Sophie took satisfaction in pointing out that the destruction of an ancient monument now worked against his interests.

Her father shifted uncomfortably.

'It gets even more peculiar,' he said at length. 'The baskets of food included apples, blackberries, plums—'

'What?' exclaimed Sophie. 'But they're not in season!'

'I inspected the contents personally, and there they were. It was all fresh, too. I have no idea how he pulled that one off.'

Sophie glanced at Bleddyn, who frowned back.

'There was also some chain mail, which looked authentic to me, but the engineer thought ancient chain mail should have rusted away long ago,' her father said. 'Didn't you read some archaeology at Cambridge? I was hoping you could look at the items we recovered from the mound.'

'Perhaps it would be better if I examined the artefacts before I see this man.'

'He's been giving the police trouble. They want a translator as soon as possible.'

'Don't you have any means of detaining him on-base?' Sophie asked. 'A brig, or something like that?'

'Oh, come on, Sophie, do you think a base that's too small for a medic will have a brig?' Her father sighed. 'It's a pity we don't, actually, because we would have been able to prevent civilians from seeing any of this.'

'Wing Commander,' said Bleddyn, 'do you know if anyone at the hospital conducted a detailed physical examination?'

'I don't think anyone had the chance. Not that it matters. We need a translator, not a doctor.'

'Sir, advances in medical practices can leave telltale signs. For example, amalgam or gold fillings in his teeth will prove he's not from the Dark Ages. If we can point out something like that, he might give up the pretence.'

Her father grunted. 'That's a good point. We'll see if it comes to that.'

They sat in silence until they arrived at Axleigh. The red bricks of the Victorian-era police station contrasted with the timber-framed buildings that lined the rest of the street.

They were still getting out of the car when an overweight, greying sergeant came out. 'I take it the train was late, Wing Commander?' he asked.

'It was. Can we talk inside, Dwight?'

Bleddyn recovered a duffel bag from his suitcase, and everyone gathered in the station's waiting room. A wireless was playing a news broadcast in an adjoining office.

'Johnson!' Dwight called out.

The wireless fell silent.

'Sergeant Dwight, I was able to find two translators,' Sophie's father said. 'Kendrick speaks Welsh, and my daughter reads Latin at Cambridge.'

The sergeant shook their hands. 'I'm glad you're here. The suspect launches into frightful rages whenever anyone goes near him.'

A towering wall of muscle entered from the adjoining room. It sported a black eye.

'Wing Commander, Miss Edwardson, Mr Kendrick, this is PC Johnson.' Dwight pointed at the burly constable. 'He arrived last Friday to replace my regular constable, Trevatt, who's been called up for national service. It was just as well he was here, too. The detainee injured Trevatt badly – broke his leg and nose – when we brought him in.'

'Gave me this black eye, too,' grunted Johnson.

'I thought you restrained him when he was still disorientated,' Sophie said. 'How did he manage to hurt two policemen so badly?'

'I handcuffed one of his arms to the bed when he first came to the hospital,' the sergeant replied. 'God only knows what he could have done with both arms free.'

'Have there been any further developments, Dwight?' Sophie's father asked.

'Folk in the village have been asking about him. I've told them we arrested someone who was interfering with construction work at the airbase, and that he's a lunatic who hasn't said anything coherent since he arrived.'

Her father nodded. 'What about the detainee himself? Apart from the violent rages.'

'He doesn't seem to know how to use the taps in his cell, and Johnson figured out he was demanding water in cups. Oh, and he hasn't flushed his lavatory, so it's getting a bit whiffy in there. Perhaps we should see if Mr Kendrick can speak to him before we take your daughter in, Wing Commander. It's no place for a lady.'

'No, I'll come as well,' Sophie told the sergeant before her father could say anything.

'If you wish, Miss Edwardson.' Dwight turned and nodded at the constable, who picked up a couple of chairs from behind the desk. 'We would normally interrogate a suspect in the conference room, but I dare not bring him out of his cell. Mr Kendrick, would you like to leave the bag here?'

'It's a house-call duffel bag,' Bleddyn replied. 'Depending on how the interrogation goes, I might be able to carry out a medical examination.'

'You're a doctor? I'm sorry, I didn't realise. Yes, a medical examination might be useful, if we can calm him down.' The sergeant took a pen and notebook from his desk. 'Are you ready to meet him?'

CHAPTER 3

1645 hours
Axleigh Police Station

The shouting began as soon as the policemen opened the door to the cells.

'That's not Latin or Welsh,' Sophie said to her father. It sounded a bit like German, but it wasn't that, either.

'There was a third language, but we can't identify it,' he replied.

'Oh, of course.' Sophie nodded. 'He must be trying to pass off an obscure Germanic language as Anglo-Saxon.'

Dwight waved them through.

A man with short grey hair occupied the barred cell closest to the door. He wasn't tall, but his muscular frame and the scar running down his left cheek gave him the appearance of a seasoned warrior. Hard dark eyes tracked the visitors. His chin and upper lip bore the lengthening stubble of a man who hadn't shaved for a week.

Sophie cast an eye over his attire. Both his trousers and his loose-fitting tunic were made of undyed linen. His hands and forearms bore more scars. Sophie couldn't see any buttons or an American 'zip', and his belt buckle was made of tarnished bronze. He was barefoot.

'Perhaps I should try Welsh first and see if we can eliminate that one,' Bleddyn whispered.

Sergeant Dwight nodded.

'Bleddyn Kendrick yw'n enw i. F'in deall bo chi'n dweud taw Brenin Arthur ydych. Ydy hyn yn wir?'

The detainee fixed his gaze on Bleddyn but said nothing.

'Bleddyn Kendrick yw'n enw i. F'in deall—'

The man interrupted with a stream of what also sounded like Welsh, but Bleddyn just knitted his eyebrows together.

At length, Bleddyn turned to Sophie and shook his head. 'I think it's a Celtic language, but it's not Welsh. Miss Edwardson, maybe you'll have more success with Latin.'

'Before I start, what are "Wales" and "Welsh" in Welsh?' Sophie asked in an undertone.

'*Cymru* and *Cymry*,' Bleddyn replied softly.

'Thank you.' Sophie looked at the man in the cell and said in Classical Latin, 'My name is Sophie Edwardson. I have been summoned as a translator. Is it true that you claim to be the legendary King Arthur?'

His stare rested on her. 'At last, I meet someone who can speak an intelligible tongue. What Germanic tribe do you belong to? Why do you not provide me with enough water? What is this strange place I have been brought to?'

Good God! He spoke with a rapid fluency that only comes with everyday usage. He had also used prepositional prefixes as separate words, even ending sentences with them – something Sophie had come across while researching British Vulgar Latin. *How* could he be fluent in a dialect that died out over a thousand years ago?

'Nobody deprives you of water,' Sophie replied when she collected herself. 'Behold the white basin in your cell.' She pointed. 'Rotate the spoked handle that sits on the right of the spout.'

His eyes darted back and forth between Sophie and the washbasin.

'It appears he speaks Latin,' her father mumbled.

Eventually, the detainee picked up an enamel cup from his bed and walked to the basin. He tried twisting the tap clockwise.

'Turn it the other way,' Sophie told him, gesturing as she did so.

'Aha!' he exclaimed when the water began to run. He filled his cup and drank four times.

The lid of the lavatory was down, fortunately – but Sophie asked him to flush it nevertheless.

He held out the cup. 'This is too small. I need a bucket.'

'One does not need a bucket to flush a latrine. Behold the chain on … the vessel above where one sits. You must pull it.'

He tried yanking it out of the cistern.

'That is incorrect,' Sophie added hastily. 'Pull it downwards, and not so hard.'

The rushing water made him jump. He released the chain too early.

'Hold it down for longer,' Sophie instructed him.

After finally managing to flush the lavatory, the detainee came back to the bars. 'Thank you, Sophie Edwardson. I have never seen plumbing like this before. I have many questions.'

'We also have many questions, but please excuse me for a moment.' Sophie turned to her companions. 'It's Vulgar Latin, not Classical or Church Latin.'

'Vulgar Latin?' exclaimed Bleddyn. 'The dialect you study?'

'It's close.'

'Wait – what does that mean?' her father asked.

'It means proving he's a fraud will be harder than I first thought.'

Dwight handed her the pen and paper.

'It's fine, Sergeant, I have my own pen and paper.' Sophie sat on one of the chairs provided. She took a notebook and pen from her handbag, and asked in Latin, 'Do you claim to be the legendary King Arthur?'

'I am sometimes called *Arthur*, but I am not a king. Was my awakening unintentional? Were you ignorant of what lay inside the resting chamber?'

'Both your assumptions are correct,' Sophie told him.

'I do not understand your language, but it has similarities to those spoken by the Germanic invaders. I am a warrior who fights for the Brythonic people and Romans within Britain – my *Combrogi*, as I call them – so I may be your enemy. Does your presence mean a Germanic tribe now occupies these lands?'

'The answers to your questions are complicated,' Sophie replied, choosing her words with care. 'Perhaps you should answer my questions first. I might be better able to give you answers when I learn more about you.'

His eyes narrowed, and then he sighed. 'I suppose I am not in a position to make demands. As you wish. My name is Gaius Ambrosius Artorius, son of Constans, son of Aurelianus. The Brythons also call me *Arthur ap Emrys* and *Arthur Cyngwr*. I am a legatus.'

'How should I address you?'

'Most people just call me Artorius.'

Sophie conveyed his replies.

'I don't know what to make of that,' said her father. 'Does he claim to come from the time of King Arthur?'

Sophie asked Artorius when he had been placed in the tomb.

'It was in the fourth year of Cynyr's rule over the Durotriges,' he replied.

'I do not recognise that name,' Sophie told him.

'Do you know Maelgwn of Gwynedd? Medraut of Camulodunum?'

Sophie shook her head. 'Can you give me references to events that were important both within and outside Britannica? Maybe the birth of Christ?'

Artorius contemplated the ceiling. 'About five centuries had passed since the birth of the Christ. The Byzantine Emperor was Justinian. Seventy years had passed since …'

Sophie looked up.

'Are you only pretending to write this, Sophie Edwardson?' he demanded. 'You have not replenished the ink in your quill.'

She turned her notebook so he could see the open page. 'With this quill, I can write hundreds of words before I need to replenish the ink.'

He stared wide-eyed at her page. 'Indeed, you can. In that case, your quill is unlike any I have seen before.'

Sophie turned to the policemen, her father and Bleddyn. 'He claims to have lived in the time of Emperor Justinian, which is the right time for King Arthur. The custom of using the year of Christ's birth as a reference point was uncommon in the early sixth century.'

'Why is he here now?' her father asked.

'I am here because someone opened my resting chamber,' Artorius replied when she put the question to him.

'How did you survive in it?'

'How much do I need to explain, Sophie Edwardson?' His eyes narrowed. 'Now that I think about it, your name is peculiar. Should you not be Sophie *Eadwarddohter*?'

Sophie shrugged. 'The name "Edwardson" passes down through male lineages. Our records of what we call the "Anglo-Saxon settlement" are poor, so you will need to explain everything.'

'A *settlement*?' Artorius glared at her. 'You call the invasion a *settlement*?'

She glared right back at him.

At length, he broke eye contact and plonked himself on the edge of his bed with a theatrical sigh.

Sophie glanced at her father. 'This may take a while.' She turned back to Artorius. 'Our records of Roman rule are comprehensive enough, but we know little of what happened after Honorius withdrew from Britannica.'

'What do you expect to happen when an oppressive empire abandons a divided people? Albion plunged into chaos and civil war. Roman against Brython, Christian against Pagan … and amid the infighting, the Germanic and Gaelic tribes invaded.'

'Were not the Germanic tribes invited as mercenaries to defend Cantium against invasion by the Picts – people north of Hadrian's Wall?' Sophie asked.

'*Pict* is a contemptuous name that Roman loyalists gave to followers of the old culture and religion of Albion, both the unconquered people of the North and the revivalists in the South. I know not why you think tribes north of Hadrian's Wall could have attacked a kingdom as far south as Cantium.'

This differed from the legends and sparse records. However, it made sense; tribes from Scotland would not have bypassed the rest of England to invade Kent. 'Pagan revivalists from nearby, then?' Sophie asked.

'Nobody attacked Cantium. Rather, it was King Guarthigern who tried to seize neighbouring lands.'

Her father cleared his throat. She ignored him.

'But you are correct about one thing,' Artorius growled. 'Guarthigern employed *Angli-Iutæ* pirates as mercenaries, offering land to those who fought for him. Through this, they gained a foothold in Albion. They drew more warriors from their homeland on the pretence of recruiting more mercenaries, until they had the numbers to overrun Cantium. They then invaded neighbouring lands and formed alliances with other tribes from Germania – the *Saxones* and the *Frisii* – to conquer more.'

'What's he saying?' her father demanded.

'I will tell you when I have his account in full.' Then, switching back to Latin, she said, 'Please continue.'

'Years of infighting had drained our strength and left us defenceless. Town after town, city after city, fell to our ruthless conquerors.'

'Did you rally eventually?' Sophie asked.

He nodded. 'I come from a family of commanders, the last of whom died when I was eighteen. I was barely a man when I first had to lead men into battle – but we won a decisive victory. I soon became a renowned warrior and tactician, admired by my allies, feared by my enemies.'

'Sophie,' her father said, 'how long—'

'All right, I'll move it along!' she snapped. 'He was describing his life story.'

'What *is* his story?'

'It's … Arthurian, and pre-Galfridian.'

'Pre-*what*?'

'I'll explain later.' Then, turning back to Artorius, Sophie said in Latin, 'Much time has passed since the events you describe. How can you still be alive?'

Artorius sighed. 'I was helping Moderatus, or *Medraut*, as he is also known, defend Camulodunum against a Saxone incursion. The enemy had captured a ballista and used it to fire pila. One struck me.' He pointed to his left shoulder.

'Pardon me, but did you not fight *against* Medraut in this battle?' Sophie asked.

Artorius frowned. 'Why would I have fought against him?'

'That is what I had heard …'

'From where?'

'From … most sources, actually.'

'Then most of your sources are wrong.'

Sophie shrugged. 'If you say so. Please continue.'

'Our physicians dressed the wound as best they could, but seven days after the battle, my jaw locked. It was a sign that my life was soon to end.'

'How did you cheat death?' Sophie asked.

'Bedwyr of the Corieltauvi brought me here. A coven of druidesses had survived near Danum despite the Romans' attempts to destroy the religion. I had won the respect of the Pagans, and the local arch-druidess had instructed Bedwyr to bring me to her if I were ever mortally ill.'

'Please continue,' Sophie urged him, glancing at her father's tapping foot and trying to ignore it.

'On my arrival, she announced her intention to put me in a deep sleep from which I would reawaken healed, for she believed the day would come when the Combrogi would need me again.'

'How long did it take to travel from Camulodunum to here?' Sophie asked.

'It took a little longer than one full day. Our drivers changed horses every twenty miles or so.'

Colchester to Axleigh in one day, by horse-drawn cart … Would that have been possible? Perhaps, if the Roman highways were still useable. 'Did this burial involve a ceremony?'

'It did, but I know not all the details,' Artorius replied. 'I respected the Pagans, but as a Gnostic Christian, I never believed such a spell could work.'

'But you were there …'

'I was gravely ill. At times, I was awake; at times, I was asleep; at times,

I was delirious; at times, pain and nausea rendered me senseless. Tarry there …' Artorius frowned at the ceiling and stroked his chin. 'The druidesses put me on a canoe to take me to the burial chamber. I remember little from when I awoke until I found myself fettered to a bed, but I could swear I stumbled from the chamber into a field. What happened to the lake?'

'Engineers drained the swamps to make farmland,' Sophie explained. 'Why was the chamber not opened immediately after you were entombed? Did your people not still need you at the time?'

Artorius shrugged. 'I remember the arch-druidess explaining that she must plant an acorn above the chamber, and that the oak to sprout from it must complete a full cycle of life.' He shook his head and sighed. 'I pleaded with them not to follow through with their plan. Even if it worked, I did not relish the thought of reawakening after my family and friends had long perished.'

Sophie jotted this down and turned to the others present.

Her father stood over her with crossed arms. 'Well, that took long enough,' he grumbled. 'What did he say?'

'He told me about a society that collapsed after the Roman withdrawal and was beset by invaders. I'll go through the details later, but he's familiar with the known history of the time.'

'Arthurian, you said before?' asked Dwight.

'More or less, and it's based on the oldest versions of the legend. He also told me he was a military leader and diplomat who forged alliances to defeat the Saxons. A lance went through his shoulder in a battle near present-day Colchester, and he developed an illness characterised by a "seizing jaw" seven days later. Might that be tetanus, Dr Kendrick?'

Bleddyn nodded. 'A "locked jaw" about a week after a penetration injury is consistent with tetanus.'

'How long can a person live after the disease manifests? If it kills within twenty-four hours, we can prove his story is a hoax.'

Bleddyn shook his head. 'It isn't that quick. Before the antitoxin, death normally occurred three to five days after the onset of symptoms.'

'All right, thank you. Artorius then explained that druidesses entombed him with enchantments that were meant to enable his revival after a long maturation time – something about the life cycle of an oak tree.'

Artorius spoke as soon as she turned back to him. 'So, Sophie Edwardson, I have answered many of your questions now, and I want answers of my own. For how long have I slept? How many years have passed?'

Well, she did promise him answers. Sophie drew her breath and replied, 'Over one thousand four hundred years have passed since the time you describe.' She braced for an outburst.

His face blanched. 'One thousand four hundred years? Why did they leave me there for so long? And the war? Do any Combrogi still live? Where are they now?'

'The boundary between the Brythons, who now call themselves *Cymry*, and the collective Germanic tribes, who are now known as the *English*, runs … from the River Sabrina to Deva Victrix.'

Artorius's jaw dropped. 'We were pushed back past the River *Sabrina*?' More colour drained from his already pale cheeks. His bottom lip began to quiver. 'Is that really all that remains of my Combrogi? And what became of my family? My wife, Gwenhwyfar? My sons, Cynon and Llachau? My daughter, Gwenhwyach?'

'What we know of a man called "King Arthur" survives only in legends, many of which are too fantastic to be true. I am sorry, but I cannot give you reliable information about your family.' Sophie actually did feel sorry for him. She'd anticipated that he would pretend to be upset by this news, but his expression of dismay was incredibly convincing. If he was lying, he was a good actor.

'I see.' Artorius brooded for a while before he asked, 'Are we still at war? If so, am I to be executed?'

Sophie shook her head. 'The war you describe ended centuries ago. Cymru and England are now part of a union of nations. Our current king has a mixed ancestry that includes Cymry blood. In fact, the man who first spoke to you when we entered' – she pointed to Bleddyn – 'is a Cymry physician.'

Artorius drew his eyebrows together. 'If I am not a prisoner of war, does that mean I am free to go?'

'That is not my decision, but our authorities will hold you for now.'

'Why?'

'Your story is difficult to believe. Brythonic Paganism vanished centuries ago, and nobody believes the druids were ever capable of the magic you describe. However, legends say that Arthur will return when we need him – and we are currently at war.'

'Legends Among the *English*?' Artorius's expression soured. 'Are you telling me the Anglii and Saxones have corrupted history so much, you now revere me as one of *your* heroes?'

Sophie frowned. 'I suppose we do.'

He straightened. 'And you think I would help you fight your current war?'

'The war is going badly. Some people want to believe that Arthur will return and save us.'

His face darkened with fury. 'Why would I help you after what you did?'

'Artorius, *we* did not do anything. What you described happened a long time ago.'

'*A long time ago?*' Artorius got to his feet and approached the bars. 'The war between our people may have been a long time ago for *you*, Sophie Edwardson, but *I* was there! I saw what your ancestors did, and the anguish still burns in my heart!' He slammed the cell bars with his palms and made Sophie jump. 'Do you think I would help the savages who burned our villages and shot our people and decapitated children and enslaved and raped womenfolk?' Gripping the bars with white knuckles, his voice faltered as he demanded, 'Do you know … do you know what your people did when they captured my son, Amyr?'

'Well then,' Sophie huffed, 'if you do not intend to help us, it seems we have no cause for concern.'

Artorius stepped back and continued to glower at her. 'Against whom are you fighting this war?'

'Why do you bother to ask that when you do not care?' Sophie demanded.

'Just tell me.'

'If you must know, the people from the various tribes in Germania have been assimilated into one nation called *Germany*. They have already invaded other nations in Europe.'

Artorius threw his head back and laughed. 'Oh, this is fabulous! You *English*, descended from Germanic invaders, now face the same threat from your old kinsmen!'

Sophie shot him a contemptuous glance before turning to her father. 'I don't think you have much to worry about. He claims to despise the English and says that he has no interest in helping us.'

'We still need to detain him until we decide what to do with him,' her father said. 'Have you found any flaws in his story?'

'Well … no, not really. I know this isn't what you want to hear, but his knowledge of the period is impressive.'

Her father frowned. 'Then perhaps Dr Kendrick can find something with his medical examination.'

Sophie turned back to Artorius, who was seated on the edge of his bed again, staring at the floor with sagged shoulders. This was going to be hard to explain. 'Artorius.' She pointed to her father and said, 'This man is my father, and he holds a military rank comparable to centurion. He wants to subject you to a medical examination. It may help to confirm or dismiss your story.'

'Do as you will,' he replied without looking up. 'I do not care any more.'

'He agrees,' she told her father.

'Sophie,' Bleddyn said, 'I'll need you to ask—'

'Excuse me.' Her father cut Bleddyn off. 'Since when did you end up on first-name terms with my daughter, Kendrick?'

Sophie stiffened.

Bleddyn furrowed his eyebrows. 'Sorry, sir, but I thought you wanted your daughter to join the QAs.'

'What does that have to do with how you address her?'

'Well, if she enters as a nursing assistant, she'll be "Sophie" or "Edwardson" to most physicians.'

Her father looked nonplussed. At length, he said, 'Well, that may be so, but she hasn't joined yet.'

'Of course, sir.' Bleddyn bowed his head. 'My apologies, Miss Edwardson – I did not mean to be impertinent. Nevertheless, the nature of my examination will require Artorius to remove his clothing. Will he object to this, particularly in your presence?'

Sophie was taken aback, but before she could reply, her father exclaimed, 'What? Kendrick, don't you think you should ask if *I* object to you stripping a man naked in front of my daughter?'

'I normally would, sir, but you were the one who suggested she join the Nursing Corps. If she does, her duties will include changing and washing wounded soldiers, and helping others with bedpans. Not to mention that she will have to deal with blood, pus, vomit, urine and excrement on a regular basis. I ask nothing of her now that wouldn't be expected of a nurse.'

Sophie glanced back and forth between the two men as it dawned on her what Bleddyn was doing.

Her father fiddled with his collar as his face turned purple. As usual, his attempts to think on his feet were proving futile.

'But although I require her presence,' Bleddyn continued, 'I must ask you to leave for the sake of the detainee's privacy. The sergeant and constable should stand nearby, but out of sight.'

Sophie's father cleared his throat. 'Well … we were only discussing the possibility of nursing. Sophie hasn't decided if she wants to join the Queen Alexandra's yet.'

Sophie had to use all her self-control to prevent a grin from spreading across her face. If nursing was now 'her' decision, her father wasn't going to mention it again.

'Very well, sir,' replied Bleddyn. 'However, I still need an interpreter.' He turned to Sophie. 'I hope I'm not asking too much on such short notice, Miss Edwardson.'

'Well, it did come as a bit of a shock, but I can help. Anyhow, I need to find out whether or not nursing is right for me.'

Her father stormed out and slammed the door behind him, leaving Dwight and Johnson to exchange uncomfortable glances in his wake.

Bleddyn winked at Sophie.

She could have kissed him. It would probably take her father months to contrive a new plan for her life.

'You need to ask Artorius about your presence, Miss Edwardson,' Bleddyn reminded her.

Artorius didn't even look up when she put the question to him. 'If you must.'

'He was non-committal, but I can stay,' she told Bleddyn.

'Sergeant, can you let me into the cell, lock it after me, and stand just out of sight?' Bleddyn asked.

Dwight hesitated. 'Are you sure that's a good idea, Dr Kendrick?'

'Well, I can't perform an examination from out here.'

'Very well, then.' The sergeant unlocked the cell, keeping an eye on Artorius and a hand on his truncheon the whole time.

Bleddyn walked in and placed his duffel bag on the opposite side of the bed to Artorius. He unfastened the latch.

'Stop, Physician.' Artorius reached over and took Bleddyn's left hand. 'You are missing the nail of your smallest finger. How did that come to be?'

'I know what he asked,' Bleddyn muttered before Sophie could translate. 'Tell him I was born this way.'

Artorius then asked if the condition also affected the smallest toe of his left foot.

When Sophie asked Bleddyn about his toenail, he furrowed his eyebrows. 'Yes, it does. How did he know that?'

Sophie was wondering the same thing. 'Where have you seen this characteristic before?' she asked Artorius.

'Sophie Edwardson, did you not say the physician was a *Cymry* – a

33

descendant of my Combrogi? I am told this feature manifested in several people from a village near Anderidos. Alas, few survived, for the villagers took refuge in the fortress when the Saxone pirate Ælle attacked. He besieged the fortress and razed it to the ground.' He glanced at Bleddyn, then at Sophie. 'Is the trait common in his family?'

Bleddyn confirmed that his sister bore the trait as well, and that his father and paternal grandfather also had it.

'The trait comes from his father's family,' Sophie told Artorius. Why was he so interested in this? She glanced at his fingers. No, he wasn't missing any nails.

Artorius looked up at Bleddyn. 'And what is your name, Physician?'

'His name is Bleddyn Kendrick,' Sophie replied.

Artorius nodded at her. 'Thank you.' He let go of Bleddyn's hand. 'I have more questions for Bleddyn Kendrick. What does he think about the domination of the English? Does he feel oppressed?'

They weren't going to get this medical examination done without humouring Artorius first, so Sophie put the questions to Bleddyn. Truth be told, she wanted to hear his reply, too.

Bleddyn stroked his chin. 'Well, let me put it this way. Does Artorius know of a queen we now call *Boadicea* in English?'

Sophie established that Artorius called her *Boudika*.

'Perhaps you should ask Artorius how Queen Boudika might have felt about her people and the Romans joining forces against the Saxons,' Bleddyn suggested. 'Would she have resented him for the crimes of his Roman ancestors?'

When Sophie translated this into Latin, Artorius glowered at Bleddyn. His hard expression then softened. 'The physician makes a valid point.' He looked at Sophie. 'Perhaps I should apologise for how I spoke to you, Sophie Edwardson. However, Bleddyn Kendrick did not answer my question about the oppression of the Cymry.'

'Artorius won't accept a dodge of the question, Dr Kendrick. He wants to know if you feel that the English oppress the Cymry.'

'No,' Bleddyn replied. 'Tell him we have a democracy, and I have the same rights as an English citizen. So no, we're not an oppressed race.'

Artorius expressed familiarity with the concept of democracy, but he thought it was inconsistent with her previous statement about a Welsh-descended king. She had to explain that the King's power was now mostly symbolic, and the country was governed by a 'senate-like council' elected by the people.

'But do the English not overrule my people in this democracy using their superior numbers?' Artorius asked. 'Does the majority not suppress the minority?'

When she asked Bleddyn, he replied, 'Well, that *can* happen, but ethnicity is only one of many things that unites and divides the British people. Anyhow, with the German threat looming, now's not the time to dwell on past grievances.'

Sophie translated this for Artorius.

He raised his eyebrows. 'Immortal gods, do I understand those sentiments! Well, then. It appears the English treat my descendants well enough today. Perhaps I should be consoled.' He looked at Bleddyn. 'Thank you, Bleddyn Kendrick.' His voice was still raw and emotional, but less despondent than it had been only minutes before.

'Can I start my examination now?' Bleddyn asked, a note of exasperation in his voice.

'I think so,' Sophie replied.

Bleddyn asked Sophie to translate and to record dictation while he carried out a head-to-toe examination. He employed an extensive repertoire of medical terms, possibly in the hope that if Artorius was a fraud who was feigning ignorance of Modern English, he might keep Artorius ignorant of his discoveries. The medical terminology barely qualified as English, and despite the number of Latin-derived terms, Sophie struggled to understand him.

When Bleddyn checked Artorius's mouth, he noted that several teeth were missing and that a premolar was chipped. Artorius claimed that he lost his teeth in battles and accidents.

'Note that I'm not a dentist, Miss Edwardson, but the patient's teeth exhibit what I suspect is an unusual amount of wear,' Bleddyn said. 'I cannot see any obvious cavities, either, although he does have a build-up of plaque … and halitosis, too.' He drew back and wrinkled his nose.

Bleddyn took a sample of hair and put it in an envelope for analysis, but he did not elaborate.

At Bleddyn's request, Artorius removed his tunic. Bleddyn had Sophie record lengths of scars along with the positions and widths of suture abscess scars. Most of these were on Artorius's hands and forearms, although Bleddyn was particularly intrigued by the circular scars on the front and back of the left shoulder, which Artorius claimed were from his near-fatal pilum wound. Bleddyn directed Sophie to record that, apart from the entrance and exit wounds, there were no scars on or near the shoulders, and to note that Artorius's shoulder mobility was normal. He specifically mentioned the absence of any scarring 'near the deltoid tuberosity' on both shoulders. Something about Bleddyn's tone gave Sophie the impression that he was trying to conceal astonishment, but she had no idea why. The flurry of obscure medical terms was numbing her mind.

'The rash around his armpits is a fungal infection,' Bleddyn said. 'I can give him something for that.' He unstopped some bottles and poured about half a fluid ounce from the smaller bottle into a measuring cup. He transferred this into an empty phial, along with a gill of clear fluid from the larger bottle, and gave the mixture to Artorius. 'Miss Edwardson, can you instruct Artorius to apply this solution three times a day until the rash clears up?'

After using a stethoscope to examine Artorius's chest, back and abdomen, Bleddyn examined the lower body. He asked Artorius to remove his trousers and undergarments. Sophie turned sideways and stared at her notes, trying to avoid forming images in her mind of Bleddyn's descriptions. Nursing probably wasn't for her, after all.

When Bleddyn finished and Artorius had re-dressed, Sergeant Dwight let Bleddyn out of the cell.

'Thank you for helping me, Miss Edwardson,' Bleddyn told her as

Johnson locked the door again. He cast Artorius a backward glance. 'I'll explain my findings later.'

Sophie nodded, and said to Artorius, 'Thank you for cooperating with us. I do not understand what Bleddyn Kendrick discovered, but we must both write reports. I will also examine the contents of the burial mound, and I may be back tomorrow with more questions.'

'Before you go, I have one request,' Artorius replied. 'The contents of my resting chamber should include personal effects. I ask that you bring me the golden pendant shaped as a wheel with eight spokes. It is a sacred symbol, and I wish to hold it close to me when I pray.'

'I know not if I would be allowed to do so, but I will ask,' Sophie told him.

'You do not believe I am who I claim to be, do you?'

Sophie had no idea what to believe any more. After considering her words, she replied, 'What I believe is unimportant. Remember, I am just a translator.'

CHAPTER 4

1900 hours
RAF Axleigh, North Lincolnshire

Sophie's father wanted to send Bleddyn to the mess hall for dinner, but Sophie insisted that he dine with them so they could discuss their findings.

'Anyway, Sophie, Kendrick, how can we prove this man's a fraud or a lunatic?' her father asked as they started with the potato and leek soup. The cook's assistant had already placed the next two courses on a sideboard, and they were getting cold. 'Any differences between his story and the known history? And what was that "pre-girlfriendian" thing you were talking about?'

'*Pre-Galfridian.*'

'Whatever. What does it mean?'

'Geoffrey of Monmouth, or *Galfridus*, popularised the Arthurian legend in the twelfth century,' Sophie explained. 'Contemporary records for the time of Arthur are poor. There were differences between what he claimed and what we presume to know, but none of these inconsistencies disprove the idea that he's the legendary Arthur. The only thing I cannot attribute to poor records is his name. He was using "Artorius" as a *cognomen*, not a *nomen*.'

The two men looked at her in perplexed silence.

'The Romans,' she explained, 'had a *praenomen* or first name, a *nomen* or family name, and a *cognomen* or personal name, or epithet. He called himself Gaius Ambrosius Artorius, which uses the Roman family name *Artorius* as an epithet.'

'So, he got the Roman naming conventions wrong?' her father asked.

Sophie shrugged. 'Conventions were breaking down when the Empire fell.' She took a spoonful of what may have been the worst soup she'd ever tasted. Even the food at Girton College was better.

'So, there was nothing else?'

'Well … most historians believe the Picts were different to the Celts of Roman Britain, but according to Artorius, they were essentially the same race before Rome divided the island. He claimed that druidesses entombed him, but the Romans supposedly eliminated the last of the druids in the second century.'

Her father raised his eyebrows. 'Well, that settles it. If the druids had been gone for hundreds of years—'

'*If,*' Sophie interrupted. 'Perhaps the Romans drove the religion underground but failed to eradicate it completely.' She tried another mouthful of soup. 'Artorius also talked about sons and a daughter – Cynon, Llachau and Gwenhwyach. He later mentioned a son named Amyr. I've seen a passing reference to a son of Arthur by that name in a ninth-century chronicle. It said that Arthur killed Amyr, but Artorius implied the Anglo-Saxons captured and killed him.'

Bleddyn cleared his throat. 'The name *Llachau* comes up in an old Welsh poem. It describes him as the son of Arthur and a great warrior.'

'I thought his only son was Mordred,' her father said.

Sophie shook her head. 'That myth arose later. Mordred was Arthur's nephew in Geoffrey of Monmouth's book. However, the notion that Arthur died at Mordred's hand is an old one.' She pulled a notebook from her handbag and turned over a few pages, looking for the reference. 'I brought some notes here, including some transcripts from the *Annales Cambriae*. Many historians believe these dry, matter-of-fact records are more reliable than other chronicles from – ah, here. "The battle of Camlann, in which Arthur and Medraut fell; and there was death in Britain and in Ireland."' She looked up. 'Artorius was talking about a Saxon incursion, not a civil war. He specifically told me that Medraut, or as we say today, *Mordred*, was an ally in this battle.'

Bleddyn pointed to her notebook. 'Perhaps something was lost in translation, but you just said they both fell in this battle. Does it imply they were fighting against each other?'

Sophie glanced at the passage again. 'Now that you mention it, it doesn't say. They could have been fighting alongside *or* against each other.' She raised her eyebrows and closed the notebook. 'That's an interesting point.'

'What Artorius said actually makes more sense, when you think about it,' Bleddyn suggested. 'According to legend, the Britons were so weakened in the civil war between Arthur and Mordred, it paved the way for the Anglo-Saxon invasion. Would a king who presided over such a calamity really be remembered as a hero?'

'Didn't you say that he claimed not to be a king?' her father asked. 'What does he claim to be?'

'A *legatus* – a Roman general. That part of his story is consistent with the oldest written accounts of Arthur.' Sophie rubbed her cheek. 'In fact, everything about Artorius … I'm not sure how to explain this, but … well, as I said before, Geoffrey of Monmouth made the Arthurian tales popular. His version of Arthur was based on his stories of older legends, which may have had a basis in history, but he made a lot of alterations. If Arthur truly existed, he would have been more like the man Artorius claims to be than the king we recognise from the popular stories.'

'So, what about Excalibur, and the Knights of the Round Table, and all that?' her father asked.

'They're more relevant to the modern tales than a possible historic Arthur.'

Having finished as much of the soup as she could stomach, Sophie took a bite of the lukewarm cabbage, potatoes and bully beef. She tried to wash it down with water.

She broke the silence again. 'If this is a hoax, he's paid tremendous attention to detail. I can't differentiate his dialect of Vulgar Latin from the one spoken in Britain at the end of Roman rule; he used the years of various kings' reigns as time references; he used old Roman place names; he appeared unfamiliar with modern plumbing and fountain pens ...' She broke off, scarcely able to believe she was entertaining the bizarre notion that the man she interrogated might actually be the real Arthur.

Her father turned to Bleddyn. 'Kendrick, what did you uncover with your medical examination?'

Bleddyn pushed his plate away, undoubtedly keen for a distraction from the food. 'It was most peculiar. I was hoping to find a smallpox or a BCG inoculation scar, but he didn't have either of them.'

'Oh – that's why you wanted me to record the absence of scars on his upper arms,' Sophie exclaimed. 'Their presence would have proven he was born in modern times. So ... he's never had those inoculations?'

'It appears not, but occasionally, an inoculation scar doesn't form,' Bleddyn replied. 'Or perhaps he didn't receive those inoculations in the arm. That was one reason I had him remove his trousers – to check for scars on the buttocks.'

'Do doctors administer inoculations in the ...' Sophie trailed off. She glanced at her father, whose frown had deepened to a scowl.

'Sometimes, but usually not. Still, I had to check.'

'There are a few inoculation objectors, though,' her father said. 'The absence of a scar doesn't prove his claims.'

'No, but that isn't the only odd thing about him. Some of his wounds had been stitched crudely; others had been bandaged when they should have been stitched. The one on his shoulder was really strange. The scar at the back is clearly an exit wound. I could only find one reasonable candidate for the corresponding entry wound, but a projectile going through a man's shoulder at that particular angle would wreck the ball-and-socket joint. Yet his shoulder mobility was normal.'

'You also noted something about his teeth,' Sophie said.

'A dentist should examine him, but I couldn't see any fillings. The missing teeth could have been lost through injury, and I didn't see any tooth decay – which I thought strange, given the state of his oral hygiene. His teeth also appeared quite worn to me. Such wear and tear on the teeth, but with little decay, indicates he ate a diet high in stoneground flour and low in refined sugar for most of his life.'

'That's what I'd expect for a pre-industrial era diet,' Sophie mused.

Bleddyn nodded. 'So, like you, Miss Edwardson, I didn't find a shred of evidence that proves his story false.'

Sophie pursed her lips and nodded. This was becoming very strange indeed.

'He can't be telling the truth,' her father scoffed. 'Perhaps there's something in that burial mound. Sophie, can you examine the items we recovered?'

'I'm really not the best qualified for that …'

'I just need to know if they're fakes.'

'Can you provide a camera with a film? I will also need a small table, a light, and some sort of a backdrop – a white tablecloth or bed sheet would be fine.'

He nodded. 'I can provide those. I'll find someone to guide you around the base in the morning and take dictation for you if necessary. Kendrick can go back to Cambridge tomorrow.'

'Actually, I was hoping Dr Kendrick would help me catalogue the contents.'

Her father frowned. 'Why? Kendrick isn't an archaeologist.'

'No, but if this is to be classified and I'm to be the most qualified person to examine these artefacts, I would at least like assistance from someone who has a scientific background. I presume your engineer is busy with the construction work?'

Her father grunted. 'Very well, then. If Kendrick agrees.'

Bleddyn shifted awkwardly, but he nodded. 'I'll do what I can.'

'One other thing,' Sophie said. 'Artorius asked me to bring him one piece of jewellery from the barrow, if that is possible. He said it was sacred to him. If nothing else, I'd like to know what it is, and how he interprets it.'

'What is it?' her father asked. 'If it's a brooch, he might be able to use the pin to stab someone, or pick locks.'

'No, it's a pendant. He wanted one shaped as an eight-spoked wheel.'

'An eight-spoked wheel?' Bleddyn exclaimed. 'That's odd. The Wheel of Dharma has eight spokes, too.'

'What's the Wheel of Dharma?' Sophie asked.

'It's a sacred symbol in Buddhism.'

Sophie's father pierced him with his gaze. 'How do you know that?'

After a moment's hesitation, Bleddyn replied, 'My sister married a Chinese Buddhist.'

'*What?*' Sophie's father wrinkled his nose. 'Your sister *married* a Chink? I suppose she now helps run their opium den?'

Bleddyn looked him in the eye. 'Don't you think that's a bit hypocritical, sir? After the British fought a war with China to force them to open their doors to British drug dealers?'

'How dare you say that about your country?' he demanded.

'He's not wrong, Father,' Sophie said. 'The history books don't put it quite so bluntly, but the East India Company was involved in smuggling opium into China.'

Her father glanced between the two of them. 'All right, I'll admit my comment about the opium den was inappropriate, but even so … your sister *married* a Chinaman? Were you fine with that?'

'I admit I had reservations,' Bleddyn replied tersely. 'Not about the man – he was an old school friend – but how the wider community would treat her and her children. The contempt some people have for people who aren't white … Well, I'm sorry to say that the Nazis aren't the only ones who believe white people should remain racially pure.'

Sophie glanced at her father with apprehension. Bleddyn's clever choice of words fell short of openly accusing him of sympathising with Nazi racial ideology, but he would not have missed the implication. It was time to bring the conversation back to the topic in hand. 'So, what about the Wheel, Dr Kendrick?'

Bleddyn shrugged. 'I'm not sure. Perhaps it's just a coincidence. Wasn't King Arthur a Christian? For that matter, could Buddhism have spread to England by the time of the Roman collapse?'

'I wouldn't think so,' Sophie replied. 'However, Artorius identified as a "Gnostic" Christian.'

'I'm sorry?' Bleddyn asked.

'There were several branches of ancient Christianity. Gnosticism was one of these. It vanished a long time ago, mostly because of anti-heresy laws.'

'Would Gnosticism have been around in King Arthur's time?' asked Bleddyn.

'Well … the Romans banned all religions other than canonical Christianity, but the Empire was beginning to crumble when they passed these laws. So yes, Gnosticism may have still been around in Arthur's time.' Sophie shrugged. 'Even so, I doubt there would be overlaps with Buddhism. Perhaps it's based on a Celtic Pagan sun wheel.'

At length, her father murmured, 'I'll think about the pendant a little more.'

The third course was bread-and-butter pudding. It was more palatable than the first two courses, but only just.

There was a knock on the door.

'Enter!' Sophie's father called out.

A signalman walked in and saluted. 'Sir, I have breaking news from Europe.' He gave Sophie's father a telegram.

'Thank you. Dismissed.'

The signalman saluted and left.

Sophie stiffened. 'It's not about Christopher, is it, father?' She glanced at Bleddyn. 'My brother – he serves on the HMS *Glorious*.'

Her father studied the telegram. 'No, it's about the campaign on the mainland.' His face hardened. 'Bloody hell, the Boche came through the Ardennes and are near Sedan. This is bad, this is very bad.'

'Why is that, Father?'

'The Germans first invaded Belgium from the north. The British Expeditionary Force was deployed to repel them – but if German forces are also at Sedan, they're in France, south of the British Expeditionary Force.'

Bleddyn furrowed his eyebrows. 'Wing Commander, are you saying our men are surrounded?'

'Not yet, but if the German forces in Sedan make a dash for the coast ...'

They said little for the rest of the evening.

When dinner was over, Bleddyn went to the barracks. Sophie was put up in the spare bedroom of the old farmhouse. She transcribed her notes of Bleddyn's medical examination from shorthand to cursive writing, washed, changed, brushed her teeth, and went to bed.

The bizarre case of Artorius and the news about Sedan kept her awake. Had Arthur really returned to the British in their time of need?

It probably didn't matter if Artorius was the legendary Arthur. He had no intention of helping the English. Besides, even if he changed his mind, what would he know about modern warfare? How could one Dark Age general help them against the efficient, well-oiled German war machine?

***

2130 hours
General Lord Gort's Headquarters
Ronse, Belgium

'Forty planes?' spluttered Lord Gort.

'Forty *bombers*,' replied Air Marshal Barratt. 'Three-man crews each. The Meuse Valley has turned into a bloody mass grave for our boys.'

Lord Gort exchanged a glance with his French liaison officer, Major Archdale, before he dropped into his chair. 'Why couldn't the fighters protect them?'

'I sent over two hundred fighters to cover them,' Barratt replied. 'Luftwaffe fighters outnumbered ours by two to one. Maybe three to one.'

'Christ almighty! The Boche have that many planes in the area?'

Barratt nodded.

'Can we try again, with assistance from the French Air Force?'

Archdale cleared his throat. 'Sir, it seems that General Gamelin has withdrawn most of the French Air Force to Paris.'

'Paris?' Lord Gort demanded. 'Why the blazes did he do that? Paris isn't their target.'

'To be honest, sir, talking to Gamelin has been like talking to a brick wall.'

'Who's on the border? Is anyone from France attacking the Germans at the Meuse?'

'Georges is, sir, but I don't think he commands enough men for it. You heard from the Air Marshal about the strength of the Germans.' Archdale frowned and cleared his throat. 'Sir, something that came up when I last saw Georges … it seems the French Air Force spotted a build-up of German artillery in eastern Luxembourg a few days ago.'

'What?' Barratt demanded. 'They *knew*?' His expression could have curdled milk.

'Gamelin believed it was just a diversion from the main thrust in the north,' Archdale explained. 'He denied the French Air Force permission to strike.'

Barratt slammed the table with his fist. 'God damn it, why didn't Gamelin tell us? *We* might have been able to hit them before they put so many bloody fighters in the air.'

'And now they're in Paris, where they can't do a bloody thing against the Germans,' muttered Lord Gort.

'I understand their commanders weren't happy about the decision, but they had orders from French high command,' said Archdale.

'The Boche aren't going to march on Paris,' Lord Gort said. 'Not with hundreds of thousands of men here, and more to the south. They need to neutralise us first. You just watch. Those German forces near Sedan are going to drive for the coast and try to encircle us.'

'And what can we do now?' asked Barratt.

Lord Gort got up and looked at the map on the wall. 'There's no stopping that spearhead now. However, they'll need to move quickly for this to work, and they'll stretch their lines.' He traced his finger from Sedan to Calais. 'Rather than attack the head of the spear, we should wait until they start moving, and then attack the shaft. Snap off the head. Then we could turn the tables and encircle *them*.'

'We still have the forces in northern Belgium to contend with,' Barratt cautioned.

'That's why we need Billotte's and Gamelin's help. We must hit the Germans simultaneously from both sides. Archdale, when you see the French commanders again, hammer some sense into Gamelin. If he doesn't free up more forces to attack the shaft of this spearhead, we'll lose this battle within a fortnight. Belgium will fall, and maybe France, too.'

CHAPTER 5

Wednesday, 15 May
0730 hours
RAF Axleigh

Armed with a camera, folding card table and white tablecloth, Sophie met Bleddyn outside her father's office. Lucy, the MTC driver she met yesterday, was there, too.

Bleddyn took the table from her, and Lucy led them to a storage hangar. She unlocked the door. 'Everything from the barrow was put in here.'

'I'd like to set the table out here,' Sophie told Bleddyn before they entered the hangar. 'Natural sunlight would be best for the photographs.'

Once inside, Sophie examined the food first. There was bread made from coarse flour, as well as cheese, apples, plums, a pear, walnuts, blackberries and raspberries. Most of the fruit and nuts were small, more like wild specimens than modern cultivars.

'Well, there's nothing here that would have been out of place in a Celtic burial mound,' Sophie murmured.

'But how could it have been preserved all this time?' Bleddyn asked.

Sophie shrugged. 'How could someone live all this time? Artorius claims magic was involved. The best way of disproving him would be to find an anachronism, such as a potato or other New World vegetable.' She picked up a blackberry. 'Mind you, I don't know where anyone could have found these at this time of year.'

'They couldn't be from the southern hemisphere, could they?' Bleddyn asked.

'When even Spanish oranges are hard to come by? Anyhow, I doubt a ship could sail fast enough to deliver fresh berries, and these are too firm to have ever been frozen.'

Sophie picked up an apple and put it to her nose. The mouth-watering but sour fragrance reminded her of cooking apples and crab apples. 'Apples lose some of their aroma in storage. The scent is too strong for this to be an old apple, and it's still firm.'

Sophie proceeded to examine other artefacts, documenting them and taking photographs as she did so. Bleddyn took notes for her. He didn't know shorthand and was slow to record Sophie's dictation, but his observations and suggestions were often insightful despite his lack of training in archaeology.

Sophie was looking for something, anything, that might suggest modern fabrication processes.

All the cloth had been woven from wool, linen or hemp. Bleddyn examined the seams carefully, but these, too, had been hand-stitched with coarse thread. The uneven hobnails in the *caligae*-style sandals had been forged by a blacksmith.

The terracotta jars and vases had all been made on a potter's wheel, and all the glass was blown. There were no seamlines or any other sign that they'd been cast. The largest terracotta jar was full of water. Bleddyn sniffed it and told Sophie that it was rainwater or well water: no chlorine. Other big jars held wine and home-brewed ale. The smaller jars contained suspensions of various herbs in water, wine, vinegar, olive oil or wool fat.

'I think these are medicinal,' Bleddyn said. He sniffed a couple, wrinkling his nose at one of them. 'This is probably elder leaf. There's rosemary, sage … and I'm not sure what the others are.'

The weapons included knives, an unstrung bow, arrows, a lance, two pila and three swords. 'There are two *spathae* and a gladius, so the swords are appropriate for the period,' Sophie observed. 'One of the spathae has a rounded tip. Interesting … see the pattern in the blade? They're made from pattern-welded steel, or maybe even Damascus steel.' They were precisely what she expected of high-quality swords made in the Dark Ages.

'I suppose one of those swords is meant to be Excalibur,' Bleddyn remarked. 'I must say, I was expecting something grander.' He picked up a strigil and held it out to her.

'That isn't a weapon,' she told him. 'It's a scraping tool the Romans used for cleaning their skin. Put it with the herbal infusions for now.' She opened a leather pouch. 'Bowstring.'

'What are bowstrings made of these days?' Bleddyn asked.

'Catgut, I think, but this one's made of hemp or linen.' Sophie rolled it between her fingers. 'It's rather thick, but I suppose a hemp bowstring would have to be thick in order to take the poundage.'

Bleddyn inspected an arrow. 'This looks like it was made for such a bowstring,' he observed, pointing to the nock.

'Was there any armour, Lucy?' Sophie asked.

Lucy pointed to a steel trunk. 'It's in there, miss.'

The shield was elliptical. Judging by the dents, chips and the partially obliterated painting of a red dragon, it had seen plenty of use. There was a splintered hole near the top.

Sophie removed two pattern-welded steel helmets – one with a full visor, the other, a Roman-style ridge helmet. Beneath them lay two suits of maille. The top suit was a quintessential Roman *lorica hamata* with short sleeves. The second one was heavier.

'Dr Kendrick, could you help hold this maille suit?' Sophie asked. 'Thank you. Interesting … the sleeves are full length.' There was damage to the left shoulder, and a brown-red residue. 'Is this dried blood?'

Bleddyn examined the residue. 'It is, but what pierced the chain mail? Good Lord, there's an entry *and* an exit site on the chain mail. Did they have armour-piercing arrows in the Dark Ages?'

'This was probably a pilum – a spear on a wooden shaft, like the ones we examined before. Their heads were like bodkin points, so yes, I think they could have pierced maille.'

'Both layers?' Bleddyn asked.

'Possibly. Artorius said it was fired from a ballista.'

Bleddyn took some scrapings of the dried blood and put it in a phial. 'It might be possible to determine the blood group,' he explained.

There was also a heavy jacket of quilted linen. It, too, had holes in the left shoulder and bloodstains. 'This must be a *subarmilis*,' Sophie said. 'If a pilum went through this as well as two layers of maille and a shield, it must have been travelling at quite some speed.'

Finally, Sophie inspected a bronze jewellery box embellished with intricate Greco-Roman agricultural scenes. She prised the lid open. It contained a silver Celtic armband, a heavy silver chain, several golden Roman-style rings with gemstones, and some ornate clothing pins and brooches. It also held the Wheel pendant Artorius had requested.

'Are you planning to give it to him, Miss Edwardson?' Bleddyn asked as she held it up.

'I'm considering it, but I need to check with my father first.'

'Just a second.' Bleddyn took it from her, procured a safety pin from his pocket, opened it, and used the point to tease open the knotted string from which the pendant was suspended. 'Artorius could use the string to garrotte someone. We should still act with caution. He only asked for the pendant.'

As they placed everything away, Sophie muttered, 'Well, Father's not going to be pleased. I haven't found a single anachronistic item or feature. For all I can tell, nothing here would have been out of place in the Dark Ages. Lucy, could you show us the barrow?'

'Yes, miss.'

As they followed Lucy across the airfield, Sophie turned to Bleddyn. 'Dr Kendrick, I really appreciate your taking dictation for me.'

He shrugged. 'You did the same for me yesterday.'

Sophie smiled. Bleddyn hadn't just deferred to her knowledge of archaeology; he'd not shown the slightest resentment when she ordered him around like a secretary. Few men had enough humility to accept a woman's authority like that.

She looked up again. 'Oh, no! Please tell me that isn't the burial mound!'

The knoll now resembled a miniature cutaway for a railway track, and the ground before it was strewn with blasted rock. Workmen were still clearing it away.

'I've never seen a burial mound as large as this,' Sophie lamented. 'This is almost as bad as demolishing Stonehenge.'

They approached the headman. Lucy saluted him. 'Lieutenant MacLean, the wing commander's daughter wishes to inspect the burial mound.'

MacLean nodded and instructed his men to take a break. He turned to Sophie. 'I hope this won't take long, Miss Edwardson. The munitions arrive next week, and we need this dump ready by then.'

'I'll bear that in mind,' Sophie replied. She pointed to a pile of green timber beside the mound. 'Was that on the top?'

'Yes, miss. This place was a wheat farm before the requisition, but the owners couldn't plough the hillock, so they left it covered with oaks.'

'And nobody thought to salvage the timber?' Bleddyn asked.

'There's barely enough heartwood in them to make it worthwhile. The soil on top was shallow, so these oaks are all stunted.'

Sophie inspected what remained of the burial mound. The man-made structure had been built atop a rocky outcrop and mounded with soil. It was not as large as she had originally thought. The engineer had retained the two long walls of the structure and incorporated these into the cutaway. The ceiling, blocking stone, back wall and floor were all gone, and the workmen were removing the substratum underneath the chamber's floor to make a deep pit. The remaining walls were now partway up the cutaway knoll.

About three feet below the man-made structure was a thick layer of clay. A wooden stump jutted out near the cutaway section. Sophie pointed this out to Bleddyn. 'This low-lying area is much like the Fens. Where we currently stand was once a shallow lake. Here' – she pointed to the top of the clay – 'was the old water level.'

'Are you saying the burial chamber was built on what used to be an island?' Bleddyn asked.

'Yes.'

Bleddyn pointed to the charcoal above the waterline. 'Was this a bonfire?'

'It might have been. It's certainly bigger than a single fireplace.'

Bleddyn bit his lower lip and pointed to some charred bones protruding from the ash. 'Those are human remains.'

Sophie shuddered.

She walked around the cutaway to examine the remaining walls. Something was odd, but Sophie couldn't put her finger on it at first. When she realised what it was, she almost screamed with excitement. 'Ble— Dr Kendrick, look!' She picked up a fragment of stone. 'See how the stone's colour is lighter where dynamite has fractured it and exposed a fresh surface?'

'The dark surface layer's called a patina, isn't it?'

'Yes. Fresh surfaces have no patina, but the darkened rock does. Now, look at the two large slabs of stone.' She pointed to the stones stuck in the two facing walls of the dump. 'They were once the inside walls.'

'They're almost as pale as the recently fractured surfaces,' Bleddyn observed.

'Exactly! It's as though the inside is newer – much newer – than the outside.'

Bleddyn hesitated. 'Could there be a more rational explanation, Miss Edwardson? Could someone have chiselled a thin layer of rock away to make the inside look new?'

'I don't think so. See that?' Sophie pointed to the nearest edges of the old barrow stones. 'That's where the entrance was, and the blocking stone would have sat right there. Do you see how the patina deepens gradually as it goes deeper into the chamber? I can't see how chiselling away a surface could attain that effect.'

Bleddyn nodded. 'Yes … yes, I see what you mean.' He looked up at her. 'It's very strange indeed.'

Sophie took photographs, hoping they would capture the necessary detail.

'Wait, what's going on?' Lucy asked. She pointed beyond the

perimeter fence. Security guards were speaking to someone who was emerging from a patch of broom.

'Was he watching us?' MacLean asked.

The stranger showed the guards some documents or papers.

MacLean shrugged. 'They're taking care of it.'

Sophie, Bleddyn and Lucy went back to the main office. Sophie had to explain the significance of what they had found and convince her father to stop work on the burial mound. They must preserve and restore it. This was the most important archaeological discovery of the century. It was even more important than Tutankhamen's tomb.

Unfortunately, he was not the least bit impressed by what she told him. 'I don't have time to start building another munitions dump,' he told her.

'But Father, you don't understand what this means! If this man really is the legendary Arthur—'

'Poppycock! He can't be King Arthur. The man is a fraud, and you weren't clever enough to figure out how he did it.'

'With respect, sir,' Bleddyn protested, 'those injuries—'

'They were faked. They had to be. I should have known better than to trust a girl and a pleb.'

Indignation burned in Sophie's chest.

'For God's sake, Wing Commander,' Bleddyn snapped, 'you're not listening—'

'ENOUGH!' George Edwardson slammed his fist onto the table. 'I've had enough of this! MI5 will have to get involved now. It will reflect badly on me, and it's entirely your fault!' His nostrils flared and the veins in his neck looked as though they were about to pop. He fixed his glare on Bleddyn. 'I paid to send my daughter to Cambridge against my better judgement, but *you*, Kendrick, *you* have just been a waste of that scholarship's funds. You're a blithering idiot who was never fit to read at Cambridge, and your father's death didn't change that!'

Sophie's blood ran cold. The colour drained from Bleddyn's face before her eyes. She glanced at Lucy, who had backed against the wall and looked as though she'd love nothing better than for the wall to open up and swallow her.

Sophie's father ordered Bleddyn into the secretary's office to write his report, 'Bloody useless piece of rubbish from a bloody useless Welshman that it will be.' Then he turned to Sophie. 'The police called before – they want you to translate for them again. Perhaps, this time, you could try to get some sensible answers out of him. If you could overcome your disposition for gullibility and work out how he's pulled off his charade, that would be delightful. Lucy, drive my daughter back to the police station.'

Sophie trembled with rage as she stormed out of his office.

She almost asked Lucy to take her back to the railway station in Doncaster so that she could leave for Cambridge and never speak to her father again. If he thought so little of her abilities in this matter, then she could damn well find someone else to tell him what he didn't want to hear.

She began to calm down and think things through after they passed the airbase gates. Her luggage was still on-base, and anyhow, she could hardly walk away from this now.

Even so, she was still seething when Lucy parked in front of the police station.

Sergeant Dwight came out of his office when they entered the building. 'Ah, Miss Edwardson. Do you wish to talk to the suspect?'

Sophie tilted her head. 'Didn't you request that I come here?'

'Request that you come? I asked your father if you were coming back today, but it wasn't a request. Maybe he misunderstood.'

Sophie sighed. 'Sorry to have wasted your time, Sergeant.'

'Oh, never mind. In fact, it might be a good idea if you speak to him. You could tell us anything we might need to know.'

'How has he been since yesterday?' Sophie asked.

'Quite morose, but he's calmed down. We're still getting awkward questions from the locals, though. Have you had any luck determining who he is?'

'No. We couldn't find anything to disprove what he told us yesterday.'

'Very strange indeed. Are we still keeping mum on this?'

Sophie nodded.

'All right. Ah, Miss Edwardson … I'm not sure if I'm allowed to ask – but if this *isn't* a hoax, could he really be King Arthur? They say he will return and save us in our darkest hour, and after the news on the wireless last night about the Meuse …'

'I didn't say he *was* Arthur, only that we cannot disprove it. Anyhow, I don't think a Dark Age warrior could help us much against tanks or planes.'

The sergeant deflated.

Constable Johnson led her to the cells.

Artorius was sitting on his bed when Sophie walked in. He stood up. 'Sophie Edwardson, I am glad you came. I am unable to converse with anyone else here, and I have missed your company. I no longer believe my captors wish to torture me. Quite the opposite, in fact. They have provided me with garments of the finest cloth.' He took the fabric of the shirt he wore in his forefingers and pulled it forward. 'I deduced that these buttons and reinforced holes are to fasten the garments. But I suppose prisoners are not allowed pins or brooches?'

Sophie couldn't help but smile. 'You do not realise the significance of a thousand years of progress, Artorius. The clothes are not of high quality by today's standards. And please, just call me Sophie.'

'These are normal now? And the tallow is also of better quality than any I have seen before. I am amazed you even provide it for a prisoner.'

Tallow? – Oh, he means soap. 'There is nothing special about the tallow, either.'

Artorius studied her expression. 'Do you now believe I lay asleep in the burial chamber for over a thousand years?'

'I am unsure what to believe. Your story is implausible, yet you do not bear characteristic marks of modern times.' She sighed. 'Irrespective of the truth, I fear that you may be taken from here to a prison, or an asylum – that is a type of hospital for the insane, and you may be held there for the rest of your life. I am sorry, but I will have no say in what happens to you.'

Artorius shrugged. 'It seems I have no place in your world, anyway. Did you bring the pendant?'

After the argument with her father, Sophie had forgotten to ask if she had permission to give Artorius the pendant. She hesitated for a moment, decided that she didn't care if he approved or not now, and took it from her pocket.

Gratitude flooded Artorius's face. 'Thank you, Sophie!' he said as he took it from her outreached hand.

'Watch, it, miss –' Johnson came forward. Sophie realised too late that she should never have come so close to the bars. Luckily, Artorius didn't try anything rash. He had already taken the pendant and stepped back.

Johnson let out a sigh. 'That was careless, miss. What did you give him?'

'It's a pendant with spiritual value,' Sophie told him. She turned to Artorius and asked in Latin, 'What sets it above the rest of the jewellery?'

'I do not know if the Wheel can help me now, but it gives me comfort. Have you seen a Wheel of Dhargh before?'

'I have not, but Bleddyn likened it to a Wheel of *Dharma*, a symbol from a non-Christian religion with large followings in the East.'

'Perhaps others have adopted the symbol and the Eight Requirements,' Artorius suggested. 'Or perhaps the Wheel of Dhargh originally came from the East. All I know is that the Christ gave one of these to Miriam Magdala before He left.'

'Are you saying that the eight-spoked wheel is a Christian symbol?' Sophie asked.

Artorius tilted his head. 'Do today's English still worship the Germanic Pantheon of Gods? The *Esar*?'

'We do not. The English converted to Christianity centuries ago.'

'All of you?'

'Well … not everyone follows Christianity any more, but nobody worships the *Esar* these days.'

'Oh! I did not expect that. Yet you are unfamiliar with the Wheel of Dhargh. Do you follow Nicene Christianity? What about the modern Cymry?'

'All modern Christian churches stem from the Council of Nicaea.'

Artorius sat on the edge of his bed, eyes downcast and lips taut.

Sophie sat in the chair Johnson had provided. 'You called yourself a Gnostic Christian yesterday. How does that differ from Nicene Christianity?'

'Well, we consider Miriam Magdala to be the principal spiritual leader of Christianity after the Christ,' Artorius replied. 'Nor do the Nicenes and Gnostics agree on the holy texts. The Nicenes rejected many gospels – those of Philip, Thomas and Miriam Magdala among them – yet added others of questionable repute, such as the Book of Revelations.'

Sophie gaped at him. Whole gospels rejected? Parts of the Bible were dubious?

Artorius went on. 'Many Nicenes of my time taught that belief in their doctrine was the only requirement for salvation. And yet, I cannot imagine that God, knowing what lies in men's hearts, would admit to Heaven those who are cruel and selfish merely because they profess the right belief. For that matter, would God be so merciless as to cast a man into Hell for eternity, and not give him a chance to redeem himself? Especially if the sin for which he was punished was not knowing who to worship, and how?'

'Some people uphold that interpretation,' Sophie replied. 'What does Gnosticism teach?'

'We believe that people who have not achieved sufficient piety will be reborn in this world, again and again, until they make themselves worthy of Heaven. But righteous actions alone do not suffice. One must also purify the soul. Only when a man eliminates hatred, greed and lust from his heart; only when such evils no longer tempt or corrupt the mind; only when one's soul becomes a reflection of God Himself; only then can one enter Heaven and become one with God.'

It didn't sound as though Artorius's Gnosticism was a fusion of Christianity and Celtic Paganism, after all. That pendant probably wasn't a sun wheel.

Artorius shrugged. 'Of course, having been called to battle and compelled to kill, I have probably not yet eliminated sufficient hatred to enter Heaven. I believe I will be reborn when I die.'

Sophie couldn't think of anything to say. This was quite a lot to digest.

Artorius frowned at her. 'Does the Nicene Church ban these ideas today?'

Sophie shook her head. 'There were times it would have been illegal, but not today. British law now guarantees freedom of worship.'

'Enough of my beliefs. I wish to learn more about the Cymry physician, Bleddyn Kendrick. He is the only person I have met who is a descendant of my people.'

'Well … to qualify as a physician, one must undergo rigorous learning and training,' Sophie explained. 'Medicine is much more advanced than it was in your time, and also much more complicated. As a mark of respect, physicians bear the honorific title "doctor" before their names.'

'Physicians are teachers?' he asked.

'The word has taken on a new meaning in English. A doctor is highly educated, but not necessarily a teacher.'

'Very well. Could you tell me more about Bleddyn Kendrick himself?'

'Only a little,' Sophie replied. 'I met him for the first time two days ago. He seems a dignified, hard-working, honest and open-minded man.' She reflected on how Bleddyn dissuaded her father from pushing her into nursing, and smiled inwardly.

'What of his family?' Artorius asked.

'His father died in a war just before he was born,' Sophie replied.

'Is he married, or betrothed?'

'He did not say he was married, although he told me his sister is married and has children.'

'Is she married to an English or Cymry man? Did he say?'

'Neither, apparently. Bleddyn said her husband comes from China – a land in the Far East.'

Artorius raised his eyebrows. 'By the Far East, do you mean the Holy Lands, Arabia, Persia, or the land beyond Persia – India, I think it is called?'

'China lies east of India.'

Artorius's eyes widened. 'East of India! That is such a long way to travel.'

'We now have means of travelling quickly. However, Bleddyn fears for the safety of his sister's husband and children in this war. The leaders of Germany consider the Germanic race superior to all others. In particular, they persecute Jews and dark-skinned races.'

'What?' Artorius drew himself up. 'They cleanse themselves of people they deem inferior?'

Sophie nodded.

'Are these people of the Far East dark-skinned?'

'Their skin tends to be a little darker than that of most people from Europe. We sometimes describe them as yellow-skinned. They have dark hair, and their eyes are a distinctive shape, narrow and tilted.'

Artorius hunched over and stared at the floor, his elbow on his knee, resting his chin between his thumb and his forefinger. 'Yesterday, Bleddyn Kendrick said that he feared a German invasion. I could not fathom why the Cymry would cooperate with the English, but it sounds as though these Germans could endanger his family.' He put his hand down and looked at Sophie. 'Over a thousand years have passed, yet the darkest side of human nature has not changed. A man who considers people of another race as vermin can plunder and kill those people without remorse. Some of the Anglii and Saxones even forced Combrogi slave-harlots to kill the children they conceived, just to stop Combrogi blood from intermingling with their own.'

Sophie's stomach tightened. 'Now I understand why you hate us so much,' she whispered. 'I am sorry, I really am.'

'Is such contempt between the modern English and the Cymry now confined to history, Sophie?'

Sophie hesitated. 'It is, but I feel I should inform you that Bleddyn might not have told you the whole truth yesterday in order to keep you calm. There are tensions from time to time. In the two days since I met Bleddyn, I have seen two instances where people treated him with contempt and made derogatory statements about the Cymry.'

Artorius's gaze hardened.

'It is ludicrous,' Sophie added, 'not least because there are probably few pure English or Cymry left after centuries of intermingling.'

'Are you sure there has been much intermingling?' he asked. 'I saw a combination of Roman and Brythonic features in Bleddyn that were common among the Combrogi of my time. In contrast, your high cheekbones, your fair hair, your great stature, all tell me that you are of pure Germanic blood.'

It was unsurprising that Artorius thought this. Bleddyn had the dark eyes and the almost olive skin of a quintessential Welshman, and a tall, big-boned girl like Sophie could not deny the Teutonic blood in her veins. 'I am taller than most women who identify as English. The differences are not as marked as you assume just by looking at the two of us.'

'Is there any barrier to the mixing of our races?' asked Artorius. 'Even a cultural one, if not a legal one? For example, if you are unmarried – I know not if you have a husband – would society disapprove if you married a Cymry like Bleddyn Kendrick?'

Sophie shook her head. 'In such an instance, people might disapprove because of class or wealth, but not race.'

'Tell me more of this world into which I have awoken, Sophie. In particular, I want to hear about your unified nation, and the war with Germany. You said they have invaded other countries. Who is at war?'

'Firstly, you need to know about the United Kingdom,' Sophie told him. 'In addition to England and Cymry, the United Kingdom includes the North of Hibernia, which we now call Northern Ireland, and Caledonia, now known as Scotland.'

'Scotland? But the *Scoti* are from Hibernia!' Artorius exclaimed. 'Did they overrun Caledonia and rename it? Do any Brythons from Caledonia survive?'

Sophie cast her eyes down. 'I am sorry, but I know little of their history. How much the Scots displaced the Brythons, and how much assimilation occurred, I cannot tell you.'

Because Canada, Australia and New Zealand had also declared war on Germany, Sophie gave Artorius a brief overview of the British Empire and explained that it included territories on continents discovered since his entombment. He asked difficult questions about the rights of the subjugated races.

When Sophie started on the subject of modern warfare, she described guns as machines that fired leaden projectiles with greater range and accuracy than arrows fired from bows. Similarly, she likened cannon to catapults.

Sophie described modern means of transport. Nothing enthralled him more than the concept of the aeroplane. She explained that they could move faster than land-based or water-based machines, and that they could drop explosives and incendiary devices on an enemy from great heights.

'Are exploding objects really useful in modern warfare?' he asked.

'I think you underestimate the power of modern explosive chemicals. A "bomb" can obliterate a building such as this one.' She gestured around the cells.

'*Hei!*' Artorius's eyes opened wide. 'If a flying legion were to attack a town, such weapons could kill by the score. Do the Germans have similar devices?'

She nodded. 'We fear the use of bombs against our cities.'

They spoke for hours, both on modern and ancient topics. Sophie was still on the lookout for a slip that could expose him as a fraud, but he did not reveal any incriminating details.

When she asked again about his entombment, he told her more than he had the day before. 'The druidesses were all dressed in white. There were no family or comrades present, for the arch-druidess insisted their presence would have destroyed the magic.' Artorius stared into space. 'Four stood around me, reciting chants and offering prayers to the god Avallach and his daughter Modron. Others transferred food and my personal effects to the tomb. They piled timber for bonfires on each side of the entrance. They sacrificed a bull on one pyre, and an Angle prisoner on the other.'

'What?' Sophie exclaimed. 'They performed a human sacrifice?' It sounded like the human remains Bleddyn noticed were from this Angle.

'Human sacrifices were not common. When a Celtic Pagan deemed a sacrifice necessary and believed that a few drops of blood or an animal's life would not suffice, they would normally use one who was sentenced to death – a criminal or an enemy prisoner.'

Sophie bit her lower lip. Human sacrifice was terrible, but if the prisoner had already been condemned … She pushed the thought to the back of her mind. 'Do you remember any more about the ceremony?'

'To prepare me, they pricked my finger with a spike made from mistletoe, and smeared my blood on an acorn. It had to be planted above the chamber. They washed my face and hands, and forced a bitter potion into my mouth. It affected my mind, and I recall little after ingesting it. They laid me on a litter and draped a white cloth over me, and that is the last thing I remember.'

'You said that you pleaded with them not to do it,' Sophie said.

'Yet they continued, for the arch-druidess had divined my future, and she was convinced I must return when Albion faces its darkest hour.'

'Artorius, your presence here is testimony to the powers of this arch-druidess,' Sophie pointed out. 'Might her divinations also be true?'

'How could I be a saviour today when my own people lost so much after my entombment? I have awakened centuries later into a world where nobody remembers what happened to my family; a world in which my remaining descendants face annihilation by a new enemy with weapons more terrible than I could have imagined.' He sighed. 'It would have been better if I had died all those centuries ago.'

Sophie barely noticed the sound of someone opening the door to the cells, but Artorius stiffened and fixed a wary eye on it. He relaxed when Sergeant Dwight entered with a plate of sandwiches.

'Lunchtime,' Dwight stated. 'You do realise it's half past two, Miss Edwardson, don't you?'

'Goodness, I'd lost track of time.'

Artorius stood back from the bars while Johnson opened the door and Dwight placed the tray on the floor.

'I must leave now, Artorius,' Sophie told him. 'I will let you eat in peace.'

'Before you go, I have one more request, Sophie,' he said as he walked forward and inspected his sandwiches. Bully beef sat between the slices of bread. 'The *vigiles* have given me salted meat again. As a Gnostic, I believe that lesser animals still experience pain and fear, and deserve more compassion than men often afford them. I would rather eat meat sparingly. Next time, is it possible for me to have an egg or some cheese instead? I would also be content with bread, vegetables and pulses.'

'It is strange that a warrior who has killed men in battle would be concerned about a chicken or a sheep,' Sophie remarked.

'If a chicken or a sheep ever attacked me with an axe, I would smite it without a moment's hesitation,' Artorius replied.

She suppressed a chuckle. 'I am unsure if men in custody have a choice in what they eat, especially with food shortages created by the war, but I will inform the vigiles – *policemen* – of your request.' She turned to Dwight. 'Artorius prefers vegetarian food. Can that be arranged next time?'

Dwight scratched his temple. 'No suspect has ever requested that before. But yes, it can be arranged.'

As Sophie left the cells with the policemen, Dwight said to her, 'Lucy's waiting for you in the common room.'

'She's probably hungry,' Sophie replied. 'I've held her up too long.'

The common room was a small, untidy kitchen, the air heavy with the smell of tea reheated in tin kettles. Sophie began to utter an apology to Lucy, only to stop mid-sentence. Lucy was sitting opposite a wireless, leaning forward with her elbows on the table and her chin resting on her clasped hands.

Dwight cleared his throat.

'The Netherlands has surrendered unconditionally to the Nazis,' Lucy said in a small voice.

Johnson groaned.

'Good God,' whispered Dwight.

Sophie swallowed. Denmark, Poland, Luxembourg and now the Netherlands were under Nazi control. Norway and Belgium were in serious trouble. If Spain and Italy entered the war, Britain and her allies wouldn't stand a chance.

Well, there was nothing they could do about it now. 'We should head back, Lucy. I'm sorry for the late lunch.'

'The canteen at the airbase will be closed now, Miss Edwardson,' Lucy replied.

'Already? Oh … what should we do?'

'There's a community feeding centre not far from here,' Dwight told her.

Lucy got up. 'That might be the best place. We're on duty, so the RAF will pay us back for the cost of lunch.'

At the community feeding centre, the waitress told them, 'We can only make sandwiches at this time, dears. We have a leg of ham, though.'

'Ooh, that sounds wonderful!' Lucy exclaimed.

'I'll have the same, please,' Sophie said. Then her mind drifted back to Artorius and his aversion to meat. 'Sorry, I've changed my mind. Do you have cheese?'

Sophie and Lucy ate in silence. The sandwiches were prepared from stale bread without butter, mustard or even margarine, but Sophie hardly noticed. She kept going through the interview with Artorius in her mind, and parts of it made her uneasy.

To someone raised in the Church of England, Artorius's Gnosticism sounded heretical. Her first instinct was to dismiss it as blasphemy, but then she recalled the narrow-minded porter at Cambridge railway station who ignored Bleddyn's advice on tobacco because he found the truth inconvenient. Was she making the same mistake? Could Artorius be right? Had the early ecumenical councils misrepresented Christ's teachings for political reasons?

Then there was the British Empire. Artorius's questions were especially confronting. Did the people they had conquered fear the British as the British feared the Germans? Had there been massacres in conquered territories? Sophie didn't know of any massacres, but Artorius speculated that these may not have been reported to the British public or had been misrepresented as battles. Unfortunately, this sounded all too likely.

The British public held Germany in contempt for its invasions of sovereign European nations, but was there any real difference between the German occupation of Poland and the British occupation of India?

Were the British really all that different to the Germans?

Only last night, Sophie had hoped and prayed for divine intervention to protect them from a German invasion. Now, she wasn't sure if they deserved it.

CHAPTER 6

1515 hours
RAF Axleigh

'Sophie,' her father said as soon as she stepped back into his office, 'I may have spoken out of turn to you earlier—'

'Yes, you did, and to Dr Kendrick as well.'

He fiddled with his collar. 'I should probably—'

'Have you apologised to Dr Kendrick?'

He continued to fidget as he glanced away.

'I contacted MI5 again,' he said after a long pause. 'They now feel this case is strange enough to warrant their attention. They want us to bring the intruder to their Doncaster office. From there they'll take him to London, where they have specialised interrogators, some of whom speak Latin well enough for the job.'

'What?' Sophie was aghast. 'They can't do that!'

'Yes, they can.'

'"Specialised interrogators"? Father, they're talking about *torture!*'

'This is war, Sophie, and he's a potential threat to our security,' her father stated.

She opened her mouth to argue, but didn't say anything. Nothing she could say here would protect Artorius from MI5.

'However,' he went on, 'the Security Service may need your help until they can move him to London. Can you stay until Friday or Saturday? Kendrick is of no further use, so I'll send him back to Cambridge tomorrow morning. They want reports from both of you. I've been instructed to hand over the film without developing it.'

It sounded as though she would be back in Cambridge by Monday after all. In light of what was happening here, the departmental meeting hardly seemed important any more. 'I suppose I should write my report, then. I need a desk and a typewriter.'

Her father pointed to an adjoining room. 'That's my assistant's office. There's a typewriter in there, but Kendrick is currently using it. Dinner tonight will be—'

'You'll be dining alone,' she stated as she walked into the assistant's office and slammed the door behind her.

Bleddyn glanced up at her, looked back at the typewriter, and pecked at the keyboard with two fingers.

'Dr Kendrick, I'm truly sorry …'

Bleddyn hit a few more keys, and then proceeded to remove the paper. 'I've finished, Miss Edwardson. Here are the notes I recorded for you earlier.' He pointed to a notebook and marched out without a backward glance, his cold shoulder wounding her.

When Sophie finished her report two hours later, she dropped it in front of her father and swept out of his office without a word.

She found Bleddyn reading a magazine in the main mess. Dinner was still over an hour away, and nobody else was present.

Bleddyn looked up when she sat beside him. 'You were quick, Miss Edwardson.' He looked back at his magazine. Judging by the cover, it was a medical or scientific journal.

'Bleddyn, don't be like this,' she begged. 'For a start, call me Sophie.'

'Just not in your father's presence.' Bitterness spilled out of his voice.

'Bleddyn, please!' She placed her hand on his forearm. 'You heard the way he spoke to me, too.'

Bleddyn glanced at her hand and looked up at her. He contracted as his expression of bridled rage softened into one of remorse. His gaze fell to the table. 'Sophie, I'm … I'm sorry. It was wrong of me – very wrong – to take it out on you like that.'

She sighed with relief. 'What he said to you was the vilest thing I've ever heard him say. He was still angry with you for humiliating him. I can't thank you enough for silencing him on the nursing issue.' She gave his forearm a squeeze. 'That was brilliant.'

Bleddyn looked up at her, a slight smile on his lips. He closed his magazine.

Sophie withdrew her hand. 'It's a pity you weren't at the police station. The chat with Artorius was more amicable than it was yesterday. He called the pendant a "Wheel of Dhargh".' Sophie described Artorius's belief in reincarnation, the importance he attributed to the act of purifying the soul, and his preference for a low-meat diet.

Bleddyn raised his eyebrows. 'That's interesting – there are similarities to Buddhism there.'

'After hearing about the Wheel, there seem to be too many similarities for it all to be a coincidence. Bleddyn, hearing Artorius describe the Council of Nicaea as a heresy – well, he lived in a time closer to those events. I mean … what if he's right?'

'You're beginning to doubt your faith?'

'Perhaps. I don't know.'

Bleddyn shrugged. 'I don't think it would matter. Before meeting Artorius, had you ever wondered what God's intentions were for non-Christians?'

'I'd always hoped He would show them mercy,' Sophie replied. 'After all, weren't they brought up believing something else was God's truth? It's just … for the first time, I'm wondering how I can be sure that *my* faith isn't a heresy, too.'

Bleddyn smiled. 'Having Buddhist friends, I first contemplated these things years ago. I believe God sent all the founders of major religions. They teach different histories, of course, and some religions have a few extra inhibitions – for example, Buddhism discourages meat and alcohol – but they're mostly consistent on ethics and morality.'

Sophie tilted her head. 'You believe that God sent more than one messenger?'

'I find that easier to believe than the notion that He sent the only one spiritual teacher to the Israelites less than two thousand years ago. If He did that, then He had forsaken everyone born before Christ, and everyone who lived in a time before Christian missionaries reached their lands. Would a merciful God really do that?'

Sophie considered this. It was an interesting idea, and an assuring one.

'He asked a number of questions about you,' she said. 'I told him everything I knew, even about your sister and her marriage. I hope you don't mind.'

'I don't, although you consider it strange that someone would marry a Chinaman, don't you?' Resignation marked his tone.

'Well … not as strange as I did before you put my father in his place over his opium remark.' That was a diplomatic way out of an awkward question. 'Anyhow, your nieces or nephews, I can't remember you saying …'

'Two nieces. I saw them on my last visit at Christmas. The eldest was nearly three years old at the time. She was quite shy at first, but eventually warmed to me.' Bleddyn smiled. 'She was quite keen to show to anyone who'd pay her attention that she could count. The younger girl was five months old, and she would break out into the most delightful smile as soon as any human face came within two feet of hers.'

His expression suddenly hardened, and he stared off into space. 'We can't lose this war, Sophie. We just can't. By God, the stories coming out of Europe … You and I might be safe if we surrender our liberty to those monsters, but my nieces, my brother-in-law, his younger brother – how many Chinese, Jews and Negroes live in Britain? The night of the broken glass, and the rumours about the Mulatto children in the Rhineland … where will they stop, Sophie? And what will they do to the Asians and Eurasians?'

A deafening silence lingered.

'You know, I was in Germany four years ago,' Sophie said at length. 'All I heard throughout the entire trip was admiration for the Führer – but I felt that everyone was on edge, as though they dared not express misgivings about the regime.'

Bleddyn raised his eyebrows. 'Go on.'

'It really came out when a couple of us went to a commercial district with some German competitors. The local girls were good hosts until I stopped and bought some hand-painted china. They wouldn't enter because the shop was owned by a Jewish family. One German girl expressed her disgust that I would support a Jewish business, and the others started glancing around nervously, as though they were afraid of being seen with me. Looking back, I think the signs were already there.'

Bleddyn stared at her. 'Four years ago, competitors … you competed in the Olympic Games?'

'Yes.' Sophie dug her nails into her palm. Curse her big mouth! She had avoided this topic yesterday because she knew Bleddyn's circumstances would never have permitted him such an opportunity.

'Wow! Which event?'

'Swimming. I didn't win anything, though. Few women take it up, and thanks to the Depression, selection for the British team was not highly competitive that year.'

'That you even made it there is still amazing,' Bleddyn remarked. 'Your father permitted you to compete at the Olympic Games? Forgive me if I speak out of turn, but I didn't think he would have approved of it.'

'Oh, if he had his way, I wouldn't even have had swimming lessons. I can thank my mother for that – and for talking him into letting me read at Cambridge. She's a very different person to my father.' It was time to move the discussion away from the Olympics. 'Did you hear about the Netherlands? It was on the wireless earlier this afternoon.'

'No, I— Oh, no!' His face fell. 'Did they surrender to Germany?'

'Unconditionally.'

Bleddyn buried his face in his hands. 'What's *happening*? Are they invincible or something?'

'It's as though they're divine punishment,' Sophie mumbled.

Bleddyn looked up. 'What makes you say that?'

'Well … Artorius asked some pointed questions about the British

Empire. He couldn't see much difference between the Nazis invading Europe and European colonisation of other continents.'

'Apart from the fact that the Germans are destroying democracies, you mean?'

Sophie relaxed a little. 'True. Most colonies had oppressive rulers before we conquered them.'

'Mind you, we didn't depose local despots for the benefit of their subjects,' Bleddyn added.

Sophie nodded. 'It's as though we're getting a taste of our own medicine.'

'We need to keep this in perspective, Sophie. Colonial history *should* bother us – but the Nazis didn't attack Britain, France or Belgium to avenge the people in the colonies. Rather, I bet the self-proclaimed "superior race" will be far more brutal to the indigenous inhabitants of those colonies.'

Sophie nodded. 'That's true. Even so, do you think Artorius has a point? Have we been hypocritical?'

'We have,' Bleddyn replied, 'and if there's one good thing that will come out of this godforsaken war, it's that we're about to learn how it feels to face an invasion. Let's hope it erodes the notion of Britain's right to rule over other people.' He sighed. 'But if we're to set things right, we need to win this war first.'

Bleddyn had managed to assuage Sophie's unease a little. He was a deep thinker, and it was interesting to talk to him. It suddenly dawned on her that they would part company tomorrow, and the thought came with a stab of disappointment. She didn't want this to be the last time she saw him. Artorius's question about her and Bleddyn sprang to mind. It was a hypothetical question … but now that she thought about it, *if* Bleddyn were to … yes, come to think of it, Bleddyn was the sort of man she'd want courting her.

She wanted him to ask for her address.

Then again, he may think it inappropriate to court someone of her social standing, and he'd hardly be able to ask her father. *She* would have to ask *him*, but one had to be circumspect about that sort of thing. It might even sound presumptuous to ask if he was engaged.

However, if she asked on behalf of someone else …

'Sophie?'

She blinked. 'Pardon?'

'You looked lost in thought there.'

'Oh – I was just going through the conversation with Artorius in my mind. He also asked if you were married or betrothed. I could only tell him that you never mentioned a wife or fiancée, or even a girlfriend. He's bound to ask again when I see him tomorrow.'

He shook his head. 'No, I haven't met anyone yet. Wait a second – you're going to see him again tomorrow?'

She nodded. 'My father will take Artorius to Doncaster, where MI5 will take him into custody. After that, it will be out of our hands.'

'But … but what does MI5 plan to do with him?'

'I don't think we'll ever find out, but my father mentioned "specialised interrogators".'

Bleddyn shuddered.

Sophie looked around, saw nobody in earshot, and pulled out a notebook and pen. 'You will be going back to Cambridge tomorrow, but if my services as a translator are required for another day or two, I won't be on the train with you.'

'So, tomorrow morning will probably be the last time we see each other?'

The hint of disappointment in his voice gladdened Sophie. She began to write her address in her notebook. 'Oh, I hope not. In fact, I was hoping for the opportunity to get to know you better.' Her throat and stomach tightened, but she maintained a calm façade as she wrote. 'I don't know where I will be after the funding cuts, but this is my home address. My mother will forward my correspondence.' Sophie tore out the page.

Bleddyn's eyes widened. 'But … but, Sophie, are you suggesting – surely not – I mean, my family is … I'm just … Well, your father – what would—'

'Oh, really, Bleddyn!' Sophie hissed, pretending to take offence. 'I never thought you, of all people, would look down on someone because of their family!'

He recoiled. 'No, no! That's … that's not what I meant—'

'Don't worry, I know what you meant,' Sophie told him with a wry smile. She pushed her notebook towards him and looked on expectantly.

Hand trembling, Bleddyn took a pen from his pocket and wrote his name. He gave an address for an RAMC hospital in Wiltshire, and one for Llanelli in Wales.

He turned the notebook back to her and was about to speak when someone rushed through the mess door.

'I heard … there's a … doctor … on-base!' the man panted.

'That would be me.' Bleddyn got to his feet. 'What happened?'

'Two men were refuelling a Magister … it caught fire! Oh God, the burns …'

'Sorry, Miss Edwardson, I'll talk to you later.' Bleddyn stashed the paper with her address in his shirt pocket and ran after the aircraftman.

Sophie got to her feet, wondered if she should follow, and decided against it. She didn't even know where the first aid kits were. It was best to keep out of everyone's way.

She looked down at the medical journal he'd left behind. A smile crept across her face. She was now sure of her feelings, and she hoped they would be reciprocated. Bleddyn was correct that her father would object to the two of them seeing each other, but that was not going to stop her.

She had been on dates before, but the men she had seen so far had all been shallow. Never had she met someone with whom she could relate so easily. His disadvantaged upbringing made his achievements all the more remarkable. Sophie was not sure she would have had the intellect and strength of character to make it through the trials he had faced. Yet despite his strengths, he was modest, almost to a fault.

Apart from his stature, Bleddyn was everything Sophie wanted in a prospective admirer, down to the fact that he didn't smoke. If that meant she had to pursue him, then so be it.

***

1900 hours
Axleigh Police Station

Artorius stared at the window across from his cell. It was open, allowing in the air. Had it been closed, it still would have allowed light to shine into the room, for its peculiar panes were made of clear glass rather than horn or wooden slats. The day had been warm and the sun still shone outside; it must be within a month of the solstice. He should ask Sophie whether midsummer was approaching or had passed.

A lock turned and the door opened. The two vigiles – no, *policemen*, Sophie had called them – approached his cell. One of them touched the box attached to the wall, a ritual that coincided with the ignition of a candle inside a glass bulb hanging from the ceiling. At least, it gave light like a strong candle. Why could he not see a wax or tallow stick, or dripping molten wax? How did the flame draw air? How could it burn so long, and so brightly, without needing to be replaced?

The larger man waved Artorius backward. After Artorius stood back, he unlocked the cell, and his colleague set a plate of food on the floor. Both of them kept their eyes on him the whole time.

After they locked the cell again, the larger man closed the window and drew the heavy black curtain across it before they left.

Artorius didn't come forward until after they had gone.

Someone had boiled onion with some sort of brown bean. There was pale cabbage and something else that looked like sliced parsnip, but it was bright orange. A mass of small white things that were probably a type of grain covered half the plate. No meat. Good. They'd heeded his request.

It was bland, though. It could have done with salt and spices.

He ate slowly, thinking about his last two meetings with Sophie. So much had changed, yet so much had stayed the same. It was still hard to believe that the Combrogi and the Iutæ-Anglii-Saxones were now as one. Then again, stranger things had happened. Artorius himself was part Roman and part Brython – what would Boudika or Caratacus have thought of him, a man whose ancestors included both their kinsmen and their enemies? Why, the Romans stripped Boudika of her lands, beat her, raped her daughters before her eyes. She had loathed the Romans as much as Artorius loathed the Anglii and Saxones. How would she have viewed the united Combrogi he fought for?

It would have confused her, no doubt, as the current circumstances confused him. Anyhow, so much time had passed. Sophie was oblivious to the crimes of her ancestors and found their history disturbing. She was truly born into a new world, one in which his struggles were a long-forgotten history. They only knew of him through legends distorted by the passage of time.

His gaze fell on the closed window and black curtain. It was thick and blocked most of the sunlight. Why start the indoor candles earlier than need be? For that matter, why block the breeze at all?

Then it struck him. After sunset, that heavy cloth would also block the light from within. The enemy had fast flying machines and bombs. If the enemy soldiers flew at night, they would find it easy to spot targets by the light they cast. The curtains must be to mask the light from within dwellings.

Artorius unstopped the wine-like rosemary infusion and dabbed it onto the raw skin of his armpit. He wished he could thank Bleddyn for this concoction. Sophie had spoken highly of the physician, and that gave Artorius comfort.

This war they were fighting must be terrible indeed. Sophie, the police officers, Bleddyn Kendrick, Sophie's father – all were frightened. Artorius could see in all of them the underlying fear of people under threat of invasion, a fear he had seen all his life. Worse still, Sophie said that Bleddyn Kendrick had nephews or nieces who were … half Chinese, or whatever the Far Eastern race was called.

Purity of the German race – what a laughable idea. The Romans once posted soldiers of all ethnicities throughout the Empire. Between that and the migration of traders, ethnic mixing had been occurring for many generations before Artorius had even been born, and another fourteen centuries had passed since. Did the Germans' stupid leaders not realise they were far too late to keep their bloodlines pure?

Not that it mattered. The most ridiculous of dogmas were often the most dangerous. It seemed that everyone felt a compulsion to defend their beliefs, and too many people resorted to violence when truth, logic and reason failed. And if these self-deluded Germans threatened to invade Albion, his kinsmen were in danger again.

But how could he help them?

Would the tactics Artorius knew and excelled at still apply? How effective were mobile infantrymen in wars with flying machines? Why, such machines would even alter the way one surveyed a battlefield and gathered intelligence.

Even if his knowledge were still useful in such warfare, the languages had changed so much. Then again, even if he spoke any language of modern Albion, nobody would give him command of a legion.

Germanic aggressors threatened this island again, but all he could do was watch the horrors unfold.

He flung his empty dinner plate against the bars. It clattered as it bounced and skittered along the concrete floor. *That wretched arch-druidess and her followers! May their Pagan gods smite them all! This fate is worse than death.*

Artorius released his clenched fists. No, he shouldn't blame them. It wasn't their fault he was useless. They foresaw the peril the Combrogi's descendants would find themselves in – but Artorius could not see how he could help.

He picked up the fallen plate.

After his entombment, the Combrogi had been pushed west of the River Sabrina. Now, he would be powerless to prevent the annihilation of his few remaining kinsmen. The druidesses had placed great hope in him, but he could do nothing. Legend revered him as a hero, but he had failed his people, he had failed his family, and he was about to fail his descendants.

He was useless. Utterly useless.

Artorius dropped to his knees and wiped the tears that were beginning to cloud his sight. *Why? Why must I bear witness to this? Is there nothing I can do?*

Still on his knees, he drew the Wheel of Dhargh from his shirt pocket, cradled it in both hands, and prayed.

God of Heaven, help me. Show me what I must do.

***

2120 hours
RAF Axleigh, mess hall

'As that girl already knows, no food after serving hours,' the cook huffed. 'You can't just click your fingers here and demand a meal at any hour you choose. Go to the community feeding centre.'

'You know perfectly well they stop serving at eight thirty,' Lucy protested.

Bleddyn glared at the cook. He had already missed lunch today, and he was starving. 'For goodness' sake, we couldn't make regular serving hours because I was operating on patients. I didn't choose to miss the regular mealtime, and it's your responsibility to make sure everyone gets fed.'

The cook looked him up and down. 'You're not in uniform yet, *Doctor*, so you can't order me about.'

'Hockey,' growled Lucy, 'Dr Kendrick may not be able to issue orders, but what do you think the wing commander will have to say when he hears about this?'

The cook stormed into the kitchen. He returned with a loaf, bottles, butter knives and plates. 'Pot's already been cleaned. Bread, Marmite and jam is all there is.' He slammed everything down on the nearest mess table. 'And hurry up! I need to clean up after you've finished.' He wandered back into the kitchen, muttering under his breath.

Bleddyn shook his head in disgust as he and Lucy put slices of bread on their plates. He spread some Marmite on a couple of pieces. 'I'm sorry about the late night and missed meal, Lucy.'

'No need to apologise. It couldn't be helped. Anyhow, Marmite on bread is probably better than whatever he cooked. We sometimes wonder if he makes his stew in a pot or a dustbin.'

Bleddyn almost choked on a mouthful. When he recovered his breath, he said, 'That accident was entirely preventable. I can't believe that man was stupid enough to smoke while working with aviation fuel. *And* he injured a second man in the process.'

'Clough's always been careless.'

The burns had been terrible. Bleddyn could not do much for the two men on-base, so he accompanied Lucy while she drove them to the hospital at Axleigh. One man needed a blood transfusion. The hospital was tiny and did not have a permanent blood supply, but instead called on a type O donor from a nearby town.

'And then someone used a high-pressure water hose to quench the flames …' Bleddyn winced. 'Thank God there were no electrical wires nearby. The wing commander needs to organise a safety training session. None of this should have happened.'

'Are you sure you want to suggest it, Dr Kendrick?' asked Lucy. 'After the way he spoke to you today?'

'Well, someone has to do it,' Bleddyn muttered.

'Will Clough and Oliver be all right?'

'They'll both end up with scarring. Clough's right eye was in a bad way, although the hospital had a Prontosil eye drop. God willing, he'll keep it.'

After taking a few bites of her Marmite and bread, Lucy said, 'Just as well we hadn't left before old Mr Black came in …'

'Ah, yes.' The ambulance had brought the farmer with the shotgun injury just as Bleddyn and Lucy were about to leave. Bleddyn had helped stabilise the man before the surgeon arrived, and then assisted in surgery while the local GP went back to his practice and a backlog of patients. 'I'm not sure what the wing commander will think of me holding up his driver to treat a civilian,' Bleddyn told Lucy, 'but they needed my help. I hope it's not usually this busy in such a small hospital.'

'It never rains, but it pours,' Lucy replied.

Now that Bleddyn had time to ponder, he recalled a peculiarity about Clough that might have been indicative of another medical condition. 'I'd also like to have a look at Clough's medical file.' He hoped disciplinary action could be postponed until after he saw the file and discussed the matter with Dr Stanley. If Clough had what Bleddyn suspected he had, the same condition might have also affected the man's mental performance.

Lucy looked at him quizzically.

'I'm sorry,' he told her, 'I shouldn't speculate openly about a patient's medical history. Tomorrow morning will be my last chance to speak to Dr Stanley.'

Lucy nodded. 'Medical files are kept at the hospital.'

Bleddyn took another bite of bread and Marmite. His mind drifted back to Sophie and her insistence that they exchange addresses. He swallowed a lump of bread that turned to concrete in his oesophagus. It was supposedly Artorius who had asked about his personal life, but Sophie hadn't insisted on his address until she learnt he had no girlfriend. The significance of this did not escape him. She was an independent and proud woman – that much was obvious – but he had never expected this.

Sophie was beautiful. She didn't bear much resemblance to Fay Wray or other women of famed good looks, but Hollywood didn't have a monopoly on beauty. Bleddyn hadn't fully appreciated how stunning she was when he first met her, because she was so ferocious when she was angry. But on the train, when she first smiled at him … Another lump of bread turned to concrete as he swallowed it.

What Bleddyn failed to understand was what she saw in him. Sure, he had his medical degree; but he had no money, and few skills apart from medicine – and he was only a houseman.

Sophie, on the other hand, had excelled in so many fields. She could play the piano. She could drive. She could swim. Hell, she was such a good swimmer, she'd even competed at the Olympic Games! She was studying for her master's, and may even go on to attain a *real* doctorate, if the chauvinistic bureaucrats would award such a high degree to a woman. She was a giant, both physically and metaphorically.

He wasn't good enough for her.

The lumps of concrete he'd swallowed now settled uncomfortably in the bottom of his heart.

CHAPTER 7

Thursday, 16 May
0700 hours
RAF Axleigh

Sophie was still angry with her father the next morning, so she went to the mess for breakfast instead of his private dining suite. She arrived at the same time as Bleddyn. They both lined up to collect bowlfuls of a mushy liquid that someone assured them was porridge. Bleddyn also took a cold, grease-laden fried egg and some toast. The cook glowered at him as they passed.

'Why's the cook angry with you, Bleddyn?' Sophie asked in a low tone as they went to a table. 'Did you force-feed him his own stew last night?'

'Lucy and I didn't get back from the hospital until after he'd closed the kitchen. Our dinner ended up being bread with Marmite and jam. Had Lucy not threatened to report him, we would have gone hungry.'

Sophie regarded Bleddyn's expression, but she could not for the life of her gauge his thoughts. He would have made an excellent bridge player. Lucy came and sat with them, dashing Sophie's hopes of a quiet chat, so she restricted herself to small talk. 'So, you didn't have his stew last night? That's probably just as well.' She took a mouthful of the so-called porridge and forced herself to swallow it. 'How badly hurt were the two airmen?'

'Very. One could still lose an eye. I want to look at their medical files this morning and discuss them with Dr Stanley. Can we do that before they move Artorius?'

Move Artorius. To a secure facility, where nobody would ever hear about him, where his captors could do anything, where he would have no recourse or legal protection. They could torture him, even silence him for good, and nobody would ever know. Her stomach churned, and it wasn't because of the porridge.

They went to the main office after breakfast, and Bleddyn requested permission to drop into the hospital to see Clough's medical files.

'And why should I let you see his files?' Sophie's father asked Bleddyn. 'He's Dr Stanley's responsibility.'

'I was involved in his treatment, Wing Commander,' Bleddyn replied, the terseness in his voice palpable. 'I noticed something that may be indicative of an underlying condition, and I would like to discuss the matter with his doctor.'

'And if you noticed it, why didn't you raise the matter with the local doctor at the time?'

'I was preoccupied treating their injuries. Another emergency patient arrived while I was there, so I didn't get the chance.'

Her father grunted. 'Oh, very well, then. Speak to him if you must. We'll call by the hospital on the way to the police station.'

Sophie tilted her head. 'You're coming?'

'I have to. The Security Service called just before you entered. They don't have anyone in Doncaster who speaks Latin. A man will be coming from London, but he won't arrive until tomorrow. Even so, they want "King Arthur" moved to their Doncaster headquarters this morning, and they want me to arrange it. Kendrick, you're to go to the train station as soon as we arrive in Doncaster. Sophie, they will need you until this agent arrives.'

'There's one more thing about the accident yesterday, sir,' Bleddyn added. 'Are you aware the patients' injuries were exacerbated when other men from the ground crew tried to extinguish the fire with water?'

'I wasn't aware of that. What about it?'

'Have the men been trained in safety awareness and emergency responses? I mean, one man was smoking near fuel, and others tried to extinguish burning fuel with water …'

'Kendrick, are you telling a senior officer how to run his airfield?' Her father's voice was low and menacing.

'You're responsible for safety on this base, Father,' Sophie said. 'Perhaps you should consider Dr Kendrick's advice before your superiors ask what you've done to prevent a recurrence.'

Her father glowered at her before breaking eye contact.

The uncomfortable silence persisted while Lucy drove them into the village. As they pulled up at the hospital, Sophie's father said, 'Kendrick, meet us at the police station when you're finished. We don't need you there, and it would be a better use of everyone's time if you joined us after you've spoken to Dr Stanley.'

'Yes, sir.' Bleddyn opened the door. 'Lucy, I may need my duffel bag. Could you unlock the boot, please?'

After Bleddyn had left, Lucy drove Sophie and her father to the police station.

Sergeant Dwight met them at the door with an apprehensive frown. 'Surely you don't propose to transport the prisoner in that car, Wing Commander ...'

'Really, Dwight, did you expect us to have a prison van? You'll have to drive him to Doncaster.'

'You want *us* to take him? With fuel rationing and all?'

'What?' Sophie turned to her father. 'Didn't you think to discuss the logistics of the prisoner transfer with the police?'

He glanced away and fiddled with his collar.

Sophie clenched her fists, took a deep breath and exhaled slowly. 'Father, *we* will have to take him to Doncaster.'

'We can't move an aggressive prisoner in the Austin.'

'Let me talk to him. He may be cooperative.' This, she did not fully believe. His incarceration was going to be dreadful, and she wasn't prepared to lie to him about it.

Lucy sat and waited at the front desk as the policemen escorted Sophie and her father to the cells.

Artorius was lying on the bed. He sat up and greeted them with an expression of mild surprise. 'You have returned with your father this time, Sophie. Have your people made a decision about my fate?'

Sophie could barely look him in the eye. 'They have. I know not what it is, but I fear it will be unpleasant. Our authorities still do not trust you, and they will ensure the British people never hear about you.' She had to pause and collect herself before she added, 'Artorius, I am sorry. I have no control over what will happen to you.'

'I never thought you did,' he replied. 'As it is, I have no place in this world. Even if your people see fit to execute me, I am prepared for death.' He looked at her with an intent expression on his face. 'I see that distresses you, Sophie.'

'It does,' she whispered.

'The Cymry physician, Bleddyn Kendrick – will I see him again?'

'That depends. If you promise to cooperate, you will be transported in a regular horseless carriage with both Bleddyn and me. They have another vehicle in which it is easier to restrain a prisoner, and they will use this if they suspect you will resist.'

Artorius shrugged. 'Even if I fought and escaped, where could I go? I will cooperate if I can meet Bleddyn Kendrick again. I hope to thank him personally.' He picked up the concoction Bleddyn had given him two days before. 'This potion appears to be rosemary in some sort of wine, not dissimilar to something an apothecary of my time would have produced. It is already working. May I take it with me? It makes little difference if I am to be executed, but if your people keep me imprisoned, then I should like to be able to treat my rash.'

'I do not see why you cannot.' Sophie's voice was hoarse. How could he be so calm about this?

'Do the policemen wish to bind me?'

'They will not bind you with rope, but they will place you in iron hand restraints.'

Artorius nodded. 'I will not resist.'

She translated his wishes and concessions to the others present. The police watched him closely as they unlocked the cell. Sophie translated their instructions into Latin, and Artorius held his hands out while the police handcuffed him.

Back in the station's office, Dwight insisted that Sophie's father fill out a form, declaring that the armed services had formally taken custody of the suspect. Her father objected, arguing that it was not the RAF's problem if the Security Service were taking him; but Dwight wouldn't back down. Artorius had been held longer than they could legally detain someone without charge, and according to Dwight, the commissioner would 'blow a fuse as it is' when he found out. 'I need a statement, Wing Commander,' he explained, 'and as nobody from MI5 has come here, it has to be you.'

Her father had just completed the form and handed it back to Dwight, when a boy of about fifteen entered the police station.

'Telegram from the War Office, Sergeant.' The boy held an envelope out.

Lucy got to her feet.

Dwight snatched the envelope from the boy's hand without thanking him and tore it open. The colour drained from his cheeks as he read the letter. 'Oh, God, no,' he whimpered. 'Oh, dear God, no.'

'Mr Dwight, please tell me … it's not …' Lucy pleaded.

'Toby. Toby, my son. He's …'

Lucy wailed and dropped to her knees. Dwight leant against the wall, his bottom lip trembling. Tears crept from the corners of his eyes and ran down his cheeks.

Sophie turned to Lucy while her father and Constable Johnson consoled Dwight. As the two men guided the sergeant to his office, Sophie overheard her father praise Dwight's brave son, and he was starting to say something positive about the life he had already led when the door to his office closed. Her father's counselling skills took her by surprise. Then again, a man who had been awarded a Military Cross in the Great War had faced these horrors before. For all his faults, he was a war hero.

Sophie, on the other hand, was at a loss. She put her arms around the sobbing Lucy and managed to get her into a chair, but beyond expressing sorrow for her loss, she had no idea what else to say. She didn't even know the nature of Lucy's relationship with Toby.

'Father …' she said when the wing commander and Johnson re-emerged.

'Lucy was engaged to the late Toby Dwight, Miss Edwardson,' Johnson said.

'Lucy, I'm giving you three days' leave on compassionate grounds, effective immediately.' Her father's normally booming voice was low and gentle. 'I can extend it if need be. I must trouble you for the car keys, though.'

Lucy pulled herself together enough to answer her commander. 'Th-thank you, sir,' she sobbed as she found the car keys and handed them to him. 'I'm … I'm sorry I can't …'

'Is there somewhere you'd like us to take you, or would you rather wait here for the vicar?' he asked.

'I'll … I'll wait here for the vicar, sir.' She buried her face in her hands again.

The wing commander patted her on the shoulder before he led Sophie, Johnson and Artorius outside to the street.

While Sophie had already known the war would claim lives, it had been something of an abstract concept until now. Dwight's and Lucy's inconsolable grief had turned the concept into a reality. A dull ache emanated from her heart, and not knowing how to console a grieving fiancée left her feeling flustered. Her brother also sprang to mind: would she ever see such a telegram with Christopher's name on it? *Please, God, spare us that anguish.*

How many more families across the country would get such dreaded telegrams before this war was over?

A tap to her elbow brought her back to the present. She turned.

'Sophie,' said Artorius, 'you said that most people can read and write. Do I assume correctly that the letter informed the *policemen* – I know not the singular term – of the death of a son in this war?'

'How do you know that?' she asked.

'I understood not the words, but I recognise the grief of a parent who has lost a child in battle,' Artorius replied in a dispirited voice. 'I have seen it many times. Too many. How is the blonde woman connected to the deceased?'

'She was betrothed to him.'

Artorius looked down and shook his head.

'Sophie,' her father said, 'it would be best if you drive, in case our King Arthur becomes violent again during the trip.' He handed the keys to her. 'Kendrick and I will sit either side of him, although to be honest, I doubt Kendrick will be much use in restraining him. Why is he taking so long at the hospital? We now need to call into the vicarage before we leave.'

'I'm surprised the post office sent the telegram boy without notifying the vicar,' Sophie murmured.

'An oversight, no doubt.' Her father glanced back at the police station door, grimaced, and rubbed his forehead. 'Dear God!' His voice was scarcely more than a whisper. 'The Great War was bad enough. I never wanted to see anything like this again.'

'*Di omnes!* Artorius exclaimed. He pointed to the road, where two cars had just passed each other. 'The horseless carriages – they move so quickly!'

'Did they not transport you from the burial mound in one?' she asked. 'What about from the hospital to the police station?'

'Until I found myself fettered to a raised bed, my recollection is fragmented. I was frantic after I awoke; they transported me in some sort of vehicle, but I cannot recall how quickly it moved.' His eyes remained glued to one of the cars as it drove away. 'Those horseless carriages passed close to each other, too. A collision would be dangerous. How do you prevent that?'

'We enforce left-hand drive.'

'Ah.' Artorius nodded. 'That makes sense. I suppose you must enforce it more rigorously than the Romans had to.'

'The Romans had left-hand drive?' Sophie asked. 'That is strange. Many places in Europe today, even those that were once part of the Empire, have right-hand drive.'

Three lorries rumbled down the street from their right. This was an unusual amount of traffic for a village like Axleigh.

A tall man in his twenties was trying to cross the road from the opposite side. He was looking the wrong way – probably watching the last lorry approach as he timed his crossing – when he stepped out in front of a car coming from the opposite direction. The car swung hard to avoid him and sideswiped the last lorry in the convoy. The lorry also swerved. Sophie winced as it closed in on the RAF car. Metal screeched on metal. Both drivers came to a complete stop and blocked the narrow street.

'WHAT IN GOD'S NAME!' thundered Wing Commander Edwardson.

The lorry driver jumped out and started berating the car driver. Sophie's father joined in the altercation, and Johnson had to intervene.

Meanwhile, the pedestrian at the centre of the accident had crossed the road. He glanced around in a furtive manner.

'Hey!' Sophie called out. 'You can't just walk away from this! You – wait, I've seen you before.' It had been at a distance, but his curly brown hair was distinctive. 'You were near the airbase yesterday.'

'Oh, yes, but … but not intentionally,' the man answered as he looked over his shoulder. 'I am an ornithologist from Manchester. I was conducting a field study when some guards told me I was too close and ordered me to leave.'

'Where is he from?' Artorius asked in Latin.

'England. He works … north of Deva,' Sophie replied. Switching back to English, she said to the ornithologist, 'Well, irrespective of—'

'He is not from your nation!' interrupted Artorius.

'Artorius, I really—'

'Your horseless carriages drive on the left side of the road.' Artorius spoke rapidly. 'He looked the wrong way before he crossed the road and stepped directly into the path of traffic. That action was instinctive. He comes from a place where people drive horseless carriages on the *right*.'

Sophie gaped at Artorius. It sounded reasonable. She glanced back at the ornithologist – or whatever he really was.

He turned and ran!

This could only mean one thing. Sophie started after him, hesitated, yelled, 'Spy!' and chased him.

The spy darted into an alley between two shops. Sophie followed in pursuit. A wall blocked his exit, trapping him.

Sophie halted, unsure what to do next.

The spy rushed at her. She put her fists up, but hesitated at the glimpse of something in his hand. He struck her left side. A thud, then a burst of agony. When he pulled his hand back, she saw what he was holding – a knife, now covered in her blood.

Pain and terror froze Sophie to the spot. The spy ducked around her and ran for the street. She tried to call out to warn whoever was closing in behind her, but all she could manage was an inarticulate moan as she fell to her hands and knees. *Oh, God!* The pain was so intense she felt sick. There was more shouting and a yelp from behind her – *Who has he stabbed now?* – but she couldn't move. Everything around her was hazy, muffled, surreal …

'Sophie! Sophie!' A hard squeeze of her shoulder brought things back into focus, and with it, another wave of pain. She looked up at Bleddyn's face. He must have just arrived.

'Bleddyn,' she gasped, 'the spy …'

'He's not going anywhere. I need to help you now.'

Sophie now saw her attacker out of the corner of her eye. Artorius was trying to choke him with the chain of his handcuffs.

Two other men approached her.

'Dr Kendrick, help her, please!' her father pleaded.

'We need to get her to the hospital,' Bleddyn said. Wing Commander, stand here. You, stand here. The cars are wedged in, hospital's only around the corner …'

Her father was still gibbering about blood loss and pointing at the ground in front of Sophie.

A large red patch running down the skirt of her dress. Her panic rose again. *I'm going to die!*

Bleddyn jumped to his feet. 'Edwardson!' A slap. 'Panicking won't help your daughter! Focus!'

'All right, all right … What should I do?'

'I need to bandage her.' Bleddyn's head came down to her level again. He took some bandages and padding from his duffel bag. 'Prop her onto her knees and raise her arms.'

Her father and the other man – the lorry driver, Sophie now recognised – did so. Bleddyn pushed the padding against her wound and bound it in place with the bandage, wrapping it around her torso. He worked quickly to apply a tight compress.

'Now, Wing Commander, stand here. You' – Bleddyn pointed to the other man – 'stand here. You need to carry her to the hospital. Squat down, keeping your backs straight. Grab each other's wrists. Yes, yes, like that. Right. Now, when I pull her forward, swing your lower arms under her legs. Sophie, I'm just going to tilt you forward a bit …' He grabbed her shoulders and tilted her forward. A wave of pain made her flinch. 'Sorry, I know it hurts,' he whispered as he pushed her back. 'Right, now stand up.'

Her father and the lorry driver hoisted her into the air.

Sophie gasped again in pain. 'Will I be all right?' she whimpered.

'You'll be fine.' He took her right forearm and placed it over the wound, then put her left hand over her right forearm. 'Hold as much pressure against the wound as you can. I'll run ahead to the hospital.'

The men carrying Sophie turned her around.

The spy was gasping on the ground. There was blood on his face. Artorius had stepped back, and the constable had taken charge of the situation.

Bleddyn turned the corner ahead, running at full speed. Her bearers carried her out of the alleyway, turned, and followed him.

A fog began to descend near the hospital. It was getting cold … It was strange that she wasn't shivering, given how cold it was … A nurse was running, people were shouting …

***

'What do you mean, only one brigade?' Lord Gort demanded.

'That's all he's prepared to send, sir,' replied Archdale. 'Gamelin still wishes to keep most of his forces near Paris—'

Lord Gort slammed his fist on the table. 'Damn it, Archdale, can't that witless Frog see the Germans aren't marching on bloody Paris? Is he providing this brigadier with air support?'

'He didn't say, sir, but I don't think so.'

Lord Gort buried his face in his hands.

A signalman poked his head in and saluted. 'Sir, Alan Brooke is on the telephone.'

Lord Gort followed the signalman into the haze of smoke and noise of the communications room. He picked up the receiver lying on the table. 'Lord Gort speaking.'

'General, it's Alan Brooke here,' crackled the voice on the other line. 'We're withdrawing to the western banks of the Zenne.'

'What?' Lord Gort demanded. 'Brookie, you—'

'The Germans have broken through the Dyle Line.'

These words took the reprimand out of Lord Gort's mouth. 'The Dyle Line?' He looked at the map, at the Belgian fortifications between Koningshooikt and Wavre. 'Did the Belgians tell you that?'

'No, I found out from RAF reconnaissance. Sir, if we try to hold our position, they'll encircle us.'

'Right, right. Do what you have to do.' Lord Gort put the receiver down. God almighty, they had trouble on both fronts!

When he went back to his office, Archdale said, 'Sir, I understand the Prime Minister is visiting Paris today. Perhaps he can talk some sense into the French high command.'

'Never mind. I need to send the Fiftieth Division north now. The Dyle Line has collapsed.'

Archdale gawked at him. 'The Dyle Line? You mean …'

'The Germans could break through our northern *or* southern flank at any time. This bloody battle is getting worse by the minute.' Lord Gort took a deep breath. 'In the meantime, go back and tell Billotte he'd better … No, better not say what had just come to mind … Tell them that if they don't want to see our forces utterly defeated, they *must* send more than a single brigade.'

'I'll do my best, sir, but it's complete disarray in Billotte's office right now.' Archdale saluted and left.

Lord Gort got up and looked at the map. *The Dyle Line.* That meant that Brussels would fall within days.

Hell, the way the Germans were moving, they might even take the city tomorrow.

Ronse was no longer a secure location for his headquarters. Communication lines from the south came from Amiens through Lille; he should move his headquarters to Lille, or somewhere nearby, and fortify the district. Those communication lines were essential; they must be kept open.

***

1400 hours
Axleigh Hospital

'She's stirring.'

'Will she be fine? Is this a good sign?'

'Her prognosis hasn't changed since you asked a minute ago.'

Sophie tried to move. *Oh … God!* Had someone split her head open with an axe? Her stomach churned. The blurred outlines of two people stood over her.

'Sophie, how are you feeling?' one of them asked. He was still blurry, but she now recognised her father's voice.

'Where am I?' she groaned.

'It's good to see you're awake, Miss Edwardson,' said the second voice. 'You're in hospital. Do you remember what happened?'

She recalled running after someone – a spy? – a bloodied knife, pain … 'I was stabbed?'

'The knife penetrated your liver, but don't worry. Livers are resilient, and they heal quickly.'

Sophie squinted at his outline, which was now coming into focus. This elderly man wore glasses. 'And you are?'

'Mr Chesterfield, the local surgeon.'

'You operated on me?'

'Alas, I didn't arrive until it was nearly over,' he confessed. 'That young doctor, Kendrick, performed the surgery while Dr Stanley supported your breathing. All I did was check Kendrick's work.' He paused. 'You're a lucky young lady, Miss Edwardson. Treating a knife wound to a liver is not too difficult for a surgeon, but Kendrick is only a house officer. His aptitude for trauma surgery is remarkable.'

'Why didn't he wait for you, Mr Chesterfield?' her father asked.

'The rate at which your daughter was losing blood demanded haste, Wing Commander. We had two accidents yesterday, which left the hospital without registered universal donors – so a transfusion was out of the question.'

Her father made an odd sound, something between a grunt and a whimper.

'So I'm going to be fine?' Sophie asked.

'I think so, but you're not completely out of danger yet. There's always the risk of infection with such injuries.'

'May I have some water?' Sophie asked. This may not have been a great idea with her stomach the way it was, but her throat was on fire.

Mr Chesterfield passed her a glass, but only allowed her a couple of sips.

'The man who stabbed me …'

'Apprehended,' her father replied. 'He had to be treated for a broken leg and nose, and now he's in a cell at the police station. He's admitted to gathering information for the Nazis.' His voice was softer than Sophie had ever heard, and his mouth was taut.

'Was he German?'

'Yes.'

Sophie tried to turn her head, but the surge of pain that came with this attempt made her settle on turning her eyes. 'You said Dr Kendrick saved me. Where is he?'

'Right now, he's probably trying to keep the other man in police custody – the one who can't speak English – out of this ward,' said Mr Chesterfield. 'I understand you're the only one who can talk to him, Miss Edwardson. I know you're feeling dreadful right now, but we may need to bring him here so that you can provide some direction. He's rather agitated.'

'It's strange,' said her father. 'Although Dr Kendrick can only communicate with him through gestures, Artorius obeys him. For that matter, Dr Kendrick is the *only* person he obeys. We almost had another crisis on our hands.'

'Artorius … he was the one who identified the spy.'

'How did he do that?' her father asked.

'He looked the wrong way before crossing the road.' She took a breath and tried to ignore her throbbing head. 'Used to right-hand drive.' Was she making herself clear?

'Ah, so that's how he … Hold on, for someone who claims … well, you know' – her father glanced at Mr Chesterfield – 'how could he deduce so quickly the spy was accustomed to right-hand drive?'

'No, not that strange. They had … I'll explain later.' Sophie had a nagging suspicion something didn't add up, but that wasn't it.

''Scuse me,' said a voice from the doorway, 'How's Miss Edwardson doing?'

'She's awake, Constable,' Mr Chesterfield replied.

'Good to hear. Sorry to ask this of her, but if she's up to it, we need her to speak to Artorius. He's just about beside himself out here, and you know what happened last time he was like this.'

'Only two minutes,' the surgeon told Johnson, 'and you must keep him calm.'

Johnson and Bleddyn came in. Bleddyn gestured to someone outside. Artorius. 'Sophie!' he exclaimed as soon as he laid eyes on her. He started towards her but halted at Bleddyn's signal. 'By the gods, the blood you were losing! Bleddyn Kendrick told me, "Sophie viva," but I scarcely believed you could still be alive. Will you recover from this?'

'There is a risk of disease, but I will probably be fine. My liver was cut.'

'*Liver?*' Artorius's stricken face fell even further. 'I have never heard of anyone surviving a cut to an organ. And yet, here you are.'

Sophie tried to smile. 'You can attribute it to advances in medicine and surgery, and Bleddyn's skill.' She glanced at Bleddyn, who had the same pallor as her father.

'Medicine *and* surgery?' Artorius asked. 'Bleddyn Kendrick is trained in both?'

'Oh – I forgot. The two disciplines are now combined.'

Artorius shrugged. 'That makes sense. I had another question, Sophie. The spy ran from us as soon as I had disclosed my suspicions, but you had not translated my words into English. Had he understood what I said?'

That was it. That was the part that didn't add up. 'You are right. He must understand Latin.'

'Well, good to see our guest has calmed down now,' Johnson said. 'Miss Edwardson, can you explain to him that I need to place him back in the cell? With all the commotion, we can't take him to Doncaster today. That'll probably happen tomorrow now.'

Sophie translated this for Artorius.

'Oh, and one other thing, Miss Edwardson.' Johnson adjusted his collar. 'It's delicate. If Artorius is going to be with us another day, he needs to know what the pile of newspaper squares beside the lavatory's for. Seems Artorius has been … using a sock for these purposes.'

This raised a smile from Mr Chesterfield, although her father and Bleddyn both remained ashen-faced.

Sophie had trouble convincing Artorius that people could possibly use paper – particularly paper with writing – for such purposes. 'Artorius, modern paper is far cheaper than vellum, and we can use printing for the mass production of writing,' Sophie told him. '*Newspapers* are especially cheap.' She took a breath. Her churning stomach and pounding headache were really taking it out of her. 'Can I explain this another time, please?'

Artorius nodded and said nothing more.

'Well, I hope that's all settled,' Johnson said. 'Time to go and leave you in peace, Miss Edwardson.'

Before Johnson escorted him away, Artorius took Bleddyn's hand in both of his, and told him in Latin that he was a marvellous physician. Sophie translated after receiving a quizzical look from Bleddyn.

'Indeed, he is,' Mr Chesterfield agreed. He turned to Bleddyn. 'However, I have one word of caution. You may have allowed yourself to become too concerned about Miss Edwardson. It's vital that you find the right balance between empathy and detachment, or else the patient you cannot save might destroy your soul. I therefore insist that you distance yourself now. By all means, call in and visit before you return to Cambridge, but leave her post-operative care to Dr Stanley and me.'

'Mr Chesterfield, how long before my daughter is able to leave?' her father asked.

'Not for another three days, at least. The stitches will have to be removed later.'

'I need to call her mother,' he mumbled.

'Bear in mind that the matron here is rather inflexible in her enforcement of the visiting hours. We should leave before she throws you out.'

Sophie was the only person in the women's ward that night. The hours of quiet contemplation left her feeling emotionally fragile and deeply upset. Anger, fear, humiliation, vulnerability … A number of emotions gnawed away at her soul as she lay alone in that ward. A small sliver of metal had almost ended her life. And Bleddyn operating on her – was it better when the surgeon was someone she cared about and trusted, or was it even more humiliating to be so weak and helpless before him?

Never before had she felt so vulnerable and insecure.

CHAPTER 8

Friday, 17 May
0745 hours
Axleigh Hospital

'Good morning, miss. Time for breakfast.'

Sophie rubbed her eyes. 'Breakfast?' she groaned. 'Already? The sun hasn't risen yet.'

'Miss, it's almost eight in the morning.' The nurse walked over to the window and opened the curtains.

Sophie squinted against the blinding sunlight. 'Oh, of course,' she murmured. Good Lord, to be so drowsy as to forget about the blackout. 'Breakfast? Thank you.'

The nurse placed a tray on an overbed table and pushed it into position. She also laid some clothes on the bedside table. 'The surgeon will come later to check on you. We've washed your clothes, although your dress is ruined, I'm afraid.' She gave Sophie another injection of morphine before she left.

Breakfast offerings were jelly, a clear soup that had already gone cold, a glass of water, and half a glass of flat ginger ale. It appeared she was still on clear fluids. That was probably just as well, with her unsettled stomach. The ginger ale stung her raw throat, but Sophie drank it anyway, hoping that it would alleviate the nausea.

After breakfast, she studied the layout of the ward from her bed.

The morphine dulled the pain, but her unsettled stomach protested even more vigorously. She would have appreciated something to read to while away the time, to keep her occupied, to distract her from the nausea and the jumble of emotions that flooded back.

It was ages before the surgeon entered the ward. 'Good to see you're looking better, Miss Edwardson.' He drew a curtain around the bed for privacy. 'Do you remember who I am?'

'You're the local surgeon, Mr …' – Sophie searched her memory for his name – '… Chesterton?'

'Chesterfield.'

'I'm sorry.'

'No need to apologise, my dear.' Mr Chesterfield placed a thermometer in her mouth. He drew back the bed sheets, opened her dressing gown, and peeled back the tape on the dressing.

More than a dozen hideous black stitches bit through her skin along an angry incision.

Mr Chesterfield studied it impassively, as though he were reading a newspaper. 'Not looking too bad,' he mused.

Sophie did not share his opinion.

Gingerly, he felt around the incision. 'Good, there's no sign of internal bleeding. There's a little inflammation, but nothing I wouldn't expect.' He checked the thermometer. 'Ninety-eight point five. Excellent. No sign of infection. Still, we should keep you on sulphanilamide for at least a week. I'll have a nurse give you a tetanus shot this afternoon.'

'When should the stitches be removed?' Sophie asked.

'In about two weeks. We'll keep you in hospital for the next three days. In that time, you should either lie down or stand; a sitting posture would be inadvisable.'

'Is there anything I should avoid?'

'Avoid getting the stitches wet or sweaty. Don't drink alcohol for at least a month. Other than that, just avoid anything that pulls the stitches or causes you discomfort.'

Sophie thought to ask one of the questions on her mind. 'Mr

Chesterfield, I remember you cautioned Dr Kendrick about caring too much for his patients yesterday.'

'Oh, yes. He was beside himself with anxiety about his work and your prognosis. Forgive me if I sound indifferent to your wellbeing, Miss Edwardson, but I've seen physicians have nervous breakdowns.'

'Would a doctor have trouble distancing himself from a patient if he was already close – say, if the patient were a close friend or family member?'

'Ideally, a doctor shouldn't treat family members or friends, but that's not always possible in a village such as Axleigh,' replied Mr Chesterfield. 'But that surely wouldn't be the case, would it? I was under the impression Dr Kendrick only met you a few days ago, presumably in relation to this alleged King Arthur.'

'Well … Wait, how did you know about the King Arthur claim?' Sophie asked.

'Miss Edwardson, the war isn't going well, and this "Artorius" – that sounds like a Latin name from which "Arthur" could be derived – appears to speak Latin, but not English. I could work it out from there.'

'Not much has escaped you, Mr Chesterfield.'

'I don't understand why they sent a houseman here, though. I don't suppose you could tell me more?'

Sophie shook her head. 'I don't think I'd be allowed to say anything more, sorry.'

'Well, not about King Arthur, but what made you ask about treating close friends and family members? Something's on your mind.'

Sophie hesitated. Mr Chesterfield may be able to tell her more about Bleddyn's reaction, but she wasn't quite ready to share her feelings.

'I'm bound by patient confidentiality, if it helps.'

'I … I exchanged addresses with Dr Kendrick the day before yesterday, but I'm unsure if he reciprocates my feelings.'

'And why should you wonder if he reciprocates your feelings if he asked for your address?' Mr Chesterfield asked.

'He didn't. I insisted on his.'

Mr Chesterfield peered at her over his glasses. '*You* made the first move? You're a bold young lady, Miss Edwardson.'

Sophie sighed. 'It was a tad impulsive. He appeared nervous when I gave him my address, but I don't know if it was surprise, or if he wasn't sure how to reject my attentions tactfully.'

He nodded. 'Well … it could be that he does feel the same way about you, and that might explain his anxiety yesterday. Yes, yes – now that I think about it, he was more detached from Mr Black when he was here the evening before last. In that case, perhaps I should have cautioned him about impropriety instead.' His expression changed to one of mock disapproval. 'Really, a girl gives him her address, and he's tearing her clothes off the very next day!'

Sophie followed Mr Chesterfield's gaze to her ruined dress. Heat flushed through her cheeks. This was not the least bit amusing. The notion that she had been … exposed to Bleddyn, greatly compounded her embarrassment. Not that it was his fault, of course. Oh, that wretched spy!

'Miss Edwardson, I do apologise if you took offence at my tasteless attempt at humour,' Mr Chesterfield said hastily. 'In truth, Dr Kendrick only cut away what he needed to remove in order to operate. It was a nurse who changed you into the hospital gown.'

'Well, that's *some* relief,' she grumbled.

'I don't understand why you need my confidence in this matter, though.'

'It's just that my father wouldn't approve. I'm not ready to tell him yet.'

'Well, if you and Kendrick do end up seeing each other, you'll have to tell your father eventually.'

Unfortunately, that was true.

About ten minutes after Mr Chesterfield left, a nurse popped her head into the ward. 'Miss Edwardson, your mother is here.'

Sophie's chest tightened.

Her mother marched in. 'Oh, good God!' She hastened over and embraced Sophie gently. 'I'd have come last night, but your father didn't even call me until this morning. What in heaven's name are you doing here?'

'I'm not sure how much I can tell you, Mother.'

Her mother clenched her teeth. 'It's bad enough with Christopher in the navy, but I thought you would be safe at least. Now your father's dragged you into something, and it's put you in hospital! How could he?'

'Mother, I'm going to be all right.' Stoicism took charge of Sophie's mood, but she had no choice but to let her mother peel back the dressing and inspect the injury for herself. Her mother looked as though she was going to be sick. She started crying instead.

'Mother, please. It will heal.'

Her mother dabbed a handkerchief to her eyes. 'I know, I know; but when you become a mother, you'll understand how much it hurts to see your child in pain.'

At that moment, Sophie's father and Bleddyn came through the doorway.

Her mother turned to face them. To Sophie's astonishment, she walked over and slapped her father hard.

'Mother!'

'What's the meaning of this, George? Putting our daughter in danger like that! *And* you didn't even call me until this morning!'

'But, Molly,' her father said as he rubbed his cheek, 'visiting hours—'

'George Edwardson, you do *not* wait until visiting hours before telling me our daughter is in hospital!'

Bleddyn sidestepped the two Titans and tiptoed towards Sophie's bed.

'Well, George?' her mother demanded. 'You'd better have an explanation.'

'It's sensitive information, Molly – so we need to step out of earshot and discuss this quietly.' Her father added the last part hastily.

The departure of her parents provided Sophie a much-desired chance to speak to Bleddyn in private. Now that she had a quiet moment alone with him, however, she had no idea what to say. Her feelings towards him were unchanged – in fact, gratitude might even have intensified them – but Sophie didn't really want to be indebted to a proverbial knight in shining armour. Mr Chesterfield had also pointed out that Bleddyn had now seen her semi-clothed while she was under anaesthesia. Things could not possibly be more awkward.

'So, you're still all right?' Bleddyn asked. 'Have either Dr Stanley or Mr Chesterfield seen you this morning?'

'Mr Chesterfield came by. He said there was no sign of bleeding or infection, so everything's fine so far, and I have you to thank for that.'

'Thank God for that,' Bleddyn murmured, eyes cast down momentarily. 'I'm sorry about that incision, Sophie. It will leave a large scar. It would have been smaller had a more experienced surgeon operated on you.'

'You don't need to apologise for anything. I'm lucky to be alive.' After a pause, Sophie added, 'I'm sorry about my mother. She's usually far more composed. You must be wondering what sort of family I have, with an incorrigible father and a hysterical mother.'

Bleddyn shook his head. 'Your mother's not hysterical, she's understandably upset.' He raised his eyebrows. 'You know, your father's been a lot more polite to me since yesterday. I'm now "Dr Kendrick" and not just "Kendrick".'

'Did he apologise for what he said to you?'

'… Not in as many words.'

Sophie rolled her eyes and sank back into the pillows.

'He's driving me back to Doncaster this morning. I'll catch the train to Cambridge, pack my belongings, and take up my post in the RAMC.'

'At … Wiltshire, wasn't it? That means you'll probably be gone by the time I return to Cambridge.' Sophie reached out and took his hand. 'But you will remember to write?'

Bleddyn hesitated. 'Sophie, if I understand what you're saying … I really …'

Her heart sank. 'You don't see me the same way?'

'It's not that – it's …' He looked around the room, and asked in a low voice, 'Sophie, surely you could do better than me?'

'Bleddyn!' she exclaimed. 'You know I don't care about class and breeding and all that nonsense.'

'I don't mean class,' he replied. 'Sophie, you're so … I mean, I don't—'

A knock at the doorway of the ward cut him off. He whipped his hand out of hers.

Sergeant Dwight entered. He wore his police uniform, although his eyes betrayed his bereavement. Another man in a suit followed him in.

'Sergeant Dwight!' Bleddyn exclaimed. 'I heard what happened; I'm so sorry … I'm surprised you're back at work!'

'With a three-vehicle accident, and a spy in the cells alongside a possible madman, I can't take time off,' the sergeant said. 'Miss Edwardson, how are you today?'

'I'm feeling sore and weak, but I'll recover, thank you,' Sophie replied.

'I'm sorry, Miss Edwardson, but it looks as though we'll need your translating services again this morning. Dr Kendrick, this is probably an unreasonable request right after an operation, but is there any chance she can come to the police station?'

'I'm afraid not.'

'This is a matter of national security, Doctor,' said the man in the suit. He flashed an identification badge. 'Craig Dutton, Security Service. Miss Edwardson is required at the police station.'

'Moving her could aggravate her injury and cause bleeding to resume,' Bleddyn explained. 'I can't allow it. If the matter is urgent, bring Artorius to the hospital. He was here yesterday.'

'Until we know who this person is, we cannot risk having him seen by any more civilians,' Dutton retorted. 'He was moved around in public too much yesterday, and it mustn't happen again. Do whatever's necessary to prepare her. If she can't walk, find a wheelchair.'

Bleddyn's expression blackened. Sophie braced herself for his outburst.

'Miss Edwardson is not to be moved.' The voice came from the doorway. 'You have *two* medical opinions on that.'

Dutton spun and faced the new arrival. 'And you are?'

'Mr Chesterfield, surgeon. Sir, as Dr Kendrick pointed out, your King Arthur was here yesterday, and Miss Edwardson fulfilled her duty as a translator only minutes after waking up from anaesthesia. I see no reason why he cannot be brought here again.'

'What? But – but how many civilians know about this case?' Dutton spluttered. 'The police and RAF were supposed to be keeping mum about this.'

'I don't know if anybody else has guessed what this was all about, but did you really expect that such peculiar events would have gone unnoticed in a village like this?' Mr Chesterfield asked. 'I will also point out, my good man, that I was a major in the Royal Army Medical Corps during the Great War. Do not presume to question my loyalty or discretion.' Hands clasped behind his back, Mr Chesterfield's voice was polite, yet as firm as steel.

Dutton turned to Sergeant Dwight.

'I won't ignore the doctors' recommendations,' Dwight told him. He looked at Sophie. 'Miss Edwardson, if we bring Artorius here, would you be up to translating again?'

'It's fine. In fact, I could do with the distraction.'

'Dr Kendrick, is the wing commander around?' Dwight asked.

'He's talking to his wife at the moment. He'll be back – but I wouldn't interrupt them if I were you.'

'I'll call the station and ask Johnson to bring Artorius around. Is there a telephone somewhere, Mr Chesterfield?'

'Follow me, Sergeant.'

Dutton stayed, casting hostile glances at Bleddyn.

Dwight and Mr Chesterfield returned within two minutes and proceeded to wait in the ward, much to Sophie's frustration. Really, why couldn't they leave and fetch him, so that she might have another minute alone with Bleddyn? Then she looked at Sergeant Dwight's face, and her antagonism melted away. One would need a heart of stone to remain angry with a man who had just lost his son.

Sophie's parents returned before Artorius arrived. Her father looked at Dwight and recoiled. 'Sergeant Dwight! I'm so sorry; I promised I'd call the vicar …'

'No need to apologise, Wing Commander. I know what happened afterwards, and I … I of all people know what you nearly lost.' The sergeant paused and glanced away, bottom lip trembling. When he had collected himself, he continued, 'We need Miss Edwardson's translating services again. The doctors say she shouldn't be moved, so we're bringing Artorius here.'

'Oh, good grief,' her father muttered. 'What's the lunatic done this time?'

'Well, that's the rummy thing. He seems to have persuaded the spy to work as our double agent.'

'*What?*'

'Wait a minute, wait a minute,' interrupted Dutton. 'We still have two doctors in the room, and what's your wife doing here, Edwardson?'

'She's here because our daughter was nearly killed yesterday,' he replied with a nod towards Sophie's bed.

'I know that, but you don't divulge sensitive information to your wife!' snapped Dutton.

George Edwardson drew himself up. 'Molly and I have been married since the Great War. I will not have you imply that my wife is a security risk. If your people had taken charge when I first called, none of this would have happened, so do not lecture me about national security.'

Dutton looked up at the wing commander's rank, massive frame and hard gaze, and he wilted.

Sergeant Dwight cleared his throat. 'Anyway, when we delivered breakfast to the detainees this morning, the spy made his offer. It turns out he was a novice in the Catholic Church before being recruited by the Abwehr.'

'He tried to flee yesterday after Artorius pointed out to me that he probably wasn't British,' Sophie added. 'It makes sense that he understood Latin, if he was studying to be a Catholic priest.'

'I don't think he's as fluent as you are, Miss Edwardson, and I understand there were some difficulties with dialects – but he was able to converse with Artorius nonetheless,' Dwight said. 'He credits Artorius with persuading him last night to offer to work for us in exchange for sparing his life. To demonstrate his sincerity, he'll divulge the code he was using to transmit back to Germany. I was on the telephone to several departments this morning before someone transferred me to a place called the Government Code and Cypher School. They've already requested we send him to their headquarters.'

'Wait a minute,' Sophie's mother interjected. 'Are you really going to negotiate with the monster who nearly killed my daughter?'

'Oh, I almost forgot. He asked me to express his apologies to Miss Edwardson. He says he panicked, and that he's glad she's still alive, so he doesn't have a murder on his conscience.'

'He *apologises* for trying to murder her?'

Sophie's father intervened. 'Molly, I don't like it, either, but the information he can provide might save many more lives. As it is, it's now in the hands of the Security Service, so I have no say in the matter.'

Molly Edwardson fumed. Sophie was a little surprised that she was not angry herself. This turn of events had left her more bewildered than anything else.

'Anyhow,' continued Dwight, 'I think Artorius would like to say something as well, and we really should ask a British citizen to translate for him, rather than trust the word of a spy who's pleading for his life. The agents MI5 sent don't speak Latin well enough for this task, so Johnson is bringing Artorius here.'

Dutton's nervous gaze darted between Bleddyn, Mr Chesterfield and Sophie's mother.

'Molly,' Sophie's father said softly, 'I think the Security Service would rather you didn't hear any more. It may be best if you stepped outside for a little while.'

'They probably won't want me here, either,' added Mr Chesterfield. 'Mrs Edwardson, the common room is down the hall. Let's discuss your daughter's recovery over a cup of tea.'

Sophie's mother followed the surgeon out of the ward, but not before casting her husband another glance that could have boiled a kettle.

Dutton turned to Bleddyn. 'We don't need you here, either.'

'I examined Artorius, and assisted Miss Edwardson when she

inspected the contents of the burial chamber,' Bleddyn explained. 'I'm already involved in this.'

'Yes, yes, but we don't—'

'Nor am I leaving my patient alone with you. You were insistent we move her despite my advice before, so I can't trust you with her welfare.'

Dutton scowled. 'Now look here—'

'What?' Sophie's father stepped in front of Dutton and glared at him. 'My daughter nearly died yesterday! Did you really expect her to leave her hospital bed this morning? *Against* the advice of the doctor who operated on her?'

Sophie smirked as she watched the agent squirm under her father's glare. Her mother must have been out of earshot, for had she heard this, she would surely have stormed back and throttled Dutton.

PC Johnson, Artorius and the second MI5 agent arrived. Sophie's father glanced at them, scowled at Dutton, and stepped away from him. Artorius was still wearing the old clothes the policemen had given him. He was in handcuffs, and Johnson had his truncheon ready.

The new Security Service agent, who was older than Dutton, looked at Sophie's father. 'Well, Wing Commander, not only did you not resolve this King Arthur matter, but you've found more for us to do. A spy and King Arthur, both in what I was led to believe is a quiet little village.'

Artorius started walking towards the bed, but Johnson put his truncheon up to Artorius's chest.

'It's fine, Constable,' Sophie assured Johnson. 'He won't do anything rash.'

Johnson lowered the truncheon.

'Are you all right today, Sophie?' Artorius asked.

'I am recovering, thank you. Our policemen brought you here because they believe you want to say something, and they need a translator they can trust. Tell me, what happened last night?'

'It appears the clergy of some Christian sects use Latin to this day, and the foreigner was studying to be a priest before he became a spy. He knew he faced execution both for espionage and for attempting to kill you, and he begged for God's mercy last night, reciting prayers in Latin. Though not as fluent as you are, I was able to converse with him. I knew that if a spy were to betray his old masters and feed them false information, he might prove valuable enough for your people to let him live.'

Sophie translated this into English.

'This much we know,' the second agent replied. 'I suppose there are people higher up who might like to know how he turned the spy, but right now, we want to know what our supposed King Arthur wants to do next.'

'Artorius, they wish to know your future intentions,' Sophie explained.

Artorius nodded. 'When we first met, I told you that I had no desire to assist the English in this war against Germania. Since then, I have learnt that much has changed since I was placed in the burial chamber. I have learnt about the society the Cymry and English have built together, and the threat you face from the Nazis. This has changed my mind.' His hard, dark eyes sparkled with resolution. 'If I can be of any service to the races of the new-age Combrogi, the countrymen of modern Britain who include my descendants, then I will help you.'

After all that had happened, Sophie was ready to believe that the man before her was indeed the legendary Arthur. Moreover, she was also prepared to believe that he actually might be able to help them. After all, if he could manage to turn a spy in one night from his prison cell, what else might he be able to do?

When she explained Artorius's offer, however, her father declared, 'This was exactly what I feared. This man is dangerous. No doubt he was making up this cock-and-bull story about not wanting to help the English, just biding his time for the right opening to present himself as our saviour.'

'Actually, Wing Commander,' said Dwight, 'when I spoke to Mr Strachey of the Government Code and Cypher School, he was enthralled by the manner in which the spy was turned. He called back ten minutes later to tell me they have an academic working for them who knows ancient Welsh, so they can verify Artorius's fluency in that language. If

Artorius does indeed speak ancient Welsh, they might have a use for him.'

'How could he be useful to them?' the wing commander asked.

'He didn't explain. Anyway, he'll be pleased to hear that Artorius has agreed to cooperate. A telegram is on its way, requesting that both Artorius and the spy be transferred to the Government Code and Cypher School. They'll send a vehicle to pick up both men directly from Axleigh.'

This drew expressions of surprise from almost everyone in the room.

The older Security Service agent shrugged. 'Well, it sounds as though the case is out of our hands now. I can't say I'm sorry.'

Dwight nodded.

Noticing Artorius's expression of impatience, Sophie told him, 'Artorius, you will be sent to another part of the country, where you will meet a scholar who has studied an old language once spoken by the Cymry – one that may be close to your native tongue. It seems this scholar has a task in mind for you.' She smiled and added, 'However, I cannot help but think it might be a waste of your other talents, especially in hand-to-hand combat. I already know the policemen had difficulty incarcerating you, and you thwarted a knife-wielding assailant while wearing iron hand restraints.'

Artorius tilted his head. 'You are mistaken, Sophie. I did not stop the spy yesterday. Bleddyn Kendrick was overpowering him as I entered the lane.'

'What?' Sophie exclaimed in English as she looked towards Bleddyn. 'Dr Kendrick, I thought it was Artorius who brought down the spy yesterday, but he tells me it was you.'

Bleddyn glanced at Artorius.

'I didn't see what happened, Sophie,' her father told her, 'but Artorius stopped to attract our attention before following you, so he was only a few paces ahead of us. Dr Kendrick was the first to reach you.'

'Strange, I never saw Dr Kendrick approaching.' Perhaps it wasn't that peculiar; Sophie had been distracted by the news of Toby Dwight, the accident and then the spy.

'I turned the corner to see you on the ground and Dr Kendrick pinning the spy,' her father added. 'Didn't you see what happened?'

'I was doubled over with the injury.' Sophie stared at Bleddyn. She never imagined this small, unassuming man would be a skilled fighter. How did he bring down a larger man with a knife?

Bleddyn fiddled with his cuff.

'Now that I think about it, that surprises me,' her father pondered aloud. 'How *did* you overpower an armed assailant, Dr Kendrick? Do you box, or wrestle?'

After a long pause, Bleddyn spoke. 'Sir, remember what I said about my Chinese friends back in Wales? Well, just as the Japanese have fighting arts like ju-jutsu, the Chinese have systems of hand-to-hand combat. My friends taught me one such art.'

Sophie's father stared at Bleddyn in much the same way as he might have stared at an egg-laying cockerel. He had held a condescending view of Asians and Asian cultures for as long as Sophie could remember, and had scoffed at the idea of learning judo or ju-jutsu instead of wrestling or boxing.

'Mind you, I'd never used it in a real fight before,' Bleddyn added.

Sophie smiled. 'You're a man of unexpected talents, Dr Kendrick.'

Bleddyn blushed and contemplated his shoes.

The older MI5 agent cleared his throat. 'Well, it seems that we're done here.' He turned to Sergeant Dwight. 'If the Government Code and Cypher School is arranging to pick these men up from Axleigh, we should take Artorius back to the cells for now. I'll also need everyone to sign the Official Secrets Act. In Miss Edwardson's case, we can bring the papers here afterwards. Sergeant Dwight, may we use your office back at the police station?'

Dwight nodded.

'Thanks. All right, who needs to sign? Wing Commander, as an RAF officer, we probably don't need your signature. Dr Kendrick will need to sign it, as will the two policemen … Is there anyone else whose signature we might need?' the agent asked.

'Maybe Trevatt, the constable Artorius injured when we first arrested him,' suggested Dwight. 'Mind you, I don't think he knows any of the developments.'

Sophie's father cleared his throat. 'My wife arrived, demanding to know why our daughter was in hospital. I related more than I would have told her had I known this would come under the Official Secrets Act.'

The agent scowled. 'Very well, then. She'll have to sign it, too.'

'That surgeon seems to have surmised a bit more than I would have liked,' added Dutton.

'He has?' Sophie's father asked. 'In that case, I wouldn't mind a second opinion on something. Dr Kendrick, if you would be so good as to fetch Mr Chesterfield?'

'Yes, sir.' Bleddyn left the ward and soon returned with the surgeon. Sophie's mother also came. Dutton opened his mouth to say something, glanced at Sophie's father, and closed it again.

'Mr Chesterfield, you've already seen more of this case than we would have preferred a civilian to see,' her father said.

'Indeed, and I've guessed it has something to do with the King Arthur legend,' Mr Chesterfield replied. 'But, as I pointed out to the boorish chap from the Security Service, I understand the importance of secrecy.'

Sophie's father nodded. 'Glad to hear it. Well, seeing as you'll have to sign the Official Secrets Act anyway, I'd like a second opinion on something. Dr Kendrick examined some scars on the detainee's shoulder a couple of days ago and noted some peculiarities about them. Now, it's not that I question Dr Kendrick's competence, but I'd appreciate a second opinion from a surgeon of your experience.'

Sophie pursed her lips. *Not questioning Bleddyn's competence now, are we?*

At the wing commander's request, Johnson removed Artorius's handcuffs, and Sophie asked him to remove his shirt.

Mr Chesterfield examined Artorius's shoulder, then took his arm and moved it in several directions, keeping his eye on the scars. He examined the skin in front of, behind, and above Artorius's shoulder, and even inspected his armpit, frowning as he did so.

'I say, this is most peculiar!' Mr Chesterfield pointed to the two scars, front and back. 'If these are entry and exit wounds, as they appear to be, the projectile would have passed between the glenoid and the humeral head, causing extensive damage to the cartilaginous surfaces and perhaps even the bone. Such an injury should never have healed properly, depriving this man of shoulder mobility. My first thought was that they had to be different scars, that there was another entry point for whatever caused the exit wound; but I cannot see any other scars.' His eyes narrowed. 'For that matter, I didn't even see an inoculation scar. However …' He inspected Artorius's right shoulder. 'Hmm. No inoculation scar there, either.' He looked at Sophie's father. 'I can only speculate what this all means, but I'm beginning to understand why the Security Service is involved.'

Sophie's father raised his eyebrows.

'If everything's said and done, we really should leave,' Dutton growled.

The second agent instructed Artorius in broken Latin to put his shirt back on.

'We part ways, Sophie,' Artorius said as he fumbled with the buttons. 'Thank you for helping me come to terms with this strange world into which I have awoken. I was so miserable to learn that over a thousand years had passed and that my people had been pushed back past the River Sabrina, but I now have a renewed purpose in life. My people – and yours – need my help again.'

Having managed to button most of his shirt, Artorius walked up to Bleddyn and extended his hand. Bleddyn raised his own. Artorius gripped Bleddyn's forearm in a Roman-style handshake, and then proceeded to pull Bleddyn into a full embrace as he said that his descendants in this time continued to do him proud.

Visibly nonplussed, Bleddyn turned his head to Sophie.

She smiled. 'He expresses his pride in his descendants, Dr Kendrick.'

After the police handcuffed Artorius and took him away with the Security Service agents, Bleddyn asked Sophie, 'Surely he means "descendants of his people"? There's no way he could know if I'm his descendant, or even if he has descendants.'

'I think subtleties in the meaning may be lost in translation,' Sophie suggested. 'I am struggling to keep up with him, you know.'

Sophie's father glanced at his pocket watch. 'Dr Kendrick, you'll need to sign the Official Secrets Act, and then I'll drive you to Doncaster station. Sophie, I'll call in here again on the way back to the base.'

It struck Sophie as odd that her father was chauffeuring Bleddyn around, but she supposed that with his driver on compassionate leave, he probably had to do so. 'I'll see you later this afternoon then, Father. Dr Kendrick … goodbye, and thank you for everything.'

'Miss Edwardson …' Bleddyn hesitated. '… It was a pleasure to meet you. May you have a speedy recovery.'

'Dr Kendrick,' Sophie's mother said. She placed her hands on his forearms. 'Mr Chesterfield told me that you saved my daughter. I didn't get the chance to thank you before.' She pulled him into an embrace that Sophie worried for a moment may have crushed his ribs.

Bleddyn's departure on such uncertain terms left Sophie feeling empty inside. There was much they both needed to say, but those words would have to remain unspoken for now. She never did have the chance to clarify why Bleddyn felt as though she could 'do better', as he had put it.

***

Sophie's mother stayed for so long the matron came past and tried to assert the hospital's rules on visiting hours.

'With nobody else in the ward, am I disturbing anyone by staying with my daughter?' her mother asked.

'It's not up to you to decide when the rules do and do not apply!' snapped the matron. 'I am trying to run a hospital here!'

Sophie's mother said nothing but gave the bossy matron a withering glare that made her depart, never to raise the matter again.

'I still can't believe that wretched spy is going to get away with trying to kill you,' she muttered after the matron left. 'Espionage and attempted murder! He ought to hang.'

'His information is too valuable. Avenging my injury isn't worth that.'

'Oh, really, Sophie,' her mother scolded. 'You're starting to take after your father, putting duty ahead of everything else. Why, you're even here to help him with this alleged King Arthur.' The slight upturn in the corners of her mouth as she stroked Sophie's hair betrayed the insincerity of her reprimand.

'Father told you this was about King Arthur?'

She nodded. 'It's a remarkable case, too, he told me.'

Sophie nodded. 'After all those months studying ancient texts, to hear someone actually speak in this dialect – really, Mother, it was amazing. Bleddyn also noticed … Well, you heard what Mr Chesterfield said about the scars.'

Her mother tilted her head to the side. 'Bleddyn?'

'Sorry – Dr Kendrick.'

'Ah.' After a pause, her mother asked, 'So, Sophie, I take it that you're fond of this Welsh doctor? Have you been seeing him?'

'No, no, I haven't been seeing him! At least, not yet, but – but how could you tell I had feelings for him?' Good grief, was her mother a psychic or something?

'I saw the way you looked at him before he left. Now,' – she tapped the tip of Sophie's nose with her index finger – 'you've just let slip that you're on first-name terms with him.'

For a woman who was so distraught at seeing her daughter in hospital, her mother had been remarkably perceptive about these things. 'We exchanged addresses two days ago. On my insistence, I may add.'

'You didn't wait for him to ask you? That's usually the way it's done.'

'Well, he might have felt it would be inappropriate to ask someone of my background,' Sophie replied.

Her mother nodded thoughtfully. 'That's possibly true.'

'He was rather insecure, and I think he feels he's not good enough – which is ridiculous. He's a doctor. Please don't tell Father yet. You know what he's like, and what he'll say about Bleddyn's family.'

'Well, sometimes, differences in upbringing can cause problems,' her mother cautioned. 'Class distinction can lead to different social and political views, different outlooks on life, and different standards on morality and ethics. Many working-class people consider us decadent, and they often have more liberal definitions of honesty than we do.'

'That's the kind of snobbish thing I'd expect from Father,' Sophie grumbled.

'No, your father would make a scene if he were here, and insist outright that your feelings are inappropriate. I'm not saying you shouldn't see a man from a working-class background – I'm just warning you not to rush into things. You are thinking of a possible marriage in the future, aren't you?'

'It's a little soon to be talking about marriage,' Sophie muttered. 'We haven't even had a first date yet.'

'Well, take your time and be sure he really is the right man. Marriages require effort and concessions from both parties. Class distinction is one possible source of contention, but conflicts will arise sooner or later, whomever you marry. When you begin seeing a man, discover his faults before you commit. Everybody has faults. Hope, but don't assume, that he will change. If you still love him and think you can live with him despite his faults, then he's right for you.'

Sophie said nothing. Her mother had probably planned this talk years ago.

Her mother resumed stroking the hair that fell around Sophie's face. 'This doctor … It is unusual to see a girl dating a man who is so much shorter than she is.'

'Most men are shorter than I am. It seems to be the fate of Edwardson and Winthrop women to resemble Amazons.'

Her mother nodded. 'True, true. Daintiness doesn't run in either side of your family, unfortunately.' After another pause, she asked, 'If it's not too personal a question, do you know how Bleddyn found the means to attend university?'

'He won the Frederick Cavendish Scholarship.'

'Ah, a scholarship. Frederick Cavendish … that's for the children of fallen soldiers, isn't it?'

Sophie nodded. 'His father died at Gallipoli.'

'Oh, goodness. Being a widow would have made life much harder for his mother. It's a competitive scholarship, isn't it? He must have been clever to win it.'

'He's highly intelligent, Mother,' Sophie told her. 'His successes also come down to hard work and self-discipline.'

Her mother raised her eyebrows. 'That reminds me of someone else I know.' A smile crept across her face. 'Yes … yes, I think I understand what you see in him, my dear. Now, we know your father is going to have a lot to say when he finds out, but he doesn't need to know just yet. You should explore your feelings for Bleddyn without interference. Just keep me abreast of what's happening.'

'Mother,' Sophie asked, 'if … if it does work out between us, what if Father remains opposed?'

'Don't worry about your father. Just leave him to me.'

PART TWO

DYNAMO

CHAPTER 9

Saturday, 25 May
1000 hours
Lys River, border of France and Belgium

'Right, men, pull up here.' Sergeant Burford pointed to the remains of a demolished bridge beside a town on the Belgian bank.

The men sighed with relief when the canoe came to a halt. Burford mopped the sweat from his brow. It wasn't even summer yet. The coming months were going to be unbearable.

He jumped ashore. 'Stay near the canoe while I find someone from the Belgian Army.'

Burford made his way towards the centre of town. The streets weren't as busy as he expected them to be on a Saturday morning. He tried to speak to a couple of people, but they hurried off as soon as he tried to get their attention.

One woman tried to bustle past, but caught sight of his badges and remarked, 'Oh – you are English.'

'Madame, I am looking for a representative from the Belgian Army.'

'They left two days ago.'

Burford grunted. So, the lieutenant general was correct. The Belgians had withdrawn from this area, leaving the British flank exposed.

She pulled her basket close to her chest as her nervous eyes darted up and down the street. 'Sir, is a battle about to be fought nearby? I have seen Germans here.'

'*What?*' The sweat on Burford's forehead chilled. 'Germans here? Already?'

'Yes. If you will excuse me, I must go home.' She hurried off.

Burford looked up and down the street. Had the Germans really pushed this far west? It would explain why nobody wanted to stop and talk …

Gunfire shattered the air. Burford spun around just in time to see his men ducking for cover. One man was down. *Christ! What can I do?*

He drew his revolver, but paused with it in his hand. It was useless at this distance. *If only I had my rifle!*

A blue car turned a corner and came towards Burford. His heart stopped when he saw the Mercedes-Benz bonnet ornament. *Germans everywhere!* He raised his revolver and fired at the windscreen.

The Mercedes veered and crashed into a house.

Jesus! He shouldn't have fired all six rounds. Burford ducked behind a lamp post that was far too thin to conceal him. If the occupants shot back, he was done for.

A door was flung open and an officer ran. Burford remained in his partially shielded position, fumbling as he pushed more rounds into the cylinder, but the fleeing German didn't look back.

Burford locked the cylinder back into place, came out from behind the lamp post, and crept towards the car. Pulse pounding in his temples, he kept his revolver raised and ready.

The driver was slumped over the steering wheel. Bullets had passed through his neck and chest. Pints of blood had spurted around him, but now, it was barely trickling from his bullet wounds.

There was a briefcase on the back seat. Burford opened it and rifled through its contents. Everything was written in German, and there were a couple of maps. Someone higher up would want these. He snapped it shut and tucked it under his arm.

The gunfire had stopped. Burford's men were emerging from their cover. They had turned the attack.

He raced up to them.

Mackenzie was lying motionless in a pool of blood, a bullet wound in the centre of his chest. A lump formed in Burford's throat.

Turner was binding Private Baker's arm.

'How bad is he?' asked Burford. As soon as he saw Baker's face, he knew the answer.

'It's bad.' Turner tied off the bandage. 'I think his forearm's broken.'

One man dead, another injured. The section was down to five men. There was no pushing on to Menen now. 'Right. Put a sling on him. He might need help getting in and out of the boat, too.'

Baker's face was taut with pain, but he replied, 'It's my arm that's injured, Sarge, not my leg. I won't be able to help row, sorry.'

'Never mind that. Turner, is there any morphine?'

'What do we do now, Sergeant?' asked Turner as he retrieved a syrette from the first aid kit.

'We're going back to base.'

'Sir, have we patrolled far enough?' Jones asked.

'The Belgians have withdrawn and left a flank exposed,' he growled. 'I just shot up a German officer's car, driving around here like they own the place. We've just about wandered into their bloody camp. Besides,' – he held up the briefcase – 'someone in headquarters will want to see this.'

***

1000 hours
Government Code and Cypher School
Bletchley Park, Buckinghamshire

Artorius paced back and forth. Nobody had come today, except for the servant who brought the morning meal. What was keeping everyone?

Since his arrival at this place near Londinium, everyone had been treating him as a curiosity to be studied. There had been another examination by a physician, and one by a *dentist* – a physician who only tended teeth. This last one had its benefits, though. Artorius had chipped a tooth at Camlann before his entombment. Druidic magic hadn't healed that injury, and the discomfort had been growing. The dentist had cleaned the damaged tooth and filled it with … Kenneth Jackson had called it a blend of metals, like brass or bronze, but it was the colour of silver. Moreover, the dentist had administered the most effective pain relief Artorius had ever received.

A knock on the door made him look up. He turned the knob, and in doing so, operated the hidden latch that kept the door shut.

It was Kenneth Jackson, the man with whom Artorius had spent the most time thus far. Like Bleddyn Kendrick, Kenneth called himself a *doctor*, but he professed to have no medical training. Apparently, he had earned the title because of his command of languages. Kenneth spoke Latin, but a stilted, old-fashioned form of it. He was also familiar with modes of speech that were similar to the Brythonic tongues of Artorius's time.

'You are late today,' Artorius said in Latin. It was still easier for Kenneth than Brythonic.

'I am, and I apologise for that.' Kenneth entered and closed the door behind him. 'I have spent much of the early morning in discussions with a colleague and my commanding officer.'

'Do your people have more questions about how I persuaded a spy to work for you?'

Kenneth smiled. 'It is better than that. We have finally convinced our immediate superior to arrange for us to meet with *his* commander. It will take place tomorrow afternoon.'

'Why do you wish to meet a senior commander?' Artorius asked.

'To introduce you to him.'

'But is it not premature, when I cannot speak any modern language? Since my arrival here, you have spent all the time in my company learning how the Brythons spoke in my time, rather than instructing me in a language that would be useful today. Would it not be more useful if you taught me English?'

'Oh, your Brythonic language – or as we call it today, *Common*

Brittonic – will be useful,' Kenneth assured him.

Artorius scratched his chin. 'How will that be so? I doubt anyone other than you would be able to understand me.'

Kenneth nodded. 'That is *precisely* why it will be useful.'

***

1750 hours
BEF Commander-in-Chief's Headquarters
Prémesques, France

Lord Gort paced around his office, glancing back and forth between the map on the wall and the seized German documents.

The map showed them in the worst position imaginable – with the sea to their backs, and completely encircled by German forces. The French Army had failed miserably in every operation since the Germans burst through the Ardennes. The Belgian Army had all but given up. The enemy now had nearly half a million French and British troops surrounded.

And yet, as bad as the campaign had been, the worst was yet to come, as attested by the documents.

A knock at the door interrupted his thoughts. 'Enter!' he called out.

Lieutenant General Pownall, Lord Gort's Chief of General Staff, walked in.

'Pownall,' Lord Gort said as Pownall saluted, 'this is a disaster.'

'Sir?'

Lord Gort pointed to the papers on his desk. 'A reconnaissance team intercepted these German documents this morning.' He picked up one folder. 'This one shows us the German order of battle.'

'Wow! That was a stroke of luck.'

'The second folder shows us their plans.' Lord Gort pointed to the map on the wall. 'The Boche will strike the Belgians here, near Thielt, with one corps. At the same time, another corps will attack us at Messines Ridge near Comines, and a third will attack at Ypres.'

Pownall studied the map. 'Sir … the attack on Thielt will make the Belgian forces contract.'

'Yes, and that will create a gap between our left side and the Belgian flank,' replied Gort. 'Oh, and the reconnaissance team found that the Belgians have withdrawn from Comines. The Germans will be attacking a weak spot there.'

Pownall pointed to Thielt and Comines. 'So, when both the Belgian and British forces contract, they will leave a hole in the front between these two spearheads, probably near Ypres—'

'Where the third corps is poised to attack,' finished Lord Gort. 'If it works, our front will disintegrate, and we'll be annihilated within days.'

'The Germans have three corps to spare for such an assault?' Pownall asked. 'Could those documents have been planted?'

'No, I don't think so,' Lord Gort replied. 'Our sergeant killed a German driver to obtain these documents. This puts us in a difficult position. I was planning to send the Fifth and Fiftieth Divisions to attack the column to the southern spearhead, but I now need them along the Ypres–Comines Canal. It's strange, but after the French have consistently failed to support attacks on that southern enemy's flank, *we'll* be the ones letting *them* down this time.'

'Actually, sir, that's what I came to tell you about,' Pownall said. 'I'd just received a telephone call from Adam. Apparently, Blanchard has told him that he cannot deliver on the three armoured divisions he had promised earlier today. The French attack from the south will only employ one unarmoured division.'

'Oh, good God, they're doing it again?' Lord Gort grumbled. 'Well, that makes the decision easier.'

'To send the Fifth and Fiftieth Divisions to Ypres instead of south?' asked Pownall.

'Not just that. Our situation here is untenable, and we have only one option left. Pownall, we must evacuate the British Expeditionary Force from Belgium and northern France.'

'Everyone, General?' asked Pownall.

'Everyone.'

Pownall cleared his throat. 'Sir, you do realise the French will claim we betrayed them, don't you?'

'Damn them,' replied Lord Gort. 'If Gamelin hadn't pulled so many divisions away from the front ten days ago, we wouldn't be in this mess now. We have no choice but to retreat. Send a message to Whitehall, Pownall.'

'Yes, sir.'

Pownall left, but Lord Gort continued to stare at the door after it had closed behind him.

Eventually, he sat at his desk and took out a bottle of cognac. He needed a stiff drink. He had just given orders for the biggest retreat in the history of the British Empire.

A trembling hand spilled the spirit as he poured it into a shot glass. *God almighty, have I left this too late?* If he had, he might even go down in history as the general responsible for Britain's collapse.

CHAPTER 10

Sunday, 26 May
0650 hours
Salisbury Railway Station

Bleddyn heaved his suitcase off the train and rubbed his eyes, trying to think what he had to do next.

A porter looked at him and smiled. 'Rough night?'

'It was. Can you tell me how to get from the station to the RAMC hospital?'

'Ah. National service?'

Bleddyn nodded.

'Just report to the stationmaster's office.' The porter pointed towards the centre of the platform. 'He'll call the relevant base, and they'll send someone to pick you up.'

Another car. It was going to be like the trip to Axleigh and Doncaster nine days ago. The armed forces must have as many chauffeurs as they had soldiers.

The thought of Axleigh made his heart sink. Nothing he would do from this point on would be as interesting as that case. He'd probably never see Artorius again. Bleddyn would have given his eye teeth to see what Artorius would do in the coming months. Was there really anything to the legendary prophecy?

No … no, his heart wasn't sinking because he would never see

King Arthur again.

Perhaps he should write to Sophie. It wouldn't be amiss to enquire about her health, after everything that had happened. It was the polite thing to do.

Or would that be a bad idea?

He snorted and lugged his suitcase to the stationmaster's office. He had a job to do.

'A car's already coming,' the stationmaster replied when Bleddyn asked how to get there. 'There'll be room for both of you.' He pointed to a woman in her mid-forties. 'Best if you wait out in front of the station.'

As they left the stationmaster's office, the woman turned to Bleddyn and asked, 'So, are you one of the doctors who'll be working with me?'

'I suppose I am,' Bleddyn replied. 'Are you a specialist, a general practitioner or a nurse?'

'I'm a theatre nurse, and I will be matron of the hospital.' She scowled. 'Well, it seems that you're Welsh, and a young doctor, too. I see I'll have to keep a close eye on you. I'll not have you sweeping one of my naïve young nurses off her feet with those dark eyes and that sweet accent of yours.'

Bleddyn stopped in his tracks.

The matron chuckled. 'Don't be so serious, young man. Look, I served in the Great War, and a sense of humour goes a long way with soldiers. You'll need to be prepared to give and take a lot of banter.'

'Wounded soldiers are up to banter after what they've been through?' Bleddyn asked.

The smile dropped from her face. 'Not always. You'll quickly learn when banter works best, and when you need to be delicate.' She extended her hand. 'Martha Wrigley.'

Bleddyn shook her hand. 'Bleddyn Kendrick, house officer. You can call me Bleddyn if regulations allow it.'

Martha smiled. 'You're happy to be on first-name terms with the matron? Well, at least you're not pretentious. Many doctors are.'

In the ensuing conversation, Bleddyn learnt that Martha had been widowed twice, and that she had two daughters. The elder girl worked in a factory, and Martha hoped her younger daughter would still be able to complete her school certificate, if the accursed war let her.

Two vehicles arrived to take men to other military bases before the car from the RAMC arrived.

It wasn't long before they turned off the road into the grounds of a magnificent manor house. Never in Bleddyn's wildest dreams had he imagined he would reside in such a fine mansion. Then again, even if he had, those dreams would not have involved shared living quarters, canteen food prepared by a military cook, and providing around-the-clock medical care. He shrugged and went to grab his suitcase, only to find a couple of porters had already emptied the boot.

The driver led Bleddyn and Martha through the main doorway into a massive entrance hall that had been converted into a waiting room. A corporal behind a desk then led them up the central flight of stairs. They turned right on the top floor and went to a room with 'Lt. Col. R. Darcy' scrawled across a piece of cardboard taped to the door.

The corporal knocked.

'Come in!' Darcy's voice was strong and stern.

The corporal entered, sprang to attention and saluted. 'Sir, the new arrivals.'

Martha and Bleddyn followed the corporal in and also stood to attention.

Darcy had short-cropped white hair. Judging by a plate with crumbs on it and the half-finished cup of tea, they had interrupted his breakfast. He looked between Bleddyn, Martha and the corporal. 'At ease, everyone. Your names are?'

'Martha Wrigley, senior sister, sir.'

'Bleddyn Kendrick, pre-registration house officer, sir.'

Darcy flicked through some files on his desk. 'Ah, yes. You two were scheduled for induction tomorrow, but I'm glad you're here.' He gestured to the chairs. 'Are you able to start early?'

'I'm a little tired after the trip, sir, but there's no reason I couldn't start a shift this afternoon,' Bleddyn replied as he and Martha took their seats.

'Like Dr Kendrick, I spent the whole ruddy night on trains and in stations – but I can start earlier if necessary, sir,' Martha said.

Darcy grunted. 'A lot of traffic on the lines heading east, I suppose?'

'Now that you mention it, sir, a lot of other trains did seem to be heading east,' Bleddyn replied.

'Heading to Kent, I expect. Actually, I want to take both of you to Kent with me today, too. We're setting up a mobile hospital there.'

'Sir, we don't even have our uniforms yet,' Martha said.

Darcy snorted. 'Uniforms are the last of my concerns now. I'm so short-staffed, I'd let you work naked if you were qualified.'

A lump formed in Bleddyn's throat. If Darcy was rushing to set up a field hospital in Kent despite being short-staffed, something was wrong.

'No doubt you've heard the news from Belgium?' Darcy asked.

'Yes, sir,' Bleddyn replied, 'and it isn't good.'

'It's worse than you've heard. Our boys have the sea to the west and the Germans on all other sides, and the Luftwaffe have won supremacy over the skies above them.'

'Sir, what are they going to do now?' Bleddyn asked in a small voice.

'They're about to retreat – and they'll be doing so under heavy fire. Casualties will be high. No doubt some of them will require medical attention on arrival back in Britain.'

'How many men will be retreating like this, sir?'

'I'm told there are three divisions stuck in northern France, with a total of a quarter of a million men between them.'

Bleddyn's jaw dropped.

Martha gasped.

'As you can imagine,' Darcy continued, 'if the Germans can take that many prisoners of war, it will bring the British Army to its knees.'

Bleddyn's head began to reel. 'What about French support?'

'I don't know what's happening in France, but the word on the grapevine is that the Germans have smashed the northern Maginot Line. If so, nothing will hold them back now. France will fall within weeks.'

Bleddyn dropped his head. His pulse throbbed in his temples. God

Almighty, what a catastrophe! The Germans were sweeping through Europe like a hurricane, flattening everything in their path. If France and Belgium fell, Europe would be controlled by Adolf Hitler, his allies and a handful of 'neutral' governments. Arthur's return would do precious little for them now.

He raised his head again. They mustn't give up. He had friends and family whose very lives might depend on Britain's tenacity, and he needed to do his part. 'We're to work in a field hospital in Dover, sir?'

Darcy nodded. 'We are, but we're not fully set up here. We only have one other surgeon so far and hardly any nurses, so we don't have many people to spare for Kent. You two have come just in time.' He glanced at the files again. 'Wrigley, I see that you were in the QAs in the Great War. Did you serve near the front?'

'Yes, sir.' The colour had drained from her cheeks, and she bore no resemblance to the jovial woman Bleddyn had met at the railway station.

'Well, you know what you're in for.'

She winced.

'Kendrick, welcome to the armed services,' continued Darcy. 'It'll be a baptism of fire. If there's anything in your luggage you don't need urgently, leave it here at the manor. We could be in Kent for up to a week, I'd guess.' He turned to the corporal. 'Collins, show these two to their respective quarters so they can leave their luggage, and then take them to the mess. They probably haven't eaten yet.'

Seven hours later, Bleddyn was in a small personnel carrier heading for Kent. He glanced at Martha, whose sense of humour hadn't recovered since the morning. She had seen this before; he could only wonder what horrors lay ahead.

***

0900 hours
St Peter's Church
Conisbrough, South Yorkshire

Sophie's mother parked the car and turned off the engine.

Sophie had never felt uneasy about attending a church service before. After her conversation with Artorius, she was beginning to question her faith – not in God, or Christ, but in Christian orthodoxy.

She opened the door. Her stitches pulled as she turned to get out of the car. It would be another four days before the abominable things were removed.

'Are you all right, dear?' her mother asked.

'I told you, Mother, it would have been easier to walk here.'

'All that way, with your injury—'

'It's easier than getting in and out of the car. You shouldn't have wasted the petrol.'

As they walked past the headstones, her mother asked, 'Did you ever find out if Bleddyn's an Anglican, a Catholic, or something else?'

'We never discussed religion,' Sophie replied. 'At least, not our respective denominations.'

'Just bear in mind, it can cause problems …'

'I'll ask, but most Welsh people are Protestants.' Sophie didn't tell her mother about Bleddyn's Chinese Buddhist brother-in-law, or that a discussion with Artorius about Gnosticism was causing her to question her beliefs. It was a little too soon for any of that.

They made their way to the pew they shared with the Percy family.

The Percys were already there. Mr Percy turned towards them. 'Good morning, Mrs Edwardson.'

'Good morning, Mr Percy, Mrs Percy,' her mother replied.

Sophie sat on the edge of her seat. It let her drop her knees to slightly below a horizontal position while keeping her back straight.

Mrs Percy looked at Sophie. 'I must say, Sophie, I'm surprised you're here today. I thought you would be in Cambridge at this time of year.'

'There have … been some problems at Cambridge because of the war. I have some free time, at least for now.' This was partly true, and vague enough not to raise suspicion.

'Ah.' Mrs Percy nodded. 'I'm not surprised, after what's happened.'

Something about Mrs Percy's tone unsettled Sophie. The Percy boys, usually grudging attendees at church, were not their normal restless selves; rather, they were positively subdued this morning. Sophie looked around. There were more attendees than usual. Some people were whispering to each other with looks of deep concern on their faces, and there was a strange tension in the atmosphere.

Her mother had noticed something amiss, too. 'Mrs Percy, we didn't turn the wireless on this morning. Did we miss something?'

'The British Expeditionary—'

The organ cut her off. Everyone stood to sing the introductory hymns as Reverend Eddershaw and his attendants entered.

As soon as the usual introductions were out of the way, Reverend Eddershaw read the story of David killing Goliath from the Book of Samuel. This had also been popular at Cambridge in recent months, although launching straight into an Old Testament reading was a significant deviation from the usual service.

The vicar closed the Bible. 'I started with this reading to remind everyone that even when defeat in battle looks certain, the righteous, through God's will, can still triumph. As such, I urge you, my fellow Englishmen, not to lose hope, despite the perils our army faces.'

Sophie bristled. Yet again, someone was talking about the 'English' at war, not the 'British'.

'As some of you have already heard,' Reverend Eddershaw went on, 'the situation in Europe has not been to our favour of late. I wish I had better news to tell you than what I bring you today. The British Expeditionary Force is now in full retreat – stuck between the Germans and the English Channel.'

Full retreat! Sophie straightened. Gasps of shock rippled through the congregation. The Percys sat in glum silence.

The vicar told them that the Archbishop of Canterbury, at the behest of the Prime Minister and the King, had designated this Sunday as a national day of prayer. He invited the congregation to join him, along with the rest of the nation, to pray to Almighty God to deliver the

British Expeditionary Force from annihilation.

Sophie's stomach twisted and turned. If today was a national day of prayer, they were in trouble. Deep trouble.

She barely heard any of the prayer the vicar had prepared, apart from the plea to God to aid His righteous followers, as He had done for David against Goliath. This plea didn't reassure her. David's shot may have caused a small army of Philistines to retreat, but killing any one warrior or commander would not have the same effect in the twentieth century.

Anyhow, David may have been a servant of God, but what would the Lord think of the British and their subjugation of so many races?

Would He view them as the lesser evil compared to the Nazis, and help them nevertheless?

No, probably not. Even David probably just got lucky. As Artorius had pointed out, God's kingdom was Heaven. Righteousness and justice did not always prevail in this imperfect world. It certainly hadn't for his people against the Anglo-Saxons.

What about Christopher? He was in Norway, last they'd heard; had the *Glorious* been recalled for this evacuation? Was he all right?

Few people went to the communion rail, and the service finished quickly. Nobody stopped to talk as everyone bustled out of the church.

'Mother, wait!' Sophie called out as her mother raced to the car. She pointed to her abdomen.

'Oh, I'm sorry, dear, I forgot.'

Her mother had been asking how Sophie felt every five minutes since they'd arrived back home. The news must really have alarmed her if she forgot it now.

'I'm truly sorry, I – we should get back home quickly.'

'Why the rush?' Sophie asked. 'What can you do back home?'

'Well … I could mound more soil around the air-raid shelter.' She sighed, her face taut with worry. 'I know it's silly, but it's all I can do right now. Dear Lord, I hope your brother's safe!'

***

There was a knock on the door while everyone was packing up. A secretary poked her head in. 'Commander Denniston is here with three people in civilian dress.'

'A commander?' Sir John Dill looked at Sir Charles Forbes and Vice Admiral Ramsay. 'You were expecting a commander here?'

'No, I have no idea … oh.' Sir Charles's expression of confusion gave way to a grimace. 'Oh, I'd forgotten – Denniston called and scheduled a meeting yesterday afternoon. It was barely an hour before this whole Dunkirk business blew up, and I forgot to call Denniston back and cancel that meeting.'

'Denniston?' asked Sir John. 'Isn't he the chap in charge of that codebreaking operation?'

'Yes,' replied Sir Charles.

'In that case, I'd like to hear what he has to say, too.' If these codebreakers had made a breakthrough, then perhaps it would be relevant to the evacuation.

'Very well.' Sir Charles looked up at the secretary. 'Let them in.'

The secretary ushered Denniston and three other men into the room. One of the older two men wore a suit that was too big for him and bore a scar across his face that Sir John regarded with suspicion. It looked like one of those duelling scars that German mensur fencers considered a badge of honour. This man wasn't a Nazi, was he?

Denniston saluted his superiors.

Sir Charles introduced everyone to the new arrivals. 'Gentlemen, Commander Denniston is the head of the Government Code and Cypher School at Bletchley Park. He and some of his men are here to make a proposition.' He turned back to the Bletchley Park team. 'You will of course recognise the Prime Minister, the Right Honourable Winston Churchill.' He pointed to the other men in the room. 'The Lord Privy Seal, Clement Attlee; the Prime Minister's chief staff officer,

Major General Hastings Ismay; Sir John Dill, who is now acting Chief of the Imperial General Staff; Lieutenant Colonel Dudley Clarke; and Vice Admiral Bertram Ramsay. At ease, Denniston.'

Denniston adjusted his collar. 'I must say, sir, I didn't expect we'd be presenting this idea in front of such a crowd.' He cast his eyes around the room and shifted uncomfortably as he and the three other men from Bletchley Park took their seats. He cleared his throat. 'Let me introduce my team. Mr Oliver Strachey and Dr Kenneth Jackson are two of our language experts, and they're here with' – he pointed to the man with the scar – 'a new recruit who goes by the name of Artorius.'

Artorius. Weird name. 'Is that a Christian name or a surname?' asked Sir John.

'More of an epithet, sir,' replied Jackson.

'Has the team in Bletchley Park assembled another of those decrypting machines – "bombes", I think they're called?' asked Sir Charles.

'Not yet, sir,' replied Denniston. 'Turing and Welchman oversee that project, and their next machine is still a few weeks away. Rather, Dr Jackson and Mr Strachey are here to propose a new idea for a code of our own.'

'All right – but we need to get back to our headquarters soon, Denniston. I hope you can make this snappy.'

Well, that was disappointing. They really needed another bombe. Nevertheless, Sir John stayed to hear them out.

Denniston cleared his throat and adjusted his collar. 'Gentlemen, could you explain your idea?'

Sir John stroked his chin. He now understood why Denniston was nervous. Denniston didn't share his subordinates' enthusiasm for their plan and was permitting them to present it against his better judgement. This didn't bode well.

Strachey spoke first. 'The idea first came to me a little over a week ago. A German spy was apprehended near Doncaster. Artorius' – he pointed to the man with the scarred face – 'happened to be there, and he not only noticed a flaw in the spy's cover, but he later managed to turn him. The spy has divulged the code he was using to transmit messages back to Germany.' He pulled out a folder. 'We'd seen it before, but we hadn't broken it. It's a substitution cypher, but a couple of interesting modifications made it deceptively difficult to crack.'

'Are you sure that the spy's information is reliable?' Sir John asked.

'Oh, yes. We looked back at all the intercepted transmissions in this code, and they're quite intelligible now. We've passed the information on to the Security Service. I understand they've already tracked down and arrested at least two other spies using this code.'

Sir Charles nodded. 'Well, that's an excellent breakthrough, I must say. However, I cannot see why you felt the need to tell me this in person.'

'Sir, our goals are not restricted to breaking the enemy's codes,' Strachey told him. 'We also devise codes that are hard to break. It so happens that Artorius may also be able to help with the development of such a code – of sorts.' He pointed to Artorius, for whom Dr Jackson was hastily explaining something in another language – Latin, it sounded like. 'Artorius doesn't speak English, but he can speak a language so rare, the Germans are unlikely to have anyone capable of translating it.'

Dr Jackson took it from there. 'In case anyone's wondering, Artorius turned the spy while conversing with him in Latin. He's also fluent in the ancient British language which academics now call Common Brittonic. If we were to place him in a major divisional headquarters, the War Office would be able to send telegrams in this language. Common Brittonic is the ancestral language of Welsh, Cornish and Breton, but it differs enough from those modern languages to render it unintelligible to native speakers today. Even if the Germans intercepted and decrypted these transmissions, it's doubtful whether they would understand them.'

'Nor would we,' said Mr Churchill. 'Our codes won't be much good if we can't understand them ourselves.' This brought a wave of stifled laughter from the room.

Dr Jackson pushed on. 'Well, I'm a linguistics expert, and I've studied these languages. If I were to work from the War Office, I would be able to communicate with Artorius in the field.'

'It's worth remembering the Americans did something similar in the Great War, using an American Indian language – Choctaw – as a code,' Strachey added.

Sir John glanced at the door, wondering if he could slip out. This new code was not the most urgent matter at present.

Sir Charles cleared his throat. 'It's an interesting idea and I'm not averse to it, but are you absolutely certain the Germans won't have people who understand it? Won't they have their own linguists?'

'I'm on familiar terms with all the world's leading experts in pre-modern Brythonic languages, and they're all British citizens,' replied Dr Jackson.

Mr Attlee frowned. 'I think I've misunderstood something. If the handful of experts in this language are all British, then how is it that this man – Artorius – doesn't speak English?'

After a moment's hesitation, Dr Jackson explained, 'That's a good question, sir. Truth be told, there's a bit of a mystery surrounding Artorius.'

Sir John frowned at him. 'I don't follow. Surely you're not planning to entrust a man who isn't a British citizen with coded messages when you don't even know everything about him and where he comes from? For that matter, what country *is* he from?'

'Oh, he seems to be from Britain,' Dr Jackson replied.

'Seems to be from Britain?' asked Sir Charles. 'Stop beating about the bush, man. Out with it. Where's he from?'

'Well ... the earliest account we have of him is that he was found near an ancient burial mound. A vague explanation was put forward to the effect that he lived in the early Dark Ages.'

'Early Dark Ages?' exclaimed Sir Charles. 'What on earth ... Wait ... *Artorius* ...' His eyes narrowed. 'Jackson, are you telling us this man claims to be King Arthur?'

'Ah ... not quite,' replied Strachey. 'Artorius never claimed to be king. In fact, I don't think Arthur was described as a king until the Middle Ages.'

'What the blazes?' demanded Mr Churchill. 'Have you all gone stark raving mad?'

Sir John scowled. Entrusting a loony who thought he was King Arthur with encoded military communications? How, for the love of God, could these men from Bletchley Park have entertained such an insane idea for more than a millisecond?

Dr Jackson handed Churchill a file. 'It is indeed an incredible claim. However, before you dismiss it out of hand, there are reports that examine the plausibility of these claims. They make interesting reading.'

Churchill opened the file and glanced at the front pages of the first two reports. 'Bleddyn Kendrick … Sophie Edwardson. A Welshman and a woman.' He closed the folder. 'If these are the most thorough investigations into the man's authenticity, there's no reason to take this seriously.'

'With respect, Mr Churchill,' Dr Jackson insisted, 'I've studied Welsh, Cornish and Breton, as well as the now-extinct languages of Old Welsh, Old Breton, Old Cornish, Cumbric and Common Brittonic. I also know the young lady who wrote that report; I lectured her from time to time at Cambridge, and she was exceptionally good at Latin. She has since gone on to undertake a master's degree in British Vulgar Latin, a dialect in which she claims Artorius is fluent. I can't confirm the specific dialect, but Artorius is certainly fluent in *a* dialect of Vulgar Latin.'

'That Welshman is only one of three doctors to examine Artorius, too,' added Strachey. 'All of them concur on his unusual injuries. We also had a dentist look at his teeth. Judging by the condition of his teeth, it seems Artorius has eaten a quintessential pre-industrial diet for his entire life.'

'Look,' said Dr Jackson, 'I can understand why you assembled gentlemen are sceptical. You are educated and intelligent men, and the idea of King Arthur's return is a fantastic one that does not sit well with the rational mind. When Mr Strachey first told me about Artorius, I thought he was having me on. Imagine my astonishment to find a man fluent in a language that hasn't been spoken for over a millennium. Bizarre as it sounds, I believe Artorius to be genuine.'

Churchill continued to scowl at the Bletchley Park men. Sir John couldn't blame him. It didn't matter how 'curious' Artorius was – this idea was bloody stupid.

Ismay intervened. 'I feel, gentlemen, that there may be further difficulties if we were to follow up on this idea. If Artorius doesn't speak English, we'll need a Latin translator to work with him, and the chance of mistakes occurring will increase with multiple translations.'

'If he really is who he claims to be,' added Mr Attlee, 'it will be hard to translate modern technical terms unfamiliar to King Arthur, and these would include almost every modern weapon and mode of transport.'

'Not to mention that having only two people who can speak the language will limit the use of this code to the War Office and just one base,' Sir John pointed out.

'Yes, well, thank you for bringing this to our attention, Denniston,' Sir Charles said with the air of a man who wanted to end the conversation quickly, 'but the idea is not practical. As it is, we've spent too long listening to this when we need to start evacuating a quarter of a million men from Europe.'

'A quarter of a million!' Dr Jackson blurted out.

Artorius tapped Dr Jackson on the elbow and asked him something.

'You're pulling them out through Dunkirk, sir?' Denniston asked as he got up.

'Good God, man, how did you know that?' Sir Charles demanded.

'Sir, we're monitoring British as well as German transmissions, and we wrote the British codes. We monitor British and German messages for any sign that our codes might have been broken.'

'Oh, yes, of course. That makes sense. Well … keep up the good work. Most of it, anyway.'

Sir John cast a contemptuous look at Artorius and Dr Jackson. The dialogue between them was becoming increasingly urgent. These men were getting off lightly with wasting everyone's time like this. Had he been in charge of Bletchley Park, he'd have fired the whole damn lot of them on the spot, including Denniston.

'With respect, gentlemen,' exclaimed Strachey, 'I think you're missing an opportunity here—'

'Mr Strachey,' growled Sir Charles, 'there may be peculiarities about this man that give superficial credibility to his claims, but it requires one considerable leap of faith to accept them in full. Nobody denies the excellent work you've done at Bletchley Park, but this idea is most fanciful and unworkable.'

Strachey started to protest, but Denniston waved a hand and cut him off. 'We've sported with Sir Charles's patience enough today, Oliver.' He bid everyone a good day and ushered Strachey to the door.

Dr Jackson and Artorius were still talking.

'Ahem …' Denniston tried to get Dr Jackson's attention. 'Kenneth, it's time we leave.'

Dr Jackson and Artorius kept talking. Artorius was getting more animated.

'Kenneth,' repeated Denniston, 'we're overstaying our welcome …'

Dr Jackson turned back to the table. 'Gentlemen, Artorius has just asked if you have enough fishing boats and … *longships* would be the best translation … for the evacuation?'

'Oh, for God's sake, this is getting ridiculous!' yelled Sir John. 'Evacuating that many men with fishing boats? And as for artillery …'

Vice Admiral Ramsay sniggered.

'I tried to explain that to Artorius,' Dr Jackson said, 'but he insisted that if modern boats really are as large as he's heard, they would be unable to approach the beaches.'

Ramsay threw his hands up. 'Well, one thing's for sure – your King Arthur certainly has no grasp of modern shipping. Luckily for us, engineers have had the good sense to build wharves to service modern ships, and there happens to be a series of such wharves at Dunkirk harbour.'

This elicited a wave of cynical laughter. Sir John didn't join in; rather, he just sank his head into his hands. *How* could Bletchley Park have recruited such imbeciles?

'Oh, they had large enough boats to require harbours in the early Dark Ages, sir.' Dr Jackson's voice was stronger, even confident. 'What they didn't have were planes and bombs. Artorius wondered if the Germans would attack the harbour from the air and thwart our retreat.'

What? Sir John jerked his head up.

Sneers slid from everyone's faces.

The ticking wall clock echoed through the room.

'Good God,' Sir John whispered. 'I'd wondered about the Luftwaffe bombing our boys, but I hadn't thought about the bloody harbour.'

'Why wasn't Sir Cyril Newall here?' demanded Mr Churchill. 'The Chief of the Air Staff would have foreseen this.'

'Stomach bug, sir, remember?' said Clarke.

'What about his aide-de-camp? Dowding or Portal could have sat in, too.'

Sir Charles glared at Sir John. 'You should have been pulling divisions out a week ago! What was that rubbish about seeing the campaign through to the end?'

'Gentlemen, stop this, please!' exclaimed Mr Attlee. 'This is an oversight, but even if the Royal Air Force had a representative here, it wouldn't stop the Germans from bombing the harbour.'

Sir John sighed. 'Indeed. The RAF has been neutralised in northern France. I can't see how they could maintain a strong enough presence over Dunkirk to thwart German bombers indefinitely.' He clenched his right fist. 'It won't be long before they destroy the bloody harbour.'

'Excuse me, gentlemen,' said Ramsay as he stood. His face had blanched. 'I will need to revise some of my plans.' He rushed out of the room without a backward glance.

Another cold silence echoed in his wake.

Sir John cleared his throat. This was awkward. 'Well, Commander Denniston, it seems that your "King Arthur" has posed an interesting strategic question. As to where he could be stationed … look, we'll have to think about that later. We may not have much further use for codes unless we salvage this operation.'

Commander Denniston nodded and turned to his men. 'Gentlemen, we should leave.'

Sir John hesitated. 'Actually, Denniston – I may have occasion to speak to Artorius again sometime in the next few days, if time permits. Perhaps he and Dr Jackson could find lodgings nearby. As a guest of the British Army, that is.'

'Thank you, sir,' replied Dr Jackson.

'That's a bad idea,' growled Churchill. 'The man's out of his mind. Or a fraud.'

'He also thinks fast on his feet,' replied Sir John. 'If his quick mind helps us win this war, I don't care if he calls himself Moses.' He pointed to the folder in front of the Prime Minister. 'That has the reports? If so, do you mind if I take it?'

***

1430 hours
Admiralty, Whitehall, London

'Tennant! I need to see you in my office!'

Bill Tennant got to his feet. 'Yes, Admiral.' Sir Charles looked as though he'd seen a ghost. This was going to be bad news.

'At ease, and take a seat,' Sir Charles said as Bill shut the door behind him. The Admiral of the Fleet groaned and rubbed his temples. 'I've just come out of the strangest meeting, but … well, someone pointed out that the Germans are sure to bomb the stuffing out of Dunkirk harbour. We may not be able to use it for much longer.'

Bill's heart jumped. 'Oh, God! Why didn't *we* think of that?'

'Why didn't anyone think of it before? It's so bloody obvious in hindsight. Tennant, if it happens, Dunkirk will descend into chaos. Ramsay's going to need a man on the ground to organise the embarkation. He'll need a captain who knows the Channel well. Someone with a steady nerve who's fought on the front line before, and someone with administrative experience.' Sir Charles looked straight at Bill. 'Someone like you. Bill, I'm sending you to Dunkirk. Go to Dover, find a ship and crew – any ship you choose – and take her to France.'

Bill swallowed, but recovered his composure and replied, 'Yes, sir.'

'Sorry to put this on you at such short notice,' Sir Charles murmured, 'but I can't think of a better man. After what you went through in the Great War, I know you'd rather stay behind that desk of yours.'

Bill straightened. 'Sir, a safe desk job is a luxury the men in Dunkirk don't have. If I'm more useful on the front line …'

Sir Charles nodded. 'That's the spirit, man! It won't be a long stay, though – not at the rate the Germans are moving. You'll have until Wednesday, I think. What we can't do by then, we probably can't do at all.'

'Sir,' cautioned Bill, 'don't expect much if I've only got three days to ferry men from the beaches. The waters are shallow, and our destroyers won't be able to come within a mile of land. Each round trip with a launch will take ages.'

'I know, I know. Just do the best you can.' Sir Charles grimaced and shook his head. He rested his elbows on the desk and put his face in his hands. 'Jesus Christ, this is a bloody balls-up. We should have seen this coming.'

'Am I to leave immediately, sir?' Bill asked.

'Yes. Godspeed and good luck!'

***

1700 hours
Dover Castle, Kent

'Pardon me,' Vice Admiral Bertram Ramsay told his driver as soon as he stepped out of the car. The anxiety had been making him ill throughout the trip. He only just made it behind the bush before his stomach heaved.

'Sir, are you all right?' the driver asked.

Bertram shook his head. 'None of us are.'

How could he have been so *stupid*? He should have anticipated the destruction of the harbour. Britain would fall, and it would be his fault.

War had changed a lot in two decades, of course. The last time Bertram saw active service, 'bombing raids' meant dropping grenades from biplanes. He had never actually seen the current aircraft in action.

No, there was no excusing this oversight. Excuses were not going to help them now. Besides, that lunatic or whatever he was, the supposed King Arthur, had seen it instantly. It still felt surreal that a man could be both as mad as a hatter and so insightful. Alas, his proposed solution would have been laughable had their situation not been so grave. Evacuating the entire British Expeditionary Force using fishing boats – not a chance. Even if they requisitioned every fishing boat in Britain, each vessel would be able to carry … how many men? Twenty? That would still amount to more than ten thousand round trips in total.

Bertram entered the tunnel, descended to the labyrinth, entered his office, and collapsed into his chair. He was still at a complete loss for what to do next. There was no way of evacuating a quarter of a million men in less than three days without a serviceable harbour. This operation was about to fail, and it had barely started.

He glanced at the photograph on his desk of his wife and sons. Helen, David and Charlie all smiled back at him from behind the glass. Many high-ranking officers would probably be imprisoned or even executed if the Nazis took control; but what of their families? Bertram had failed his King, his country, even his wife and boys …

He picked up the photograph and studied it. The photo was from their holiday on the Isle of Man last summer, only a few months before the outbreak of war. There were several ferries in the harbour behind where they had been standing. Those ferries were the only means of transport to and from the island.

Could they help?

No, not really. The draughts of those ferries were still too deep to bring them close to the beaches.

Something else in the background caught his eye. It was a tugboat, manoeuvring a ferry. Charlie had pointed to them in wonder. Bertram had tried to explain what the tugboats were doing, but didn't think his two-and-a-half-year-old really understood it.

Could they be of any use? They were smaller than the large vessels they towed, and they could move into shallower waters; but they lacked speed and carrying capacity. They would be hardly any better than fishing boats.

Unless …

Of course! Bertram sprang to his feet. *Not all is lost! Not yet!*

He put the photograph back in its place, grabbed a notebook, and began sketching out a plan, from initial concept to communication, fuel supply and coordination. They wouldn't be able to recover artillery, but from what Bertram had heard, the army needed to replace it, anyway.

The Royal Navy would have to requisition small boats in major harbours around the British Isles, starting with those near Kent. There were quite a few on the Thames, and Ramsay would speak to fishermen from Dover in person. He did not want to send civilians into a war zone, but they needed help, and fishermen were experienced sailors.

It was still all rather hasty, though. So much could still go wrong. Were there any more oversights? If only he could spend more time on it! But alas, time was a luxury he didn't have.

CHAPTER 11

Monday, 27 May
0900 hours
HMS Wolfhound, offshore from Dunkirk

Bill Tennant and his officers stood on the bow of the ship and peered through his binoculars.

Dear God.

German aircraft were already bombing the town and the docks. Bill winced each time he saw part of it disappear in a cloud of dust, and cursed his inability to stop the onslaught. The sound carried belatedly over the water, but the bombs were falling so fast there was no way to tell which boom corresponded with which flash of an exploding bomb.

'Gentlemen,' he told his officers, 'the evacuation may not go according to plan. A degree of improvisation may be required.'

'That's an understatement if ever I heard one, sir,' Commander Conway grumbled.

Minutes passed, and then an hour. The only consolation was that no Stukas came out farther to attack the *Wolfhound*.

It was nearly two hours before the Luftwaffe planes cleared from the sky. God only knew how many thousand bombs they had dropped in that time. The once mighty harbour was up in smoke.

'Conway, we need to go ashore,' Bill told his second in command. 'However, any ship trying to moor in the harbour now risks catching fire.'

'I wouldn't worry about that, sir,' replied Conway. 'We'll choke to death on that smoke first.' He pointed to a beach north-west of town. 'That'll be our best landing site, I think.'

Bill clenched his teeth. 'And we can't bring the ship any closer to land there, lest we beach her.' Ferrying men by whaler lifeboat was going to be excruciatingly slow. If only the Royal Navy had more motorised launches!

Indeed, it took nearly an hour for Tennant and his eight officers to row from the *Wolfhound* to the beach.

They walked to Dunkirk. The Luftwaffe must have hit an oil storage tank, for a dark cloud of smoke rose from the harbour like an ominous typhoon. The foetid smoke was already settling on the wreckages and rubble that greeted Bill every way he turned. He passed a leg projecting from underneath a collapsed house. A girl in her early teens with a bloodied face sat on the kerb, sobbing. Alas, they couldn't stop and help.

As they approached the harbour, the stench of wood smoke and burning rubber became overpowering. It looked even worse on closer inspection. Rubble everywhere. Several mangled bodies lay on the street amidst the debris. Soldiers were milling about farther back from the harbour, many of them watching Bill and his men.

'Where do we go now?' Clouston asked. Anxiety had thickened his Canadian accent.

'We need to find Colonel Whitfield,' Bill replied. 'He's been coordinating the evacuation until now.'

Clouston surveyed the remains of nearby buildings. 'Do you even think he survived, sir?'

'Well, there's only one way to— Ow!' Bill's ankle rolled as something gave way underfoot.

Conway extended his hand. 'Sir, are you all right?'

Bill tested his ankle by putting weight on it slowly. It held up. 'I'm fine.'

An army lieutenant approached and saluted. 'Are you here to evacuate us, sir?'

Bill nodded. 'The man coordinating the evacuation so far – Whitfield – do you know if he survived the bombing?'

'Nobody really knows what's happening or who's in charge, sir, but everyone's saying that we have to go to the bastions near the sea.'

Bill read fear, anger, agitation and despondency on men's faces as he made his way to the bastions. Bellows in English drifted in from afar, but strangely enough, some of the cries sounded more like drunkenness than despair.

There were several bastions, all of them robust mounds of soil and concrete. They had been made to withstand a bombing, thank God. Men were congregating at one of the doors. This must be Whitfield's office.

'Out of our way, we need to speak to Whitfield,' Bill ordered the soldiers as he and his men pushed their way through.

As Tennant's eyes adjusted to the dark, a man broke away from a radio set and approached them.

'Colonel Whitfield?' Bill asked, trying to make out the epaulettes.

'Yes.' Whitfield looked Bill up and down, eyes resting on his epaulettes and his sleeves. 'A naval captain. Are you here to evacuate the BEF?'

'Indeed. Captain William Tennant, at your service. I am here at the behest of Vice Admiral Bertram Ramsay and Admiral of the Fleet Sir Charles Forbes.'

'Captain Tennant, I … Will the Royal Navy be taking control of this embarkation?'

'My superiors think it's the best solution, Colonel,' Bill replied. Whitfield's question made him uneasy. The various branches of the armed services were not exactly renowned for cooperation.

Whitfield nodded. 'Yes, yes indeed, that makes sense. I-I just hope they've let you know what you're in for.' He drew a cigarette from his shirt pocket with a trembling hand.

'I understand it's been difficult so far,' Bill said, probing for information. At least Whitfield appeared willing to relinquish control.

'*Difficult*, you say?' Whitfield snorted. 'Yes, well, I-I don't care for that euphemism, Captain – it's a bloody shambles! Order has broken down. Hundreds of men arrive in town every hour, most of them separated from their units. They come here, not knowing if they're supposed t-to stand their ground and fight, or get on a boat, or just crawl into the nearest wine cellar and get plastered. We have drunk soldiers running amok and looting, and … and hundreds of soldiers and civilians died in this morning's bombing raid.' He patted his pockets down.

'We saw what they did to the harbour. It's going to impede the evacuation.' Bill obliged the colonel by lighting his cigarette.

Whitfield handed him a sheet of paper. 'Here's a list of the various headquarters. At least, th-this is the most up-to-date version; something's bound to change by the end of the day. I heard from Lord Gort's office early this morning th-that they expect the front will collapse soon, and that the Germans could be driving down the beaches by tomorrow evening.'

Oh, God, thought Bill. A day and a half? Was that all the time they had?

'It wasn't just the harbour they bombed either,' Whitfield continued. 'The Luftwaffe bombed a traffic jam at … at Poperinge. We still don't know the death … how many were killed.' He drew on his cigarette. The tremble in his hand abated a little. 'Well, I wish you luck, Captain. I wish you all the luck in the world, 'cause you're going to need it!'

***

1000 hours
Dynamo Room, Dover Castle

Bertram gathered the paperwork. 'Denny, let's go. Let's hope this works.'

'Yes, sir,' replied his aide-de-camp.

As they left the office, they almost collided with an approaching signalman.

He sprang to attention. 'Sorry, Admiral, but we've just received a message from Tennant. The bombing raid left no useable wharves in the harbour.'

Bertram nodded. 'Thank you.'

'Looks like this new plan is about to be put to the test, sir,' Denny remarked.

149

They went outside and found a driver. 'Take us to Saint Luke's church in Ramsgate,' Bertram ordered.

'Yes, sir.'

Forty minutes later, they arrived in Ramsgate and made their way to the church hall. Bertram was about to find out how successful the harbour master he'd contacted yesterday had been at recruiting local fishermen for this impromptu meeting.

The sight of nearly one hundred men seated before a small lectern greeted Bertram when he walked in. The verger was also present, no doubt wondering about the unsolicited use of the hall. He looked at Bertram, glanced at his uniform, nodded, and left.

The man standing beside the lectern turned to Bertram and Denny. 'Sirs, I'm Toby Smith, here on behalf of the harbour master. I hope we've arranged this to your satisfaction.'

'Thank you,' Bertram replied.

Toby took a seat.

'Begging your pardon, sir,' one of the fishermen called out as Bertram stepped behind the lectern, 'but Mr Smith said you needed to talk to us fishermen. We were wondering how long this build-up in the harbour was going to last. You see, our livelihood's fishing, and, well, most of us haven't been able to go out these last couple of days. We understand this is important for the war, but we've still got to put food on the table for us and our families.'

A few men nodded.

'Gentlemen, I hear your concerns,' Bertram replied, 'and believe me when I say that I don't like this occupation of a civilian harbour any more than you do. Unfortunately, it may last up to another week. We're entering a critical stage in the war.'

'Are you going to evacuate the army from France to 'ere?' another man called out. 'We 'eard yesterday in church that they was in deep trouble.'

Bertram nodded. 'We are, but you mustn't talk about it outside this hall. If the Nazis listen to our civilian transmissions and believe we've given up hope, they might believe there will be little point in attacking the Royal

Navy in the Channel. That is why we haven't let the BBC report much about our operations yet. And as for making this rescue happen – well, it is for that reason, gentlemen, that you have been called.'

Bertram's words were met with silence.

'You may not be in the armed services,' he continued, 'and some of you may have been rejected because you work in an essential industry. However, Britain needs your help now. We must evacuate our boys as quickly as possible from Dunkirk in France.' He sighed. 'German bombers have just destroyed the harbour there. The ships we plan to send – destroyers, requisitioned ferries and other large vessels that can move hundreds of men at a time – will need to drop anchor a mile from the beach.'

'So you need small craft, like fishing vessels, that can get closer to the beach?' Smith asked.

'Precisely. The main purpose of small vessels will be to ferry men from the beaches to larger boats. Your fishing boats are small enough to come close to land, but they're larger and faster than the whaler lifeboats on destroyers and ferries. The ships can then make the round trip back to Ramsgate or Dover.'

More nods.

'Each small vessel could be going back and forth to Dunkirk for several days, and it will be dangerous,' Bertram warned them. 'The Germans are closing in, and you could well be fired upon while rescuing soldiers. There are mines in some places, U-boats could be patrolling the waters, and aeroplanes are raining down bullets and bombs. We cannot order any civilians into a war zone, but on behalf of our soldiers, I'm *begging* for help. If we lose the British Expeditionary Force, we'll lose the war.'

Another heavy silence descended on the hall in the wake of Bertram's plea.

'Well, if I'd been able to join the army, I'd prob'ly be in the thick of it by now, anyway,' piped up a young fisherman. 'I can't think about me own safety when the Nazis have been firing on our boys for weeks now.'

This elicited a chorus of agreement.

'Like you, Fred, I was knocked back 'cause I'm in essential services,' called someone else. 'This rescue's prob'ly the most essential service I can do!'

This drew an even louder chorus of approval.

'Admiral, I have a couple of questions,' an elderly fisherman said. 'While I'm happy to do my bit for king and country, I don't s'pose there'll be enough of us to make much of a difference, will there?'

'You'll be the first,' Bertram replied. 'I've already arranged for the recruitment of other fishermen and small boat operators from around the coast, but they won't arrive until tomorrow at the earliest.'

'Another question, sir. I don't know if I got enough diesel to get to France and back. What with rationing—'

'All participating craft will be entitled to refuel from naval stores free of charge,' Bertram reassured him. 'We'll also provide water, first aid kits and ration packs for any vessel that sails over, and anyone who participates will be paid daily at an ordinary seaman's rate. Now, is there anyone who is not willing to go? Some of you may have families, for example. We won't judge anyone who walks out now.'

'You should leave, Nick,' one fisherman said to the young man sitting beside him. 'You have a wife and a baby, and without casting the nets I can manage the *Porpoise* on my own.'

'Dad, if you're injured or killed there, nobody can sail the boat back,' the younger man hissed. 'Most soldiers, bless 'em, wouldn't even know port from starboard.'

'Son, please,' the old man pleaded, 'what if little Charlie grows up never knowing his dad?'

'Then tell him I died a hero, trying to stop him from growing up under the bloody Nazis!'

The old man stopped arguing.

In the end, nobody left.

'Gentlemen, on behalf of the British Army, the Royal Navy, the entire country, I thank you!' Relief flooded through Bertram's veins. Fishermen could be rough, unpolished, even uncouth, but the men before him had nerves of steel and hearts of gold. These fishermen, these diamonds in the rough, were about to participate in the biggest rescue in the history of the

Royal Navy. The country would be indebted to them forever.

'We have men distributing rations and first aid supplies from warehouse number three,' Denny explained. 'There will also be coordinates and directions to help you avoid dangerous stretches such as mined waters. We'll send the first small boats at 1800 hours, so everyone should collect fuel this afternoon.'

Denny took a registry of names and vessels. To Bertram's disappointment, the assembled sailors had only forty-one boats between them. Still, the fishermen were giving everything they had.

More would come in soon, anyway. It turned out Admiral Preston had already conducted an audit of small craft throughout Britain. The Royal Navy and the Ministry of Shipping would be requisitioning suitable craft by now.

After they'd concluded with the fishermen, Bertram and Denny went to the docks. The smell of fish and salty air had an invigorating effect on Bertram after the sleepless night in the tunnels. If this operation were to succeed, up to a quarter of a million men would land in south-eastern England – more, if the French asked for help. The navy intended to use Ramsgate primarily as an embarkation port, with Dover as the main point for disembarkation of the men from France; but Bertram considered it prudent to have a few services here. Amid the chaos, some vessels were sure to drop evacuees back here in Ramsgate.

'Take us to Dover,' Bertram told his driver as he and Denny climbed back into the car. 'Not the castle – the port.'

Bertram continued to dwell on the evacuation plans. Kent would be unable to house the entire army, so he was planning to send most men straight back to their barracks. Tidworth had offered to take the bulk of the French and Belgian evacuees, and to assist in redeploying them in central and southern France. Nevertheless, if there was going to be a beach evacuation, men would arrive back in England without boots or clothes. Most of them would undoubtedly be dehydrated, and some would be injured …

'Sir, we're at Dover.'

'Huh? Already?' He must have fallen asleep. 'Thank you.' He stepped out of the car. The salty air and screeching seagulls again pushed back the fatigue.

Buses were already amassing to take soldiers to the railway station. There were engines and carriages waiting in the nearby shunting yards to ferry men to their respective barracks. Denny had already contacted local schools and churches to see if they could provide emergency accommodation, just in case the numbers overwhelmed the railway and created a bottleneck.

The army had erected temporary administrative offices as well as water and clothing distribution tents. Medical personnel paced around in front of a field hospital tent.

'Wait … what are they doing there?' Denny pointed to a couple of people in civilian clothes near a field hospital.

'Let's find out,' replied Bertram.

They approached. A middle-aged woman sprang to attention. A younger man followed her lead.

'Who are you, and why aren't you in uniform?' demanded Bertram.

'Martha Wrigley, senior sister, sir,' replied the woman.

'Bleddyn Kendrick, pre-registration house officer, sir,' replied the man. 'We arrived for duty at Salisbury yesterday, and our commanding officer brought us directly here.'

'Is something wrong?' An RAMC lieutenant colonel stepped out of the tent, saw Bertram, and saluted. 'Lieutenant Colonel Darcy – is there a problem, Admiral?'

'It's irregular that you have people on duty without uniforms,' Ramsay said.

'Admiral, I was so short of staff, I had to pick these two the day they arrived. I was under the impression we would have been inundated by now, but Dover is quieter than I expected.'

'Ah, yes.' Bertram sighed. 'Alas, the enemy bombed the harbour at Dunkirk, and that has complicated things a little.'

'What?' exclaimed Darcy. 'Sir, does that mean this rescue's already failed?'

His two subordinates exchanged nervous glances.

'We're trying a contingency plan,' Bertram replied. 'With any luck, you'll have your hands full tomorrow. In the meantime, if your new recruits don't have uniforms, send them to stores to pick some up. There are spare clothes for men who will have had to strip before wading out to rescue boats; they might have some RAMC uniforms.' He glanced at Wrigley. 'Although I doubt they'll have anything for the QAs.'

'Yes, sir. I'll send Kendrick over; he can let us know if there's anything suitable for Wrigley.'

Bertram and Denny passed supply tents with clothes, marquees with water, other mobile hospitals, and marshalling areas. Hawker Hurricanes roared overhead as they made their way across the Channel. Never before in living memory had Dover been such a hub of activity – and things had barely started.

This evacuation had to succeed. Bertram's planning would mean the survival or collapse of Britain. It was damn lucky he'd been present when those codebreakers had announced their ridiculous plan. Had it not been for that lunatic, one critical oversight might have gone undetected until it was too late. Pray to God that there would be no more.

Bertram looked up at the sky. Perhaps … perhaps Artorius wasn't mad. After all, he had just prevented the collapse of this whole rescue. Was that really just chance?

Could he really be King Arthur?

***

1130 hours
Cabinet War Rooms, London

A madman or a miracle? Whatever Artorius was, he had seen that complication in Dunkirk immediately. Such a sharp mind warranted further attention, and Sir John Dill had invited Artorius and Kenneth Jackson to the map room.

'Now, remember,' he told Dr Jackson, 'everything here – *everything* – comes under the Official Secrets Act. What you see and overhear in these rooms must not be repeated outside to anyone. Make sure Artorius knows it, too.'

Artorius spent a good fifteen minutes familiarising himself with the situation map on the wall. He seemed incredulous about its detail and accuracy, from what Sir John could understand through Dr Jackson's sporadic translations. He thought he had picked up an inaccuracy in Kent. Sir John had to explain through Dr Jackson that the Wantsum Channel had silted up long ago, and the Isle of Thanet was no longer an island. Artorius then proceeded to reflect on the role of Kent in the Anglo-Saxon invasion of Britain for longer than Sir John cared.

Artorius and Dr Jackson then started to argue over something.

'What is he saying?' Sir John asked.

'My apologies, General. Artorius was having trouble accepting just how quickly the battle was moving, and how up-to-date our information is. I had to explain radios and telephones to him.'

Sir John rolled his eyes. Someone should have explained radios to him *before* he came here.

Artorius continued to study the map, tracing his finger along the horseshoe-shaped front line of British, French and Belgian soldiers, encircled by the sea and by the Germans. He pointed to the cluster of men in Lille and asked something.

When he was done, Dr Jackson looked at Sir John and asked, 'Artorius wishes to know how long you think it will be before your enemies slay all the men trapped in this region.'

Sir John cleared his throat. 'I doubt the Germans will kill them *all* before they surrender.'

Dr Jackson translated this for Artorius, who drew his eyebrows together. Several sentences passed between the two men.

'I really wish you would keep me abreast of the conversation,' Sir John muttered.

'Sorry, sir,' Dr Jackson replied. 'Artorius was astounded that soldiers would surrender and not die fighting. Apparently, when the Anglo-Saxons invaded England in his time, taking prisoners was not a standard practice unless the prisoner's life had some political leverage – for example, the son of a Saxon king.'

Sir John adjusted his collar. 'Does Artorius understand that such an action would be a war crime today?'

'That's what I was explaining to him, sir.'

Sir John sighed. This idea of bringing Artorius to the planning rooms had been a mistake.

Artorius asked which army was between the British and the Germans on the north-western front.

'They're from Belgium,' Sir John replied. 'Explain to him that Belgium is the country within this black line.' He followed the international border with his finger.

Artorius stiffened. He said something to Jackson, who translated, 'He wishes to clarify that most of Belgium has now fallen to the Germans.'

'It has,' Sir John said.

After another exchange, Dr Jackson said, 'Artorius wants to know if the ruler of Belgium plans to surrender, or retreat, or die fighting, and when he will act.'

'I'm not sure,' replied Sir John. 'That's up to the politicians, not generals like us.'

Artorius and Dr Jackson conversed a little more. Artorius pointed at the map a couple of times, glancing at Sir John as he did so.

At length, Dr Jackson said, 'Sir John, I hope I don't sport with your patience too much by telling you this, but Artorius says that you and your fellow commanders should remain abreast of political discussions. If Belgium surrenders, then a massive hole will open in your flank.'

Sir John frowned. 'Does he anticipate Belgium will surrender without warning?'

'Given how quickly the battle lines are moving and how much of Belgium has already been taken, Artorius believes their collapse could be imminent. He also believes that it will be in Germany's interests if they surrender without warning, and he suspects they may be trying to coerce the Belgians into this.' Just as Artorius had done, Dr Jackson pointed to a build-up of German divisions near the stretch of the flank held by the Belgian Army. 'This build-up of forces here is too far away to be engaged in the battle directly, but they will be well-positioned to take advantage of the hole in our flank if Belgium surrenders without warning.'

'Good God,' Sir John muttered. Artorius was right. With so many forces near the Belgian lines, the Boche must have been planning a major thrust.

'There's more, sir,' Dr Jackson continued. 'If the Belgian part of the front collapses suddenly, the German forces will make their way to the beach and drive along the coastline. They could cut off our means of retreat within a few days. Artorius said you would need to use flying machines – aeroplanes – to get them out.'

Sir John's temples began to throb. Artorius still didn't understand the capacities and limitations of modern technology; the notion of evacuating the BEF in aeroplanes was pure fantasy. Unfortunately, the pending complication he foresaw was no fantasy, and Sir John should have seen it for himself.

'Willingham,' he said to a duty officer, 'get hold of Admiral Keyes.'

'Our liaison officer with the King of Belgium, sir?' Willingham asked.

'Yes.'

Sir John stood over Willingham as he worked his way through various telephone exchanges until he reached King Leopold's headquarters.

'Ah, hello,' the duty officer said. 'To whom am I speaking? … Admiral Keyes, I'm calling on behalf of Sir John Dill. He wishes for an update on any potential discussions between the Belgians and the Germans.' His face tensed. 'Ah, I see. Admiral, if you'll excuse me for a minute while I let Sir John know.' He looked up. 'General, King Leopold is in a private meeting with German diplomats at this very moment. Admiral Keyes has been denied permission to speak to him.'

The room spun before Sir John's eyes. *Oh, Jesus Christ!* There was no doubt about it – King Leopold was negotiating terms of surrender. These negotiations would take … how long to come into effect? Twenty-four hours, if that. He turned to Jackson and Artorius. 'Dr Jackson, I'll have to call this meeting to an end. Are you able to find your way out?'

Dr Jackson nodded. 'I understand, sir.' He led Artorius out of the room.

Sir John wiped the cold sweat from under his collar. *Jesus*, why hadn't he seen this before?

He turned back to the duty officer with the telephone receiver. 'Is Keyes still on the line?'

'Yes, sir. Would you like to speak to him?'

Sir John took the receiver. 'Admiral Keyes?'

'Yes, Sir John?'

'Can you reach Lord Gort?'

'I can, sir, but wouldn't an encrypted message be safer?'

'There's no time. Warn Lord Gort that Belgium will surrender overnight, and that the Belgian sections of the front line will fall at daybreak tomorrow.'

'Overnight?' asked Admiral Keyes. 'Are you sure it will be that quick?'

'There's no doubt about it. The Germans are amassing forces near the Belgian stretches of the front line, poising for a thrust. If Belgium surrenders, and we don't have reinforcements in place, they'll take Dunkirk within two days.'

***

1340 hours
BEF northern flank, Belgium

Alan Brooke slammed on the brakes and skidded to a halt just behind a convoy of Third Division trucks.

A private guarding the vehicles saluted him.

'Take me to Montgomery!' Alan called out to the private as he jumped out of the car and grabbed his briefcase.

'Yes, General.'

As Alan followed the private, anxiety seeped back into his chest and gripped his heart. The BEF was on the knife-edge of a total defeat. After considering and eliminating possibility after possibility, Alan could only think of one solution that might work. There was but one commander who had any chance of relocating his division in time.

The private led him to a farmhouse. Monty must have requisitioned this as an office.

Alan immediately spotted the familiar silhouette in an oversized jacket talking to men in reserves outside. Montgomery looked up as Alan approached.

'At ease, Monty,' Alan said before Montgomery could salute him. 'We have a situation developing, and you're the only one who may be able to fix it.'

Monty turned to his men. 'Sorry, we'll have to leave it there.' He looked back at Alan. 'My office is this way, General. If you'll follow me …'

'Oh, never mind confidentiality – everyone will find out soon enough,' Alan replied. 'The King of Belgium is negotiating with German diplomats at this very moment. Belgium is about to surrender, perhaps as early as tonight or tomorrow morning. Seeing as their forces hold about eighteen miles of our north-western front—'

'You want me to disengage here and relocate the Third Division to the north-western flank?' As usual, Montgomery didn't need prompting.

'Yes. The other divisions can cover you here. It's the relocation that will be hard to pull off, and you're the only one who I think has any chance of doing so.' He unrolled the map and held it against the farmhouse wall. Monty obliged him by holding the other end. 'If the Third Division can cover the Yser River to the Ypres–Comines Canal near Diksmuide, that would be enough. The river's wide enough west of Diksmuide to slow the Germans down. But to get there … this is the only route I could see, and even it involves two river crossings. Then you'll have to drive through no man's land in front of our guns … I don't like it, Monty, but the roads are just too congested behind the front line.'

If Montgomery was at all apprehensive about it, he gave no indication. 'Lieutenant General, during the idle months in France, I had the Third Division train for precisely this sort of thing. Allow me to show you the modifications we've made.'

Monty led Alan outside. He showed him to the back of one of his vehicles. 'One thing we found is that when moving under the cover of darkness, it can be hard to see the vehicle in front of you. We had a few collisions before we worked out how to fix the problem. These rear lights and shades cast light onto the axles, which, as you see, we've painted white. This makes our trucks clearly visible, but only to someone directly behind them. Our men now have no trouble following a convoy in the dark without alerting our presence to anyone else.'

As his commanding officer, Alan knew Monty had not sought permission to modify the vehicles in this manner. Bernard Montgomery's one significant fault was his tendency to undertake unilateral action without consulting his superiors first. And Alan didn't care about that one bit. If the modifications worked as Monty claimed, they would save the BEF. He looked up at Montgomery. 'Are you sure you can do this?'

'It shan't be the least bit difficult, sir,' Monty declared. He went on to describe the operation as if the division were going on a picnic.

Alan wished he could believe it would be that easy. Montgomery's division was the best in the corps, but this near-impossible task was all that stood in the way of total defeat.

***

2230 hours
Dunkirk Beach

Bill Tennant watched as another whaler laden with troops pushed off from the beach. By Christ, this was wretchedly slow. There was hardly any point in continuing the operation.

Men on the beaches were growing weak from lack of food, water and sleep, so the naval crews had to row. Each round trip in a whaler took nearly an hour to deliver twenty-five men. It had been eight hours since they started loading her, and the *Wolfhound* still wasn't full.

The naval presence and the promise of an evacuation had restored order in Dunkirk, but it was only a matter of time before the troops realised that they offered false hope.

'We'll be going until Christmas at this rate,' growled Conway.

'I doubt the Nazis will give us the luxury of that much time,' Bill replied, his neutral tone belying his mood. 'Things will get more interesting when the Luftwaffe returns. I've also advised Ramsay to close Route Z.'

'That'll slow the ships down, sir,' Conway remarked.

'It will, but the Germans can fire on our ships from Calais. Anyway, the trip from Dover to Dunkirk isn't the slowest part.' He didn't let Conway know how disheartened he felt. Men needed to have faith in their leaders. Morale could easily plummet if they could sense their commanders were dispirited.

'I understand Ramsay's planning to send small boats to help out?' Conway asked. 'Fishing vessels and whatnot?'

'That will help a little, but we'll only be able to rescue a fraction of the BEF in the little remaining time we have.' Bill hesitated, and then finally let his guard down. It was not as though the stiff upper lip was going to shield his men from reality for much longer. 'Frankly, Conway, I feel our government will need to negotiate a treaty with Hitler before the end of June.'

'Either that, or we should brush up on our German.' Conway turned his binoculars to the harbour. 'Clouston seems to be keeping order well; he has the men lining up, but if we can't move them out fast enough …' He frowned. 'Captain, there's something out there on the water.'

'Is it a ship?' Bill asked.

'No, but I can see waves breaking out to sea.' He pointed to something off the beach. 'It looks like a pier or a jetty, but I thought this harbour only had wharves.' He handed Bill the binoculars.

Bill looked to where Conway had pointed. 'It's not a pier. It's the mole, the breakwater. Remember, we passed it coming … Wait a minute.' A crazy idea entered his mind. 'Come on, let's take a closer look.'

They walked into the harbour and approached Clouston.

'At ease,' Bill told Clouston as he saluted. 'I'd like your opinion on a matter, actually. Come with us to the mole.'

'Yes, Captain.'

The breakwater was intact, as was the causeway connecting it to the mainland. The Germans had bombed the stuffing out of the harbour, but they'd missed this. The swell betrayed shallow waters on the eastern side, but the land on the western side of the breakwater, the inner side to the harbour, dropped quickly into the depths. Bill pointed to it. 'Clouston, if we ran long gangways from the ships, do you think a destroyer could berth here? Do you think the land drops away fast enough?'

'Berthing along here?' Clouston peered into the dark water. 'It looks deep enough, but are you sure about having ships moor alongside this, sir? It's a bit flimsy.'

'It's holding up to the battering waves, isn't it?' Conway asked.

That was good enough for Bill. 'We'll have to take the risk. Conway, send orders to the fleet and a message to Lord Gort. I want ships to dock along here, and troops redirected to this breakwater. Clouston, I want some anti-aircraft guns around here. See if any of these army chaps can muster some up. We should check the western mole, too.' A spark of hope ignited deep within his heart. If they could stop the Germans from blowing this up, they might yet save the army.

CHAPTER 12

Tuesday, 28 May
0100 hours
Lieutenant General Alan Brooke's Headquarters
Armentières–Lille Road, France

Alan donned his trench coat and stepped outside into the pouring rain. Montgomery's division was going to drive past, and Alan had to see them.

Vehicle after vehicle drove past, recognisable by the light shades and the now mud-flecked white axles. In order to get this far, Monty had made the first river crossing. So far, so good – but the most difficult stretch was yet to come.

When Alan was satisfied all the Third Division's convoys had passed, he went back inside and listened to his wireless. 'Let me know if any encrypted message comes through, Perkins,' he muttered to his signalman. Between sickening anxiety and a developing toothache, there was no chance of sleeping tonight.

Montgomery still had to drive in front of their guns, through no man's land, and hope the Germans wouldn't see them in the dark. This was the most dangerous part of their journey. He lowered his head and massaged his temples as he waited beside the radio. Thousands of civilians had choked all the roads within their perimeter. How could the British Army hope to fight a war when they kept getting in the way?

Guilt stabbed him for allowing such a heartless thought to cross his mind. These civilians were running for their lives. Many of them had lost everything except for the clothes on their backs. Some were injured, and God only knew how many had already been killed. And soon, the British would retreat, leaving these people to the mercy of their invaders. *That* was the worst part about this whole godforsaken battle.

'Sir,' Perkins said, 'we have an encrypted message from the Twelfth Lancers.' He handed Alan a note.

Belgian artillery moving away from positions. Explanation requested, none given yet. Anticipate 12th Lancers will soon hold front line. Urgent request for backup.

Alan scrunched the note up in his fist as tightly as he could. Sir John Dill's prediction had been correct; the Belgians were laying down arms overnight without warning the British Army. Treacherous bastards. The Lancers were just a regiment; they wouldn't be able to hold for half a day against a full German division. Now, Monty's ability to redeploy the Third Division was all that stood between the BEF and total annihilation.

Alan kept listening to the broadcasts. No significant reports of gunfire came in. It seemed as though Monty really was slipping though, right under the Germans' noses.

Transmissions reporting enemy engagement increased in frequency as the pre-dawn light turned the sky from black to grey. Unencrypted messages from the Twelfth Lancers came in; they were under heavy fire.

But where was Monty?

Alan kept listening. Seconds turned into minutes, and an hour passed. The light was increasing; the German panzers would begin moving soon. More reports came in from the Lancers, but no word about Montgomery. Helplessness and despair pounded Alan's soul.

He couldn't take much more of this. He got up and started pacing back and forth. *Jesus Christ, where's Monty?* If this operation failed …

'Sir,' Perkins called out. 'The Twelfth Lancers report the arrival of reinforcements. It's the Third Division.'

The first wave of relief quenched Alan's burning anxiety like water. Monty had made it! A little later than expected, but in time to plug the hole.

Transmissions started coming in from the Third Division as well as the Lancers. At 0700 hours, Colonel Ryan reported that the Lancers had completely withdrawn, and requested that the regiment be allowed to rest.

'I can't grant him his request,' Alan told Perkins. 'Instruct Ryan to deploy the Twelfth Lancers along the canal east of Diksmuide. They must destroy bridges and disperse any German engineers who try to amass on the other bank.' That ought to be enough to prevent the Boche from crossing the river for a day, after which, the BEF would withdraw again.

'Right away, General.'

Crisis over, Alan got up. He needed a cup of tea. No, coffee; tea wasn't strong enough. He was struggling to hold back tears of relief. Thanks to the chief of staff's foresight and Monty's seamless command, they had averted a blow that could have destroyed the BEF within two days. Bernard Montgomery could be arrogant and prone to egotism at times, but he was the best commander in the British Army.

Alas, this was only the first of many possible catastrophes. Would the exhausted Lancers be able to prevent the Germans from crossing the lightly guarded canal for a whole day?

This whole operation was still precarious, and Alan could only oversee his own corps. What about I Corps? Barker had been erratic of late. What about the French? One wrong move, one breakthrough on either flank, and the BEF would collapse.

***

0815 hours
Diksmuide, Belgium

Edward Mann followed the road south along the canal. He drove under a railway bridge – fortunately demolished – and stopped at the Morris CS9 light armoured cars beside a road bridge. There were just a few sparse houses and a hotel here; terrace housing lined the other bank. This must be the outskirts of Diksmuide.

As he got out of the car, Sergeant Brown approached him and saluted. 'Sir, the enemy knows this bridge is standing. We saw a German staff car crossing it just as we arrived.'

'Didn't you stop it?' Edward demanded.

'We shot at it, sir, but it kept going.'

German reinforcements wouldn't be far away, and this bloody bridge was too big for them to destroy with the CS9's anti-tank guns.

Edward peered over the wall at the bank of the canal. 'Wait, who are they? Ah, Belgians.' It looked as though they were wiring the bridge with explosives, too. Excellent.

But then his relief gave way. *They were disassembling their work.* 'Hey, what are you doing?' he cried out. 'The enemy are on their way!'

A Belgian lieutenant looked up at him and shrugged. 'Our government has surrendered. What are we to do?'

'If you take it apart, you'll be assisting your conquerors,' Edward pleaded. 'At least leave it for us to finish!'

The Belgian lieutenant shrugged and said something in Flemish to his subordinates. They stopped what they were doing.

Edward was about to ask Brown to find a signalman when he espied a French major approaching from the north. He and Brown turned and saluted.

'Lieutenant,' the major said, 'I am Major Bernard of the Third French Army Division. Our forces will secure this bridge. You may now stand down.'

'Yes, sir,' Edward replied. If the French were taking over the guard of this bridge, then they wouldn't …

Wait, this is strange. 'Major, where are your men?'

'They will be here very soon,' the major reassured him.

'Well, in that case, we will stay and hold it until your forces arrive.'

The Frenchman scowled. 'You will not follow my orders, then?'

Edward looked him in the eye. 'I take orders from British commanders. I will stand my men down when yours arrive, and not before.'

The major loitered as Edward instructed Brown's team to set up a Vickers beside a nearby warehouse. He lingered on the bridge, looking over the edge from time to time at the Belgians and their partially wired explosives.

Another CS9 arrived and stopped. The men got out. It was Sergeant Owen's team.

'Owen, have you heard anything from Brooke about a French battalion patrolling this canal?' he asked Owen.

'French? No, sir. I've not heard of any French in this area.'

Edward went to attract the French major's attention, but couldn't see him. 'Hey, where did he go?'

'Where did who go?' Owen asked.

'The French major who was standing on the …' Edward trailed off. 'Did anyone see the French major leave?' he called out to Brown's team.

The men looked around. 'Where'd he go?' one of the privates asked.

The major couldn't have returned to this bank without walking past Brown's team. He must have crossed the bridge and kept going. A knot formed in Edward's stomach. This was bad, this was really bad …

An Austin Utility drove towards them and stopped. The driver got out and approached Edward. 'Lieutenant Smith of the Monmouthshire Engineers. We're demolishing bridges and barges along the canal.'

Edward saluted. 'Second Lieutenant Edward Mann of the Twelfth Lancers. Sir, a man claiming to be a French major tried to order me to stand down, and then scarpered over the bridge when I refused. I think he was part of a fifth column.'

The colour drained from Smith's cheeks. 'Good God! The Germans must be within bloody shouting distance!' He looked over the bank and pointed to the Belgians. 'Who are they?'

'Belgian engineers, sir,' replied Edward. 'They'd started priming the bridge for explosives before they got the order to surrender.'

'If their work's still in place, that'll be the fastest way to bring her down.'

'Good luck persuading them to help,' grumbled Edward. 'The war's over for them.'

'Oh, I think I can persuade them. Back me up, Mann.'

Edward and Smith climbed down the bank. Smith asked the Belgian lieutenant something in French. When the Belgian shrugged, Smith drew his pistol and pointed it straight at the man's chest. Edward did the same. The Belgian lieutenant began to stutter a protest, but Smith shouted him down and raised the pistol to the man's head.

Smith's 'persuasive tactics' worked. The Belgian lieutenant ordered his men to show Smith the fuses and detonators, and as far as Edward could deduce, explain how they had wired the explosives. They abandoned everything and wasted no time dissipating.

Although Smith worked quickly to rewire the explosives, knowing the Germans were breathing down their necks made the passing minutes fly. Edward kept glancing between the engineer and the road on the other side of the canal, listening for vehicles, hoping they wouldn't come just—

'Take cover!' yelled Smith.

He and Edward scrambled up the bank.

Edward only just made it when the first explosive went off. Five more followed in rapid fire. The western side of the bridge disappeared in a cloud of smoke, and the centre of the unsupported arch collapsed into the water. A wave splashed against the canal's retaining wall.

Thank God for that. One more calamity avoided.

Part of the bridge still projected out from the opposite bank. The road on the other side dropped away. This could mean ...

Smith dusted himself down. 'Will you be moving downstream, Mann?'

'Not yet, sir,' Edward replied. 'German forces can't be far away.' He pointed to the remnants of the bridge on the far side of the river. 'See how the road rises to the bridge over there? German drivers probably won't even see the bridge is gone until they're almost on it, and I want to be here waiting for them.'

'Well, send some men with me,' Smith ordered. 'I'll need cover if I meet the Boche downstream.'

Edward turned to Brown. 'Sergeant, take your team and follow the lieutenant.'

'Yes, sir.'

Smith drove off, and Brown and his men followed in their CS9.

Edward turned to Owen. 'How many Bren guns does your team have?'

'Four, sir.'

'Right. Set up two each side of the road. Aim your guns at the opposite bank. I want two men to take the vehicles down the road – just out of sight from the river. Where they park will be our rendezvous point.'

'Yes, sir.'

Edward took up his position with two privates at the corner of the hotel on the southern side of the road. They had a good, clear shot of the far side of the bridge. Now the wait …

'Owen, don't open fire until I do!' he called out.

'Understood, sir!'

Would this trap really work?

Where minutes flew past when the bridge was still standing, seconds now crawled as slowly as caterpillars. Edward's heart pounded. Where were the Germans? He should just about smell the bastards by now …

A soft rumbling from the eastern side of the canal heralded the pending arrival of vehicles. It grew louder. Edward's already racing pulse stepped up a notch.

A column of motorcyclists skidded to a halt just in time. A flurry of German expletives floated through the air.

'Open fire?' one private asked as he stared down the Bren gun's sights.

'Not yet,' whispered Edward. His right hand trembled with excitement, but he needed to time this.

The motorcyclists hadn't had time to turn back before two personnel carriers towing artillery came up behind them. More shouting. The heavy vehicles screeched to a halt, nearly driving the motorcyclists into the canal. Perfect.

'FIRE!'

It was almost unsporting. Krauts fell as they ran for cover. The personnel carriers were soon riddled with holes; God only knew how many were still inside. There was some return fire, but it was erratic and went wide of the mark.

The Lancers kept firing until there were no Germans in sight, and then withdrew and regrouped down the road. The CS9 and Austin Twelve were parked outside a farrier's.

'Now I see why you were waiting, sir!' Owen exclaimed, eyes bulging with triumph. 'That was one hard kick to the balls if ever I saw one!'

'Good to be able to bite back for a change!' Edward felt as though he could fly, but he needed to focus. At least this gunfight had cured his fatigue. 'All right, men, we'll rest for five minutes.' He pulled a packet of cigarettes from his pocket. 'Have one if you want, then we'd better move along. This won't be the last time they try crossing today.'

***

1530 hours
Wormhoudt, France

'Fahey, we gotta go now!' Parry yelled at Brian.

They sprinted down the road, bullets and tracer spluttering the dirt around them. A three-tonner slowed as it passed. Parry scrambled aboard, and Brian grabbed hold of the back tray. He had one leg over the edge; one of the men inside reached forward to help him—

BOOM! Brian slammed into the tray and pain shot through his leg.

'Jesus, she's on fire!' someone yelled.

The men inside almost knocked Brian over.

'The ditch, there!' one man shouted.

Everyone darted for cover.

Once below the level of the grass, one private began to load a charger clip into a Lee–Enfield.

'No, don't,' a sergeant told him. 'We're surrounded. It's time to surrender.'

Surrender. The word sank into the pit of Brian's stomach.

'Gimme the rifle.' The sergeant took it from the private, removed the charger clip and bolt, and raised it butt-first above the ditch. After a few seconds, he slowly got to his feet. 'Everyone, stand up, hands where they can see them. Don't make any sudden movements.'

Brian got to his feet. He winced as pain fired through his injured leg.

The Germans approached and surrounded them, rifles ready, but nobody fired. Their uniforms were not what Brian had expected. They were wearing some sort of cape, or poncho, over the top of a black uniform.

He sighed. His combat days were over now; he was going to be in a POW camp until the end of the war.

Oh, well. At least he would get out of it alive. They'd put up a terrific fight and had kept the Germans back from the main road for almost a day. With luck, his sacrifice had helped many others escape. Brian had managed to take out a few Germans before his capture, too. If every Tommy could boast that, they'd win the war.

A German officer discussed something with his men. A couple of enemy soldiers came forward and made everyone stand in a line. They proceeded to inspect the captives for weapons.

The Germans found a photograph on the man beside Brian. 'That's my fiancée,' he explained.

The German soldier threw it to the ground.

'Hey—' the man called out as he stepped forward, but the German shoved him back into line.

'You will not take the photograph with you,' their commander stated. 'No photographs, no letters.'

'But you can't do that!' exclaimed someone. 'You are allowed to confiscate weapons—'

The German commander pointed his pistol at the man's chest. 'You will do as we say!'

There were no further protests as the Germans searched for and removed all personal effects from their captives. They even took the dog tags, for some bizarre reason.

When they had finished, their commander pointed west and shouted, 'March!'

One of the soldiers lowered his hands as he started to walk, but a German sergeant jabbed the muzzle of his rifle into his chest and yelled, '*Nein! Hände hoch!*'

'We're not going to try any funny business – we've surrendered.'

'*Hände hoch! Hände hoch!*' screamed the sergeant. There was no mistaking what he meant. The prisoners were going to have to march to wherever they were going with their hands raised above their heads. Nobody said anything, but Brian groaned inwardly. How far would it be in this muggy weather? He was knackered, and with his leg, this march was going to be the death of him.

They soon joined another group of captives. Brian didn't recognise anyone other than Parry; most of these men were from the Second Warwickshires. He and Parry were among a handful of attachés from the Royal Artillery.

Another German non-commissioned officer came and inspected them. 'You can lower your arms,' he said in English. He pointed along the road. 'March that way.'

They had scarcely walked two hundred yards when someone collapsed. Several Warwickshires went to help him up, but one of the Germans yelled at them, 'No! Away!'

'But he can't walk; he's got a bullet wound to the leg,' another man explained.

The German NCO drew his pistol and pointed it at the fallen man.

'Hey!' cried a British captain. 'What are you—'

BANG.

Silence.

Brian's skin went cold as a wave of horror drenched him.

'But – but he'd surrendered!' stuttered the captain. 'You can't—'

'March!' screamed the German officer.

Anguish welled up inside Brian. He wanted to fly into that pistol-wielding monster and tear him apart, limb by limb.

No, that wouldn't help. They'd shoot him before he could get his hands on him.

What did the Germans have in store for the rest of them if they were prepared to commit such a brazen crime?

The Germans proceeded to shoot – no, *murder* – two more prisoners who collapsed as they marched. They came across a few more soldiers along the way who had surrendered or were injured. Again, wounded soldiers unable to walk were shot on sight.

Tears welled up behind Brian's eyes with every murder. Deep loathing and revulsion replaced what used to be fear of the enemy. It was bad enough losing friends in battle, but war was war. This was far more personal, far more depraved.

And his leg wasn't getting any better. By the time they had gone a mile, it was threatening to collapse under his weight. *God, I'll be next!*

Parry grabbed Brian's arm and put it around his shoulder. 'Can someone help me?' he hissed, not quite loudly enough for the Germans to hear.

Another man helped prop up Brian's other arm.

They reached an intersection where another company of Germans held more prisoners. The NCOs spoke among themselves, and the new company ordered them to turn left, away from the road and towards … Brian racked his brain. Esquelbecq? Was that the name of the village? Well, they would be under the direction of another company; with luck, *these* ones would treat prisoners of war properly.

It was starting to rain when they were taken off the road and onto a farm. Their captors led them around a row of massive poplar trees to a barn. Brian sighed. This must be shelter from the rain.

Wait a minute. We can't all fit inside. Why do they want us in there anyway?

The captain from the Second Warwickshires was pleading on

their behalf as the Germans herded them in. 'Listen! My men are tired and thirsty! I demand that you treat us in accordance with the Geneva Convention! Don't pretend you can't understand what I'm saying! You know—'

'Silence!' screamed a German NCO. He rammed the captain in the solar plexus with the butt of his rifle. 'You will not make demands! Everyone, inside!'

Brian was among the last to be bustled into the overcrowded barn. The stifling air was heavy with the stench of cow manure and body odour. There was barely enough standing room.

'For the love of God, there isn't room for the wounded to lie down!' protested the captain.

'English pig!' snarled a German lieutenant. 'There will be lots of room where you are going!'

A curious mix of panic and serenity swept through the barn. The Germans clearly had no intention of letting them live, but what could anyone do to stop it? All the captives could do now was make peace with God in their final moments.

'What are you doing?' Brian heard the captain's voice again. 'No – no, please, you can't—'

'GRENADE!'

Brian didn't see it, but everyone pulled away from something that landed on the floor.

Someone threw himself over it.

BANG! Brian's ears rang, but the brave man's body shielded his comrades from the worst of the blast.

Several more grenades came through. At least one more man sacrificed himself to save his compatriots. The explosions, the jostling, the shouts, the screams … it was total pandemonium. Something hit Brian's left arm.

And then … the jostling and screaming subsided. The only sound came from the moans of the wounded.

'They've stopped,' Brian whispered.

'I wonder what they're planning next,' muttered someone beside him.

One of their captors appeared at the door. 'Five out!' he yelled.

Nobody moved.

'Five out!' the German yelled again, gesturing as he said it.

Grudgingly, a man began to move, then another. The German counted them, '*Eins, zwei, drei, vier, fünf.*'

Brian was standing near the wall now. He peered through a gap in the boards.

The Germans made the five captives form a line, turn away from them, and kneel before a ditch. 'Please,' he could hear one man begging, 'one last cigarette—'

'Kneel, English swine,' a lieutenant ordered him.

Five Germans lined up, one behind each prisoner.

The first man raised his rifle and fired.

'*Oh, Jesus!*' Brian exclaimed.

The next man fired. Then the next. Then the next. Then the last. Five shots, five murders. Each burst of gunfire made Brian's chest explode with fury and terror. He reached for his knife, intending to stick whoever hauled him through the door, but it wasn't there. Of course it wasn't; they'd surrendered all weapons. He couldn't even take one of these monsters as they led him to his death.

'Five more! Five more!' yelled the German at the door.

'Well, I'm not going out!' spat one Scotsman. 'I'm not gonna make it any fucking easier for them than it already is!'

Eventually, someone moved.

A strange sensation of calmness came over Brian. 'Well, we know what's going to happen to us all,' he mumbled. 'There's no point in delaying the inevitable.'

Brian shuffled past a private who took his hand. 'I don't know who you are,' he said, 'but I need to shake hands with you.' The lad barely looked old enough to serve, and his bottom lip was trembling.

Brian limped to the edge of the field as the Germans directed him. His mother entered his thoughts; she was about to lose a son. *Oh, God,*

Mum, I'm sorry. I'm so sorry.

His leg screamed as they forced him to his knees. Out of the corner of his eye, he could see gunmen lining up behind his fellow captives.

This was the end.

'*Eins!*' cried out the lieutenant.

BANG. The first man fell. They were starting at the other end; Brian would be the last.

His heart was now beating so hard he wondered if it would burst before they shot him.

'*Zwei!*'

BANG.

He began thinking of the pointlessness of war.

'*Drei!*'

BANG.

Really, what was the use of it, when all it did was kill so many young men like him?

'*Vier!*'

BANG.

I'm next. Brian's heart slammed against his breastbone.

'*Fünf!*'

He tensed.

BANG.

The bullet kicked him forward. His face hit the ground. It took a split second for the pain to come, but by God, it was intense. Warm moisture began pooling underneath his chest. *Damn, it's not instant …*

***

Brian awoke to see a dark grey sky before him. He was on his back.

Gradually, the events of that afternoon began to come back to him.

Had he died and gone to Heaven?

No, he shouldn't feel pain in Heaven.

Hell, then?

Nope, too cold and wet.

He was still alive.

Pain stabbed at his chest as he tried to move around. He groped around and found his glasses.

Wait, didn't I land face first? They must have turned him over to check if he was dead. They didn't check too carefully, then.

Nine corpses lay in the ditch with him. Brian looked back at the barn in the fading light. It was filled with bodies, and there were others lying around the front and sides of the barn. His own shirt was soaked with blood, which was now congealed.

It was drizzling, too. Brian began to shiver. He needed to get out of the cold and rain.

His chest and right leg wouldn't allow him to stand. His left arm throbbed with each futile effort to use it, too.

He managed to roll himself onto his belly, and he began using his two good limbs to crawl towards the barn. It was slow, agonising work, and the effort made him draw even harder for air through his injured chest.

It was dark by the time he was under the barn's roof and out of the drizzling rain.

The groaning told him that he wasn't the only one to survive the massacre.

One man sitting against the wall turned his head gingerly towards Brian. 'Another one alive? Were you one of those they lined up and shot?'

'Yes,' Brian wheezed. 'I passed out. What'd they do?'

'Bastards shot up the barn,' the man groaned. 'A few men tried to run and got cut down as they fled.' He winced and caught his breath. 'Bastards. This isn't war, this is murder. Some men weren't too badly hurt. They've already left. Trying to get to Dunkirk.'

'Will they find … their way?' Brian gasped.

'Dunno, but everyone's saying to follow the pillar of smoke. They'd just better hope they don't run into those bastards who shot us again.' He panted and leant against the wall. 'Bastards. Murderous bastards.'

Brian rested his head on the leg of a corpse and gasped. He couldn't keep his eyes open any longer.

***

2000 hours
King George III Hotel, Whitehall, London

The door opened. Kenneth Jackson re-entered the room with a tray. 'You are still not familiar enough with the use of cutlery,' he told Artorius, 'so I think we should eat in privacy and practise it again. I have vegetable soup, an omelette and bread.'

'Have you heard anything more of the battle?' Artorius asked him. It was so *infuriating* being stuck at an inn, unable to communicate with the outside world.

'A messenger relayed that Sir John Dill wishes to meet us again tomorrow.'

Artorius kept his gaze on Kenneth Jackson.

'That is all I know. Artorius, they tell the public little, lest it cause a panic or inform the enemy of our movements. As it is, you know more about what is unfolding than the ordinary citizen.' Kenneth sat the tray down and gave Artorius the soup. 'It is customary to eat soup first.'

Artorius stared at the bowl of soup. Indeed, he was among the first to learn of the battle's developments; but he was still little more than a spectator. For all he knew, the Germans had already tried their advance. Was it repelled, or was the defeat of Britain now inevitable?

'Artorius!'

Artorius looked up.

'Did you hear anything I told you about the spoon?' Kenneth demanded.

'I did not. I apologise, but I worry about this battle.'

'The request for another meeting is a good sign. If the enemy had succeeded in the manoeuvre you saw, Sir John Dill would not have time for another audience with you.' Kenneth pointed to the spoon.

'Now, pay attention. There is etiquette in the way one eats soup.'

***

2300 hours
Lieutenant General Alan Brooke's Headquarters
Armentières–Lille Road, France

Alan Brooke dropped into his seat and put his head in his hands. He took deep, deliberate, slow breaths. The stress would kill him for sure. The meeting with Colonel Ryan earlier that evening had particularly shaken him. There had been a near miss in the town of Diksmuide, where a sapper and a second lieutenant from the Twelfth Lancers had blown a bridge only minutes before the Germans arrived. *By God*, had the Germans taken that bridge, this retreat would have already failed.

Luckily, the new perimeter they were going to establish tonight would be tighter and easier to defend. The Twelfth Lancers needed to rest. God willing, he might even be able to send some regiments to the coast for evacuation tomorrow.

The telephone rang.

Alan picked it up. 'Brooke speaking.'

'Sir, Major General Alexander is on the line,' the operator told him. 'Should I put him through?'

'Yes.'

A click.

'Alec?' Brooke asked.

'Here, sir.'

'Alec, I must say, I'm a little surprised you're calling me,' said Alan. 'Your commanding officer is Barker now.'

'Indeed, sir,' replied Alec, 'but I fear he may be letting us down a little. Our corps is meant to cover from Poperinge to Proven, but that particular flank was supposed to be covered by the Third Medium Regiment. However, Barker has withdrawn this regiment, and to the best of my knowledge, hasn't replaced it. I'm not sure what his reasoning is, but I fear this action may have created a gap on our left flank.'

Letting us down a little? That was Alec – an unflappable aristocrat who understated even the gravest of problems. 'Yes, I see what you mean,' Alan replied. 'Have you tried talking to Barker about it?'

'I've tried, sir, but … well, he didn't really give me a coherent reply, to be honest. Sir, my division has nothing to spare at present. All my regiments are either engaged or in reserve, on Barker's orders. I was hoping that II Corps might be able to fan out and cover it.'

'Yes, yes … thanks for letting me know, Alec. I'll see what I can do. Are there any other problems in I Corps? I understand there was a large build-up of enemy troops at … Wormhoudt, I think it was.'

'Oh – Thorne has already withdrawn from there. He lost a couple of regiments, though. Again, he wanted backup for them – but Barker didn't allow it.'

'Well, at least *most* of the corps got out.' Alan hung up.

Christ almighty. If II Corps didn't have enough to deal with, he now needed to patch up Barker's hole.

It was a pity Alec didn't take the initiative and send a reserve regiment there despite Barker's orders. Nevertheless, the fault was ultimately Barker's, and at least Alexander had warned Alan.

After pondering awhile, Alan eventually settled on the Fourth Royal Northumberland Fusiliers and the Royal Hussars. They were probably the best-rested regiments at present, which wasn't saying much, and deploying them would deplete his strategic reserves significantly.

'A message from the Fifth Division, sir,' Signalman Perkins called out. 'They're having trouble withdrawing from the Ypres–Comines Canal, and have almost been flanked by German infantry. Some battalions have already been cut off.'

Dear God. Bad news kept coming thick and fast. The BEF's situation was still precarious. So much would hang in the balance for the next few days.

CHAPTER 13

Wednesday, 29 May
1730 hours
Cabinet War Rooms, London

Another bloody meeting with Churchill. *And* at such short notice. Sir John had another appointment scheduled.

He met Sir Charles Forbes and Sir Cyril Newall outside the conference room before they entered. 'Well, let's hope this meeting will be shorter,' he whispered. The three heads of the armed forces had convened twenty minutes earlier in Sir John's office and discussed the operational changes they wanted to bring into effect. Now, the three commanders would support each other and present a unanimous front in this meeting with Churchill.

The Prime Minister was already sitting inside, puffing on a cigar. Sir John suppressed a cough. Men tended to smoke excessively when they were nervous, and there was no escaping the stench of tobacco in this poorly ventilated underground bunker. On the other hand, tobacco did conceal other odours of men who had slept erratically for days, and washed accordingly.

'Gentlemen, sit down,' said Churchill, his bulldog-like face wearing the same frown it always wore. 'I don't think you're aware, but Lord Halifax has lost confidence in our ability to win this war. In the crisis meeting with the War Cabinet yesterday, he argued that we should negotiate a truce with Herr Hitler, using Signor Mussolini as an intermediary. It almost came to a vote of no confidence in my leadership.'

'What the devil?' exclaimed Sir John. Lord Halifax had been one of the architects of the failed appeasement plan. Was the fool really considering a peace treaty with the Third Reich?

Churchill nodded. 'With the fate of the British Expeditionary Force in the balance and the Germans about to deliver what could be a decisive blow, Lord Halifax believes we can only hope to preserve our sovereignty if we negotiate for peace now. I reminded everyone present that we would not be negotiating from a position of strength. Herr Hitler will surely impose terms on us that would leave us vulnerable should he later choose to break the treaty, and he has proven that he cannot be trusted.'

Sir John let his breath out. Churchill could be insufferable at times, but they'd just changed prime ministers. To do so again after just a couple of weeks, and to appoint an appeaser like Halifax …

'Even so,' Churchill continued, 'a devastating loss in northern France will further erode the distinction between pessimism and pragmatism. Lord Halifax may have more supporters next week if I cannot give Parliament encouraging news about Dunkirk.'

Sir Charles cleared his throat. 'I'm pleased to say the operation is proceeding more quickly now. We had evacuated twenty-five thousand up to yesterday, mostly men detached from units. The field commanders are beginning to send regiments to Dunkirk in an organised manner, and we've already rescued at least thirty thousand today. It may be as many as fifty thousand by midnight.'

'So, around seventy-five thousand men will be back by midnight,' Churchill mumbled. He tapped his cigar into the ashtray and drew on it again. 'It already exceeds the bleak expectations we had on Monday – but it's still less than a third of the entire expedition. Are we able to extend the operation?'

'God willing, we can,' Sir John replied. 'The new perimeter is holding.'

'On a more pessimistic note, Mr Churchill,' said Sir Charles, 'we've lost three destroyers today, as well as other vessels.'

'*Three* destroyers?' Churchill exclaimed. 'We can't afford losses like that to continue!'

'Indeed not, sir, which is why I've withdrawn our eight best destroyers from the operation. It has come to my attention that we need to modify ships' cannon and guns so they can elevate to ninety degrees. The German Stukas can release a bomb from a vertical dive with deadly accuracy, and our ships cannot fire on them when they do. This leaves them dependent on protection by the Royal Air Force.'

Churchill furrowed his eyebrows. 'With eight destroyers in reserve, what ships are involved in the rescue?'

'We're still using older destroyers, lightly armed ships like personnel carriers, and smaller vessels such as corvettes. Civilian craft are also helping – although they, too, have suffered losses.'

'Civilians?' Churchill asked.

'Passenger ferries, mostly. We're also using small craft for the beach rescues, but mostly with naval crew on them. Apart from professional fisherman and ferry crews, we haven't sent many civilians.'

Churchill scowled. 'Did the idea of recruiting fishermen come from that King Arthur lunatic?'

'It did – and it's working,' replied Sir Charles.

'King Arthur lunatic?' asked Sir Cyril.

Churchill drew on his cigar again. 'As much as we are fortunate that he made his observation when he did, it would be unwise to have anything further to do with a man who believes he's a mythical king.'

'Wait – who's this King Arthur chap?' asked Sir Cyril.

'Three days ago, just after the first meeting about this retreat – the one you missed because you were ill – Bletchley Park codebreakers came to meet Sir Charles with a ludicrous idea of transmitting in ancient Welsh as a code. It turns out one of the men who knows ancient Welsh also thinks he's King Arthur. Anyhow, let's move on,' he added just before Sir Cyril could ask any more questions. 'I don't want to hear any more about King Arthur. What's causing the losses? We gave Park permission to send fewer squadrons with larger numbers over to Dunkirk. I had reservations, because if the Luftwaffe strikes when the RAF has no presence in the skies …'

'It's a mix, Mr Churchill,' replied Sir Charles. 'Only one destroyer was sunk by an aeroplane. The Kriegsmarine claimed the other two. Mines are also a problem – in fact, a civilian ferry struck one this morning. Minesweepers have opened the Ruytingen Pass route, and we're sending more patrols east of the Kwinte Buoy in order to keep the Kriegsmarine away from our ships.'

'It sounds as though you're putting all your eggs in one basket,' Churchill said. 'Suppose the German U-boats come from the west?'

'To do that, sir, they'll need to come the long way around Scotland, and they'll have to run the gauntlet as they pass Scapa Flow, Plymouth, Portland and Portsmouth. I understand the French Navy has reinforced their north-western coastline, too.'

Churchill drew on his cigar again. 'The RAF's losses haven't been anywhere near as high as the naval or army losses. I feel they could do more to alleviate the threat posed by the Luftwaffe.'

Sir Cyril cleared his throat. 'Sir, we only have a few thousand trained pilots, compared to the hundreds of thousands of men in the army and navy. Furthermore, Dowding is preparing for the next stage of this war.'

'What do you mean?' Churchill asked.

'Well, the army has been forced into retreat, and is unable to retrieve artillery or vehicles. How long will it take to replace the tanks or the anti-tank guns abandoned near Dunkirk?'

'It could take several months,' said Sir John. He steeled himself for the next part.

Sir Cyril nodded at him and turned back to Churchill. 'If the BEF couldn't hold back the German invasion of Belgium with their artillery, what hope do they have of thwarting an amphibious landing in Britain without it?'

Sir John adjusted his collar. *All right, rub it in.*

'However,' continued Sir Cyril, 'such an amphibious landing would be vulnerable to attack from the air. The Germans know this, so before they try to invade Britain, they will launch an aerial assault against the Royal Air Force. Now, we increased the intake of cadets at the beginning of the war, but those first recruits won't be ready for another couple of months. The few thousand pilots we currently have may be all that stand in the way of a German invasion. Dowding can't afford to lose many pilots before we start fighting for control of the skies over Britain.'

'Sir Cyril has a point,' admitted Sir John. 'As much as I want better RAF cover for the evacuation, we need to look ahead.'

'Very well,' grumbled Churchill.

Sir John looked at his watch. He might just make this meeting with Artorius after all – though he had better not let Churchill know about it. There was one more contentious issue Sir Charles wanted to raise …

'One final matter, Prime Minister,' added Sir Charles. 'The evacuation of wounded soldiers is proving difficult, especially from the beaches. I advise that we leave the wounded behind and prioritise the evacuation of uninjured men.'

'Good grief,' exclaimed Churchill. 'And how many of them are going to die if we do that?'

'How many will die if we try to take the wounded? A stretcher takes up more space on the boats than two men.'

'Not to mention that many of the wounded will no longer be medically fit for duty,' added Sir John. 'The front line might still collapse any day, so our priority must be to rescue able-bodied men as quickly as we can.'

Churchill's expression remained sour.

'Mr Churchill,' pleaded Sir John, 'I hate Sir Charles's request as much as you do – but this rescue is costing the Royal Navy dearly, and if the perimeter breaks, the evacuation ends. Anyone we don't have back by then will be killed or captured, and that will include every able-bodied man who lost his place on a boat to a stretcher. The situation calls for *triage*, as the medical profession calls it.'

The Prime Minister lowered his eyes and slumped his shoulders.

'May the Lord forgive us for abandoning them,' he muttered. 'However, I understand what you mean. Very well. Do not evacuate the wounded.'

***

1807 hours
Office of the Chief of the Imperial General Staff
War Office, London

'You had a special unit of soldiers?' Dudley Clarke asked in broken Latin.

'I did,' Artorius replied. 'Each tribe or kingdom raised its own army, but I also maintained a maniple of hand-picked warriors. Those chosen were skilled in the use of the multiple weapons and were proficient in unarmed combat, and they needed to be good horsemen. They also needed to know forest craft. This maniple supported and helped to train regular legions, but I also called on these men for difficult operations, such as the slaying of commanders or kings behind enemy lines.'

Dudley Clarke looked to Kenneth Jackson, who translated Artorius's words for him. He was asking another question when he looked up and greeted a newcomer. Artorius turned around. It was Sir John Dill.

Dudley Clarke said something to Kenneth before he saluted Sir John and left. Kenneth explained to Artorius, 'We have our meeting with Sir John Dill now, but Colonel Clarke would like to continue this discussion at a later time.'

Shadows of fatigue encircled Sir John Dill's eyes, but Artorius could not read despair in them. This was a good sign.

Sir John said something to Kenneth, who turned to Artorius and explained, 'The leader of the nation requested an impromptu meeting with Sir John and other military commanders. Sir John has only just returned, and apologises that he kept us waiting.'

Artorius nodded.

'He thanks you again most earnestly for your advice about the

Belgians,' Kenneth continued. 'Sir John regrets that he did not notice this before you pointed it out.'

'I made the same mistake once, and it cost me dearly,' Artorius replied. He shuddered at the memory.

Sir John Dill beckoned them to follow him. He led them again to the room with tables in the middle bearing *telephones* of varying bold colours. These again drew Artorius's attention, but Sir John instead pointed at the map on the wall.

'I see the British forces occupy a smaller area,' Artorius mused, 'but it appears your perimeter has not been breached. How many men have you rescued?'

Kenneth asked this question, and after listening to Sir John Dill's reply, told Artorius, 'The number is between fifty and sixty thousand. Sir John also hopes to evacuate many more over the coming two days. The front line is better defended now, and the navy has become more efficient at evacuating the soldiers.'

Artorius blinked. These staggering numbers were hard to fathom. Oh well, at least the situation had stabilised; that was the main thing. It was now time to consider other matters. 'What of the civilian population?' he asked. 'How much do they know of this, and how are they reacting to these unfolding events?'

After a lengthy exchange with Sir John Dill, Kenneth told Artorius, 'So far, this operation has been kept secret. The public are extremely worried, with the last major announcement having been made during the day of prayer last Sunday.'

'Are you telling me you had the people pleading to God three days ago, and they have been left in this state of fear?' Artorius asked. 'If so, it is time to reconsider what you tell them. One thing I learnt is that it is nearly as important to instil confidence in the civilians as it is to instil confidence in the soldiers themselves.'

But how best to do it? Artorius pondered.

'Kenneth,' he said at length, 'was this day of prayer held across the entire nation?'

Kenneth nodded. 'It was.'

'Then it is time they hear that God has answered their prayers.'

CHAPTER 14

The hinges of the letterbox squeaked. Sophie put her knitting aside and went to the front door. She bent to pick up the mail, noting only slight discomfort where the stitches had been a couple of days ago.

There was only one letter addressed to her, and it had her supervisor's name and address on the back. She tore it open, wondering what had happened while she was in hospital.

Dear Sophie,

I received your letter about your injury, and I am most sorry to hear it. I pray you are recovering well.

I am writing to tell you that government officials arrived here this morning. They anticipate that the Luftwaffe will bomb English cities. To ensure the preservation of our antiquities in the event of an attack on Cambridge, irreplaceable items are being relocated to a safe facility.

Unfortunately, many artefacts upon which your project relies will thus be inaccessible for the duration of the

A hollowness filled Sophie's chest. She had known this could happen, but that knowledge did not lessen the disappointment. Not that she or Dr White could do anything about it, and of course, they must ensure the preservation of those antiquities.

She wandered into the living room.

'Any telegrams?' her mother asked. Since the outbreak of war, she always asked about telegrams first.

'No telegrams, just this from Cambridge.' Sophie held the letter out.

Sophie's mother took the letter and read it. 'Oh, no! Sophie, I'm so sorry. I know how much this means to you!' She embraced Sophie.

'I can understand why they're doing this, Mother.'

'Well, let's hope they reinstate your scholarship after the war,' her mother said as she released her. 'It can't go on forever.'

'I won't be able to recommence if we lose,' Sophie murmured. She looked at the wireless, which had been on since breakfast.

The BBC had cancelled all scheduled programmes and was only broadcasting news about the battle in Belgium and France. The deputy chief of staff announced that Belgium's surrender had left the British Expeditionary Force with a compromised northern flank. Everyone was predicting the imminent collapse of the BEF, and that this was likely to result in Britain's capitulation.

'*I have before me the telegram sent by His Majesty the King to the commander-in-chief of the British Expeditionary Force, Lord Gort,*' the newsreader announced, his voice unusually low and hesitant. '"*All your countrymen have been following with pride and admiration the courageous resistance of the British Expeditionary Force during the continuing fighting of the last fortnight. Faced by circumstances outside their control in a position of extreme difficulty, they are displaying gallantry which has never been surpassed in the annals of the British Army. The hearts of every one of us at home are with you and your magnificent troops in this hour of peril.*"'

'It's a consolatory message,' her mother said softly. 'There's no hope for them now.'

Sophie couldn't take any more. She went outside and wandered to the back of the garden, where their land backed onto a stream.

Despite the ongoing conflict between her parents over the allocation of garden space, neither of them had touched the area behind the hedgerow – although her mother had started the gradual process of replacing the privet with hazel. They left this area as an untamed wilderness to prevent erosion along the stream. It was home to birds, voles, red squirrels, and an assortment of other wildlife. Christopher used to play 'Robin Hood' here when he was younger. It was a good playground for a child, and a good retreat for an adult.

She walked over to the massive oak with the swing hanging from a low branch. Her parents intended to fell the giant ash that also grew on their property for timber, and let smaller trees take its place. She hoped they would leave the oak alone. This tree and this swing had sentimental value.

Sophie eased into the seat, the old ropes squeezing her forearms on either side. She started rocking back and forth, fingering the left rope absentmindedly.

A strong wind tugged at the uppermost branches and swished the leaves, but the trees and hedgerow diffused the gale at ground level, where it merely rustled the leaves. This overcast and blustery morning reflected Sophie's mood perfectly. She had witnessed the miraculous return of Britain's greatest hero, but he had returned too late. Perhaps he could never have saved them, anyway. After all, England now made up most of Britain; he was centuries too late to prevent his people – the Welsh – from being driven into a tiny corner of the island. Now, history was about to repeat itself as German invaders again threatened the inhabitants of the British Isles.

Sophie and her family would be safe in the event of a German occupation, unless one of them were to join a resistance movement. The Nazis didn't much like the French, though; how would they treat Britain's Celtic races? Then there were non-European ethnic minorities, not to mention Jewish and Polish refugees. What would the Nazis do to Bleddyn's in-laws and his Eurasian nieces? Would Bleddyn end up imprisoned or killed trying to stop them from harming his nieces?

Sophie would probably never find out. The invasion would create such chaos, it was unlikely she would ever hear from him again.

Her studies terminated, her country's sovereignty at stake ... Her world was crashing down around her, and she could do nothing to stop this calamity unfolding. An overwhelming sense of helplessness enveloped her. For the first time in years, she began to cry.

***

1300 hours
Office of the Chief of the Imperial General Staff
War Office, London

There was a knock at the door.

'Can you get it, Clarke?' Sir John asked without looking up from the report Sir Charles had given him. He could barely tear his eyes away from this. This might work, after all.

A click. A squeak of hinges.

'It's Newall and Dowding,' Sir Charles said.

'Sorry I'm late,' Sir John heard the Marshal of the Air Force say. 'Look, I know you only invited me here, but because this could be relevant to Fighter Command, I thought Sir Hugh ought to join us and hear this directly.'

Sir John looked up and nodded. 'Please, be seated. I'd only just started going through the report Sir Charles has given me.'

'It's good news,' Sir Charles said as the RAF commanders took their seats beside him. 'Despite the bad weather, we're evacuating men faster today than we have since this operation began. There haven't been many Luftwaffe raids, either.'

'Well, the weather is hampering flights – both ours and theirs,' Sir Hugh explained.

Sir Charles nodded. 'Furthermore, our reinforcements in the Channel have kept the Kriegsmarine at bay. We'll have over one hundred and twenty thousand men back home by midnight if this keeps up. Even better, we might do it without losing any ships.'

Sir John rubbed his temple with a trembling hand. The last few days had just about shot his nerves to pieces, but it now looked as though they might salvage something from this godforsaken mess.

'As such, this morning's BBC announcement was premature,' continued Sir Charles.

'It took me by surprise, too,' said Sir Cyril.

'Oh, I assure you, it was well considered,' Sir John replied.

Sir Charles frowned. 'The Germans surely know about the rescue now, so I don't see the point in keeping this hopeful news from the British public.'

'I was speaking to that man, Artorius – through Dr Jackson, of course,' Sir John told them.

'Artorius?' asked Sir Cyril. 'Who's … wait a minute, is this the man I heard about yesterday? The King Arthur chap?'

'Excuse me?' asked Sir Hugh.

Sir John sighed. 'Gentlemen, I have a portfolio back in my office, which ought to explain everything, if you care to follow me after this meeting. Anyway – to answer your question, Sir Cyril, yes, the same man. He was worried that a major defeat such as this could demoralise the British public. In order to minimise the public perception of Dunkirk as a major defeat, he suggested we remove all hope, and then give some of it back.'

Sir Charles frowned. 'Why is that?'

'Artorius said that people without hope will surrender to what they believe is the inevitable, even if the consequences are unthinkable. Defeatism may be taking root in the public, after the news they've been hearing. Artorius told me that one tactic he used was to make the people believe things were worse than they really were, and then deliver the positive news belatedly. He claimed it worked wonders for reinvigorating a fighting spirit in people who were on the verge of despair.' Sir John shrugged. 'At least, it sounded reasonable. I thought it was worth a try.'

'Well, we certainly have a despondent public mood right at the moment,' muttered Sir Charles. 'It could be a good idea, but I wouldn't tell Churchill it came from Artorius if I were you. You heard what he said yesterday.'

Sir John snorted. 'Churchill doesn't know what we owe him.'

'It may not be quite as much as you think,' Sir Charles replied. 'Yes, that fishing boat suggestion was a good idea, but the majority of evacuations are coming from the breakwaters. Tennant's been able to use those as makeshift piers.'

Sir John shook his head. 'It's not just that.' He explained to the others how Artorius foresaw the quick surrender of the Belgians, and how the Germans were poised to take advantage of their collapse.

'Good grief,' muttered Sir Cyril. 'If their plan had worked, Lord Gort would have surrendered by now, wouldn't he?'

Sir John nodded.

'This Artorius chap sounds like a brilliant tactician, then,' said Sir Hugh. 'I can't fathom why Churchill doesn't want anything to do with him. It's a peculiar name. Who is he, and where does he come from?'

'That's actually a difficult question to answer,' replied Sir John.

'Truth be told, we have no bloody idea who he is or where he's from,' muttered Sir Charles. 'Hell, there's even doubt over *when*.'

Sir Hugh frowned at them. 'What on earth do you mean?'

'You'll have to peruse the report I mentioned,' replied Sir John. 'It will answer your questions. No ... no, it won't. It will explain things, but you'll come away with more questions than you have now.'

'Anyway, what does this man's advice mean in terms of the current retreat?' Sir Cyril asked. 'For how long do you intend to delay this public announcement?'

'Just long enough for despondency to set in. Artorius also advised that when we do eventually let the public know about the evacuation, we should use some rather extravagant language. After the national day of prayer, I think we should present this rescue as a "miracle" that answered our prayers.'

'So, when should that time be?' asked Sir Cyril.

Sir John stroked his chin. 'Perhaps ... we should do it when about half the men have been rescued, and report an older rescue count. That way, even if the Germans compromise the evacuation soon after the announcement, we could still present a partial success *and* an improvement on the original announcement. Do you think forty-eight hours' time would be suitable?'

Sir Charles shook his head. 'No, we'll have to do it tomorrow at the latest. Enough civilian sailors and fishermen are involved for their communities to notice, and the movement of thousands of troops by rail is hardly inconspicuous. Telephones can spread a rumour from Kent to Edinburgh within minutes, so we won't be able to contain this for much longer.'

Sir John nodded. 'Good point. I suppose at the current rate of evacuation, we'll have half of them out by tomorrow, anyway.'

'Indeed,' agreed Sir Charles. 'However, so that the evacuation can proceed as quickly as possible, there is a matter we need to address. Captain Tennant and Lord Gort have clashed over how and where to evacuate the men. Lord Gort doesn't want too many vessels on the breakwaters, lest the Luftwaffe hit them. Tennant, on the other hand, wants to maximise their use, because he can load men onto ships much faster using the breakwaters than from the beaches, even with the fishing boats helping. Now, I know Gort outranks Tennant, but I would rather a naval man manage the embarkation, and Gort's interference isn't helping. Could you intervene, Sir John?'

'You don't think that Lord Gort has a point?' asked Sir John.

'Tennant's judgement in this matter is better,' replied Sir Charles. 'The bad weather isn't just keeping aircraft grounded; it's creating a swell that's hampering the beach rescue. We should embark men as fast as possible while we have a reprieve from the Luftwaffe. The meteorologists predict this gloriously foul weather will clear up tomorrow night.'

'Very well,' conceded Sir John. 'I'll see what I can do to change his mind. It won't be easy, though; Lord Gort is not always receptive to suggestions that came from the safety of the War Office.'

'Perhaps it would be sensible to recall him,' Sir Hugh said. 'I don't say that because he's clashing with this Tennant chap; whoever commands the rearguard will probably be captured. It wouldn't be good for morale if the Germans were to capture such a renowned general.'

Sir John nodded. 'Indeed. We'll have to order him back. Lord Gort has the heart of a lion, and he'll see the campaign through to the end unless orders prevent him from doing so.'

'Excellent idea,' agreed Sir Charles. 'That would also make it look like a tactical withdrawal. He might consider it a disgrace if he were replaced without any given reason, and I certainly don't want that. I know the man's service record. I'm just not sure if he's the right person to lead the evacuation at this time.'

Sir John sighed. 'I know what you mean.' Like many fine

commanders, Lord Gort was not always perceptive of his own fallibility. 'Well, let's hope whoever replaces him as commander-in-chief of the BEF would be more amenable to letting your man Tennant run the operation as he sees fit.'

***

1800 hours
King Albert's Holiday Villa
De Panne Beach, Belgium

Bernard Montgomery couldn't help but admire the trappings in Lord Gort's latest temporary office. Would the Germans plunder this royal villa of its splendid artwork, chinaware and Persian rugs?

No time to wonder about that now. Most other generals were seated, awaiting the arrival of the commander-in-chief. Bernard took the spare chair beside Alan Brooke.

Lord Gort walked in. His dark-ringed eyes and washed-out expression betrayed internal defeat. Bernard clenched his teeth. A commander should never let his subordinates see him lose hope. He leant over to Alan Brooke. 'It looks as though Gort's had it. How's he going to inspire confidence in his leadership?'

Brooke replied with a solemn nod.

To be honest, the precarious nature of the situation meant that everyone was under strain. Worst of all was Lieutenant General Barker of I Corps.

Lord Gort cleared his throat, and everyone fell silent. 'Men,' he told the assembled commanders, 'I received a telegram from the Prime Minister this afternoon.' He unfolded a piece of paper. 'From now on, Whitehall wants me to report from De Panne every three hours. I am also to nominate a corps commander to take over the BEF, and I am to return when they request, which they indicated may be soon.' He looked up again, ashen-faced. 'I feel cowardly, retreating and leaving anyone else in this mess, but I have no choice. To quote the telegram verbatim: *"This is in accordance with correct military procedure and no personal discretion is left to you in the matter. On political grounds it would be a needless triumph to the enemy to capture you when only a small force remained under your orders."'*

Bernard never suspected Lord Gort would take the opportunity to retreat unless ordered to, anyway. Hell, the man had a VC, and … was it one or two bars to a DSO? Lord Gort had his faults, but cowardice was not one of them.

'The orders for the corps commander are as one would expect' Lord Gort read from the telegram again. '"*The corps commander chosen by you should be ordered to carry out the defence in conjunction with the French and evacuation whether from Dunkirk or the beaches, but when in his judgement no further organised evacuation is possible and no further proportionate damage can be inflicted on the enemy he is authorised in consultation with the French Commander to capitulate formally to avoid useless slaughter."'*

Lord Gort sighed. 'Men, Dunkirk will be our last stronghold. We will need to transfer our headquarters there, and the northern front – II Corps – should withdraw behind I Corps tomorrow. I will also send some of our more insightful commanders back to Britain to begin preparations for home defence.' He fixed his gaze on Alan Brooke. 'I know you feel as I do about leaving our men behind, but we need sharp minds to take control of the British Army after this unfolding defeat.'

Lord Gort recommended Brooke for a higher position? Bernard hadn't expected that. It was a wise decision, but he was under the impression the two men didn't get along.

'Brooke, have you pulled all divisions off the front line?' Lord Gort asked. 'How many men do you still have?'

'Yes, sir. The Third and Fourth Divisions are both quite strong, with a total of twenty-five thousand men between them. The Fifth and Fiftieth Divisions are now down to only two brigades each, with …' – he swallowed, and continued with a slight quiver in his voice – '… with only about a thousand men in each brigade.'

'Good God, man!' Lord Gort exclaimed. 'Is that all that's left of those divisions? Two brigades? I hope they're not all missing in action.'

Brooke shook his head. 'Some of the exhausted brigades have already left for England, General. At least, those who came away from the Ypres–Comines Canal …' His voice wavered slightly at the end.

Lord Gort nodded. 'Well, we should count small mercies. Have you chosen a corps commander to replace you when you leave tonight?'

'I know of only one man I would be happy to see take over the corps. Major General Bernard Montgomery will be assuming command in my absence.' He turned to Bernard. 'Monty, I'm sorry to drop you into this, but as you see, I'm under orders.'

'Understood, sir.' It took all of Bernard's restraint to keep his voice and expression neutral. He wasn't sure what stunned him more – that he had been given the command of the corps when there were other lieutenant generals in the room, or that Alan Brooke, who had been so composed throughout the whole campaign, was now blinking back tears. So, Brookie *had* been feeling the strain of the past few days. He'd held it together brilliantly until now.

'Good,' Lord Gort said. 'Montgomery's probably one of the best choices for this job, come to think of it.' He surveyed the room. 'Regrettably, in such a withdrawal as we find ourselves, whoever is in the rearguard will undoubtedly be captured. We will have to sacrifice a corps in order to save the rest of the British Expeditionary Force. Monty, I want you to transfer one of your small divisions – Fifth or Fiftieth Division – over to I Corps. Barker will need men from a rested reserve if he's to hold the line as long as possible.'

A groan at the back of the room made Bernard turn his head. Barker had buried his head in his trembling hands.

Lord Gort explained to everyone how and when he wanted withdrawals and evacuations to occur. After withdrawing through I Corps to the beach at De Panne, II Corps was to leave via the beach after midday tomorrow, where a number of small vessels were helping to transfer men from the beaches to destroyers and ferries waiting off the coast. Similarly, he wanted III Corps to withdraw behind French lines and evacuate from Dunkirk.

Unfortunately, the instructions he gave to Barker on the withdrawal of the defensive perimeter probably went unheeded. Barker was now quite beside himself, and Bernard doubted he was capable of executing these commands. This was a disaster in the making.

'It sounds as though you're trying to evacuate most of the BEF tomorrow night, sir,' Brooke said, wiping his cheeks.

'I am. Meteorologists are predicting the weather tomorrow will continue to hamper Luftwaffe attacks. The weather the day after tomorrow will be fine, and that will mean an onslaught from well-rested enemy pilots. Brooke, now that you've handed over command, it's time for you to leave.'

Alan Brooke stood up. 'Well, good luck, Monty. I … I feel like a coward, leaving my men like this, but at least they will be in capable hands.'

Bernard stood and saluted his superior. 'I won't disappoint you, sir.'

Alan shook his hand. 'Monty, all hell will break loose the day after tomorrow. You need to arrange the evacuation of the corps, but that doesn't mean you have to be the last man out. I'm going to recommend you for corps command, so … so for God's sake, get back safely.' By now, the tears were running down his cheeks and his voice faltered on every syllable. He saluted Lord Gort and left.

After the meeting, Bernard went and spoke to Lord Gort. For the sake of the entire BEF, something had to be done about Barker.

'Sir?' Bernard stood to attention and saluted.

'At ease, Monty. What is it?'

'General, you seem to think that most of I Corps will be captured.'

Lord Gort nodded. 'Alas, I don't see how to avoid it.'

'Actually, sir, if the commanding officer executes the perimeter withdrawal correctly, it might be possible to evacuate a large number of French soldiers and most of I Corps, and perhaps the commanding officers as well. However, you must remove Barker from the corps.'

Lord Gort looked Monty in the eye. 'That's an insolent thing to say of one of your superiors, Monty.'

'Sir, I don't give a damn if it's disrespectful. Barker has jeopardised the BEF several times already. He's lost his nerve. Just look at the state he's in.' Bernard pointed to the distraught Barker, who hadn't moved from his seat. 'Do you think he even heard half your orders? The officer in charge of I Corps will also need to liaise with the French. Now, the First Division was transferred to I Corps about a week ago. Their commander, Alexander, would be a good man to lead this evacuation.'

Lord Gort continued to glare at Bernard.

'General,' Bernard insisted, 'you need someone with a steady nerve, the respect of his men, and diplomatic sensibilities. If you want to rescue as many men as possible, you must look at the suitability of your commanders, not their ranks.'

Lord Gort grunted. 'You know, Monty, you're right.' He raised his head. 'Barker! You're to leave for England tonight with Brookie.'

Barker rose to his feet. 'Sir, you mean … you mean that I can go home? That I won't be captured?'

'I will appoint Major General Harold Alexander as acting commander of I Corps,' Lord Gort told him.

Barker saluted and thanked Lord Gort several times over, relief washing over his face. Bernard refrained from scowling, but it was disgusting to watch. How did Barker ever become a lieutenant general in the first place? Why, the fool was so happy to be leaving the battlefield, he was oblivious to the fact that his career was over.

CHAPTER 15

Friday, 31 May
0010 hours
Port of Dover

'Brookie.' Someone shook Alan's shoulder. 'We're back in England.'

'Already?' He could have sworn he'd lain down only a minute ago. Alan rubbed his eyes. Lieutenant General Ronald Adam came into focus.

They stepped onto the deck, where they were bustled along as everyone streamed off the destroyer.

'The men should make way for us,' Adam growled.

Alan looked Adam up and down in his undergarments, and then looked at himself. 'To be fair, most of them won't know who we are.'

The first thing Alan did was find a distribution tent and replace the clothes. Once decently attired, he approached a midshipman and asked who was coordinating the rescue.

'Vice Admiral Ramsay,' came the distracted reply. 'Look, men are to—'

'Ramsay? Bertie Ramsay?' It was heartening to learn that a competent officer was in charge.

The midshipman tilted his head. 'You know him?'

'I'm Lieutenant General Alan Brooke, and I would like to see Ramsay, if it's convenient for him.'

The midshipman saluted. 'Certainly, sir. Follow me.'

Alan followed the midshipman past various other tents. They

passed a queue in front of a mobile field hospital. A couple of men were standing beside a pallid-looking corporal. 'He's been throwing up all day,' one of them said to the young medic bending over him. 'We think it's something he ate. He collapsed on the boat coming here.'

'He's severely dehydrated,' the medic replied; he had a Welsh accent. 'Help me get him onto a bed; he'll need IV saline.'

The midshipman found a driver and directed him to take Alan to see Ramsay.

The car passed marshalling sites and bus convoys, and went up a hill towards the massive fortress. They went over a moat and through a small gate in the wall, and took two sharp turns before stopping. The driver killed the engine. 'Do you see that doorway, sir?' He pointed to a tunnel in the side of a hill. 'The offices are down there. Follow me.'

The tunnel went down and straight. It was just as well these cliffs were of pale chalk. It would have been impossible to see by the feeble light had the walls of the tunnel been any darker.

The driver led Alan past a number of side tunnels until they came to a right-hand bend, where it opened up into a wide corridor full of personnel, tables, pinboards, secretaries, typewriters and telephones. Vice Admiral Ramsay emerged from a side room, sipping from an enamel mug.

'Bertie!' Alan called. 'I should have known you were running this.'

'Good Lord, if it isn't Alan Brooke!' There were shadows under Bertie's eyes, but his gaunt face lit up when he saw Alan. 'Good to see you got out of Dunkirk safely, Brookie!' He came over and shook Alan's hand warmly. 'You look exhausted!'

'So do you, Bertie, so do you. I don't think we'll have long to rest after this, unfortunately. That was a brilliant idea, enlisting fishermen for the rescue.'

'Oh, that idea.' Bertram waved his free hand casually. 'I picked it up from someone else. Well, a variant of it, anyway. Now, Tennant tells me there are at least a hundred thousand men still over there. Is that correct?'

'It is. Lord Gort is planning to evacuate all of II Corps tomorrow, some twenty-six thousand men there alone, as well as most of III Corps.

The Boche tend not to move their artillery after dark, so it's easiest to send people to the port at night.'

'Tennant thought as much, but thanks for letting me know. The weather forecasters are predicting fine conditions for the morning after, so we may only have one more day before the German pilots return to the skies. Anyway, can I get you anything? Tea, perhaps?'

Alan shook his head. 'Thank you, but no. I need to brief the CIGS, and then I just want to go home.'

'All right, then. I'll arrange for a driver to take you to the War Office directly.'

The sun was just starting to lighten the horizon as Alan's driver took him through the Kent countryside. Alan wound down the window and enjoyed the clean air, far removed from the soot and smoke that had spilled out of Dunkirk and blanketed half of Belgium these past couple of days. The tranquillity brought relief to his ringing ears, but it also left Alan feeling hollowed-out in the middle, as though he had no right to enjoy such a pleasant drive. A battle raged only fifty miles away. How long would dear old England stay like this?

The roads through London were relatively quiet at this early hour, and it wasn't too long before Alan was at the War Office. When he met Sir John, he reiterated his prediction that they only had another twenty-four hours, and that the next evening would be the busiest so far. He hoped he'd articulated himself properly and hadn't mixed numbers up. A fog of fatigue was enveloping him and muddling his mind.

'Brookie, you look dead on your feet,' Sir John observed. 'Go home. We'll need you back soon, but rest first. Where do you live?'

'Hartley Wintney, sir. It's near Winchfield station, and the trains are regular enough.'

'Well, I'll at least have a driver take you to the station.' He pointed to his telephone. 'You should call home, too, and let your family know you're on your way.'

***

Two nights had passed since the Germans shot them and left them to die. Brian had seen a French farmer, but the man didn't render assistance to any of the wounded, the swine.

No, he wasn't a swine. He was terrified. The Germans who had massacred their captives also controlled this area. No wonder the farmer didn't dare try to help.

Pain. Brian had already endured more pain than he thought possible. Every laboured breath, every movement of his punctured chest was agony. But the thirst tortured him more. His throat smouldered, and he couldn't even collect the rainwater from tantalising showers that fell only feet away.

One by one, the moaning men around him were falling silent. They suffered, but were too weak to scream. Some begged God to take them quickly. Yesterday, the man who spoke to Brian on the first night here had tried to do himself in with two .303 rounds. He had pointed one to his head and tried to detonate it by bashing the primer cap with the ball of the second round. His feeble attempts hadn't worked, but he was lying motionless this morning.

The man had tried to take his own life. He'd failed, but he'd tried. Would God forgive him for such a sin?

Yes, surely He would, for He would know what this man had already endured.

The rumble of an engine grew louder and then stopped abruptly. Doors slammed. German voices drifted into the barn. Had they come back to finish off the survivors? If so, would it be cold-blooded murder, or an act of kindness? Brian had loathed the entire German nation only yesterday, but he was now too weak to care.

Please, God, may this end soon.

Three men entered the barn and covered their noses, muffling their exclamations about the stench of death and decay. Brian shifted slightly.

On seeing him move, one of the new arrivals stopped, knelt down beside him, and asked something in German.

'I don't … understand,' replied Brian.

'*Vous êtes Français? Brittanique?*'

'*Brittanique … plutôt,*' Brian gasped.

The man looked around. 'Why are there no weapons here?' he asked in French. 'No helmets, no guns …'

'We had … surrendered.'

The German's expression darkened in disgust. '*Ach, du Scheiße!*' he exclaimed. 'You were captured by the *Schutzstaffel*. The SS do not take prisoners.'

The Germans moved the survivors out into the field and used their jackets to prop their heads up. Brian caught a glimpse of a Red Cross armband on one of the jackets.

The movement had caused his chest wound to start bleeding again. The man who had spoken to him even removed his own shirt and used it as a makeshift compress.

A lump formed at the bottom of Brian's parched throat as lost hope flooded back into his mind, combined with remorse for the hatred he had felt towards these medics when he first heard them speak. *These men … they're not like the bastards who left us here to die.* 'Please,' he whispered, 'water …'

The shirtless medic unscrewed a canister.

'*Nur ein bisschen,*' another one called out. '*Er muss operiert werden.*'

He offered Brian the briefest of sips from the canister.

The medics loaded the survivors into the back of a truck. Before leaving, a couple of them became animated about something else. They went to the ditch, and returned with another survivor. The man from the ditch was laid beside Brian. It was Parry! He was still alive!

They were at a German casualty clearing station within an hour. A doctor gave Brian morphine and began assessing the casualties to decide who needed surgery most urgently. A nurse gave him another all too brief sip of water. 'It will … take time; others need operations first,' she said in hesitant English. 'You may have some water, but only a little. You have operation soon.'

Now that the morphine was kicking in, Brian didn't feel the thirst so badly anyway. He glanced at Parry, who was now on a bed across from him. Like Brian and everyone else, his injuries were severe. There was no guarantee he would survive. But thanks to the decency of the German medics, at least he had a chance. They all had a chance.

Brian hoped and prayed that their rescuers would be spared in the coming battles. Whatever side of a war they were on, it was a travesty when men of honour died.

***

0830 hours
Waterloo Station, London

Alan Brooke paced up and down on the platform, hands clasped behind his back.

An elderly woman walked up to him and peered into his face. 'Excuse me, but are you with the British Expeditionary Force?'

'I'm afraid I am – or rather, I was, until last night,' he replied.

'Is it true that not all is lost, and that the navy is rescuing our boys?' The tone of her voice was both hopeful and pleading. She held up a newspaper with 'OUR BOYS SAVED?' emblazoned across the top.

After everything he had seen, Alan felt 'Narrow Escape' would have been more appropriate. Nevertheless, he confirmed that a rescue operation was underway.

'May God bless you then, and may He bring our boys back safely!' she exclaimed. 'You know, we're all so very, very honoured by your heroic efforts there—'

'Yes, yes, thank you,' said Alan. 'But if you'll excuse me, my train is just pulling in.' And not a moment too soon.

She gave him a big smile, patted him on the elbow, and left.

Alan found a compartment. A newspaper with the headline 'OUR HEROES DEFY HITLER' had been left on the seat.

Alan didn't feel heroic at all. Too many men had died, and too many were still in mortal peril while he was safely back in England. The evacuation may have been going as well as could be hoped, but a retreat was still a retreat.

Alan awoke when the train lurched forward. Good grief, he'd only sat down for a minute and nodded off! Afraid that he might overshoot his station if he fell asleep again, he paced up and down the corridor to stay awake. This tactic was not without its drawbacks. Newspapers and radio stations across the country were all talking about the evacuation. Every Tom, Dick and Harry assumed a man in a uniform was part of the British Expeditionary Force, and everyone he passed wanted to congratulate him, extend condolences or prayers, offer him cigarettes, and so forth.

Alan did not want to talk to anybody, least of all about Dunkirk. He just wanted to get home, see his family, and find out about Tom.

Tom. His oldest son had been gravely ill, but Alan had only been able to think about him in passing this last week. Oh, God, was he all right? Would Benita know?

Winchfield station couldn't come fast enough.

It was the longest train ride Alan had ever taken. He had barely hopped off the train when his younger two children almost bowled him over and fired questions at him.

'Kathy, Victor, your father's been through an ordeal, and he's tired.' Benita's level voice chided them gently.

Alan put his arms around them and looked up at his wife. 'Well, I'm pleased to see them, but I thought today was a school day.'

'For heaven's sake, Alan, I couldn't send them to school today with you coming back!' His wife's calm demeanour started to crack. She hugged him. 'Oh, God, we were all worried sick about you!'

'Have you heard any news about Tom?' Alan asked. 'He developed appendicitis before I had to lead the corps north. Last I heard before the enemy cut our communication lines, there were complications ...' He trailed off. For all he knew, his oldest son could have been dead for a week.

Benita nodded. 'I've still been getting news, and Tom's all right. He's still in a field hospital in France, but he's getting better.'

Tears of relief welled behind Alan's eyes.

'Come on, Alan, let's get you home.' Benita took his arm.

'Benita, I'll need to go back to the War Office as soon as possible,' he told her apologetically. 'The newspapers are talking about a miracle, but this is still a defeat, and we need to work out what went wrong before the Germans try to invade us.'

'You can worry about that later. Rest first. God, Alan, I'm relieved to see you. We heard rumours about an evacuation, but until that phone call—'

'Wait – rumours? I saw headlines in the newspapers—'

'Speculation. Whitehall plans an official broadcast this afternoon. Mind you, it's probably their worst kept secret right now.'

Despondency still weighed Alan's heart down, but for now, he had a reprieve. His son was alive, and he could finally get a proper rest.

***

1600 hours
St. James's Park, London

This massive manicured garden was a good retreat from the concrete, brick and bituminous material that encapsulated modern Londinium. Unfortunately, even here, Artorius could not escape the foul stench of the air – although it was a little better than it was at the inn. Coal, rock oil and tar had largely replaced timber, tallow and plant oils as the fuels of choice by the millions who now lived in this city, and these rock fuels emitted such foul smoke when burned. And then, of course, there was *tobacco*, some exotic dried leaf which released a noxious smoke when burned. For some bizarre reason, people actually seemed to enjoy.

Perhaps this tobacco was addictive, like cannabis. Yes, that would make sense. Cannabis, too, gave a putrid smoke. Intoxication and addiction were the only incentives to burn it. Cannabis also fuddled the mind like an overindulgence in wine and ale. If this tobacco had the same effect, it was disconcerting that so many people working at the War Office indulged in its smoke while carrying out their duties.

'I thought you might like to leave the hotel, after all that work on the *dictionary*,' Kenneth Jackson explained. He pointed along the lake. 'Our King lives in a palace that way. Would you like to see it?'

'Would he grant us an audience?' Artorius asked.

'We would not be allowed in,' Kenneth replied. 'We can only see the front from this side of a fence. However, if we are lucky, we might see the changing of the guard.' His voice and eyebrows both rose on that last comment.

Artorius looked at him. 'Kenneth, you make it sound as though watching the king's guards change is entertaining.'

Kenneth recoiled slightly and glanced away.

Artorius couldn't help but think that he'd said something offensive, but Kenneth offered no explanation.

'It has been two days since we have spoken to any of your commanders,' Artorius said at length. 'What is happening?'

'I showed you the *newspaper*. All is going well now. Sir John Dill not only considered your tactical advice valuable; he has even taken your advice on public reporting. This bodes well, Artorius, and you have proven your worth.'

'And yet, there is only so much I can do from here.' Artorius watched a duck land on the water.

'Give the commanders time to finish with the current retreat. After what you have done, they will surely accept your help. In fact, you will probably end up with a more important planning role than the one I envisaged.'

'To help, I need to see your current methods in action. I am too unfamiliar with modern … you call it *technology*. Kenneth, I would like to visit the battle front.'

'What? In the middle of an evacuation?'

'If they are sending boats, surely they can accommodate a passenger. Could some of these fishing vessels do with an extra hand? Is there a vantage point from which I could witness some of the fighting on the mainland of Europe?'

Kenneth's eyes had widened. Artorius could not expect his translator, who was not a combatant, to enter a battle front. 'Perhaps a place from which I could witness the disembarkation in Britain, then?' Artorius asked.

'Well … we could go to the War Office and ask,' Kenneth suggested. He looked at his watch. 'It would have to be tomorrow, I think.'

They walked a little farther.

'Artorius,' Kenneth asked, 'Sophie Edwardson wrote in her report that you were hostile to the English and that you had no interest in helping us in this war. Now, you are desperate to help, and are even prepared to risk your life to do so. Why did you change your mind?'

'My people live among yours, and they are threatened by these Nazis,' Artorius replied. 'To refuse to help you would be to abandon them. Sophie was accompanied by a Cymry physician, who reminded me … who reminded me so much of one of my own sons.' The words caught in his throat. He turned his face to the lake. 'I must help them. They are all I have left.'

***

1900 hours
Admiral Abrial's temporary office
Bastion 32, Dunkirk

Bill Tennant glanced from Admiral Abrial and General Fagalde to their chiefs of staff, who were standing poised above him like vultures waiting to feed. He then looked at Major General Harold Alexander, now commander-in-chief of the retreating British Expeditionary Force. Were the French commanders opposite them telling the truth, or were they trying to coerce their relatively low-ranking British compatriots into doing their bidding?

'Gentlemen,' Alexander told Abrial and Fagalde, 'I was not witness to what Lord Gort promised you, but my orders are to evacuate. As much as I would like to help, neither my orders nor our resources will allow me to help defend the perimeter for a further three days.'

General Fagalde scowled at him and drummed his fingers on the desk. 'Major General, I hope you do not mean that the French Army is to cover the British Army withdrawal.'

'Sir, understand that we are also helping to extract as many French troops as possible,' Alexander said. 'All who can be saved, will be saved.'

'Except honour,' hissed Abrial's chief of staff.

Admiral Abrial cleared his throat. 'There seems to be some confusion about what Lord Gort's orders were. Perhaps we should go to see him.'

Bill shook his head. 'I'm afraid that's not possible. Lord Gort left earlier today.'

'What?' demanded Abrial.

'You are lying!' growled Fagalde.

Bill dug his nails into his palms.

'Kindly do not accuse Captain Tennant of lying,' said Alexander. 'Lord Gort has already departed for England, in accordance with instructions from Whitehall. *I* am now commander of the British Expeditionary Force, and my orders are to retreat as quickly as possible.'

'*Major* General Alexander,' growled Abrial, 'if you leave so quickly and expect the French to sacrifice themselves to cover you, your actions will bring great shame upon the British Army.'

Bill shifted uneasily. Abrial did have a point there.

'I will contact Mr Eden and clarify my orders,' Alexander suggested.

Fagalde nodded. 'That may be the best course of action. Let us meet again at 2300 hours.'

Bill and Major General Alexander left.

As they stepped outside, Bill turned to Alexander. 'Major General, I don't know if you have an office yet, but my office has radios and even field telephones within walking distance.'

'Lead the way, Captain.'

Bill glanced at the sky as they walked to Bastion 28. The clouds were breaking up. By dawn, there would be nothing to hamper the Luftwaffe pilots, and the onslaught from well-rested pilots would surely be horrific.

When they arrived at Bill's office, Alexander called Whitehall. Bill checked the shipping schedule and loading rates. 'The bad weather's really hampering beach rescues tonight,' he muttered. 'And Lord Gort wanted the whole of II Corps evacuated tonight. They're at De Panne … Driscoll, if you can get in contact with their commanding officer, get him to redirect five thousand men to Dunkirk. There's no way we'll get the entire corps off the beaches. Oh, and I want the *Basilisk* and the *Codrington* to dock at the breakwaters when they arrive, too. Their crews have done so before.'

'What about the small craft, sir?' Driscoll asked.

'They'll have to go back with anyone they find. Tell Ramsay not to send any more tonight – the seas are too choppy. We'll need them tomorrow, especially if the Germans bomb the breakwaters.' He was glad Alexander had relinquished more control to him than Lord Gort had done.

'Yes, Mr Eden,' Bill overheard Alexander say, 'but I must impress on you that prolonging the evacuation may not help more men get away. The BEF may simply be wiped out. Speed is of the essence here. … Yes, I understand, but I need an answer as soon as possible. … Good, thank you.' He hung up and looked at Bill. 'Eden needs to consult a few people. He'll call back.'

It was an hour before the telephone rang again. Alexander picked it up directly. 'Hello? … Speaking … Yes, Mr Eden … Yes … I'd just like to clarify – by "50:50 basis", do you mean that we should slow the evacuation of British servicemen until the number of French evacuees reaches parity, or is the ratio to apply from this point onwards? … Good, good. And as for the end of the operation … Midnight tomorrow?

Understood. Thank you, sir. Goodbye.' He replaced the receiver.

Bill frowned. 'Sir, what was the answer about the parity?'

'It applies from this point on,' Alexander replied.

Thank goodness. That would be easier to manage, especially with the five thousand men from II Corps. 'I'll have the men form two lines at each breakwater – one for the French, one for the British. It'll be imprecise, but it's more important that we keep the lines moving.'

At 2300 hours, they returned to Abrial's office.

'Gentlemen,' Alexander said to the French commanders, 'I have a reply from the Secretary of State for War. He wishes me to hold my position until midnight tomorrow, while we evacuate the French and British soldiers in equal numbers.'

'Only another twenty-five hours?' exclaimed Abrial. 'But that will not give us enough time! Anyhow, we contacted Mr Churchill, and this is his reply.' He handed Alexander the telegram. 'This telegram comes from the Supreme War Council in Paris. As you can see, your own Prime Minister has agreed to evacuate the British and French, his own words, "arm in arm". You will also see he has ordered the British to extend their presence for another three nights so that we can also evacuate our men.'

Bill's heart sank into his stomach. Had the Prime Minister really promised that, over Mr Eden?

Alexander studied the letter. 'I'm answerable to the Secretary of State for War,' he replied. 'I will hold my position until midnight tomorrow – that is, for a further twenty-five hours.'

Fagalde's face contorted with rage. 'You're going against your Prime Minister's orders?'

'As I told you, General,' replied Alexander, 'I answer directly to the Secretary of State for War, Mr Anthony Eden. Less than an hour ago, he told me to hold the line for another day, not another three days. We are assembling both French and British soldiers at the moles as we speak. As per our instructions, Captain Tennant is now evacuating the French alongside the British in equal numbers.'

'Then I shall close the harbour until you agree to your Prime

Minister's request!' Abrial declared.

'Oh, don't be bloody stupid!' snapped Bill.

'How dare you?' bellowed Abrial as he rose from his seat.

Bill stood, too. 'If you close the harbour—'

'Speaking to an admiral like that—'

'—you'll impede the rescue of—'

'If you were a French captain—'

'—your own men—'

'—I would have you court—'

'Gentlemen, please! Enough!' Alexander had risen and put his hands between Abrial and Bill.

They sat down, but Abrial continued to glower at Bill. 'Major General Alexander, I hope you will report Captain Tennant's insolent behaviour.'

'Captain Tennant should have watched his tongue,' Alexander replied, 'but we're all under a lot of strain. I think what he was trying to say is that if you close the harbour, we will have to make greater use of the beaches, which are farther away from most of the French divisions than the harbour is. I will also point out that the French, like the British, are exhausted and low on munitions, and I do not believe that either army can maintain the perimeter for much longer.'

Abrial glared at him.

'Admiral,' said Alexander, 'I do not think it will serve either of our interests for you to slow the evacuation in such a manner. However, your men are welcome to board British vessels on a 50:50 ratio. Whether we leave via the harbour or the beaches, we are terminating this operation tomorrow night.'

Abrial's expression could have curdled milk. 'Then I cannot stop you,' he hissed. 'But this is a betrayal some of us will never forget.'

***

2300 hours

For the first time since the evacuation began, one of Bernard Montgomery's ideas had come unstuck.

'The vehicles are too far from the water's edge, sir, and the fishermen are having trouble spotting men in the swell,' his aide-de-camp called out to him over the blustery wind. 'Can we make another makeshift pier?'

Bernard shook his head. 'We committed all our surplus vehicles to make that one, Sweeney.' It was stupid not to check the tides first. He looked around at the units amassing on the beach. Most of them were also low on drinking water, and dehydration would weaken anyone still here tomorrow. It would be worse if the clouds cleared and men were in the full sun on the sand.

Some more vehicles came along the beach.

'Are those trucks ours?' Sweeney asked.

Bernard shook his head. 'They belong to I Corps. They're withdrawing the perimeter.'

'Wait – are you saying we won't be behind the front line tomorrow?'

Bernard nodded. All hell would descend on those who were still here at sunrise.

He scanned the beach. This was not going to work; it was now time for the contingency plan. 'Anderson!' Bernard called to the brigadier, now acting major general, who had succeeded his command of Third Division.

'Yes, sir!' Anderson ran over and saluted.

'At ease. Anderson, it's apparent we won't be able to send anyone else home via these beaches for a while. We need to rendezvous at Bray-Dunes beach, behind the new defensive perimeter.'

'Understood, sir.'

Bernard nodded. 'More regiments from II Corps will converge here in the next couple of hours. Many of them won't have radios, so they won't know about the change in plans.' He paused and took a deep breath. The insufficient number of radios was one of several complaints he had about the outfitting of the BEF. 'I need you to remain on the beach here until

0200 tomorrow morning and redirect men. I will go to Bray-Dunes to oversee the embarkation. If need be, we'll withdraw to Dunkirk.'

Anderson nodded. 'Yes, sir.'

Bernard followed the beach south-west with his aide-de-camp and his brigadier general staff.

A burst of machine gun fire came too close for comfort. Bernard's heart skipped a beat when Charles Sweeney hit the ground beside him. While other men fired back at their elusive assailant, Bernard checked on his ADC.

'It's not deep, sir, and he's still conscious,' another soldier said as he took some bandages out of a first aid kit and began to bind Sweeney's head. The blood trickled from above his hairline, but it didn't look deep.

Well, at least he wasn't seriously hurt. Bernard could admonish him then and there. 'Sweeney, there's a reason the army issues those tin helmets! Why, for the love of God, were you not wearing one, you nitwit?'

'Following the example set by my commanding officer, sir,' replied Sweeney.

Bernard shook his head. Sweeney was a loyal man, but he had a cheek at times. Truth be told, Sweeney reminded Bernard so much of himself when he was the same age.

He looked at the sand dunes in the direction from which the shell had come. Their attacker had probably slipped away into the darkness.

They filtered through the defensive lines I Corps had established and arrived at Bray-Dunes beach. Bernard looked at the sea. 'Damn it,' he muttered under his breath. There were ships off the beach, but the small boats dared not come too close to the choppy waves. He glanced at the sky. Even more stars were shining through than before. This was not good …

'General,' called a signalman, 'the naval representatives in Dunkirk wish to know how many more men we have.'

'Let them know we had about twenty thousand left at midnight, and the beach evacuation is proving difficult.' He'd sent five thousand to Dunkirk earlier that night; if he could send more, all the better.

The signalman coded the message and transmitted it. This was a slow process; Bernard wanted to know what to do with the remaining men *now*. Still, it would be unwise to let the enemy know where most of the evacuations were taking place. His patience was running as low as their time, but it would still be reckless to hurry this.

A message came back, and the signalman decoded it. 'Sir, Captain Tennant requests that you transfer all remaining men to Dunkirk for evacuation.'

Bernard closed his eyes and took a deep breath. This was their best hope.

Troops streamed past for hours, and Bernard had officers direct their men to follow the beach to Dunkirk. The wind began to calm, much to Bernard's consternation. Fishing boats and yachts came back inshore, but the calmer weather would also mean the return of the Luftwaffe after sunrise. Why couldn't the seas have calmed around sunset? If they had, more men would have departed via the beach by now.

The flow of troops slowed to a trickle. Anderson himself came past at 0300 hours. Bernard waited another half an hour, but nobody else came. He was confident that nearly all the men from II Corps were now en route to the breakwaters at Dunkirk. He turned to his ADC and his BGS. 'Sweeney, Ritchie, it's time for us to leave.'

They left the beach for the road and began to walk to Dunkirk.

The eastern sky was beginning to lighten at 0400 hours. Dunkirk was still a couple of hours away on foot.

A truck came by. Bernard hailed it, and the corporal driving put his head out of the window.

'Are you heading to Dunkirk?' Bernard asked.

'Yes, sir. Do you need a lift?'

Bernard got into the cabin beside the driver, while Sweeney and Ritchie hopped in the back.

The trip was excruciatingly slow as the truck lurched from one bone-rattling pothole to another, but it was faster than walking. Bernard kept glancing at the sky. Sunrise was now dangerously close. How much light did the Luftwaffe pilots need?

The harbour was teeming with men, but the various petty officers directing the crowds were keeping order well. There was a destroyer docked on the breakwater before him. The metal monster looked foreboding, towering over him in the low light; yet it offered the promise of rescue, and reminded him that he was nearly home. There were two more ships behind this one, and Bernard could make out the silhouettes of ships moored alongside the breakwater on the opposite side of the harbour. The embarkation was proceeding efficiently. This Captain Tennant was doing a splendid job, as were the sailors under his command.

On seeing Bernard's rank, an ensign saluted him. 'General, if you're leaving this morning, you should bypass the queue and go straight to the front of the lines. Senior officers have priority.'

Bernard nodded. 'Thank you.' He turned to Sweeney and Ritchie. 'Follow me.' Not everyone in the corps had embarked yet, but they needed no further direction from their corps commander now. Bernard's role was finished for the time being, and he had orders from Brooke.

He walked along the breakwater, passing men he had seen in his division, and hopped aboard the HMS *Codrington*.

The sun still hadn't quite risen when they sailed out of the harbour, but it was already light. The destroyer raced ahead at full speed.

'Hell, these naval chaps are a bit reckless, aren't they?' Sweeney exclaimed. 'There could be mines or wrecks or anything through here.'

Bernard pointed to the sky over Dunkirk. 'That's why they've thrown caution to the wind.' Dozens of aeroplanes dotted the skyline on the horizon. The Luftwaffe were already closing in. 'The farther we are into the Channel, the less likely they are to come after us.'

Sweeney shuddered. 'Bloody hell, look at 'em all! Just as well we're not in the midst of all that.'

'Well, it would have made the day more interesting,' replied Bernard, retaining his composure.

Sweeney was right, though. It was going to be a horrendous day for those still in France, and not all the men from II Corps were safe yet. He bowed his head and prayed silently that Alexander would pull through this. It was just as well Barker was no longer in command of the rearguard.

CHAPTER 16

Saturday, 1 June
1215 hours
Bastion 28, Dunkirk

Another bomb exploded nearby. The shockwave pulsed up the legs of Bill Tennant's chair.

'By God, that was close!' exclaimed Major General Alexander.

The constant drone of aeroplane engines and the continuous rattle of machine-gun fire were making Bill's skin crawl. 'I need to check how things are going,' he announced as he stepped outside. A sense of relief he knew deep down to be unfounded washed over him. His instincts urged him to leave the enclosed bunker where he was blind to what was going on around him, even though the logical part of him knew the bastion was the safest place to be. They were made of thick concrete and had so much soil mounded over them they would probably even withstand a direct hit.

Clouston was still keeping the lines moving on the breakwater despite the constant threat from the air. The man had a nerve of iron. Near misses had reduced the walkway to the eastern mole to little more than a narrow plank.

There were casualties on stretchers near the breakwater's gate, and sailors were conveying them to one of the ships along the breakwater. Bill went over and hailed a nearby officer. 'Lieutenant, we were ordered to prioritise the evacuation of able-bodied men!' He pointed to the casualties. 'What are those men doing here?'

'Sir, they're from a field hospital that was abandoned in last night's withdrawal. The medics brought them here, and the men – well, some of the soldiers in the queue started loading them before we told them otherwise. Should I tell them to unload, sir?'

Bill hesitated. Unloading them would waste more time. 'No, just get the boat loaded and on its way. But send the rest of the injured to the nearest casualty clearing station!'

'Yes, sir!'

A destroyer pulled away from the mole and nudged past the wrecks with the delicate grace her crew had honed over the past few days. As soon as the ship's bow was pointing out of the harbour, the engines burst into full power and she tore away.

Bill looked up at the sound of a falling bomb – *and the whistling stopped! It was right overhead!* He hit the ground and braced for the explosion that would end his life.

A crash. Debris rained down around him.

Slowly, Bill opened his eyes again.

An unexploded bomb sat barely ten yards from him in an impact crater.

'Thank the Lord,' he whimpered as he got back to his feet.

'Jesus, that was bloody good luck,' gasped a lieutenant beside him. He shot Bill a weak smile. 'Must have scared the devil out of you, too, Captain. Never thought I'd ever hear you swear like that.'

Now that the lieutenant mentioned it, Bill realised he had indeed let fly with an expletive. 'Yes, well, you'd better hope you never hear it again,' he replied curtly, annoyed with himself. 'It's sheer luck that you lived to tell the tale this time. Well, come on, get that thing roped off!'

'Yes, sir!'

The situation was becoming untenable. Bill passed half a dozen soldiers who were firing back at the low-swooping bombers with Bren guns – not that they had much chance of hitting them – and went to the bastion.

'Sir,' Driscoll told him as he walked in, 'the *Basilisk* has sunk.'

'What?' exclaimed Bill. 'Couldn't she be towed?'

'The Luftwaffe struck her a second time, sir.'

Jesus Christ. Three destroyers by the middle of the day, and nearly twenty vessels in total.

Alexander looked up at him. 'Tennant, do you need to reconsider the evacuation?'

'Sir, Vice Admiral Ramsay will be reluctant to commit more vessels if this keeps up.'

Alexander fiddled nervously with the end of his moustache.

'The Germans haven't been all that active at night, though,' Bill added. 'I suggest we send a coded telegram to Ramsay, requesting that he not send any more boats before sunset. We'll need more time to get everyone away, though. Can the BEF hold out here for one more day?'

Alexander stroked his chin. The stubble was almost a beard now. 'They're not just bombing the harbour and boats, you know. The front line is really getting pounded.'

Bill bit his bottom lip.

'Even so, I think we could manage another withdrawal to just outside Dunkirk tonight. Are you sure those breakwaters will last another two days?'

'If not, we'll request another flotilla of small vessels,' replied Bill. 'Both moles are useable at present. The Germans might think we've abandoned the rescue if ships stop coming during the day, and ease up on the harbour.'

'Let's hope so,' Alexander said. 'As it is, an extension may go some way to appeasing our French comrades after last night.' He nodded. 'Very good, then. We'll work according to this plan for now, but we should also consult with our respective superiors in Whitehall.'

Bill saluted again and turned to Driscoll. 'Send a coded message to Dover.'

***

Bleddyn splashed water on his face. He hadn't slept for two days. The operating tent was stifling under the summer sun. Alcohol, cresol, ether, blood, sweat and vomit all saturated the air he was trying to breathe.

God, we need relief!

The Royal Navy was supposedly only evacuating able-bodied men, but what passed for 'able-bodied' was anyone able to board a boat. The medics had been dealing with an endless stream of soldiers with broken bones, flesh wounds, festering wounds that needed dressing, burns, dislocations – including a soldier with a dislocated knee who had used his rifle as a walking stick – dehydration, gastroenteritis …

There were also a few cases of abdominal, lung and head injuries that required urgent attention. How some of these men were able to swim out to a boat or even walk along a pier, Bleddyn couldn't understand – although some of them may have been injured aboard the boats. The fishermen certainly had been.

As for the medics in Dunkirk … He did not want to think about that.

Well, one surgery down; a thousand more to go. Bleddyn stepped back into the waiting room – or whatever that tent was called – to see at least twenty casualties on stretchers before him. '*Arglwydd mawr,*' he muttered under his breath. They weren't supposed to be rescuing patients on stretchers!

All right, who first? The man taking shallow gasps of air was probably the most critical. Bleddyn ripped the bloodied shirt open. There was a penetrating chest wound caused by either a bullet or shrapnel. He palpated around the wound and listened with his stethoscope.

'Jack,' Bleddyn said to the orderly, 'get the other end of this stretcher. I'll take him in first.' There was no time to scrub properly; rubbing his hands down with disinfectant had better be enough.

'Ah, Doctor!'

Bleddyn turned. A gaunt man of about fifty had called out to him. He was probably a high-ranking officer, but Bleddyn didn't recognise the rank insignia yet.

'One of my men has been in here since this morning, and people keep passing over him,' the officer said.

'What's wrong with him?' Bleddyn asked. He realised belatedly that he had forgotten to salute, but he was too tired to care about protocol now.

'Broken arm, protruding through the skin. I just checked on him, and he's going pale and clammy.'

'He'll have to wait.'

The officer scowled. 'Now look here, Doctor, I happen to know what shock looks like—'

'I'm sure you do.' Bleddyn cut him off. 'But this man has a collapsed lung, and he could die within minutes.' He turned to the orderly and nodded. They picked up the stretcher.

'Good God, what have you doctors been doing all day?' demanded the officer.

'Been working non-stop, we have!' Bleddyn retorted over his shoulder. 'If you want to help, tell whoever's running this we need a relief team!' As an afterthought, he added, 'And medicines! And supplies! And linen!'

Bleddyn felt dreadful for ignoring the officer's request, for a man going into shock certainly needed help; but he was learning the hard way what 'triage' meant at a casualty clearing station.

Would he face disciplinary action for insubordination?

Oh, never mind – there was no time to worry about that now. He had to drain the chest cavity of his patient before it was too late.

***

1800 hours
War Office, London

Sir John Dill had just got back to his office to find Dr Jackson and Artorius waiting there. *Oh, no. What are they doing here?* He opened the door. 'Please, come through.' He slumped in his chair and cradled his head in his hands.

'Sir, is everything all right?' inquired Dr Jackson.

'I've just come out of a meeting with Churchill,' he moaned. 'By God, the man is insufferable! The Germans have bombed the stuffing out of our boys at Dunkirk, and the men on the ground think the embarkation would be safer at night. Sir Charles and I have just spent a full hour trying to persuade the Prime Minister to approve their request. Bloody hell, it was only yesterday that he … Oh, never mind.' Sir John bit his lip. He'd already blurted out too much.

'Is he worried that it might slow the rescue?' Dr Jackson asked.

'He is – but we've lost so many ships today.' He looked up. 'Anyway, what was the reason for your visit? I wasn't expecting you today.'

'It was a little impromptu, sir. Artorius has been getting impatient in the hotel. I'm unsure if this is a good idea personally, but he asked if he could witness the battle or the evacuation first-hand. Is there a vantage point from which he could observe it?'

Sir John shook his head. 'It's too dangerous.'

'Artorius knows it's dangerous, sir, but he's … prepared to take that risk.' Dr Jackson swallowed. 'Even if he cannot render assistance, he wants to learn more about modern warfare, so that he can assist with future battles.'

'Dr Jackson, I'm grateful for what Artorius has already done, but now is not the time for me to work out what role he should have next. We really need to get this retreat over and done with. Can I get back to you when it's over? Just a couple more days.'

Dr Jackson spoke to Artorius in Latin. Artorius pursed his lips and scowled, looked at Sir John, and softened his expression. He nodded and replied.

'Sir John, Artorius notes that you are exhausted, and he apologises that he insisted on seeing you at this time.'

Sir John grimaced. Exhausted wasn't the word. Still, they would have to start planning the next phase of the war as soon as possible.

He watched Dr Jackson and Artorius leave. It was damned impertinent of Artorius to make such a request. Then again, it *was* thanks to him that the BEF hadn't already collapsed.

It was an interesting notion, too. Could they make better use of him?

Was he really the legendary Arthur, here to deliver Britain from a great peril?

If they did find a role for him, how would this war unfold?

***

2010 hours
Bergues–Furnes Canal, France

'Lieutenant Langley!' the signalman shouted to Jimmy, 'Major General Alexander orders all units along the canal to withdraw immediately after sunset!'

Jimmy wiped the sweat from his forehead. 'And not before time,' he muttered, probably too softly for the signalman to hear him over the din. The constant firing of .303s inside this farmhouse was making his ears ring. So many close calls today, so many deaths …

'Lieutenant.' One of his corporals was peering over the windowsill. 'Near the tree line.'

Jimmy craned his neck. German infantrymen were moving something large into position. 'Bloody hell, a cannon! Concentrate your fire on the men operating it.'

Unfortunately, the distance and fading light thwarted their efforts. They eventually felled one man, but the Germans kept moving their cannon into position.

Then it lurched.

They've fired!

The world exploded.

***

Jimmy blinked. A white ceiling came into focus before his eyes. 'Where am I?'

A man in a doctor's coat came over. 'Lieutenant? Do you remember what happened?'

Jimmy tried to think through the haze of a pounding headache. He recalled shooting at Germans near a cannon, a lurch and a puff of smoke, an explosion, being flung backward … 'I was wounded?'

The doctor nodded. 'Apparently, you came under heavy fire.'

'How – how many more injured? Anyone killed?'

'I don't know. The man who brought you here didn't tell me any more.'

More recollections came. Jimmy had asked if everyone was all right, but he couldn't remember anyone answering. There had been a jolting sensation, pain shooting up his arm … 'Am I in a German or a British hospital?'

'This is a British casualty clearing station.' The doctor sighed. 'Alas, I fear you may have been better off if the Germans had captured you. We're out of many key supplies, and all I can really do for you is to control bleeding and hope for the best.'

'Oh well, I suppose that means I'm going home soon,' Jimmy murmured.

The doctor grimaced. 'I really wish you were, but they're … not evacuating the wounded.'

'Huh?'

'If you want to leave, you'll have to be able to walk.'

'That's all right. My legs are fine.' Jimmy tried to get up.

Whoa. The room spun around so violently he had to lie back down. His head threatened to explode.

The doctor put a hand on his shoulder. 'Perhaps not just yet.'

No, he had to go. 'But I have to, if – if I don't get away, they'll capture—'

'They're extending the evacuation, so you'll have some time to get your balance back,' the doctor assured him. 'It would be better to rest for now.'

***

2300 hours
Bastion 28, Dunkirk

'It looks as though it'll be an uneventful night, thank God,' Bill Tennant said to Major General Alexander. 'The first ships have docked and are loading smoothly.'

'And no sign of the Luftwaffe. Of course, their pilots are probably exhausted by now.' Alexander had rings under his eyes. He sipped his tea. 'Captain, a sub-lieutenant on one of the ships gave this letter to me, but you need to read it, too.'

Bill held it up to the weak light of the hurricane lamp. It was from Sir John Dill.

If all proceeds as planned, tomorrow night will be the final night we evacuate British soldiers from Dunkirk. If the remaining British rearguard does not exceed one brigade, Major General Harold Alexander is to hand command over to a brigadier, and leave on the night of the 2nd of June. Captain William Tennant and all Royal Navy staff are to depart at the same time, and must announce the end of the evacuation of the BEF by unencrypted radio transmission. Royal Navy ships plan one last rescue of French and remaining men in the British brigade on the night of the 3rd of June, embarkation to be organised by French commanders.

Bill frowned. 'That's odd. I wonder why—'

Someone cleared his throat behind Bill. It was Conway, standing near the entrance to the bastion. 'Captain Tennant,' he said, 'Major Newman of the Twelfth Casualty Clearing Station is here to see you.'

'Tell him to wait until I've finished—'

Newman stormed in without invitation. 'Captain, what was the meaning of sending us more casualties? We can't cope with the ones we already have! Men who would recover given proper attention are dropping like flies! I've run out of sulpha drugs; we're low on morphine; we've no running water; no antiseptics—'

'Now look here, Major …' Bill growled.

'Captain, perhaps I should handle this,' said Major General Alexander. He indicated a vacant chair. 'Please, Major, take a seat.'

Bill exhaled. Alexander was right. Newman may have been out of line, but the poor doctor was near the end of his tether. Hell, everybody was now – except for Alexander, whose patience never seemed to run out.

'You're commander of the BEF, sir?' Newman asked as he settled into the chair.

Alexander nodded. 'What is left of it, at least.'

'General, please …'

'Major,' Alexander said softly, 'I am not unsympathetic to your pleas, but I do not have the resources to help you. You do understand why we're not evacuating casualties, don't you?'

'I do, sir,' said Newman in a faltering voice, 'but surely you can do *something* for them? Men are dying for want of better care. Can any of the ships docking here drop off supplies?'

'It would take too long to unload ships,' Bill replied before Alexander could speak. 'The army is critically low on ammunition, but I dare not request more, because unloading it will slow the evacuation.'

Newman's bottom lip began to tremble. 'What about a hospital ship? Can't *anyone* take casualties?'

'Again, the logistics are problematic,' Alexander replied. 'We have limited time in which to dock as many vessels as possible.'

An epiphany struck Bill. 'Wait, General.' Why didn't he think of this before? 'It may not slow us down if the hospital ship comes during the day.' He turned to Newman. 'We've stopped loading men during the day because of the aerial attacks on our ships. However, if a clearly marked hospital ship docked during the day – well, surely the Luftwaffe would respect the Geneva Convention.'

Alexander's eyes widened. 'Of course! And if it arrived during the day, loading the wounded onto it won't impede the evacuation of able-bodied soldiers. Right. I'll send the request using an unencrypted telegram. That way, the Germans will intercept it, and they will know it's a humanitarian request.'

Tears glistened in the doctor's eyes. 'Thank you, gentlemen, on behalf of all those under my care!'

'Don't thank us too quickly, Major,' cautioned Bill. 'It won't arrive until after sunrise.'

Conway ushered the doctor out.

'Oh, damn it,' Bill mumbled after the doctor left. 'We forgot to ask how many patients he has.'

Alexander shrugged. 'There are probably more casualties than the ship can take, anyway. We'll just load as many as we can.'

***

2345 hours
Port of Dover

A new team had come to relieve Darcy's medics. They had brought much-needed supplies, too.

Bleddyn had never felt so depleted in all his life. His eyes itched and his head throbbed from lack of sleep. It was worse than the hunger and thirst. Nor would he ever forget what he had seen over the past couple of days. His fingers fumbled and trembled as he tried to unfasten his surgical gown. *Oh, God, can I endure the whole war like this?* He wasn't sure if he would last another week. Would he let his country down, and his family? Then there was Sophie … Well, this just proved he wasn't worthy of her. Her brother was on the front line, as her father had been in the Great War; and here he was, barely able to cope with treating those brave men who had been wounded in battle.

Darcy looked up at him from the hand-washing basin. 'Well, Kendrick, I told you it'd be a baptism of fire. You handled it well for your first time.'

'I did well?' Bleddyn asked, unable to believe it. Hell, Darcy had sworn at him when he hesitated to perform an amputation.

As though he read Bleddyn's thoughts, Darcy grinned and said, 'Oh, that amputation – don't take what I said personally, son. Every triage surgeon hesitates the first time he faces that dilemma, and needs a kick up the bum to do what's best at the time, but still not fully right. In fact, I just repeated what my superior said to me the first time I was in that predicament.'

Still not fully right. That was putting it mildly. 'I was wondering if I'd ever forgive myself.'

'For amputating, or for hesitating and trying to call a surgeon who was up to his neck with other operations?' Darcy grimaced. 'Don't dwell on it. Now that you've done it once, it'll be easier to do next time.' He stared off into space. 'Never gets easier to live with, though. The Great War was like this, and, oh God, I hoped I'd never see the likes of it again.' He looked back at Bleddyn. 'I meant what I said, Kendrick; you handled both the scalpel and the pressure better than most new recruits would have done. I'm glad to have you in my hospital.' He clapped Bleddyn on the shoulder. 'It's time we both got some rest. But first, I want to check on some of the patients on the ward.'

'I'll come and check, too.'

They ran into Martha on the way. She, too, looked burnt out, and barely acknowledged Darcy's thanks before she left for her sleeping tent.

One of the new doctors was on the ward, monitoring fewer patients than Bleddyn had expected to see there. He was still pondering this when someone called out, 'Ah, the young Welsh doctor!'

It was the officer Bleddyn had clashed with earlier. His stomach tied itself in knots.

'I'm glad to find you again,' the officer said. 'I owe you an apology for the way I spoke to you earlier. I was too concerned for the welfare of one of my men to notice how much pressure you and your colleagues were under.'

Bleddyn let go of his breath.

'It's easy for us to forget that you're responsible for every injured man who passes through this hospital, not just those we know. I do realise you're doing the best you can.' The officer extended his hand.

'No offence taken, sir,' Bleddyn replied as he shook the officer's hand. 'I was brusque as well, and I'm sorry I couldn't do anything for your man at the time. However, you're wrong about this being the best I can do. It's the best I can do under the circumstances.'

The commander returned a wry smile.

'By the way, is your man all right?' Bleddyn asked.

'He is now. After you told me to speak to whoever was in charge, I saw Vice Admiral Ramsay and let him know the medics were overwhelmed. A relief team was already on its way, although on my insistence he had some of the casualties taken to the hospital at Dover.'

So that was why the hospital had cleared so quickly.

'How about the patient with the … collapsed lung?' the officer asked.

Bleddyn pointed to the patient's bed. 'It was touch and go, but I think he'll make a full recovery.'

Darcy regarded the officer. 'You're Major General Montgomery, aren't you?'

'I am, but I'm afraid you have the advantage, Doctor.'

'Lieutenant Colonel Ronald Darcy.' The surgeon saluted. 'I was one of the medics who treated you in Palestine. I doubt you'd remember me, though; we weren't sure if you were going to pull through.' He turned to Bleddyn. 'So, Kendrick, you're already upsetting generals. They say the best doctors in the Medical Corps have no respect for authority, so it sounds like you have a promising career ahead of you.'

'Now, now,' chided Montgomery as he waved a finger at Darcy. 'We don't need you old cynics corrupting innocent young minds.' He sighed. 'Well, I'm dead on my feet, and I'd best be off to my barracks. You both look as though you could do with some rest as well. My apologies again, and thank you for all that you've done here.' He gestured around the ward.

'Well, well, well,' Darcy muttered as Montgomery left.

'Sir?'

'Montgomery shouldn't have tried to interfere with our work, but not many generals care enough about their men to enter a hospital and see how they're being treated. There, Kendrick, is a man worthy of the sword and baton on his shoulder.' He looked back at Bleddyn. 'Well, it doesn't look as though we need to check on anyone now. Let's get some rest.'

CHAPTER 17

Sunday, 2 June
0100 hours
Bray-Dunes Beach, France

Major David Strangeways held his watch up to the faint moonlight. Bloody hell, it was already Sunday morning, and he was still stuck in France! Would they get out tonight? They had better. The Germans would overrun this beach shortly after sunrise.

Death and destruction, chaos and confusion, panic and pandemonium – what David had seen these past few days would haunt him for the rest of his life. Yesterday had been the worst. Of the three hundred men in the battalion at the beginning of the campaign, less than half withdrew to the crowded beach after sunset.

Worse still, it wasn't over. What would happen if Germany tried to invade Britain? Would the army again crumble in the face of the German onslaught?

'They didn't send enough boats,' one man complained as he scanned the water.

'Actually, they did,' another replied. 'Look out there. The Germans blew this place to kingdom come.'

Wrecks of small craft littered the shallow waters, and there was at least one larger vessel farther out. Craters, corpses, vehicles and debris littered the beach. All gave testimony to the horrors of war, and the carnage of yesterday.

David shuddered and pushed the thought to the back of his mind. He had to get his men home before they faced another day of this. There were too many others waiting to be rescued from the beach here. 'Well, men, I don't think we'll be departing from here anytime soon,' he called out. 'Let's try for Dunkirk harbour.'

A wave of groans swept through the battalion. David couldn't blame them. Trudging for miles through sand was the last thing exhausted men wanted to do. However, there was another reason they needed to move. German infantrymen occasionally penetrated the front line to fire at the masses of British troops on the beach. They claimed lives every time, and usually retreated into the dark before anyone could return fire.

David and his men had been marching for less than an hour when a stranded boat caught his attention. 'Halt!' he ordered when they were close. She seemed undamaged, but where was her crew?

The barge appeared to be afloat. Perhaps she had been beached at low tide. The crew might have abandoned her when bombs were raining down around them, but why hadn't they returned? Did they not realise she was unscathed? Had they been killed?

Oh well. David had sailed pleasure yachts before; how different would a barge be? Could he operate her?

'Men, this could be our boat home,' he told them as he started to undress. 'I need to check if she's seaworthy.'

He waded out and inspected her hull from the outside. There was no serious damage above the waterline, and she was afloat, bobbing unanchored in the waves. The rudder appeared intact, too.

David climbed aboard. She had a large cabin with a carpeted dining room and plush leather sofas. This was a luxury cruise barge.

The mast, sails and rigging all seemed to be in order. He tried the rudder from aboard. It yielded.

Finally, David went below deck, just in case she had a slow leak. He had no torch handy, but he couldn't feel any pooling water as he groped around in total darkness.

He climbed back onto the deck and shouted to his men, 'I think she's fit to sail! Come aboard!'

Excited chatter rippled through the men up as they clambered onto the barge.

David found a lieutenant who knew enough about sailing to operate the wheel while he adjusted the sails. The breeze filled them, and she started to move.

The hull touched the sand beneath them. David drew his breath. Was there too much weight aboard?

The yacht rose again and drifted out into deeper water.

'We're off!' he declared.

The men cheered.

The sailing barge was slow, and the sun was well and truly up by the time they were near the White Cliffs of Dover. Those ivory cliffs protruding from the turquoise sea, symbolic of dear old England, had never looked as beautiful as they did today in the morning sun. The First Battalion of the Duke of Wellington's Regiment had escaped from that hellhole in Dunkirk, and they were back home.

Well … nearly home. David wasn't sure exactly where they were, but that didn't really matter. He just had to follow the coastline until he found a place to dock. He turned the barge west.

It wasn't long before he steered her into a large harbour with an odd assortment of naval vessels, ferries and fishing boats, and a huge commotion ashore. The sound of cheering welcomed David's ears. It felt good to be home, and it was reassuring that the British public were still behind them.

'Major,' one corporal said apprehensively, 'there are reporters with cameras there. I can see some ladies, too.' He pointed to his underclothes. 'Most of us stripped to wade out to this barge. We can't meet the public like this!'

This was indeed a problem. They needed to find some cloth, and quickly. So, what could … Oh, yes. 'Corporal, take those curtains down and bring me one of them. Wear it like a kilt. I want anyone not properly covered to get below deck until we can bring back clothes!'

***

'Eleven hours.'

'What was that?' Bill Tennant asked his signalman.

Chief Petty Officer Driscoll looked up. 'Sorry, sir – just murmuring to myself. Eleven hours until sunset, when the bombing should stop.' He sighed. 'Eleven … long … torturous … hours.'

Bill nodded. His head felt as though it was full of soaked newspaper. Luckily, not many British soldiers remained in Dunkirk – except for the wounded, and they might get some of them away soon. The Royal Navy hoped to move thousands of French soldiers tonight, but Bill would soon be out of this wretched hellhole. He just had to make it through the next eleven hours.

His eyes fell on the message he'd received last night. The Navy planned one more operation after tonight to rescue French soldiers, but they specifically wanted him to send an unencrypted transmission tonight, announcing that the BEF had been evacuated. Why was that?

Ah, of course. With luck, the Germans would interpret such a message as an end to the rescue, and the Luftwaffe would stop trying to hit the breakwaters. The ships' crews were familiar with the routine now, providing no more craft sank in the harbour and created new obstacles. If the French could send their men to the breakwaters in an orderly manner, the Royal Navy wouldn't need a presence on the ground.

BOOM! Another uncomfortably close explosion made Bill jump. Night couldn't come fast enough. He just had to make it through one more day … just one more day … just one—

'Captain Tennant!' Driscoll called out. 'I'm getting a distress call from a ship nearby. The HMHS *Paris* has been hit by a Luftwaffe bomber.'

HMHS? The hospital ship! 'Any casualties?' Bill demanded.

'I'm not sure, Captain. The engines are out, and she's requesting a tugboat. Her captain apologises, and says they'll be unable to retrieve any of the wounded.'

Seething bile trickled into Bill's stomach. Mines were indiscriminate and U-boat crews were unable to see a ship's markings, but pilots would have seen the Red Cross from the air. Besides, their transmissions had made it clear that only a hospital ship was coming. This was a war crime. The British had better win this war, if only to make the Germans pay for this.

'Very well,' Bill growled. 'Get her coordinates and call for a tugboat. Let's hope she's not taking water on too quickly, and they can get her back to England.'

Bill would also need to let Major Newman know they couldn't evacuate any of the wounded. Men who could not walk would have to surrender to the Germans, and Newman would have to make do with his dwindling supplies in the meantime. He sighed and put his face in his hands. Newman had been distraught last night, and Bill did not relish the thought of telling him this news.

***

1300 hours
War Office, London

Alan Brooke took slow, feeble steps towards Sir John's office, his weak grip on his briefcase barely enough to prevent it from dropping to the floor. The two days of rest had not restored his energy or dampened his anxiety. Yes, they had evacuated most of the British Expeditionary Force safely; but they had still suffered a loss of historic proportions. The German menace continued to loom over them, and Alan had doubts about the ability of the now weakened British Army to resist what the Third Reich was sure to attempt by autumn – the invasion of Great Britain herself.

The magnitude of the task ahead was overwhelming. Despondency set in whenever Alan thought about it. However, time was of the essence now, and this was why he was already back at the War Office. Hell, he would have been back yesterday had he not needed to see a dentist.

He knocked on the door of the Chief of the Imperial General Staff's office. Sir John called him in.

'At ease, Brookie,' Sir John told him as he saluted. 'Good to see you back at work so soon, although you still look under the weather. Please, take a seat.'

Alan obliged. 'I would have rested longer, sir, but I doubt the Germans will permit me to do so. You said you had a new assignment for me? The sooner I start the better.'

'It's good that we're of the same mind there,' said Sir John. 'Do you realise that Lord Gort has recommended you for another post and a promotion?'

Alan blinked. 'He has?' Lord Gort had made it clear that he thought Alan failed to inspire confidence, and had even threatened to replace him.

Sir John nodded. 'I know the two of you have had your differences, but Lord Gort now understands you had a better grasp of the situation than he did, and he said that you led your corps well. In fact, he's also recommended you for investiture into an order of chivalry. His Majesty has approved such awards in principle, and he will be investing commanders into the Most Honourable Order of the Bath over the coming days.'

What? 'Sir, I already have a CB ...'

Sir John shrugged. 'Well then, the next level up is Knight Commander – and in your case, it's not before time, either.'

Alan gaped. Did this mean ... did this mean he would become a *knight*? He would have been ecstatic had he not been sick with worry right now. 'But, sir, after I presided over such losses ...'

'We didn't lose because of you, Brookie.'

That was true, but as a senior commander in the British Army, Alan couldn't shake a sense of responsibility for the failures that led to this defeat. He had been calling for better training regimes these last four years, but could he have pushed harder?

Never mind the past now. It was time to get down to business. 'Anyway, Sir John, I fear that we only have weeks to do what we should have started years ago. You will appreciate that we need to go back to barracks, rearm, and prepare for an invasion.' He opened his briefcase to retrieve his notebook. 'We also need to organise training exercises, especially those that will refine coordination between the different branches of the armed services. The Germans were good at probing for weak spots, and when they found one, they wasted no time in putting their weight behind a thrust – usually with coordinated strikes from the Wehrmacht and the Luftwaffe. We need to practise until the British Army and the RAF work as one unit, not as separate divisions of the armed forces. How quickly will our industries be able to supply us with new artillery? Oh, and if they're considering new designs, we did find limitations in our artillery and tanks. Among other things …' He looked up to see a grimace on Sir John's face. 'Sir?'

Sir John sighed. 'Alas, I don't think you will care for your new post, Brookie. Mr Churchill believes we should try to halt the German invasion of France. He wants you to go back to take command of the forces that remain in central France, and to re-form the British Expeditionary Force there.'

Alan stared at Sir John. 'Please tell me you're joking!'

'The Prime Minister believes the risks associated with another European campaign are worth trying to keep France in the war.'

'But, Sir John,' Alan pleaded, 'we've lost so much artillery, and the troops are exhausted! The French command has disintegrated, and most of their remaining forces are spread along the Maginot Line and communication within their ranks has broken down, and disciplined German units are poised ready to strike south!' He paused for a breath. 'General, why did we bother with the rescue at Dunkirk if we're just going to throw our boys straight back into the fire?'

'Brookie, you're not telling me anything I haven't already said to Churchill.' Exasperation spilled out from Sir John's lips. 'There is no convincing him otherwise. I'm truly sorry, but he insists you return to re-form the British Expeditionary Force in central France. We haven't set the date yet, but it would be as soon as we can rest and rearm a division. It won't be much longer than a week, that's for sure.'

Alan fell silent. He could feel every slow, powerful, deliberate heartbeat as it radiated from the centre of his chest. They had experienced unimaginable losses over the past few weeks, yet *this*, this act of utter stupidity and recklessness, was the blackest moment of the war so far.

'Brookie,' continued Sir John, 'Mr—' The telephone rang. 'Excuse me. Don't go just yet.' He picked up the receiver. 'Hello, Chief of the Imperial General Staff speaking … Oh, hello, Stuffy, how are you? … Not bad, not bad, under the circumstances. … Artorius and Dr Jackson? They're staying at the King George the Third Hotel here in Whitehall … You do? I don't think the rooms have individual telephones, so you'll have to call the hotel reception. Is there anything else? … Good, good. … My pleasure. Goodbye.'

'"Stuffy"?' Alan asked. 'Sir Hugh Dowding?'

'Yes.' Sir John put the receiver back in place. 'He was asking about …' He frowned. 'I'm not sure how much I can tell you, Brookie.'

'Understood, sir.'

Sir John waved a hand. 'To hell with it. I suspect you'll end up with a central planning post before much longer. We've just had an "interesting" person turn up, and we're still not sure what to make of him. It was this man who pointed out that you would have been preoccupied with the evacuation, and told me we needed to bring the negotiations between King Leopold and German diplomats to Lord Gort's attention. I understand your corps dealt with it; how important was that warning?'

'Sir John, I do not exaggerate when I say that had it not been for that warning, we would have lost the BEF.'

Sir John nodded. 'The fishing vessel idea to aid beach evacuations was also partly this man's idea, although Ramsay refined it.'

'Sir,' said Alan, 'I cannot overstate how valuable his contributions have been. Is there any chance he can make Churchill see sense?'

'Oh, I very much doubt that. Churchill thinks he's mad.'

'What the blazes?' Alan spluttered. 'Why, for the love of God, would he think that?'

Sir John scratched the back of his ear as he avoided Alan's gaze. 'Well … to cut a long story short, this man claims to be King Arthur returned from Avalon. Well, something to that effect.'

Alan stared. He blinked. 'You can't be serious?'

Sir John pressed his lips together hard and nodded. 'The weirdest thing is, both medical and linguistic experts are convinced he's real. Anyhow, he's offered to help. We will need to filter any such advice he gives through competent officers, of course, because he can be astoundingly ignorant of modern technology, society and warfare. Still, he has a razor-sharp mind that can put things together quickly, and he's already proven his worth.'

Blood pounded through Alan's temples. The Prime Minister was sending men back to France to face certain defeat, and the War Office was taking advice from someone who thought he was King Arthur … This couldn't be real. It was all just a bad dream, surely.

'We need to keep quiet about this, of course,' Sir John cautioned. 'I have no idea what would happen if the public ever caught wind of it, and I don't want to find out.'

'Is there … anything more I should know, General?'

Sir John shook his head. 'I don't think there's much more we need to discuss, Brookie; but as I was saying before the telephone rang, Mr Anthony Eden wishes to see you in Whitehall when you leave here. It's about this deployment back into France.'

'Thank you, sir.' Alan stood up, saluted, and left. He was going to let the Secretary of State for War know precisely what he thought of his new mission.

***

1500 hours
Doncaster Railway Station

Sophie's mother stopped the car. 'Darling, I'm so sorry ...'

'There's not much anyone can do about it,' Sophie said. 'I need to clear out my dormitory, and my office.'

'What will you do now?'

'Register with the Labour Exchange, perhaps join the Auxiliary Territorial Services or the Mechanised Transport Corps.' She looked at her mother. 'I can type and I know shorthand. I can also drive.'

Her mother raised her eyebrows. 'Somehow, I don't think your father would like the idea of you changing car tyres and oil.'

'Are you saying I shouldn't?'

'Not at all. I hope, though, that you're able to find an assignment that lets you stay in England. Your brother is already on the front line ...'

'With the retreat from France, England may become the front line,' Sophie replied.

Her mother sighed. 'That is true.'

Her mother followed her into the station.

They met Mr Percy near the ticket office. He turned to them. 'Mrs Edwardson, Sophie, how are you?'

'Well, thank you,' Sophie's mother replied. 'And you?'

'Very well today, very well indeed.' His grin stretched from ear to ear. 'After that miracle at Dunkirk, we all have much to give thanks for.'

Miracle. Sophie sighed. She had been elated when the miracle was first announced, but it didn't take long for her to realise that this was not a victory at all.

Mr Percy's grin slipped a little. 'I must say, you don't appear to share the sentiment.'

'When you come from a military family, you learn to see through such propaganda,' Sophie's mother replied. 'The evacuation means our forces haven't been annihilated, but we've well and truly lost this battle. It's the worst defeat in our history.'

The grin fell completely from his face. 'Oh, good grief, you're right.' He shrugged. 'Still, it could have been much worse. "He who fights and runs away may turn and fight another day" – Cicero, wasn't it?'

'Tacitus – and we'd better hope the next battle turns out differently,' Sophie replied.

'I'm sure it will,' Mr Percy said. 'Are you going back to Cambridge?'

Sophie nodded. She would eventually have to tell people her programme was finished, but she didn't want to do so today.

'Alas, I'm going to Edinburgh. I'm not sure when I will see you next, but I wish you a pleasant journey.'

It was another hour before the train to Cambridge pulled into the station. As it slowed down, Sophie's mother reminded her, 'Remember to call when you arrive.'

'I will.' Sophie stood. 'Oh, and if I receive any post, will you let me know?'

Her mother got to her feet, too. 'I can, but you're only going to be away for a couple of days – were you expecting any … Oh, of course.' She smiled. 'You're waiting for a reply from Bleddyn, aren't you?'

'I wrote to him last Friday, but I haven't heard back from him yet.' Sophie hesitated. 'It is rather a long time now …'

'Darling, don't worry. Men take ages to write. Besides, he may be tied up with this Dunkirk business.'

'Really?' Sophie asked. 'He should only have just started in Wiltshire. Why do you think he might be in Dunkirk?'

'He won't be in Dunkirk – but there may be medical teams in Dover treating men as they come back to England. If he's in Dover, he may not have received your letter yet. It's too soon for you to worry about his inattentiveness.' She hugged Sophie. 'Your degree may be a disappointment, but let's pray for a happy outcome here.'

The carriage was full to overflowing, but Sophie found a seat and retreated deep into her thoughts, scarcely aware of the noise and bustle around her.

What was Artorius doing? Perhaps he hadn't come too late to save them – but would he be able to?

Should she contact the Security Service again and ask if they wanted a translator to work with him?

No, probably not. There would be no shortage of classics scholars working for them. If they needed her, they would have already called.

***

1600 hours
King George III Hotel, Whitehall, London

Artorius climbed the stairs until he reached the first level. Was this the appropriate wing and level? His room was on the right near the stairs, but it would pay to check. He held up the key and examined the metal plate attached to it. The figures did not match.

Oh, how silly of me. He turned the tag attached to the key around. *Now* they matched. Curse this new numbering system. Kenneth Jackson was adamant that these 'Hindu–Arabic' symbols were easier to work with than Roman numerals, but to someone unfamiliar with them …

He inserted the key in the door and turned it. Before he entered, a bell rang behind him. It came from the direction of the *lift*, that mobile platform that took people from floor to floor, if they knew how to operate it.

Kenneth Jackson stepped out. He looked at Artorius, sighed, and then scowled.

He followed Artorius into the room and shut the door behind them. 'Where were you?' he demanded.

'I have barely left this room, never mind this villa, since I arrived here. I tire of the constraint. Is it any surprise that I would want to explore this new world a little more?'

'Artorius, you cannot just wander off whenever you choose!'

'I used to command armies,' Artorius stated. 'I am unaccustomed to taking orders from a translator.'

'Artorius, it is for your own safety. You do not speak the language, and you do not know how our technology works … For example, suppose you were hit by an automobile?'

Did people really think he was such an imbecile that he could not work these problems out? 'I have already deduced the conditions under which vehicles stop for pedestrians by observing when and where pedestrians cross the roads. As it is, all I did was visit the manicured garden nearby. The bustle, the traffic, the stench of the smoke from the rock oil your countless horseless carriages burn – I cannot say I like modern Londinium.'

Kenneth sighed. 'You do not speak English. People will know you are a foreigner in a time of war, and they may think you are a spy.'

Artorius laughed.

'What is funny?'

'Kenneth Jackson, an effective spy needs to be able to speak the language of the people he infiltrates. People may mistake me for a foreigner, but only an idiot would think I could be a spy.'

'Well … what you say is true … but panicked crowds are not known for their intelligence. There are people who will distrust anyone they believe is a foreigner, so you could arouse unwarranted suspicion.'

Artorius sighed and collapsed onto the bed. Kenneth did have a good point there, and he should have realised it.

Kenneth cleared his throat. 'I have received a message. Sir Hugh Dowding wishes to meet you. He has requested our presence tomorrow night.'

'Who is he?' Artorius asked.

'He is a … legatus of our flying forces.'

Artorius straightened up. *Flying forces!* What did the legatus of the flying forces have in mind for him? 'Does this mean I will be working with flying machines?'

Kenneth shrugged. 'I do not know what he has in mind. He has invited us to dinner; I am sure we will learn more then. Do you remember what I taught you about knives and forks, and what to eat and not eat with your hands? I think it will be in a private dining room, but we should still revise modern dining decorum …'

Artorius barely heard him. This was the best news he had heard since his awakening. *Flying machines.*

***

Bill Tennant stood on the breakwater and watched the *St Helier* pull away. It was over. That ferry contained the last of the able-bodied British soldiers.

'Well, sir, that's it,' murmured Clouston. 'Only Major General Alexander left.'

'And the wounded,' Bill murmured.

Clouston sighed. 'We can't save 'em all, sir. We've sent many thousands back.'

Bill nodded.

He and Clouston went back to Bastion 28, where Alexander and Conway waited with General Fagalde of the French Army, and Chief Petty Officer Driscoll and Able Seaman Collins of the Royal Navy. There were still thousands of French troops in Dunkirk, but it was up to General Fagalde to manage the last night of the evacuation.

As instructed, Bill had Driscoll send an unencrypted radio transmission in Morse code to Dover Command: 'BEF evacuated'. He then bid goodbye to General Fagalde.

'And the Royal Navy will be back tomorrow evening?' Fagalde asked.

'We will be monitoring your transmissions, and if your people are still holding out, then yes, the Royal Navy will return tomorrow,' Bill reassured him. 'When our ships come, make sure your men are ready to step aboard without delay. We sent an unencrypted message to ensure the Germans know the British have left. We hope they will interpret such a message as the end of the rescue and stop trying to bomb that breakwater.'

'Sir,' said Clouston, 'I'd like to return tomorrow night on one of the rescue boats.'

Bill gaped at him. The man hadn't even slept for five days, keeping order on the breakwater the whole time. 'Is there no limit to your energy, man?'

'I'll have all the time in the world to rest when I'm dead, sir. I grew up in Montréal, and I speak French, so I might be useful tomorrow night.'

Bill shook his head. 'Who to send will be Ramsay's call, not mine, but you can let them know when we return to Dover. Damn it, Clouston, you're a dedicated man.'

There was one ship still in French waters. She was offshore, fully loaded, and awaiting Bill and Alexander.

The major general came out of a storeroom with a megaphone under his arm.

'What's that for, General?' Bill asked.

'Captain Tennant, I was hoping to impose on you one last time. Some of our men could be stuck behind enemy lines, but they might try to make their way to the beaches under the cover of darkness. Could we do one last patrol?'

Bill rubbed the front of his temples. His eyes burned for lack of sleep, he could barely think straight, and his abused body threatened to cave in at any moment.

'Captain, I know it's quite a demand,' Alexander said. 'The truth is, after we promised Major Newman a hospital ship, and it never arrived … well, we're leaving too many men behind as it is, and it won't rest easily on my conscience. I know it sounds silly, but if there's any chance we can rescue even one man stuck on the beaches … well, I have to try.'

The bags under Alexander's eyes betrayed his torturous fatigue — yet he was determined to do this. Bill nodded. 'As you wish, sir.' He understood what Alexander hadn't said, and he felt the same way. 'There are still a couple of fishing boats off the northern beach. They'll find our boys if any are stuck there, but there may be men trapped in other parts of the harbour front, or perhaps just south of here.'

As Collins took the launch through the harbour and past the beaches, Alexander bellowed, '*Is anybody there?*' through the megaphone over and over again. They listened during the major general's pauses, and Bill peered through his binoculars. No reply came from British or French troops, although some Germans returned fire, and some of it came too close for comfort.

Bullets from one such burst ricocheted off the bow, causing everyone to hit the deck.

'This is getting dangerous,' Alexander declared. 'I don't think we'll be able to rescue any more men this way. Take us to the ship whenever you wish, Captain.'

'Collins, we're done here,' Bill told his able seaman.

'Yes, sir.'

Germans were firing machine guns from the beaches at the destroyer. There was little chance of being hit at this distance, but Collins took them to the far side of the ship nonetheless. Petty officers relayed messages as soon as everyone was aboard, and the engines began to rumble within two minutes.

Exhausted though he was, Bill stood on the deck and watched the French beach as the ship began to pull away. His bottom lip and hands began to tremble under the weight bearing down on his heart and soul. It was much the same after Jutland; he had held it together throughout the battle, but after the danger passed, he went to pieces. His only chance to avoid making a spectacle of himself was to find a bunk before anyone could speak to him.

These post-battle nerves were irrational, really. Although Bill could not help but fixate on the dead and the wounded, he also knew he had evacuated far more men than anyone had initially thought possible. Hundreds of thousands of men owed their escape to Bill and his men.

The task had almost broken them all, but Operation Dynamo had been an outstanding success.

CHAPTER 18

Tuesday, 4 June
0700 hours
12th Casualty Clearing Station, Dunkirk

'Wassat?' Jimmy Langley awoke to rumbling. Was it thunder? No …
vehicles. 'More wounded?'

'I think it's the Germans,' the doctor whispered.

Germans. This was it. Jimmy would have left two days ago had the
Luftwaffe not bombed a hospital ship. If the Germans were prepared to
attack hospital ships, were they going to take prisoners?

A heavily built German officer stepped through the door, followed
by three subordinates. All of them bore rifles.

Jimmy's heart forced its way up his throat and into his mouth. *Oh,
God, is this the end?*

The medic stepped forward and spoke, trembling hands raised in
front of him. 'D-do you speak Eng-English?' he asked.

'A little,' the officer replied in a deep voice.

The doctor turned slowly and deliberately, and pointed at his Red
Cross armband. 'I am Ma-Major Philip Newman, medic. There are only
medics, casualties and a ch-chaplain here.' His voice went hoarse as he
asked, 'Do you – do you respect the Geneva Convention?'

Cold sweat oozed from the pores of Jimmy's throbbing head.

The German looked at him, and then looked around the room. He lowered his rifle and signalled to his subordinates to do the same.

The entire room exhaled with relief.

'I see these men are … what is it you say … "in a bad way", but we cannot move injured prisoners of war now,' the officer explained. 'Do you need food? Water? Medicines?'

'We need all of it,' Newman replied. He pointed to Jimmy. 'For example, this man needs surgery on his arm, but I cannot even clean and dress his wounds. Please, in the name of all that is good and merciful, we need help.'

The officer nodded. 'I will see what I can arrange.'

***

0900 hours
Outskirts of Dunkirk

Erwin sipped his coffee as he listened to the short-wave radio. The crackling voice announced that the German flag had been hoisted in Dunkirk. It heralded the end of the fighting and a German victory, but something deep inside Erwin shifted uncomfortably at this news. The 'German' flag now bore the emblem of the *Nationalsozialistische Deutsche Arbeiterpartei*. They had performed a miracle in the way they had rebuilt the German nation after its collapse during the Great Depression, but to define all of Germany by one political party left little room for individuality – and some things about the NSDAP left lingering doubts in Erwin's mind.

The flag over Dunkirk … a victory, but not a total one. The Wehrmacht may have won this battle, but they had squandered an opportunity to end the war. That halt order had been a mistake. Had they continued to drive two weeks ago, they would have smashed through disordered British lines and taken hundreds of thousands of prisoners, not just tens of thousands.

Oh well. At least Erwin had forced Molinié to surrender. Why had that idiot barricaded himself in Lille? One risky manoeuvre and a siege, and he captured forty thousand prisoners of war – the strongest blow in those last days of the campaign.

The sound of someone clearing their throat broke Erwin's thoughts. He turned around to see Hoffmann standing at attention.

'*Generalmajor*, we have found a Jew among the captured rearguard French soldiers. You told me you wished to be notified about Jewish prisoners of war.'

Erwin nodded. 'Take me to where you are holding him.'

'I had the men bring him here, sir.'

Erwin stepped outside the communications tent. Hoffmann gestured to two of his men, who dragged a French prisoner towards them. Damn. He could not prevent subordinates from witnessing what Erwin planned to do next. Oh, well. As it was, the men needed to know how he wanted to deal with Jewish prisoners in the wake of the Führer's well-publicised comments.

The Jew's face was bruised and bloodied. They dropped him at Erwin's feet. One of them spat on him as he lay face down on the ground.

'That's enough,' said Erwin.

'But, sir, he's only—'

'I said that's enough.'

The private saluted and backed away.

The French soldier lay on the ground, panting.

'Hoffmann,' Erwin asked, 'how did you know he was a Jew?'

Hoffmann handed him some papers, a dog tag and a Star of David pendant.

Erwin examined them. The man's papers identified him as a Jew, but the dog tag did not list a religion, and the surname 'Pascal' didn't sound *too* distinctly Jewish.

Pascal struggled to prop himself up on trembling arms.

Erwin knelt and offered him some water from his can.

'What is the *Generalmajor* doing?' whispered one private. 'He doesn't intend to spare this worthless Yid, does he?'

'Hold your tongue, Private!' Hoffmann hissed.

Erwin made eye contact with the prisoner. 'Pascal, the Führer has made it clear he does not want us to take Jews as prisoners of war, but to shoot them on capture instead,' he said in French.

Pascal stiffened. The water-can slid from his fingers.

Erwin threw the Star of David aside and scrunched up the identity papers. 'Therefore, it is best for you to pretend these were lost, and that you are a Catholic, like most of your countrymen. Now, remember, the food in a prisoner of war camp will not be kosher. It would be unwise to raise suspicion, though.'

Pascal nodded and cast his eyes down. '*Je comprends,*' he whispered. '*Merci.*'

Erwin picked up his water-can and stood. 'Put him with the other prisoners. You are not to tell anybody he is Jewish, and you will treat him the way you would expect to be treated if you were a captive.'

'But, sir—'

'Private, did you not understand my orders?'

The private who tried to argue shut his mouth and saluted. He and his compatriot hauled Pascal to his feet. The Jew was unsteady, and the privates had to support him as they took him to the makeshift prison camp.

Erwin looked at Hoffmann. 'And that, Captain, is how I want Jewish captives to be treated.'

Hoffmann pressed his lips together and clasped his hands behind his back. 'With respect, sir, the orders not to take Jewish prisoners came from higher up, and the men know it.'

'Technically, I haven't received orders,' Erwin replied. 'We only have the Führer's supposed wishes from the wireless.'

'And if formal orders come through?' Hoffmann asked. 'Would you disobey them, and insist that we disobey them, too?'

'Yes, Hoffmann, I would,' Erwin replied. 'You see, if I had allowed the men to kill that Jew, then each of us would have to stand before God on the Day of Judgement and explain why we murdered a man in cold blood. I doubt He will accept the excuse that we did so because the laws of our country demanded it. The laws of man can be flawed, as we know all too well. Even the Son of God died because of the laws of man.'

'Do you think God cares much for the people who killed His son, sir?' Hoffmann asked.

'That same son begged the Father from the cross itself to forgive His tormentors, Hoffmann.'

Hoffmann lowered his eyes. 'You make a good point, sir.' He looked up, hesitated, and asked, 'Even so, are you not worried about the consequences in this life if the Führer finds out?'

Erwin shook his head. 'Not really. I've just been awarded the Knight's Cross for capturing Molinié and his corps. With this and a *Pour le Mérite* from the Great War, I am now one of Germany's most decorated soldiers.' He smiled. 'Some people higher up may not approve of my act of mercy, but after what I have achieved, I am confident they will overlook it.'

'Yes, sir. That is all.'

'Very well. Dismissed.'

Hoffmann saluted and left.

Erwin took a deep breath. Erwin had been telling the truth when he said he didn't fear the consequences of his superiors finding out, but that the Führer's announcement on the radio had been part of a disturbing trend.

There was no doubt the Führer was a great leader. Germany's redevelopment under his leadership was testimony to that. Nor was there any doubt that this war was necessary to reclaim what France and Britain had taken from them with the Treaty of Versailles.

But some of the NSDAP's anti-Jewish and anti-Romani statements were nothing short of hysterical. It was the same for the denigration of the 'Rhineland Bastards'. Personally, Erwin couldn't understand why German women would ... have children ... with Negroes, but the rhetoric about the 'contamination of the Aryan race with Negro blood' was going too far. And as for the notion that the 'negrification' of

Germany was a Jewish/French conspiracy to weaken the superior Aryan race … Erwin shook his head. Utterly ridiculous.

Yet this rhetoric intensified as each year passed. Where was it going to end? They had removed prominent Jews from public offices and universities. The *Kristallnacht* had been a particularly worrisome event. There had even been rumours that they were sterilising part-Negro children and euthanising the disabled – although Erwin was sure these rumours weren't true.

Pray to God they weren't true …

'*Generalmajor* Rommel!'

The signalman interrupted Erwin's thoughts. He turned and nodded to the man as he stood to attention.

'General von Rundstedt has requested that all officers above the rank of colonel report to his new headquarters at 1100 hours.'

This was probably about the next campaign. Paris would be their next target, and they would need to start within the next two days. Erwin pushed aside his doubts about the Nazi Party for the time being. It was time to focus on the task ahead, and the betterment of the German nation.

***

1500 hours
Office of the Chief of the Imperial General Staff
War Office, London

'*Tell me he didn't do that!* Sir Charles leapt to his feet. 'That rescue cost us four thousand sailors and dozens of craft! By God, we lost six destroyers! And you're telling me, after all that, you're sending men back into France?'

'I hear what you're saying,' Sir John Dill replied, 'and believe me, I've already begged Mr Churchill not to do this. He *insists* we try to halt the German invasion of France. And like you, I fear we could see an encore to the Dunkirk evacuation.'

'Don't get your hopes up,' the Admiral of the Fleet snarled. 'We don't have the men or the ships for it.'

'And we can't afford to lose more pilots before they turn on Britain,' added Sir Hugh.

Sir Cyril nodded.

'Then please make that known to our Prime Minister,' pleaded Sir John. 'I *cannot* make him see sense on this issue.'

'The Prime Minister's an idiot!' exclaimed Sir Charles.

'There is a reason for this madness, though,' Sir John said. 'Mr Churchill hopes the French will send their naval fleet to British ports before the Germans overrun them. It won't be easy to convince them to do so if we abandon them now. Would you rather such a large fleet remain grounded, or worse still, fall into German hands?'

Sir Charles turned, looked at him and sighed. 'Yes … yes, that is true. Even so, we're gambling on the French government doing the sensible thing with their naval fleet as they crumble.' He resumed staring off into space.

At least Sir Charles was calming down now.

'Are you sure there is no hope of stalling the Germans in France?' Sir Cyril asked.

Sir John shook his head. 'It would take a miracle. France will fall within two months, and then the Germans will turn their attention to Great Britain. It will be harder, of course, for they'll need to make an amphibious landing.'

'They made an amphibious landing in Norway,' Sir Charles reminded him. 'And if we don't recover some of your artillery from southern France, your men could be shooting at panzers with .303s.'

'That is not a prospect I look forward to,' agreed Sir John. 'We must continue to push our case with Churchill, but never mind about that now. I invited you three gentlemen here for a drink. The British Army owes around two hundred thousand lives to the Royal Navy and the Royal Air Force.' He unstopped a decanter of whisky and filled four small glasses. 'I hope this Glenfarclas is a good drop. Aged twenty-five years in oak. You'd probably know more about Scottish whisky than I do, Stuffy.'

Sir Hugh shrugged. 'I'm more of a Dalmore man myself, but a twenty-five-year-old Glenfarclas should still be fine. Mind you, it isn't me you should be toasting. Keith and all the boys under his command who flew to and from Dunkirk every day are the ones who made the sacrifice. Keith sends his apologies, by the way. He was too tired to come.'

'I also invited Tennant and Ramsay, but they declined,' Sir John said.

'I'm not surprised,' Sir Charles told him. 'They had trouble waking Bill when he got back to Dover yesterday morning. He hadn't slept for days.'

'It wasn't just that he was tired, actually.' Sir John dropped his gaze. 'It turns out one of the commanders under his command – a man who'd been helping to load soldiers in Dunkirk – went back on the night of the third. Canadian chap who knew French, it seems, and he thought he'd be useful in that final evacuation of French troops. We know from another boat that they were attacked by Stukas and sunk. He ordered the other boat to proceed to Dunkirk, but when they came back … well, they couldn't find any trace of the sinking vessel.'

'Oh, good God.' Sir Charles stared at him. 'I heard about an RAF rescue boat being hit with our boys on it, but I didn't realise one of them had been serving directly under Tennant.'

'It's upset Tennant greatly,' added Sir John. 'Apparently, his last words to Tennant were that he'd have plenty of time to rest when he was dead. And now …'

'He's *missing*,' said Sir Charles. 'Let's pray the Germans rescued them, and he's now a prisoner of war.'

A morbid silence hung in the air.

Sir John raised his glass. 'Well, let's propose a toast to all the men who risked life and limb to rescue the British Expeditionary Force.'

Sir Charles was slow to return to the table and pick up his glass. 'And to those who did not return. May their sacrifices not be in vain.'

Each man raised his glass and sipped.

'Hmmm,' murmured Sir Hugh. 'Not bad, not bad at all. There's one man we forgot to toast, though: Artorius. Legend claims King Arthur will return to deliver Britain from great peril, and Artorius has actually done that.'

'Yes and no,' growled Sir Charles. 'He's saved us once, but he hasn't delivered us from peril. All we've gained is a little more time. About two months, maybe three.'

'It will be a two-pronged assault,' added Sir Cyril. 'Germany will try to weaken us using a naval blockade, and they'll step up their attacks on shipping. They used their air force to great effect in Dunkirk, and they'll do the same here.' He looked out of the window. 'So far, the only civilians to see the war directly have been merchant sailors and the fishermen of southern England; but I fear that when the bombs start falling on English soil, it will be total war, unlike anything in living memory.'

Sir Charles added in a serene tone, 'It's a lovely day outside, you know.'

Where was the Admiral of the Fleet going with this comment? 'Well, yes,' agreed Sir John, 'I suppose it is ...'

'Did you realise the centre of a tropical storm – a hurricane or a cyclone – is also calm? There was a case in Australia at the turn of the century, where a pearl-fishing vessel dropped anchor and harvested oysters one sultry day. The captain checked the barometer, and the pressure had dropped to less than nine hundred bars – the lowest barometric pressure ever observed at sea level. The weather was hot and still, but he knew precisely what it meant: a cyclone had formed around them while they were fishing. He was in the eye of the most powerful storm mankind has ever seen.' Sir Charles put his glass down and stared at it intently. 'It's a fitting metaphor. Belgium and the Netherlands have fallen; Norway's making its last stand; Hitler has a foothold in northern France; Spain and Italy are likely to join Germany. A cyclone is sweeping through Europe, gentlemen, and our island sits right in the eye.'

A clock chimed in the adjacent room.

Sir Hugh took another sip and put his glass down. 'Then we'd better get ready for it. Gentlemen, have any of you given further consideration to the idea Mr Strachey and Dr Jackson proposed?'

'To … Oh, God!' Sir John shook his head. 'Artorius was getting impatient and wants to do more for the war – I was meant to get back to him by now. As it is, I think he would be more valuable as a tactician, but we'll need a good translator to work with him.'

'Dr Jackson has already recommended someone, and she'll be easy to find,' said Sir Hugh.

Sir John frowned. 'She?'

'Her name was in that file you procured from Mr Churchill,' Sir Hugh told him. 'Artorius first appeared at an RAF training airfield near Doncaster. Now, it so happens that I served alongside their base commander, George Edwardson, in the Great War. We were both in Number 16 Squadron of the Royal Flying Corps, as it was then. George was the grandson or the great-grandson of a viscount or a baron – I can't remember the details – and he was rather toffee-nosed about it. He went back to his home near Doncaster to manage an inheritance. It was because he tied himself down to one region that he hasn't risen above the rank of wing commander, despite an unbroken service record.' Sir Hugh waved his left hand dismissively. 'Well, that and the fact that he doesn't have much between the ears. Anyhow, he called on his classics-educated daughter to translate when they first found Artorius. I had dinner with Artorius and Dr Jackson the night before last, and it transpired that young Miss Edwardson is fluent in Latin. She also has some familiarity with his particular dialect.'

Sir John scratched his chin. 'How is she familiar with his dialect?'

'She was researching Latin in the British Isles during Roman rule, or something like that,' Sir Hugh explained. 'She's probably the best qualified translator in the country. Nor would it be difficult for me to track down the daughter of one of our officers.'

The others nodded.

'Where do you want to place Artorius?' asked Sir Charles.

'The best location would be a place where all three branches of the armed services could work with him. I was considering posting him at Bourneford airbase in Wiltshire.'

'Ah, yes, Wiltshire … that's close to V Corps barracks,' Sir John observed.

'Not too far from Portland and Portsmouth naval bases, either,' added Sir Charles.

Sir John nodded. 'You've certainly thought it through, Stuffy. Yes, it's a good place to put such a cryptographer. And of course, if *our* experiences are anything to go by, it would be sensible for the commanders in those bases to brief him on operations.'

'Do you think it would be better to keep Artorius here and send Jackson to the field, so that we may be able to keep Artorius closer to us?' Sir Cyril asked.

'No,' replied Sir John. 'I think Artorius will go doolally if we confine him to an office in London. Sir Hugh's idea is better.'

'In addition to that, he needs to learn first-hand about twentieth-century technology, and how it's changed the nature of warfare,' Sir Hugh added. 'He was already trying to plan for an aerial assault when I spoke to him last night. Some of his suggestions were logical, but he couldn't understand the need for large landing fields, or why a bomb crater can be dangerous for planes. He'd assumed they got airborne by flapping their wings like birds.'

Sir John's attempt to suppress a laugh ended in a snort. 'Yes, I know what you mean. However, do you think this young lady – Miss Edwardson – would agree to work for us? Bear in mind she will be privy to classified information, and she could be placed in danger.'

'We can ask,' replied Sir Hugh. 'If Miss Edwardson is willing to help, are we in agreement that we should send Artorius to RAF Bourneford?'

'I like the idea,' Sir John told him.

Sir Cyril nodded. 'Go with it, Stuffy.'

'By God, this is completely insane,' muttered Sir Charles. 'Our sovereignty is at stake, and we're planning to seek counsel from a man who believes he's King Arthur.' He drained his glass. 'Right. Count me in.'

1800 hours
Girton College, Cambridge

Sophie stopped in the doorway to the dining hall. It struck her that this would be her last dinner at Girton College. A chapter of her life was about to close, and unless they reinstated her scholarship after the war, it would close for good.

The strange thing was, she had learnt more about Vulgar Latin in late Roman Britain from Artorius than she would from all the stone relief carvings and fragments of parchment she could ever hope to find – yet she would never be allowed to use this information.

For that matter, where was Artorius now? What plans did the cryptographers have for him?

It had been the most tumultuous month of Sophie's life: the loss of her scholarship, British defeats in the war, meeting Artorius, meeting Bleddyn, being stabbed and hospitalised, and the news of the Dunkirk evacuation. Her mood had seesawed from despondency to ecstasy and back again.

Sophie was not the only resident whose studies had been terminated because of the war, and the dining hall was quieter than it had been only a month ago. Most girls were sitting near the wireless. People all but slept beside it these days to avoid missing an update about the war.

The BBC was broadcasting a commentary on the now complete Dunkirk evacuation. All British news outlets had spent the last few days portraying this evacuation as a victory. The press had been ecstatic about a miracle, but in reality it was a terrible defeat that could have been much worse. Nor had anyone reported the number of lives lost. It was only a matter of days before thousands of families across Britain, perhaps tens of thousands, would receive devastating news.

Thoughts like this just added to Sophie's despondent emotional state. Who was she to bemoan the loss of her dreams and aspirations when others were losing their lives, fighting to protect the freedoms she enjoyed?

There was but one course of action for her to take. She must do her part for the war effort.

She turned her attention back to the wireless. Now that most of the soldiers had cleared from Dover, reporters were interviewing anyone connected to the operation, from fishermen involved in the rescue to bus and train drivers. It was time for the BBC to stop trying to paint this evacuation as a victory, and look towards the next phase of the war. Nevertheless, Sophie did hear in passing about a medical team from Wiltshire that was 'tirelessly working, day and night, tending to injured heroes' and about the 'countless lives' they had saved. Was Bleddyn part of that team? If so, her mother was right. He wouldn't have received her letter yet.

The newsreader then announced that they would play an excerpt of the Prime Minister's speech to the House of Commons.

'*When Napoleon lay at Boulogne for a year with his flat-bottomed boats and his Grand Army, he was told by someone, "There are bitter weeds in England". There are certainly a great many more of them since the British Expeditionary Force returned.*'

The Germans had already cut down those bitter weeds once to clear a path to France.

'*Sir, I have, myself, full confidence that if all do their duty, if nothing is neglected, and if the best arrangements are made, we shall prove ourselves once again able to defend our island home, to ride out the storm of war, and to outlive the menace of tyranny … if necessary, for years; if necessary, alone.*'

That comment was a slight to soldiers from the dominions and colonies.

'*At any rate, that is what we are going to try to do. That is the resolve of His Majesty's Government — every man of them. That is the will of Parliament and the nation. The British Empire and the French Republic, linked together in their cause and in their need, will defend to the death their native soil, aiding each other like good comrades to the utmost of their strength.*'

Sophie shook her head in disbelief. There was no saving France now – the Germans had a secure foothold behind the Maginot Line.

'*We shall go on to the end. We shall fight in France; we shall fight on the seas and oceans; we shall fight with growing confidence and growing strength in the air!'*

The hair on the back of her neck prickled at Churchill's rising words.

'We shall defend our island, whatever the cost may be. We shall fight on the beaches; we shall fight on the landing grounds; we shall fight in the fields, and in the streets. We shall fight in the hills; we shall NEVER surrender!'

The background chatter in the dining hall increased and several girls applauded this proclamation. By the time the noise had decreased and Sophie could hear the radio again, she only caught the end of the final sentence:

'… were subjugated and starving, then our Empire beyond the seas, armed and guarded by the British fleet, would carry on the struggle, until, in God's good time, the New World, with all its power and might, steps forth to the rescue and the liberation of the Old.'

The 'New World' was almost certainly a reference to the United States, and again ignored the fact that Canada was already fighting with Britain. Unfortunately, America's experiences in the Great War had fuelled an isolationist movement. Roosevelt didn't have the public support for another European war.

For what it was worth, Churchill's orations were raising morale. Sophie hoped someone else was handling the strategic side of things, and just using Churchill as a rousing figurehead. Everyone seemed to have forgotten about his role in the Gallipoli campaign during the Great War. How did Bleddyn feel about that, and the man whose disastrous plan brought about the death of his father?

Sophie was halfway through her dinner when the college mistress approached her. 'Miss Edwardson, there's a telephone call for you. Air Chief Marshal Sir Hugh Dowding wishes to speak to you.'

A cold knot formed in Sophie's stomach. Her father's superiors had never contacted her before. Had something happened to him? She may not have been on good terms with him, but blood is thicker than water.

She followed the college mistress back to her office. The telephone was a new and uncommon model, with a receiver and a mouthpiece built into the one handset. Sophie picked it up, but had to think which way to hold it, more accustomed as she was to the candlestick design. The mouthpiece was probably the end with the cord attached, so she put this part to her mouth and the other end to her ear. 'Hello?' she asked timidly. 'Sir Hugh?'

'Hello, am I speaking to Miss Sophie Edwardson?'

'You are, sir.'

'Miss Edwardson, are you alone at present?'

'The college mistress was here a moment ago, but she's left to give me privacy.'

'Good,' said the Air Chief Marshal. 'I'm calling in relation to a bizarre incident that occurred about two weeks ago. I presume you know what I am talking about, though I ask you to be circumspect about what you say aloud over the telephone. Spies could be tapping the lines.'

So, that's what it was about. Sophie let her breath out. 'Was there any more you needed to know, sir? I was under the impression someone else had taken control of that incident.'

'The man you spoke to has offered to help us, and after considering his involvement in certain recent events, we will take him up on his offer. I wondered if you would like to become a signaller or driver in the Auxiliary Territorial Service in Wiltshire. At least, this will be your official job description. We actually need you to continue working in the same capacity as before.'

Involvement in recent events? Did this have anything to do with Dunkirk? … And Sir Hugh wanted Sophie as *a translator for Artorius?* The gravity of it dawned on her, and she could barely contain her excitement – but it also left her perplexed. 'Sir, I'd be willing to help – but surely … Well, I'm rather surprised – I mean, don't you have other people who …' – she caught herself just in time – '… have the required skills, as well as the appropriate level of security clearance?'

'You've been recommended for your specialist knowledge on this topic.'

Ah, Artorius's dialect must have been causing some confusion with other translators. 'In that case, Sir Hugh, I'd love to help!'

'Excellent. Are you able to come to my headquarters in Bentley

Priory? We can talk a little more about it here. Understand that you will be privy to some confidential material if you take this job, so I cannot discuss this any more until you've signed the Official Secrets Act.'

'I can come tomorrow, sir.' Sophie took out her pen and jotted down his instructions for travelling to Bentley Priory. She now appreciated the practicality of the one-handset mouthpiece and receiver combined. The design lacked aesthetic appeal, but it left a hand free for writing.

'Thank you very much for your cooperation, Miss Edwardson,' said Sir Hugh. 'I must say, though, that when I called your father first, he gave me your home address. Your mother guessed what this was about, and she was not happy that I'm trying to recruit you for follow-up work. She told me about your injury, and how you sustained it. I cannot promise this job will be free of danger.'

'I'll speak to my mother, sir, but I'm sure she'll understand,' Sophie assured him. 'If I can do my bit for the war effort, I'll jump at the chance!'

Sophie put the receiver back. She opened the door and attracted the college mistress's attention. 'Professor Wodehouse, may I please make another call? It's important.'

The college mistress nodded.

Her mother was indeed unhappy to hear that she would be working for the RAF. Sophie reminded her that this was an extremely important job, and that she was finally able to do something significant for the war. She added that she could learn plenty from the 'man in question', and that someone would have to nail her to a wall to stop her from going. Her mother gave her blessing in the end, but grudgingly.

Sophie had put the receiver back before she recalled that Air Chief Marshal Dowding had said the airbase was in Wiltshire. That was in the same county as Bleddyn!

She went back to the dining hall. Her meal had gone cold, but she barely noticed this as she bolted it down in an unladylike manner. All her Christmases had come at once. The War Office had offered her a job, they specifically needed her linguistics expertise, and she would work with Artorius. She would learn so much about the Late Roman period and early Dark Ages! Would the War Office declassify this one day, so she could publish what she would learn?

To top it off, she would also be close to Bleddyn, allowing her to pursue a proper courtship instead of a long-distance one.

Sophie almost collided with another linguistics student as she left the hall. 'Oh – Betty! Pardon me!'

'Sophie? I'm sorry, I heard about your scholarship – but you look rather cheery …'

'I've just been offered a job!'

Betty's eyes widened. 'Really? Where?'

'The Royal Air Force needs ATS recruits in Wiltshire.' Sophie had to contain her excitement and begin the deception. 'It won't put my studies to use, but at least I'll be doing something useful for the war. Anyway, I need to repack my belongings, so I must get back to my dormitory now. I hope you can complete your degree despite this accursed war.'

Betty smiled. 'Thanks, Sophie. Best of luck with the new job!'

Sophie walked briskly, almost breaking out into a skip, as she headed to her room. Britain's prospects looked grim, but the legend said that Arthur would return in Britain's hour of need – and he had. Sophie was certain they could not lose this war now. Even better, she was going to play a crucial role in their deliverance. She couldn't wait to start.

COMING SOON

The Darkest Hour, the second instalment in the *Artorius* series.

ACKNOWLEDGEMENTS

I owe a debt of gratitude to the many family members, friends, and critique partners on Scribophile who helped me to polish this manuscript.

I've consulted too many historical sources to list, but I should specifically mention *Dunkirk: Retreat to Victory* by Julian Thompson, and the 2004 BBC docudrama *Dunkirk*. Specific details about the Wormhoudt Massacre including Brian Fahey's personal account come from *The Forgotten Massacre* (2nd Ed.) by Guy Rommelaere.

For the Arthurian legends, including the earliest Welsh sources and historical references, "Hero of Camelot" (http://www.heroofcamelot.com/about) has a good repository of material and links, and was the starting point for my research.

ABOUT THE AUTHOR

T. J. Farlow grew up in Australia, but he has also lived and worked in Germany, where he and his wife welcomed their first child. Modern Germany is of course very different to Germany at the time of this novel. T. J. has long been interested in the boundary between history and mythology, the place where stories such as the Iliad, the Odyssey and the Arthurian tales sit. He's also held a lifelong interest in science, and has a PhD in chemistry. He holds a black belt in Taekwon-Do and enjoys edible gardening.

***

If you enjoyed this book, help spread the word by sharing it with others or writing a review online.

To find out more about T. J. follow him online or visit his website.

Facebook: T. J. Farlow
Instagram: tjfarlowauthor
Website: tjfarlowauthor.wixsite.com/farlow

www.ingramcontent.com/pod-product-compliance
Lightning Source LLC
Chambersburg PA
CBHW032057050726
47590CB00001B/306